THE BYBLOS
DISCOVERY

THE BYBLOS DISCOVERY

DAVID CULLEN

Culpro Books

The Byblos Discovery
First published 2011

ISBN: 978-0-9559911-5-8

www.lulu.com/davidcullen
Facebook: David Cullen Books
e-mail: davidcullenbooks@btinternet.com

Published by Culpro Books
an imprint of Cullen Productions

"Murder is often a way of preventing something worse from happening"
- Dr Frederic Wertham, 1895-1981
American psychiatrist

"I and Ali are the fathers of this nation… And from Ali's descendants are my grandsons al-Hasan and al-Husayn, who are the masters of the youths of Paradise, and from al-Husayn's descendants shall be nine… the ninth among them is their Qa'im and Mahdi"
- hadith quoted in the *Ikmal* of Al Saduq

For Jenna and Jaime,
the real Paradise and Love

And for JoBo,
the last in a short but illustrious line

GLOSSARY
قاموس المصطلحات

Byblos – Greek name of the Phoenician city Gebal, today known as Jbeil in Arabic. It is 37 kilometres north of Beirut, Lebanon. Founded around 5000 BC, it is the oldest continuously inhabited city in the world. 'Byblos' in Greek means papyrus; it is the derivation of the English word 'Bible'.

Houri – In Islam, houris are the companions of humans and djinni who enter paradise. They have great beauty and are noted for their white eyeballs and black pupils. They can be male and female. In European usage, houris are voluptuous, beautiful, alluring women.

Djinn – Origin of the English word 'genie'. In Arabic folklore and Islamic teachings, djinni, humans and angels make up the three sentient creations of God. Djinni can be good, evil, or neutrally benevolent. In modern usage it can also mean a seductive, beguiling female.

al-Mahdi – In Islam, the prophesied redeemer, the Guided One, who will rid the world of error, injustice and tyranny alongside Isa (Jesus).

ad-Dajjal – In Islam, the Great Deceiver.

A Glossary of Arabic Words and Phrases used in the book is on pages 354 and 355.

Lebanon

Cast in order of appearance

A dead man, walking

Omar Arif – *Assistant First Secretary of the Permanent Mission of Iraq to the United Nations.*

Carla Chedid – *a member of the Lebanese Department of General Security.*

The Damascene – *a mercenary, an assassin.*

Love – *a houri, protector of The Secret.*

Paradise – *a houri, protector of The Secret.*

Brother Malek – *keeper of The Secret.*

Captain Maroun Khoury – *Lebanese Department of General Security.*

Abu Yussuf – *a private investigator based in Jbeil.*

Madame Gourhant – *a client of Abu Yussuf.*

Captain Jihad Merhi (Abu Samer) - *Lebanese Internal Security Force.*

Albert Gourhant – *distrusted husband of Madame Gourhant.*

Gisele Merhi - *wife of Jihad, formerly an agent of the Lebanese Department of General Security.*

Sergeant Deeb el-Gharib - *Lebanese Internal Security Force.*

Captain Fadi Lattouf – *chief of the Civil Police of the Palestinian Security Force in the Beirut refugee camps.*

Nada Lattouf – *wife of Fadi Lattouf (and with the patience of a saint)*

Acting Captain Selim Himo - *Lebanese Department of General Security.*

Lana Lattouf – *daughter of Fadi and Nada Lattouf.*

Wissam Lattouf – *youngest son of Fadi and Nada Lattouf.*

Major Ghanem - *Lebanese Internal Security Force.*

Three members of The Circle of Haouch Moussa

PROLOGUE
مقدمة اثنين

30 December 2006
9 Dhu'l-Hijja 1427

Al-Kazimiyah, north-east Baghdad, Iraq 06:00

He had not slept that night.

Those who are about to die never do. He had spent the last hours praying and eating. His last meal was chicken and rice with a cup of hot water and honey. He had then read verses from the Qur'an and snacked on Milky Way candy bars.

They came for him just before 06:00. He was already dressed in grey trousers, a white collarless shirt and his thick woollen overcoat, protection against the chill during his last moments. Absentmindedly he stuffed a couple of Milky Way bars into his coat pocket and then picked up his Qur'an as he turned to face the four hooded men. Their eyes were hard, mocking and yet, perhaps, just a little fearful.

Good, he thought. Let them be afraid. He wasn't.

He walked out through the cell door. He knew where he was going.

The irony of the time and place was not lost on him. It was the announced first day of *Eid ul-Adha*, the Festival of Sacrifice, when Muslims celebrated the willingness of Ibrahim to sacrifice his son as an act of obedience to God, a sacrifice which was changed on God's command to the sacrifice of a goat. Today, he thought, he would be the sacrificed goat. The scapegoat. No doubt afterwards they would slit his throat.

The place was Camp Banzai, previously military intelligence headquarters, now perversely renamed Camp Justice. He knew the gallows well, he had been there often.

There was pandemonium as he entered the room, masses of people were in there, all shouting and screaming in his direction. All Shi'a traitors, collaborators with the invaders. Sunnis would never behave this way, he told himself. "Down with the invaders," he shouted back. "Down with the invaders!"

He did not tarry. With his four hooded praetorian, he climbed the steps. He noticed a mobile phone in someone's hand below.

Even the men on the gallows were now shouting, chanting "Muqtada, Muqtada, Muqtada!", mocking him with the name of the young Shi'a, the fourth son of Grand Ayatollah Mohammed Sadeq al-Sadr and son-in-law of Grand Ayatollah Mohammed Baqir al-Sadr, both of whom had been murdered by the old regime along with many other family members.

He sniffed in disdain. "Muqtada?" he sneered mockingly. "*Allahu Akbar!* The Muslim Ummah will be victorious and Palestine is Arab!"

"Go to hell!" screamed a voice.

"Is this the bravery of Arabs?" he asked.

The noose was placed around his head, the knot on the left side of his neck.

"Long live Mohammed Baqir Sadr!" screamed another voice. "Go to hell!"

"The hell that is Iraq?" he responded.

"Please, I am begging you not to!" shouted a sudden voice of reason. "The man is being executed."

He looked around but he could not see who had spoken. It was like a circus. A zoo. Animals, all of them. He began to recite the *shahada*, the Islamic creed. "*Allahu Akbar.* There is no God but Allah. Mohammed is the messenger of Allah. God is greatest. *Allahu Akbar*. There is no God but Allah. Mohammed is the messenger of Allah. God - "

The platform dropped.

Even above the noise, the cheering and the cursing, a loud crack was heard.

He was dead.

4 years later...

28 June 2010
16 Rajab 1431

Upper East Side, New York City, USA 17:30

Omar Arif, Assistant First Secretary of the Permanent Mission of Iraq to the United Nations, walked down the steps of the four-storey brownstone mission building at 14 East 79th Street, between Madison Avenue and Fifth, and turned right.

He walked at what he hoped looked like a leisurely pace. There were two reasons why he could not be seen to be rushing: one was the heat – it had reached 98 degrees Fahrenheit in Manhattan that day and anyone rushing would be sure to attract attention to themselves. And that was the second reason also – he must not attract attention to himself. Every fibre of his being was telling him to hurry, get a move on, run. But if anybody from the Mission – or, worse, anybody *watching* the Mission – saw him acting in any way out of the ordinary, questions would be asked. And the last thing he wanted was questions. He had too many answers.

He passed the five-storey townhouse at number 17, the home of New York Mayor Michael Bloomberg, and then turned right into Madison Avenue.

As it was, he was already doing something out of the

ordinary – he was not going straight home to his apartment up on 92nd. But that could be explained, if anyone asked. He was enjoying a Monday evening out in The Big Apple. Nothing wrong with that, he was not a prisoner he was a diplomat (well, actually, he was nothing more than a middle-ranking civil servant, but he had diplomatic status).

He crossed Madison at 78th and a block further down turned left, heading for the 77th Street subway.

Midtown, New York City, USA 18:00

The lobby of the Grand Hyatt Hotel next to Grand Central Station on 42nd Street is opulent, big, busy and bustling. The constant background musak of the lobby's huge cascading waterfall means that if you talk intimately, quietly, to the person next to you you cannot be heard by those passing or even those sitting just a few feet away from you in the central area near the elevators. It is a perfect place for a clandestine lovers' tryst, a private business deal – or a meeting of spies.

Carla Chedid sat in one of the double settees, a polystyrene cup of not-at-all bad Café Americano from The Market, the foyer café, on the table in front of her. She was dressed in an already-short white cotton summer dress that had ridden up as she had sat down, and her olive thighs were now attracting surreptitious glances from two middle-aged businessmen sitting at ninety degrees to her. She smiled coyly as she tossed back her long black hair, at first pretending not to notice – then suddenly looking directly at her two admirers, challenging. Caught out, the men blustered, fumbled, looked away, spoke gibberish, one of them actually asking the other "Did you see The Mets last night?"

She grinned. Hell of a game, boys, hell of a game. But on a scale of one to ten you stood a cat's chance in hell with her. Her heart – and her body – belonged elsewhere. For you, she would not be dancing.

She reached forward for her coffee, took a sip and put the cup back down on the table. She noticed them looking again. Was it her fault the dress was low cut?

From her Guess purse she took out her HTC mobile phone to check the time.

He was late. He'd better show. He *would* show. She was his handler, and like every good handler she had enough on her agent to ensure strict obedience. The publication of just one of the photos she had of Omar Arif playing stick-the-tail-up-the-donkey with a firm-buttocked and astonishingly hung young man from Hell's Kitchen would be enough to end the Iraqi's diplomatic career and probably give him a free face-down swim in the Hudson River.

She finished her coffee and treated the businessmen to a slow, sensual lick of her lips (in your dreams, boys) before taking her make-up bag from her purse.

Just as she finished applying Mac's cherry electric lipgloss, she saw him on the escalator, rising up into the foyer from the 42nd Street entrance. When he came over, they would kiss for pretence's sake, just in case anyone was watching. After all, what could be more natural than two Middle Eastern UN diplomats meeting and hitting it off, strangers in a foreign land and all that? He was Iraqi, she was Lebanese, but as far as the Americans were concerned that was the same place!

But as he came towards her she could see that something was wrong. She stood up, something she would not normally do, smiling anyway. "*Habibi,* I thought you had forgotten." She spoke in English, her voice deep and accented.

"I – I am sorry I'm late." There was sweat on Arif's brow.

She took his hands and pulled him towards her, the action reminding him of their need to kiss. He pecked her on the cheek and pulled away. "We need to talk," he said lowly.

"Of course we do, Omar." She noticed the two businessmen exchanging raised eyebrows with each other and knew what they were thinking. *We need to talk* – the universal signal of a relationship end. Was the Arab jerk actually breaking up with the – what was she? Puerto Rican? And a perfect age. No longer a babe, not yet a cougar.

"No, we really need to talk." Arif said lowly, staring straight into her eyes.

"All right. Over dinner."

"Now."

She held in her irritation, flaring her nostrils. Somebody needed a good slap. But this was also worrying. What was vexing him so? "Okay..." She opened her purse, ostensibly checking that she had put away her make-up and telephone. She did not carry a gun on the streets of Gotham, but there was something else in her bag - a ten centimetre long piece of solid olive wood. It was carved into the shape of a cross with the cross beam uneven to fit comfortably between a person's fingers. A Holding Cross. She had been given it a few years ago. "We cannot talk here."

"Yes, we can." He did not say it in English, which made the two businessmen look up as they heard the sudden foreign language. But they would have no way of understanding Kurdish, one of the two official languages of Iraq for the last six years.

For a moment Carla did not move and did not speak. Slowly she sat down. "*Tayyib,*" she said in Arabic. "Okay. But speak Arabic, my Kurdish is not good." She grabbed Arif's arm as he went to sit down next to her. "But first you can get me another coffee."

He nodded and went to move off, but she held onto his arm. "And a pastry. The raspberry Danish. You know us Lebanese and our sweet teeth." She smiled without warmth.

As Arif went across to the café, the two businessmen stood up to go, obviously disconcerted by the lapse into the foreign – and to them hostile-sounding – tongue. She ignored them.

Five minutes later Arif returned with two poly-cups and two grease-proof bags. As he laid them on the table, Carla said

"*Shou?* What?"

He sighed, sitting down next to her. "I have found out something terrible. Terrible. It is my own fault, I should not have been listening."

"What is it? You have weapons of mass destruction after all?"

"Please."

"*Aasif.* Sorry. But what is wrong with you?"

Leaving the grease-proof bag on the table, Arif leant forward and carefully tore it open to reveal an almond-encrusted *pain aux chocolat.* He touched the top of the cake with his index finger but did not pick it up. He looked over his shoulders, first one way then the other. There were many people about, but perhaps there was safety in numbers. He took a deep breath and said, "Sajida was right."

Grand Central Subway, New York City, USA 18:45

Passing by the shoeshine 'boys' outside Grand Central station, Arif used the subway entrance by the Park Avenue overpass. Earlier he had planned to take a short trip five blocks west to Times Square to check out the action after he had met with Carla, but now he did not feel in the mood so he made his way to the northbound platform. He would catch the express to 86th Street. Then it would be a six-block walk to his apartment on 92nd.

Carla was not happy with him. She had wanted proof of his accusation that Sajida was right – but he had none. How could you prove something like that? He had simply overheard the conversation. There would be nothing written down, no file on a computer somewhere, the knowledge was too sacrosanct, too precious, too unbelievable. Too holy? Only a handful of people alive would know it, those who were in on it, those who were waiting for the right time. It would be knowledge and word-of-mouth only. There would be no tangible record. It was too dangerous.

So, sorry Carla, there was no material proof. And the physical proof was elsewhere. You had asked him to report 'anything and everything' and he had. Job done. What you did with the information was up to you. Arabs should not be spying on Arabs anyway, they should be on the same side, especially when they were surrounded by The Great Satan.

The subway was throbbing with the evening rush hour, the northbound platform crowded with people going home. And it was so damn hot down here, mirroring the sweltering summer weather above. The Blue Jays were playing at The Yankees tonight, so the Line 4 express train would be extra full all the way to 161st Street. The Line 5 would not be much better. Perhaps he should change his plan and catch the Line 6 local?

There was a blast of stale but very welcome air and an anticipatory shuffling and moving forward as the 4 train approached. He would catch this, he decided. It was stifling down here, he needed to get out. He would have to stand but as it was the express it was only two stops.

Someone bumped into his left arm, and at first he thought it was a pathetic attempt at a pickpocketing. But he looked to his left to see a tall, stunning blonde woman smiling at him apologetically, mouthing "Excuse me!" above the din of the arriving train.

"No problem!" he mouthed back smiling and quickly turned as the train doors opened and the crowd moved forward.

On the train he stood shoulder to shoulder, back to back, front to front with his fellow travellers, hemmed in tightly, facing the doors as they closed. He noticed that the woman who had bumped into him had not got on, but was still standing on the platform smiling at him, her head tilted slightly to one side. Her gaze followed him as the train moved off, and it made him frown.

She was beautiful but she had the strangest, most discon-certing eyes. It might be a trick of the light refracted in the train's glass, but they looked like they had no colour. The irises were white, almost glowing, the pupils blacker than black...

Like a houri.

He stiffened, fear shooting through his body as the train re-entered the tunnel and he lost sight of her. *In the name of Allah!* There, Carla, there was your proof!

He thought of the bump into his arm...

Omar Arif was dead before the train reached its next stop at Lexington and 59th. But no one knew it. The body, eyes open but dull, remained held in the upright position by the crush of passengers. Only at 161st Street when the Yankee fans disembarked did the body fall, landing with its head on the platform, feet still in the car. People waited, looking, expecting the idiot to pick himself up. But he did not.

And never would.

Murray Hill, New York City, USA 22:00

Carla Chedid stood naked at the window of her thirtieth floor apartment on East 39th Street and looked north over the lights of Midtown. The room behind her was in darkness so there were no reflections to spoil her view of the Upper East Side way beyond. Nearby she could see the United Nations Building backing on to the East River. She knew that just to the west of it, although it could not be seen from her elevated angle, was United Nations Plaza. At number 866 was The Permanent Mission of Lebanon to the United Nations, where she had been stationed for the last five years.

For five years she had been the 'permanent representative' of the External Security Unit of the Lebanese Department of General Security at the United Nations, unbeknownst to Ambassador Salam or anyone else at the Mission, who thought she was an Assistant Counsellor. In fact she was a Gatherer – of information, facts, ideas, theories, thoughts, anything and everything that may or may not affect the security of Lebanon. And in the intriguing world of Lebanese politics, that meant watching your own kind as well as foreigners.

Five years... and she had not been home. Five years of effective exile. The things she had done for her country – she could write a book. Five years ago she had not been as quick as she could have been, she had been two minutes late in getting to Nejmeh Square in Beirut, one hundred and twenty seconds too late to stop a seismic event in the history of Lebanon. There had been reasons for it, but it was a mistake she would never make again. That was why she had been exiled and given yet another new name. She was too good an operative for the DGS to lose but the name Zahia Zalloum, code-name The Djinn, was now permanently linked to the darkness of 14 February 2005. So she had become Carla Chedid.

She stretched upwards, the muscles of her small, thirty-something body still taut, her gluteals hard. As she brought her arms down, she ran her fingers through her long black hair, massaging her own scalp. Then she leant forward, shaking her hair over her face then flicking it back. In the light from Manhattan outside, she walked away from the window and went over to the dresser, picking up her ornate black and gold hair clip and fastening it in her hair.

She looked at the man on the bed, lying naked and satisfied in the shadows. The man with the long hair now sticking with sweat to the sides of his face, hiding the hole of his missing left ear. In this light she could not see the scars on his body, but she knew where they were, every one of them. She had counted them often. She had licked them often.

"You think it is true?" asked the voice from the bed.

Carla shrugged. "As we both know, strange things happen in the Middle East. For example, who would have guessed the identity of Hariri's killer?"

"But this sounds ridiculous."

"Preposterous, I admit."

"You do not believe in a second coming?"

She smiled. "You being rude?"

"For once, no." He reached out and turned on a bedside light. He raised himself on his elbows, admiring her hairless body.

She came over and sat on the edge of the bed, in turn admiring his hairless body, caressing his right thigh. "Do we have *al-mahdi*? Or *ad-Dajjal*? Indeed, do we have anybody? It is only hearsay." Her fingers reached his groin and stopped. "But one thing I do know, Marwan." She patted his thigh and stood back up. "The world is not ready for *Yawm al-Qiyamah*[*]. Or Armageddon. This needs to be sorted, if it exists. And stopped. They need to know." She walked over and took her purse off the top of the dresser.

"What are you going to do?" he asked.

She shrugged. "If there is anything to it, it is too dangerous to commit electronically by whatever means, even voice." She rummaged inside the purse and brought out the Holding Cross. For a moment she was distracted, caressing the wood with her fingers, she looked over at the bed and said gently "I always carry you with me."

Then she said, "I am going back."

---

[*] Judgment Day

PART ONE
الجزء الأول

THE RETURN
عودة

30 June 2010
18 Rajab 1431

Coastal Highway, Lebanon 18:00

The ninety-one kilometre journey from Beirut to Tripoli is nominally timed at two hours. Maybe someone had done it once in that time – or maybe they had just made it up. When your journey includes extricating yourself from the car park at Rafic Hariri International Airport to the south of Beirut, the drive through the eastern periphery of the capital, the volume of traffic on the coastal highway and the crazy drivers, the trip between Lebanon's first and second cities is likely to use up more than three hours of your life.

The woman called Love was tired as she drove her black Jeep Wrangler Ultimate over the Nahr el Jaouz (River el Jaouz) and continued northwards on the highway. The journey from JFK Airport in New York had taken over thirteen hours; firstly American Airlines Flight 44 to Paris and then Middle East Airways Flight 206 to Beirut. Club Class helped, of course, but travelling was simply tiring no matter your seat pitch or how well (or not) you were treated.

She would have liked to have driven with her blonde hair blowing in the wind, but she had had to leave the Jeep's removable hard top on while it was parked for four days at the airport. The windows were down but it was still warm in the car. But she did not sweat. Never had done, never would do.

The traffic on the highway was thinning now she had passed

the fishing port of El Batroun so she could increase her speed. Shortly she was passing Chekka, the Mediterranean Sea clearly visible again on her left after the highway's little inland detour.

Soon now she would be home, and she was glad. She had her job and she had done what had to be done.

But she wanted to be with Paradise again.

Tripoli, Lebanon 18:40 – 20:00

Tripoli is the most conservative, the most Middle Eastern, the most Islamic of Lebanon's cities. The Old City is dominated by the Ottoman-restored Castle of Saint Gilles which looks down upon the maze of souks, madrassas, khans and hammams below with the benevolence and protective instincts of a big brother.

Although she was not from these parts, Love felt at home here. She was religious but without favour – she regarded Sunni, Shi'a, Druze, Christianity and all the rest as merely sects of the one true deity, different rooms in the same father's house. The piety of Tripoli calmed and inspired her.

She parked the Jeep in its usual place in the Parking at Al-Nejmeh Square, unloaded her rucksack from the back and walked eastward down Khaled Chehab Street. The evening sun was lowering in the west but it was still bright and hot.

To her right was the Great Mosque with its mix of Western and Islamic architecture and the minaret which so obviously used to be a Christian bell tower during the building's previous incarnation as the twelfth-century Crusader church of St Mary of The Tower. To her left she passed the fourteenth-century madrassas of al-Khayriyat Hassan and al-Nasiriyat. Then she crossed over towards the entrance of Souk al-Sayaghin, the gold market.

The souk was narrow and shaded by a half-covered wooden ceiling. As in any market, there was hustle, there was bustle. Traders stood outside their shops beckoning in passers-by, offering that 'special price'; elsewhere voices seemed to be raised in the most terrible of arguments but in reality it was purchasers and sellers going through the usual haggling.

Instead of going down in to the souk, Love stopped at the entrance by the juice stand on her right. The owner of the stand smiled when he saw her, placed his right hand on his heart and gave a small half-bow. "*Salaam*," he said quietly, reverentially.

Love returned his smile. "*Salaam*. All is well?"

"*'eeh, madame*. It is."

She nodded and walked past him behind the juice stand.

Into the Hammam al-Nouri.

The now abandoned and derelict Hammam al-Nouri bathhouse was built in the fourteenth century. In its day it was the crown-jewel of all the hammams in Tripoli, noted for its smaller than usual dressing room and tepidarium and larger than usual hot water steam hall surrounded by private bathing alcoves. Multi-coloured marble was used on the floors, fountains and basins, and the bright decoration of the walls and ceilings can still be seen even though the place is in disrepair. Looking up from inside, the domes in the roof are perforated with green and blue glass roundels, giving the day-time illusion of a thousand stars in the heavens.

It was quiet inside, dim, but no longer damp as it would have been in the days when it was in use. Love trod softly, respecting the tranquillity of the place. She stopped in the middle of the steam hall and said softly "*Ahlan...?*", her voice magnified and echoed by the domes above.

She heard a noise. A shadowy figure appeared in the dressing room entrance way. Love turned towards the shadow but said nothing more as she placed her rucksack on the floor.

Suddenly the figure moved, running with an alarming speed, grabbing Love before she even had a chance to straighten up. Love felt herself being crushed, hands were in her hair, on her face...

Then lips were on hers, in affection not lust. Her face was covered in kisses.

After a mutual hug which lasted a lifetime, the other figure pulled away and Love looked at the mirror image of herself. Same body, same height, same blonde hair, same face, same white eyes with the so black pupils.

The other one said, "Sister, I have missed you so."

Love reached out and caressed the other face. "And I have missed you, my darling Paradise," she said to her identical twin.

"I have already filled the bath for you," smiled Paradise.

"Thank you, sister, that is much needed."

"And there is spiced lamb to eat. Or are you not hungry?"

"Oh yes, I am. I didn't eat on the planes."

"How did it go?" Paradise bent down, picked up the rucksack and handed it to Love.

"Fine. A successful conversion. Thank you." She took the bag.

"Just the one?"

"Just the one. A fool who was listening when he shouldn't have been. The one who was overheard has been dealt with by the disciples. It was in his favour that he reported the eavesdropper himself, but now he is on two strikes. If he needs to be converted, they will call us again."

"My turn next time."

"Of course."

"Now you go and bathe, the food will keep until you are ready. You can tell me later how you did it."

They hugged, lingering on the final extra squeeze. "Oh I missed you so," said Love. "It is not right, we should not be apart. We are the same person, after all."

"And I missed you too much. But as we said before, America is hardly ready for one of us let alone two. We'd have been too noticeable."

"Hiding in plain sight?"

"There is that."

"Or we could have put the lenses in so that we did not stand out. We could have even forced ourselves to dress differently."

"Next time, yeh?"

"Next time – Oh! I have something for you." Love put the bag back down on the floor and crouched over it. Unzipping and rummaging, she pulled out a blue crescent-shaped object. "I have one too." With a deft flick of her left wrist the object opened to its proper shape and she handed it over. A New York Yankees baseball cap.

Paradise beamed. "Sister, thank you!" She flipped it onto her head.

Love put hers on. She stood back up, taking her sister's hands. "Now we're two All-American girls!" she laughed.

"Or," chuckled Paradise, "two All-American *houris*."

Love could hear the call to *salat al-Maghrib,* sunset prayer, from the mosques outside as she leant forward in the bath for her sister to reach over and wash her back.

The alcove was illuminated by candles, the flames casting shadows up the walls and into the domes above. There was no electricity in the place, meals were cooked on a portable gas stove in another room. And, of course, the water was cold. But the women had gone through much worse things during their training than not having hot water to bathe in. They had learned to like the effect it had on the skin, that moment when you eased yourself into the water and your whole epidermis corrugated. And it made your hair shiny too.

Love had told Paradise about New York: following the fool from the Mission, seeing him meet his girlfriend in the lobby of the hotel (it looked like he might be finishing with her – well, how right he had been!), the trip into the subway, the syringe under her false nail into his arm, his face at the end as he looked into her eyes from inside the subway car and had realised what had happened. It had been perfect, a sublime conversion.

"You are always so skilled," Paradise scooped water over her sister's back.

"And so are you, my dear."

"When I need to be, yes. But you... you make it an art form."

"The gods like art."

"Oh indeed they do."

Love stood up, the water rolling from her fair skin. Turning round, she held out both her arms and Paradise helped her climb out. As she dried herself on a thick cotton towel, Love asked "So we're happy that The Secret is safe?"

"We have ensured that it is so, as we are charged to do."

"Until *Yawm al-Qiyamah*, then the whole world will know. But should The Secret be moved? We normally do when there has been a breach."

"The thought had occurred to me," Paradise took the towel and began to dry her sister's back. "This was not a serious breach, our action was pre-emptive. The leak plugged before there was any spillage. But the final decision is not ours."

"We must ask Malek."

"Yes, we will visit the treasure of life in the morning."

1 July 2010
19 Rajab 1431

North Lebanon 05:30

They left early, just before the end of *salat al-Fajr*, dawn prayer. The shops in the souk were closed, the juice stand covered over. No one was about. The sun was just pushing in from the east, the night sky retreating rapidly before it. It was going to be another clear, hot day.

At al-Nejmeh Parking they unscrewed the hard top off the Jeep and left it occupying their usual space. It would be safe.

Then they were off, Paradise driving, Love next to her in charge of the backpacks containing water, fruit and chocolate. They were dressed identically in white cotton sleeveless vests, camouflage combat trousers and desert boots. In the back of the car were two khaki cotton shirts which they would put on later in deference to their destination. Each of them had tied their hair back into a simple ponytail. They wore no make-up – beauty never needed it.

They took the highway south-east out of Tripoli to Zgharta then turned due south onto the main road following the Nahr Jouiet. Soon the road began to rise, leaving the river behind, and they were climbing into Mount Lebanon, past olive groves and vineyards, forests of cedar, oak and pine trees, the land becoming more rugged, the vistas more spectacular. They stopped just south of the busy summer resort of Ehden, pulling over into a quiet area for their refreshment and relief.

As they leant against the Jeep, they looked out over the stunning Qadicha valley, the Maronite holy valley, below. The place was tranquil. They could see orchards of apples and mulberries, and farms, green arable land. From way down they could hear the sound of bells from one of the many monasteries and churches below.

While Paradise finished her second peach, Love felt into one of the front pockets of a backpack and brought out two small, flat plastic cases. "Here, we'd best put these in now. We don't want to frighten the holy men." She offered her palm with the two cases in it.

Her sister smiled, taking the case furthest from her. "What's the score?"

"I lead thirty-two to thirty."

Slowly, tentatively, Paradise opened the case. Then she grinned, opening it wide and holding it out. "Green!"

"Thirty-two thirty-one. You're closing." Love opened her own case, raising it up to her face and leaning forward slightly. With great care she put the brown contact lenses into her eyes.

Deir Qozhaya, Lebanon 08:30

They drove down into the valley past the village of Aarbet-Qozhaya, Ehden now well above them. Soon they could see the red roof of their destination: the ancient Monastery of Saint Anthony of Qozhaya.

Qozhaya is a word of Syriac origin, meaning 'the treasure of life'. To the six monks and two hermits who inhabited the vast monastery this meant Jesus Christ, to whom they had dedicated their lives. As well as the fifty-room monastery, there were two caves. One cave was used as a church. It had a man-made facade of pink stone with three arched bell towers, lower arches, windows and a doorway leading into the cave behind.

The other cave was less pious but nevertheless useful: previously it had been used to imprison the insane, in the hope that Saint Anthony would cure them miraculously. The chains used to constrain the inhabitants can still be seen on the walls.

Now with their shirts on and contact lenses in, Paradise and Love drove into the courtyard in front of the monastery. They were well-known here, they did not need an appointment.

They had come to see Brother Malek.

They were shown into their usual small meeting room on the third floor. Brother Malek would be with them shortly, they were informed. Whether the monks that lived here ever wondered why one of the long-stay pilgrims was regularly visited by two young women (and identical young women at that – apart from their eyes: one had green, one had brown) they did not know. There must have been curiosity, but the regular, handsome donation given to the monastery for Malek's board and lodging ensured no questions were voiced openly.

They had brought one of the backpacks in with them, leaving the other under the seat in the Jeep in a forlorn protection against the heat. Thankfully they had eaten their chocolate on route. The bag which Love now placed on the heavy pine table contained fruit, confectionery, fizzy drinks and other items, their usual little gift for the Brother.

They were standing by the window admiring the magnificent view across the valley to the Deir Qannoubine, the Qannoubine Monastery – the seat of the Maronite Patriarchs for four hundred years until 1800 (1215) - when a voice behind them said, "*Al-salaam 'aalaykum.*"

The twins turned and said together "*'aalaykum al-salaam,*" both giving a little bow of the head.

They had not heard him enter, they never did. He always moved in silence, like a wraith. He was dressed in a black full-length cloak, a *burnus*, with the hood up. Poking below the hood, his beard was long, wispy and bushy, the natural black pigmentation fighting to an inevitable defeat against the grey of age.

His right hand indicated the bag on the table. "My gift?" His voice was deep.

"As always," said Love.

Malek opened the bag and peered in. He asked, "The situation has been resolved?"

"Yes," nodded Love. "In the manner specified. A permanent conversion."

"How exactly?"

Love held up her left index finger, saying nothing.

Malek nodded. "Then the leak is sealed. Once again, only the trustworthy know The Secret. The disciples."

"And half of those we have already permanently converted, as instructed and as necessary," said Paradise.

"God will be pleased. You have both proved worthy protectors of The Secret. Your commander has proven to be a good friend."

"When will it be time?" asked Love. "When will the world know The Secret?"

Malek looked back into the bag. His hand went in and brought out a box of Al Fakher two-apples flavour *ma'asel*, shisha tobacco.

"There is cherry in there too," said Love.

Malek spoke as if there had been no diversion. "The time is not yet right. We must keep a close eye on events. The Secret will be revealed when God says so. But I think it will not be long now." He picked up the bag, keeping the tobacco in his left hand.

"There is one other thing," said Paradise.

The hood turned towards her.

"We must consider whether The Secret needs to be moved."

"We always move The Secret when it has been compromised," said Love.

Malek remained silent for a while. Then he said, "But you told me you had resolved the situation."

"Yes," nodded Paradise, "but we must not become careless or

complacent. It is not for my sister and I to decide – we are merely protectors – but we make the point with recommend-ation. Moving has served us well in the past."

The hood nodded. "As has your idea of keeping yourselves many miles from that which you are the protectors of." Malek knew that the twins had not yet let him down or failed in their duties. "That is a masterful stroke. If anyone ever finds out you are the protectors - "

"Which they will not," said Paradise.

Malek stopped. A full minute later he went on, "Then they will expect The Secret to be with you, not many miles away. If you are ever compromised that gives me time to ensure The Secret is safe. To alert the disciples." He put his hand into a pocket of his robes and brought out a Samsung mobile phone, holding it up. "However... I take your counsel well. Maybe it is time to move The Secret."

The women were nodding.

"Perhaps," suggested Malek, "to somewhere where the reception is better?"

The women smiled. "I think that is a good course," agreed Paradise. "Your decision is sound, as always." She had learnt in the past that it was best to let Malek believe the ideas came from him.

"Where will we go?"

Love walked back over to the window, admiring the Qadisha Valley for what she now knew would be the last time. "We have been here in Tripoli and The Valley for some time."

"We should move further south," Paradise was still standing by the table.

"We were thinking..." continued Love.

"Maybe Charbel," suggested Paradise.

Deir Qozhaya, Lebanon 10:30

From his small cell-like eyrie in a top far corner of the

monastery, Brother Malek watched the two women drive off in their Jeep. They were good, he thought. Very, very good. His own personal *houris*. They were efficient – and lethal. Protectors of The Secret. And they would be of even more use in the future, once The Secret was revealed.

He turned away from the window. They were right, of course. It had always been accepted protocol that a breach, any breach, would necessitate a move. He had been here at Qozhaya for some time now, so that in itself was also reason for a move. Too much familiarity, too much routine, led to complacency.

They were going to try to secure a place for the pilgrim Brother Malek at Deir Mar Maron, the Monastery of Saint Maron and Saint Charbel, in the Jbeil District. That was logical, a Christian pilgrim would be expected to move from one sacred shrine to another. So he would need to prepare The Secret for transportation.

But not before a little indulgence...

Next to his small basic mattress on the floor was a dark blue carrying case, about forty centimetres square with brown reinforcements on each corner and a brown leather handle on the top. He went over and knelt down next to it, unhooking the clasps and opening the lid. Carefully he took out the pieces: the water jar, the body, the plate, the hose, the bowl, assembling them carefully. His *argileh*, his shisha pipe.

He already had charcoal and matches. Water he would get from the latrine downstairs. Then he would settle down and enjoy a two-apples smoke.

He looked at the assembled seventy centimetres high *argileh* in admiration. It was certainly a work of art, a one-off piece, a fitting climax to the career of the artist, the sculptor, the genius who had made it. The artisan who had so tragically died on the same day as he had completed it.

The artistry, the filigree, was beautiful and delicate. Stunning yet subtle multi-coloured shapes and patterns adorned the body and the bowl. The bowl was not glass but pure crystal. And the body, the plate and even the tongs were not base metal. They were pure twenty-four carat gold.

It was the most expensive *argileh* in the world.

Two hours later, after a satisfying and thoughtful smoke, Brother Malek used the residual water in the bowl of the *argileh* to wash his hands and face, wetting the floor of his cell as he did so. Packing the pipe away in its box, he pulled his mattress into the centre of the small room, covering the wetness. Standing at the end of the mattress with his hands raised, he said "*Allahu Akbar.*" Then he bowed and began to recite "*Subhana rabbiyal adheem...*". God is most great. Glory be to my Lord Almighty...

Kneeling on the mattress, the Christian Brother Malek continued with the Muslim *Dhuhr* prayer.

3 July 2010
21 Rajab 1431

Ras en Nabaa, Beirut 21:00

Captain Maroun Khoury of the Lebanese Department of General Security was a slim, fit-looking man whose looks belied the fact that he was in his fifties. Bald on top, he kept his hair at the back and sides cropped short, not quite shaved, blending in with the trim greying beard on his face. He was the Chief of the External Security Unit of the DGS, a unit whose existence was unknown even to senior members of the Lebanese parliament. After all, who would believe that Lebanon had, or needed, its own equivalent of the CIA or the SIS-MI6? He reported to no one except the Director General of General Security, currently Major General Wafic Jezzini.

Khoury's team was divided into sub-units of Gatherers, Listeners and Watchers. They gathered, listened and watched anything outside, or originating outside, Lebanon's borders that might affect the security of the country. A very wide brief, even for a country as small as Liban.

It had been a busy day as usual. The United Nations Special Tribunal for Lebanon – which was investigating the 2005 assassination of former Prime Minister Rafic Hariri – was due to report in the autumn and issue indictments, and Khoury's team were the only people in Lebanon who had seen the first draft (obtained by clandestine means, of course). There were powerful groups inside and outside the country that would not like what the Tribunal had to say. Also it was the fourth anniversary of the 2006 'summer war' between Israel and Hizbullah, and the usual annual threats of a repeat of the bombing of Lebanon were being issued. Khoury wondered wryly how anybody could get to sleep in Lebanon during the summer with the constant noise of sabre-rattling!

But one of the privileges of rank was that he could go home each night, unlike some of his field staff who could sometimes be away on assignment for months, if not years. Khoury lived in Ashrafieh, just a kilometre away from the DGS building. He longed to make the healthy walk across the park, up past the Lycée Franco-Libanais, across Elias Sarkis Avenue then through to his apartment just south of Abdul Wahab el Inglizi Street, but protocol forbade it. He had to go by car.

To him this was nonsense. He acknowledged his rank and the sensitivity of his position, but surely it was easier to put a bomb under a car than under a person? And he was skilled in self-protection and evasion techniques to thwart any threat to his person in the street. And anyway, few knew that his unit even existed.

It was an argument he had had with successive Directors General, but none of them would listen. The only concession he had been granted was that he could drive himself instead of being assigned an official driver and bodyguard.

So at 21:00 that Friday evening, Maroun Khoury drove his Mercedes M-Class SUV out through the entrance of the DGS building and headed home.

Ashrafieh, Beirut 22:00 – 23:59

At the last minute, Khoury decided to pop up to Spinney's in Mar Mitr for some weekend shopping, so it was another hour before he arrived back at the Ottoman-era building where he lived. The building and the tree-lined street were in darkness, which meant just one thing – another Beirut power cut!

Shopping bags in hand, he began to climb to his apartment on the fifth floor, one from the top, using his mobile phone to light his way. If he couldn't get fit by walking to and from work, Beirut's frequent power failures and the stairs would ensure he did not turn to flab!

The gated, see-through elevator in the middle of the winding staircase was stopped between the second and third floors. As he went past, he shone his phone inside to confirm no one was trapped – and it was also a handy excuse just to take a little rest.

He was breathing heavily, but not gasping, by the time he reached the fifth floor. Putting down his shopping as he stood outside the ornate wooden door of his apartment, he felt in his pocket for his keys. He sniffed. The cleaners must have washed the stairwell today, he could smell jasmine.

He was just offering the key to the lock, holding the phone in his left hand, when a voice from above said *"Massah el-khair,* Moro."

He froze, key in mid air, controlling his breathing, aware of his gun in the well of his left armpit under his jacket. For a moment he did nothing. Then he said to the door "Well, well..."

Slowly he turned, the light from his phone moving at the same speed as his gaze, across the landing, up the stairs to his right.

The first thing that came into view at the top of the stairs was a pair of pink trainers. Then knee-ripped blue jeans. The light progressed upwards over a plain pink T shirt, then shone on the long black hair with the ornate hair clip and then the smiling olive face.

Khoury relaxed. "If I'd known you were coming - "

"You'd have baked a cake?"

"I'd have met you at the airport." He turned the key in the lock and opened his door.

Slowly she began to walk down the stairs. "And spoil the element of surprise?"

He smiled. "You always were one for the dramatic. Here,

come in." He bent down and picked up his shopping bags.

She reached him as he straightened and planted a kiss firmly on his lips.

The lights came on like fireworks exploding.

During all the years she had worked for him she had never been into his apartment, even during the brief but intense two-month period when they had been lovers. She was taken aback by how modern it was, totally in contrast to the antiquity of the building. She sat down on the wide cream leather couch. "Nice place."

"*Merci ktir.*" Without even asking, the first thing Khoury did was to prepare and activate the filter coffee machine. Only then did he begin to unpack his shopping. "You have eaten?"

"No."

"I have falafel, hummus, tabbouleh... All Spinney's best, except the tabbouleh which was from Monoprix yesterday."

"You are kind, thank you."

Khoury paused with his head inside one of the open-plan kitchen cupboards. He said, "I'm surprised they let you in the country. There are still those who would like to find out exactly what Zahia Zalloum knows about Hariri's killing."

"Zahia Zalloum is not here. Carla Chedid is. Zahia is missing during operations, has been for five years. Carla's papers are not false, I would not be flagged up at Immigration."

"True."

Khoury had finished unpacking and was busying himself with plates and food. Carla stood up and went over to the gurgling coffee machine. She found cups in the second cupboard she opened.

"Why are you here, ZiZi?" Khoury was pulling leaves from a romaine lettuce.

"CiCi."

"What?"

"Carla Chedid. CiCi."

"To me you will always be - "

"What will I always be, Moro?" She was up close to him, two cups of coffee in her hands. He could smell her perfume, mingled with her musk from the flight.

Putting the lettuce onto a plate, he picked up some tomatoes on the vine. He wanted to say she would always be a temptation, the best and most skilful lover he had ever had, but instead he said "My most skilled field operative."

"Would you like me to wash your tomatoes?" she asked innocently. She placed the coffees on the work surface, reached out and pulled two fruits off of the vine.

Khoury grinned, unable to come back with a witty retort – but oh how he remembered her washing techniques! She could do it with one hand. As she turned on the tap and ran the fruit under the water (indeed with one hand), he said "Tell me."

She shook the fruit, leant over him and placed them on top of the lettuce. "It's probably nothing and I am being over-cautious. But I didn't want to put it in writing or tell you over the phone, just in case The Listeners have listeners. It could be delicate. Can I wash your *khiyar*?" She stretched across.

"I'll wash my own cucumbers, *merci*." Khoury snatched the two small cucumbers out of her hand. "Why don't you - "

"Bathe," she said. "May I bathe? It was a long journey and I came straight here after dropping my bags at the hotel."

Their eyes met. Khoury could have sworn the cucumber in his right hand grew a little bit. "Of course," he smiled. "Sorry. I did not think. It is through there, down the hall. Next to the bedroom. I'll get you some towels - "

"No, no," her hand touched his arm. "Just tell me where they are, I'll find them. We'll talk over dinner. As I say, it might not be important or even real."

"Okay, as you wish," said Khoury, wondering whether he should offer to wash her back.

Or other parts.

*

"One of my UN contacts," Carla crunched down on a leaf of lettuce with tabbouleh balanced on top. "A gay Iraqi."

"Naughty boy." Khoury scooped hummus onto a piece of *khobz*, flat bread, and popped it into his mouth.

"He has never been very productive. But he overheard something at his Mission. He was very keen to report it to me."

"Keen?"

"As in keen to keep me happy so that I did not send his superiors certain, er, recreational photos I have of him."

"Zi – CiCi you are outrageous."

"I had a good teacher, Moro. Anyway, from what he'd overheard he claimed that Sajida was right."

Khoury stopped eating, frowning. "Sajida? Who, what or where is Sajida?"

Carla explained it to him.

Khoury nodded. "Oh Sajida, of course." He laughed, sipping from his glass of *arak*. "The rumour. The Great Secret. The Second Coming. The Messiah. Well, we are two thousand years on from the last one! *al-Mahdi*. Nobody believed Sajida, of course."

"Perhaps they did not want to believe."

"There was no proof."

"There still isn't. But you understand why I could not tell you except in person."

He nodded. "But what's it to do with us, with Lebanon?"

She sat back, wiping her mouth on a paper napkin. "Telling you this now makes me feel like it is all indeed stupid nonsense. Non-believers dispute that there was ever a Messiah in the first place, let alone a Second Coming." She sighed. "Was I foolish to return?"

He reached out and touched her hand. She did not pull away. "No, no you did right. And it is good to see you again after all these years."

"And you too."

"But what has it got to do with Lebanon?" he repeated.

She leant back in her chair, her hand naturally moving away from his. "Apparently The Great Secret is being kept here in Liban."

"Here?"

"On the basis that it would be the last place the searchers would look. Saudi definitely. Syria maybe. But little old Liban? Who would think it?"

"So we are near *Yawm al-Qiyamah*?"

"Who knows?"

"Can't fight Judgment Day."

"Who says?"

Khoury laughed out loud. "Shall we sit more comfortably?" He nodded over into the living area. "I have baklava if you would like some."

"My teeth are always sweet."

Five minutes later he came to join her on the couch with more coffee and a box of baklava. He sat close but not too close. "Where are you staying?" he asked.

"The Hotel Albergo."

"Just round the corner? Very nice. But I hope my departmental budget can take it! I have an idea. Stay here. No, no - " he held up his hands. "No hidden agenda, I promise. I have spare rooms, it makes sense. And this place is secure, nobody else knows you're back and we can keep it that way."

She was smiling, shaking her head. "You don't have to sell it, Moro. Or add riders. I'll stay here tonight and tomorrow we can decide what to do, if anything."

She popped a baklava into her mouth and for the first time in his life Maroun Khoury wished he was wrapped in layers of filo pastry and covered in a sugar sauce...

Beirut 23:59

In her assumption that The Listeners have listeners, Carla was right. In the complex, sectarian driven world of Lebanese politics and government, distrust and intrigue between the factions is mandatory not optional. The Listeners have listeners, The Watchers have watchers. Spies spy on spies, narks nark on narks. It is a given. Known and accepted.

As the Chief of the External Security Unit, Maroun Khoury was not blind to the obvious. At least once a week he swept his apartment for hidden devices, using the officially-issued Super Sweep 2000 professional bug finder.

Listening devices can be hidden in anything: power sockets, lights, telephones, picture frames, pens, calculators, absolutely anything – even walls. A major benefit of the Super Sweep 2000 is that it will not only sweep for listening devices but, if left in a room, it will continuously monitor, detecting any devices that may be brought into the room even before they are hidden. So with his weekly sweep and the machine's constant monitoring, Khoury was happy that his apartment was clean.

But he was wrong.

It was a question that had been asked through the ages: who guards the guards? The Super Sweep could detect any listening device, concealed or brought into the room. But it could not detect itself and the special adaptation that had been made to it prior to issue: the tiny listening device concealed deep within it.

And so at 23:59 that night, someone listened and transcribed and then picked up the telephone...

4 July 2010
22 Rajab 1431

Deir Qozhaya, Lebanon 09:00

The Jeep Wrangler Ultimate, with the hard top on, was waiting in the courtyard when Brother Malek and one of the monks came out of the monastery. Although it was already thirty degrees, even up here in the valley in the mountains, Malek was wearing the *burnus* with hood up. He said a few words to the monk, embraced him, and then walked towards the Jeep. He carried a small backpack and the small dark blue *argileh* case.

Love was waiting by the open back door of the vehicle, and Malek experienced just a little shock when he looked into her eyes. It had been a long time since he had seen either of the *houri* without their lenses in.

Silently he climbed into the Jeep, throwing his bag onto the seat next to him and placing the case gently next to it.

Love made sure the hem of his *burnus* was tucked in, slammed the door and climbed into the front next to her sister. The car moved off.

"Everything is arranged?" Malek threw back the hood and scratched his head. He shook his unruly bush of hair. He was grateful that the air conditioning was on.

"Yes," Love half-turned in her seat. "They are expecting the pilgrim Brother Malek to arrive today, scheduled to be staying for at least three months."

"And The Secret will be safe there?"

Paradise looked at him from the rear-view mirror. "We are satisfied."

Malek looked back. "Then I am too."

"We have made financial arrangements," continued Love. "A donation. But they have asked if you would like to work as well while you are there."

"Work?"

"The Monastery has much land. They grow fruit and vegetables and produce wine and jams, to sell locally and to the visitors. They ask all lodgers to help out."

Malek sniffed. "I may be too busy praying."

"As you wish," Love turned back.

"But then again, I would wish to fit in. Maybe I can do a little work somewhere quiet and unobtrusive. I don't wish to be involved with the hoards of pilgrims and tourists. Couldn't I stay in the hermitage? That would be an ideal place for The Secret."

"It has not been used as a hermitage for fifty years," Paradise was concentrating on the less than perfect road leading back up to Ehden. "It is now a shrine to Saint Charbel."

Malek nodded. After a moment, he said "Lebanon's patron saint by acclamation. I wonder what Saint Maron thinks about that, it is his monastery after all."

"I would think the saints are above petty human-style squabbles," said Love.

"Indeed..." Malek looked out the window at the valley disappearing below. "Where will you be?"

"We will be down in Jbeil," answered Paradise.

"Old Byblos! We are going where the crowds are now."

"It is better than being alone," explained Love. "Too conspicuous."

"But in Jbeil you are within easy reach of me at the monastery in Annaya," nodded Malek, understanding. "Good. Do you have anything for me?"

Love leant forward and rummaged in the bag between her

legs. She passed a silver tube over her shoulder.

Malek took the cap off the end and slid the *Romeo & Julietta Churchill* cigar into his palm. He looked up to see Love dangling a lighter over her shoulder, which he accepted. "Should I open a window?"

"Try it," said Paradise. "But you may get too hot. Do not worry, the smoke does not affect us."

Malek lit up carefully, starting with quick, sharp puffs and then a long sensuous draw. Reluctantly he had to exhale. "I was contacted by the disciples," he announced.

Love turned in her seat, her white and black eyes intense. Paradise's identical eyes looked at him via the mirror.

Malek said, "I think more conversions might be necessary."

Ashrafieh, Beirut 19:00

As it was a Sunday, Maroun Khoury allowed himself the luxury of leaving the office earlier than he normally would. He did, after all, have an incentive back in his apartment.

Much to his disappointment, CiCi had slept in one of his spare bedrooms last night. It was expected but, like any man, he lived in hope. Their time had passed, but the passion, the lust, the abandon of their two-month affair never left his mind even though it was many years ago now. He wondered if he would ever see her belly-dance again? Well, she was staying in his apartment, so it would be now or never.

They had discussed the matter of The Second Coming over their breakfast croissants and *labneh*, Khoury being a little distracted by the fact that Carla wore her pink T-shirt – and nothing else, as a surreptitious glance confirmed.

The Sajida statement and the inferred prophesy had surfaced now and again over the years, but nothing had ever come of it, and Khoury had thought that it had at last been consigned to history, filed under Lies and Misdirection. He did not believe it, never had.

It was not that he was non-religious – he was as good a Maronite as the next man – but religion had nothing to do with this. If Sajida was right all along then the world was looking at *ad-Dajjal* not *al-Mahdi*.

As discussed with Carla, he had set The Listeners and The Watchers in motion, and he had contacted the latest unit of the DGS, The Readers. This unit was not under his command (yet) but they would be looking at all e-mail and text activity flowing into and out of Lebanon and looking for trigger words and phrases.

Carla had agreed that she would not be taking an active role in the investigation. There were still too many people in Lebanon and adjacent countries who would very much like a conversation with her about her knowledge of the Hariri assassination five years ago. She would be returning to New York tomorrow morning.

Which meant, reflected Khoury sadly, that he had one last night with her.

He must make the most of it.

"CiCi? Carla?"

The apartment was silent and still.

"ZiZi? Zahia?"

Nothing. He felt the reassuring bump under his left arm but he did not draw his gun. She had not said she was going out. But then again she had not said she was staying in. But where did she have to go to? He probably knew better than she did the identities and the quantity of people who wanted to talk to her, and that worried him – until he saw the note on the coffee table.

Moro. Have gone to pick up my stuff from the hotel. C xxx

What an over-reactive idiot! he chided himself. And he liked the last three letters of her note. Did it bode well for the coming night?

He would take her out to dinner – his favourite local restaurant, which he considered one of the best in Beirut, was

Abd el Wahab up on the same street as her hotel. Then he would suggest an early night, as she had an early flight tomorrow.

And who knows? Maybe she would dance for him. For old times' sake...?

There was a knock on the door. Good, she was back.

He went across and opened the door, smiling.

And then stood back, his eyes wide...

Ain el-Mreisseh, Beirut 19:15

The memorial statue to Rafic Hariri is larger than life.

The stunningly accurate suited figure of Lebanon's assassinated former Prime Minister stands with hands in pockets in a special garden overlooking the site of his murder outside the St George Hotel, his wise-owl face seeming to say "I knew it would happen."

The small woman in a headscarf and dark glasses had been there for five minutes. She was not the only one pausing to reflect, to pay respect, but she knew she should not linger. For her, it could be dangerous.

The taxi that had brought her from the Hotel Albergo was still waiting. With a nod, she climbed back in. "*Yalla*. Back to Ashrafieh Street, *s'il vous plait*."

Ashrafieh, Beirut 20:00

Carla got out of the taxi two streets away from Khoury's apartment. Old habits never die, they just harden. She enjoyed the feeling of the Mediterranean sun on the left side of her face as she walked northwards, wondering when, if ever, she would be back in her homeland again. She loved this Land of The Cedars, but there were people in it who did not love her. So tomorrow she would return to her exile. But tonight she would enjoy her last evening, she would take Moro out for dinner and then suggest an early night. She had already checked in online and printed out her boarding card for the first leg of the journey to Paris, so the rush in the morning would be reduced. Who knew? They might even get some sleep.

Then again, they might not.

She skipped lightly up the stairs to the fifth floor, her thirty-something legs firm and untiring. She had a spare key that she had found concealed in a lampshade in the hallway (old habits never die...). He might not be back yet, in which case she would destroy the note she had left for him and then get herself ready for the evening.

She went into the apartment and immediately knew something was wrong. It was still. Too still. And there was a smell.

Of body, of faeces... of death.

Her left hand went to her hair and pulled out the hair clip, in one smooth motion pushing the metal clasp back so that the needle underneath was exposed. The micro-syringe was not loaded but she could easily kill someone with the needle alone.

"Maroun? Moro?" she called quietly, trying to keep her voice normal in case she had got this all wrong. Which she knew she hadn't.

There was no reply. It was quiet. So, so quiet. Keeping her back to the wall, she moved swiftly over to the window, glancing out at the small Juliet balcony. As she turned back she saw his feet sticking out from behind the couch. *Oh God, Moro.*

But she did not rush over. His assailant might still be here, and she would make the perfect target bending over him.

Carefully, her movements as silent as a djinn, she explored the apartment: the kitchen, the bathroom, his bedroom (she noticed there was an open bottle of Ksara red wine on his bedside table), her bedroom, the third bedroom. In cupboards, under beds, behind furniture.

She was alone.

Grim-faced, she went back out into the lounge, quickly

kneeling by the side of Maroun. He looked up at her, smiling. But she knew he could not see. And the ligature so tight around his neck that in some places it had broken the skin and sunk inside him, told her that the smile was a rictus grin.

Captain Maroun Khoury, Chief of the External Security Unit of the Lebanese Department of General Security, was dead. Slaughtered like an animal. His hands were at his sides but his fingers were bent like claws, a reaction to his final excruciating moments. On his shirted chest was a sheet of paper.

A single tear rolled out of Carla's left eye. Was this to do with her? Had she returned to Lebanon and brought death in her wake? In his position, Maroun would have lots of enemies, lots of people who wanted him dead, both foreign foes and, sadly, internal foes. Anybody could have done this.

But she knew she was kidding herself.

She reached out and lifted the piece of paper off his chest. She already knew what it was.

She was looking at her online check-in boarding pass for her flight tomorrow. It was a message to her.

She stayed kneeling on the floor next to the body for ten minutes, just in case his soul had yet to leave. Then she sat back on her heels, angry, sad but resilient. She had shed her tear for Maroun. Now she needed to dust the place and then leave and leave quick.

But one thing was for certain.

She would now be staying on in Lebanon.

PART TWO
الجزء الثاني

THE DISCOVERY
اكتشاف

5 July 2010
23 Rajab 1431

Jbeil, Lebanon 09:00

For the oldest continuously inhabited city in the world, Jbeil has some surprisingly modern suburbs, commercial districts of glass-fronted office buildings in which twenty-first century life continues apace. But this evidence of the latest inhabitants of the city is ignored by the thousands of tourists who come each year to see the old town, the Byblos of history, with its fishing port and sheltered old harbour, stone buildings with red-tiled roofs, the many Roman and pre-Roman ruins, the Crusader castle, the church of Saint John the Baptist with its Byzantine origins, and the souks.

Dating from the Ottoman era, the souks are a maze of intersecting alleyways, sometimes no more than two metres wide, with old stone buildings and covered arcades. Nowadays the Byblos souks are mostly geared towards their tourist visitors, with souvenir shops, modern boutiques, cafés and restaurants, but in some parts traditional trade still exists: a baker, a spice emporium, a gold merchant, a bookshop.

And, in the souk furthest away from the modern travellers, up near the Roman road and backing onto the cemetery, a *Muhaqqiq Khass* – a Private Investigator.

Abu Yussuf was originally from Palestine, but with his medium complexion, medium height, medium weight and medium age, thinning dark hair and neatly trimmed moustache, he could pass as a native of any country in the Levant. His non-descript appearance served him well in his current profession.

He was sitting behind his desk observing the sobbing, grim-faced woman sitting opposite. "Madame Gourhant, I am a busy man," he lied. He was anxious to get back to his game of solitaire, and he cast a glance at the pile of playing cards he had hastily scooped into his drawer. Okay, the woman could represent some well-needed money – especially if he stretched the job out and asked for daily retainers – but it was summer, it was hot and, really, could he be bothered?

The small, ineffective fan in the corner of the room clanked from side to side. What little coolness it produced did nothing for the humans but it seemed to provide a welcome updraft for the flies. There were at least three gliding about the room.

"He has done it before," sniffed Madame Gourhant, gathering herself together after a five minute weeping indulgence. "But back then I was young and things were different in Liban. Now we are liberated and we have rights."

By 'we' Abu Yussuf presumed she meant woman-kind. If so, perhaps not as many rights as you imagine, he thought. But he kept his reflections to himself. "And what would you like me to do?" he asked.

With a mighty sniff, Madame Gourhant pulled herself up from her slouch, tears ceasing. "I want you to find evidence. Evidence that I can use in a divorce."

"You do not have any evidence already, to support your allegations?"

"I have the evidence of a wife's feelings, her intuition. But it is not evidence that will stand up in a divorce hearing."

"No, that is correct. You know that divorce in Lebanon is... complex, shall we say? Were you married here before a religious court? Or were you married abroad?"

"I was married here. In church."

"You are a Maronite?"

"Yes."

"In which case, there is no concept of divorce, as you must know. You will be petitioning to have the marriage annulled. How long have you been married?"

"Thirty years."

Abu Yussuf's eyebrows rose. Then you were on a hiding to nothing, dear lady. Nullity meant proving vices that existed at the time of the marriage. "May I ask, madame, how old you are?"

She did not bridle at the question. "I am fifty-two."

"And your husband?"

"Eighty-two."

His only reaction was a slight cough, but he could feel his cheeks rising in mirth. Quickly, he pulled a cigarette from the packet on the desk and busied himself lighting up. He turned the packet to face the lady, eyebrows raised. She shook her head.

This could be the perfect summer job for him, he thought. Would a man of eighty-two really be committing adultery? Technically it was possible, physically also to a lesser extent. But there was great truth in the saying that when you reached a certain age you'd rather have a cup of tea than be bothered with the effort of having sex!

So, the lady wanted evidence her husband was sipping from another cup. If he was, Abu Yussuf would prove it. But whether the lady would be given the evidence was another matter. It would be useless to her without the historical evidence also. It might be more useful if he sold it to the husband, turn a double profit.

He pretended to have given it much thought. "It is something I could take on. I charge two hundred and fifty thousand pounds a day, plus the same amount on hand-over of the evidence."

"What is that in dollars?"

Abu Yussuf took his new pirated Apple iPhone from beneath the playing cards in the drawer, found the calculator application after three attempts and tapped in some figures. He announced "One hundred and sixty-six dollars."

Madame Gourhant nodded. "That is acceptable."

"I do, of course, have other cases. Naturally I will charge you only for days worked." Both lies were said with a straight face.

"Of course. You would like a payment in advance?"

"Two days, if you would be so kind madame. And do you have a photograph? Of your husband?"

"I do." She rummaged in her bag and passed over a folded A4 sheet of paper with the tips of her fingers, as if she was pleased to get rid of it.

As she was counting out cash onto the desk, Abu Yussuf opened the paper and smiled at the printed photograph of a fat, bald, lugubrious old man. Eighty-two? He looked ninety-two! Was he worn out by the copious amounts of illicit sex? Or simply by being married for thirty years to this *sahira*?

This, thought Abu Yussuf, *muhaqqiq khass extraordinaire*, was going to be easy.

Ashrafieh, Beirut 09:30

Carla sat on the edge of the bed in her opulent room on the fourth floor of the Hotel Albergo gently rubbing her temples with her fingertips.

She had not slept well, but was it any wonder? Her erstwhile lover, her friend, her boss was dead. Murdered. And she could not report it. She was *persona non grata* in Lebanon, in fact she was probably *persona* on several hit lists, and so her return, even under a different name, must be kept *sub rosa*. Maroun would have to wait for his body to be found by someone else.

That was bad for the body and its potential decomposition, but good for her. She could start investigating a murder which no one knew had happened yet. No one except the murderer, of course.

Was it anything to do with her? No, no one knew she was in

the country. Mortal threat was part of the job description of the Chief of the External Security Unit. It might be connected to a case the unit was involved in, or a past case, or someone with a vendetta against the ESU or even against Maroun personally (Lebanese memories have no time constraint). Or perhaps one of the factions had decided, simply, that the ESU needed a new Chief. Murder was the weapon of expediency in the world of 'intelligence'.

But the manner of the murder was unusual. Car bombing was the preferred and accepted method of removal, or shooting if necessary. Garrotting to the point of near decapitation was unusually brutal. Indicating, perhaps, a personal nature to the crime.

For the thousandth time she wondered if she was doing the right thing. Should she just go, flee back to her exile in New York, pretend to be as surprised as anybody at the eventual announcement of a new ESU Chief? (The announcement, when it came, would not give any explanations as to why, it would just say that Captain Walid Ibrahim or whoever was assuming the duties of Unit Chief from that day. Maroun would not be mentioned. No one ever received any thanks for a job well done – even if they had been murdered in the line of duty.)

She looked at her watch. She was far too late to get her Middle East Airlines 10:25 to New York via Paris now. She could always rebook, of course, the next flight was at two in the morning – but who was she kidding? She owed it to Moro to find out why he had been killed.

Subconsciously her hand went up to her hairclip.

And she owed it to him to exact revenge.

But she would need help. To whom could she turn without endangering herself?

Her thoughts were interrupted by a knock on the door and the announcement "Housekeeping."

She went over and looked through the security peephole. The maid was there, pale blue uniform with white hat and pinafore, with her trolley of towels and maid-paraphernalia behind her.

"*Un moment, s'il vous plait!*" called Carla. This was perfect timing, she needed to get out of this room despite the opulence of its oriental rugs, inlaid wooden furniture and crystal chandelier. She would go to the rooftop pool, relax in the sun, maybe have a swim (did they rent costumes? If not, she would send out for one). And she would think.

Grabbing her key card, she threw her Guess handbag onto her shoulder. "*Bonjour,*" she said as she opened the door.

"*Bonjour, madame,*" greeted the maid. She was holding an armful of clean towels.

"It's all yours."

"*Merci.*" The maid stepped back to let Carla leave and then went inside, leaving the room door open.

Carla walked down the thickly-carpeted corridor towards the lift, still thinking about the murder of Maroun Khoury and what she was going to do now.

Where did she even begin?

Ashrafieh, Beirut 12:00

Carla enjoyed her morning on the roof, sometimes swimming, sometimes just floating in the pool, sometimes sitting on a lounger in the sun and enjoying the views northward over east Beirut to the shimmering Mediterranean beyond.

The swimsuit that had been purchased for her from a nearby boutique suited her perfectly, a one-piece costume, black with a gold pattern and mesh sides, complementing her long black hair and tanned olive body.

At midday she slipped on a white cotton robe (compliments of the hotel) and declined the offer to eat at the poolside. She was not hungry and she needed to begin her investigations while – and she grimaced as she had the thought – the body was still warm.

She had thought all morning about who could help her.

There was one person, just one person out of the two million plus in Beirut, who might be able to. If he was willing.

Down on the fourth floor, she padded along to her room, bipped her key card and went in, kicking the door closed behind her. She had already extended her stay by one night so she had no need to worry about checking-out times –

Her head was wrenched backwards as a rope was whipped around her neck.

Instinctively Carla's hands went up, grabbing the ligature, trying to get her fingers under it. She felt one of her false nails ping off. The rope was was tight, so, so tight.

The person behind crossed their arms and pulled.

Carla's mouth opened but no air could come out. Or go in. She was being shaken from side to side like a rag doll.

Giving up on the rope, she reached up and behind, grabbing hair, pulling. Pulling, pulling, pulling. She was winding the hair round and round in her hands as she pulled. But the pressure on her neck increased. Popping sounds started in her ears.

Then she let her legs go from beneath her, dropping to the floor on her rear, pulling the assailant down with her by the hair so that she would not simply drop and hang herself.

The attacker's chin banged painfully on the top of Carla's head, but she heard the hollow clunk as lower teeth bashed into top teeth. There was a grunt from above. The rope loosened. Quickly Carla rolled to the left, grabbing the now uncrossed hands which were still holding the rope but were now in front of her. Mouth open, gasping for air, she pulled the assailant off balance, onto one knee. Let's get a look at you...

She was staring into the face of the maid.

The maid's hat had been knocked off and long blonde hair cascaded down over her face. Blood was trickling from her mouth. Behind the hair, glowing white eyes stared at Carla, sending a shiver through her body. A *houri*?

Carla yanked at the rope. The maid yanked back. For a few seconds they went back and forth. Then unexpectedly the maid shoved Carla backwards. Carla staggered for a few steps and then fell over, back onto her backside. But the shove had given her distance. As the maid stood up, ready to come forward, Carla reached up and pulled out the clip from her hair, flicking it open, exposing the needle. "Okay *habibi*, you want some?" she panted, grinning. Her robe had fallen open to reveal the swimsuit underneath.

The maid stopped, breathing heavily, nostrils flared, the bizarre eyes staring unblinkingly, the bloody mouth expressionless. The rope dangled from her right hand.

"Who are you?" Carla had the needle protruding between the index and second fingers of her left hand. Tentatively she moved forward, giving little threatening thrusts. "What do you want?"

The maid backed away, looking at her curiously, her head slightly tilted to one side. "Your eyes," she said. "Are you one of us?"

Carla frowned. "My eyes are not like yours."

"But they are black. They are beautiful. Opposite."

The maid reached the door, feeling behind for the handle. She said, "You will be converted. *al-Mahdi* wants your soul."

"*What?* What are you talking about?"

"You will not stop The Second Coming." The maid pulled down on the handle.

"Oh, I won't won't I?"

"*Allahu Akbar.*" In a flash the door was open and she was gone.

Carla dashed over, the needle still held out in front of her. She looked left then right along the small corridor. No one.

She ran to the lift and stairwell, looking over the stairs, listening for footfall.

Nothing.

For a minute she stayed there, listening, aware. A couple came out of a room further down. Quickly she closed the robe, exchanging nods with the couple as she went back to her room.

She locked and chained the door, leaning against it, breathing heavily.

She flexed her jaw, rubbing the joint below each ear with her right hand and simultaneously reforming the hair clip with her left. Tentatively she ran her fingers over her neck. She could feel the welt.

Was this what had happened to Moro? If so then she knew she was completely responsible for his death. They had tried to get her too.

In the name of God.

She went over and knelt down by the side of the bed, like a child about to pray. Then, not for the first time in Beirut, the woman previously known as Zahia Zalloum, and sometimes as The Djinn, began to cry.

Jbeil, Lebanon 16:00

The slap hurt Paradise's face like the simultaneous sting of a hundred bees. The force of the blow knocked her head five centimetres to the side but she stood her ground, accepting her punishment.

"You stupid bitch," said Love, anger in her eyes. "We do not fail in conversions, do you hear me? Never!"

She raised her hand again and Paradise screwed up her eyes but did not move away. They were in their new accommodation, a disused and boarded up shop behind the old Mayadoun Bookshop on Rue St John just inside the northern medieval ramparts of the old town.

"I... I am sorry, sister," Paradise lowered her head in shame. "I did not expect her to have such skills of resistance. And you should have seen her eyes. They were so, so black. But I have no excuse. Please punish me more."

"Oh no," Love shook her head, putting her fingers under her sister's chin and lifting her head back up. "You would like that too much. If the controller finds out you have failed, we will be recalled."

"But our job here is not done."

"We can be replaced. There are others."

"What about Malek?" sniffed Paradise.

"He must not find out, never. Otherwise we will be done for."

"But it is not your fault, I am the one who failed."

"We are the same person. Two halves of one whole. What is visited upon one is also visited upon the other."

Suddenly Love whipped her hand back sharply across her sister's face, again knocking her head to the side. This time Paradise staggered one step backwards, reaching out and grabbing Love's arms to steady herself. She looked across into eyes as white as hers. "Do it again," she whispered. "I am not sufficiently chastised."

"No. My refusal is your punishment."

Disappointed, Paradise lowered her eyes. "Yes *uhktee*."

"We are agreed?" asked Love. "We say nothing about this?"

"Yes *uhktee*. But what about the woman?"

"We will revisit her. She sounds intriguing. The eyes of a djinn. She will be a good conversion."

Paradise smiled. "That is good. That is right."

The hardness left Love as she reached out and caressed her sister's chin. "I have started your lip bleeding again."

"It is my punishment. I deserve to bleed."

"No," said Love. "No, you don't. I will look after you as you always look after me. Here, let me wipe it."

She pulled Paradise's face towards her, leant forward and with soft laps of her tongue began to lick the blood from her sister's lip.

6 July 2010
24 Rajab 1431

Jonblat, Beirut 09:00

Captain Jihad Merhi of the Lebanese Internal Security Force was pissed off. A state, he reflected, that he seemed to be in permanently nowadays.

Today was the funeral of Grand Ayatollah Mohammed Hussein Fadlallah*, who had died on Sunday, and dignitaries from around the Middle East were attending. Such was the great man's standing that a day of national mourning had been declared in Lebanon, which meant that banks and public offices were closed. But as the ISF was not a public office in that sense, Merhi was not only at work but also his unit was expected to provide 'discreet security' at the internment at the Al-Hassanein Mosque in the suburb of Haret Hureik later (non-discreet security would be provided by other entities).

After years of staff cuts, Merhi really did not have the manpower to provide a 'for appearance's sake' presence. His officers could be better used assisting with the enquiries into the clashes between UNIFIL (the United Nations Interim Force in Lebanon) and a number of residents down south last week (there was an allegation that a French battalion had destroyed acres of tobacco plantations, for reasons unknown), but his objections had been overruled, as usual, by his boss Major

---

* *The Shi'a cleric, described by some as the 'Spiritual Mentor' of Hizbullah.*

Ghanem.

On top of this, and to add to his pissed-offery, Ghanem had told him to prepare a risk assessment for the joint visit of Saudi King Abdullah and Syrian President Bashar al-Assad at the end of the month, including detailed security arrangements for their discussions with President Michel Suleiman at the Presidential Palace at Baabda.

So the small, slim, powerful, currently chain-smoking, often whisky-drinking, fifty-one year old Merhi was not happy.

And the last thing he wanted was a telephone call.

His mobile phone rang at 09:03.

Merhi was intent on his computer screen and at first he did not hear it. It took a few moments for his mind to register that there was a ringing coming from somewhere. He frowned at the phone on his desk but then realised that the sound was coming from behind him, from his uniform jacket draped across the back of his chair.

Cursing, he turned in his seat, fumbling into an inside pocket. It was probably his wife Gisele wanting him to pick something up on the way home tonight. Couldn't she just have text?

The phone stopped ringing as he pulled it out.

1 MISSED CALL

Damn and buggery. Well, the light of his life could ring back, or he would ring her later when he was less busy (using this criteria, that would be about next Easter).

Leaving the phone on his desk, he turned back to his screen.

The phone rang again.

UNKNOWN

Merhi picked it up and stared at the screen. So it was not Gisele. Not many people were privileged to know the mobile number of a Captain of the Internal Security Force, and those that did were all 'plumbed in' to the phone's memory. The

Caller ID would show. This lack of name meant Stranger. If it was a spam phone call, someone selling something, he would castrate them and serve them their testicles dipped in chocolate on ice cream topped with a strawberry sauce.

The phone stopped ringing.

Good, better all round perhaps.

He had just typed in his estimate of the number of armoured vehicles needed for the journey from Baabda to the Prime Minister's Office at the Grand Serail when the phone rang for the third time.

He snatched it up in irritation, this time pressing the green key. "Who the fuck is this?"

There was silence at the other end.

"Hello?" shouted Merhi.

A deep voice said, "Captain Merhi?"

He couldn't tell whether it was male or female. "Who is this?"

"Is this Captain Merhi?"

"Who are you?"

"Jihad Merhi?"

"How did you get this number?"

There was a pause. Then: "You gave it to me."

"Who is this?"

"It is best if I do not say."

"If you're pissing me about - "

"Five years."

"What?"

"Five years ago. You gave me your number."

Merhi fell silent, feeling the fingers of history creeping up his spine. "Five years...?" he said quietly.

"Yes. I would like to meet you again."

"Five years was a long time ago."

"Yes, it was. Can we meet?"

"Is it about what happened?"

"No."

"Then...?"

"Can we meet?"

"Why?"

"I... I need your help."

Merhi's mind was racing, tumbling back five years to a turbulent time in Lebanese history. "Are you - ?"

"Please do not say it! Do not say my name!"

"But..."

"Please. Can we meet? It is a matter of life or death. Mine."

Merhi was quiet again. Then he said slowly, "Okay."

"I know you will be busy today, with what is happening. Do you remember your little code you had with your Palestinian friend?"

"My little code?"

"When you arranged meetings?"

"Oh. Yes."

"So on that basis can we meet on Thursday? At 13:00?"

Merhi was working it out... The named time less twenty-six hours... Tomorrow at 11:00. "Yes."

"You name the place."

He plucked something. "Outside the *Voix du Liban* building in Ashrafieh?" It did not matter, the place would always be the same and it was not there.

"Yes. Thank you. *Merci ktir.*"

"Are you all right?"

"I hope so."

"Can you tell me what this is about?" There was no response. "Hello? Hello...?"

Jbeil, Lebanon 10:00

Private investigator Abu Yussuf yawned and looked at the time on his iPhone.

It had been a long ten minutes since he had sat down at this table outside the coffee house in Rue Cheralam, near the small but popular Ahiram Hotel on the northern coast road. His subject, eighty-two year old Monsieur Albert Gourhant, suspected adulterer and sex fiend, was in the barber shop opposite.

Abu Yussuf signalled for a second espresso and took a long draw on his cigarette, idly running his fingers across the phone's touch screen. His first full day on the job of following the old man and he was bored already – admittedly a boredom assuaged by the quarter million Lebanese pounds a day his client was paying him.

He wondered for how long he could prolong his nice little summer earner. How long did it take to confirm an eighty-two year old's infidelity or fidelity? Actually possibly a long time if he was, say, a once a month man, which was quite possible due to Monsieur Gourhant's age. A younger man would just take a few days, a week at the most.

A *muhaqqiq khass* less scrupulous than himself might drag this out for months and just sit in his office and do nothing and lie about his investigations. But not Abu Yussuf. He would let it take a month at the most and, to prove to his client that her quarter million a day was money well spent, he would give her a schedule of her husband's movements, hour by hour, location by location. The fact that he would also try to sell the schedule to Monsieur Gourhant was just good business practice.

The screen on his phone suddenly changed and he quickly pulled his fingers away, aware that he had pressed down too hard and had opened an application. He frowned in curiosity, then smiled with the pleasure of a skinflint when he realised he had hitched a ride on someone else's WiFi.

It was the GPS application, one he had not been in before. This was good, it gave him something to play with. A visit to a Lebanese barber's shop was always more a social event than a business transaction, especially on an unexpected public holiday such as this, so the subject would be in there for at least an hour, chatting, philosophising, sorting out the problems of the world.

Abu Yussuf watched as the number of satellites found above were counted out on his phone. Ten and rising! Was nowhere private anymore?

He looked over at the barber shop window. Well, there was no privacy for you Monsieur Albert Gourhant. Your wife was watching you.

Grinning, he opened Google Maps and began to play.

Ashrafieh, Beirut 11:30

Paradise smiled as Love held out the two contact lens cases. They were sitting in their Jeep outside the Hotel Albergo. As always, Abdel el Wahab el Inglizi Street was busy and crowded with traffic, but they had simply double-parked. Taxis did that.

Paradise chose the case nearest to her and slowly opened it. Her face lit up. "Green! I win again."

"Thirty-two thirty-two," nodded Love. "We're equal. As we should be." She opened the other case, leant forward and put in the brown contact lenses. Then she looked at her sister, blinking. "All right?"

"Yes. You still look beautiful. Even with human eyes." Paradise had not put in her contacts. She did not need to, she was staying in the car.

"If I need you, you'll know." Love bent across, kissed her sister on the cheek and then got out of the car. Her blonde hair was tied up and she was dressed in a smart dark grey two-piece suit and open-necked white blouse, a look which hinted at corporate uniform.

She walked through the tall, ornate gates of the hotel, past the small garden area and up the marble steps into the opulent foyer. Over at Reception, she said "Taxi for Room 431."

The male clerk tappy-tapped on a keyboard and looked at a screen below the level of the counter. He nodded and picked up the telephone. "I will let her know you're here."

Love waited, watching the clerk intently. Already he had

confirmed that her prey was still at the hotel. Now she just wanted to know whether she was in. The clerk would not have the chance to tell the prey that there was an unrequested taxi waiting downstairs, he would be asleep before the words left his mouth. "She has asked me to help with her luggage." Love stretched out, touching his arm.

The clerk raised a sardonic eyebrow. "We have porters to do that – hey, are you all right?"

The taxi driver had suddenly pulled her hand back and grabbed the side of her head, screwing up her face. "*Kakhbah!*" she gasped, her brown eyes glaring at the clerk. "No!" she looked back towards the entrance. "No, no, no!"

Turning away from the Reception counter, she ran back out.

Carla Chedid was not stupid. After yesterday's attack on her at the hotel it was obviously too dangerous for her to spend another night there. At first she had thought of going back to Maroun's apartment, but that was a non-starter, people might be knocking at the door wondering why the Chief of the External Security Unit had not reported in. And even if they weren't, poor Maroun would be well and truly over-ripe by now. So she had checked in to the Sofitel Le Gabriel on Avenue de l'Indépendance, a few blocks away.

But she was curious. Curious as to the murdering maid at the Albergo. That the maid had killed Maroun was beyond doubt: she had tried to kill Carla in exactly the same way. But how did she know about Carla? And why, anyway, would she try to kill her if this was a hit against the ESU Chief?

The two answers were obvious. She knew about Carla because she, or someone, had been listening. Despite Maroun's precautions, despite his conviction that his apartment was clean, it wasn't. Carla well accepted that the ESU was only one group of many Listeners operating in the maelstrom of Lebanese politics.

As to the second question, there was no need to kill Carla

because of Maroun's murder: she had not been there at the time, she had not seen anything. So, she was being targeted 'in her own right', as it were. Why? Because of something The Listeners had heard. What? What knowledge did she possess that would get her murdered? What knowledge had she passed to Maroun that had necessitated his elimination? Well, there was only one thing, wasn't there?

The knowledge that Sajida was right.

Although Carla had not stayed at the Albergo overnight, she had not checked out. Dressed in her ripped-knee jeans and pink T shirt, she was returning now to pick up her small suitcase and pay her far-from-small bill. She knew she needed to be careful. Yesterday's attack had been in the middle of the day. She would watch the staff carefully, although obviously the tall, blonde female assassin was not an employee. But she might try the same cover twice. She might be waiting.

Abdel el Wahab el Inglizi Street is naturally narrow, as are many of the old streets of Ashrafieh. Cars were parked on either side and the traffic was heavy and moving at a slow pace thanks to a Jeep that had double-parked outside the Albergo.

It was as she was standing on the kerb opposite the hotel, waiting to cross the road, that her eyes passed over the Jeep and then went back again with a jolt.

Her face hardened, fists clenching. Well, well, well...

Ripping the hairclip from her head, she dashed out between the slow-moving cars to a cacophony of horns and shouts. A woman driving a beige Ford Explorer with three children inside called her a son of a donkey.

In the Jeep, Paradise looked up to see what all the shouting was about.

Carla saw the startling white eyes as she reached the open window of the Jeep. Her left hand lunged outwards and grabbed the woman by the throat.

Paradise clawed at the small but vicious hand on her throat, eyes looking at the needle that was coming towards her. Her air was instantly restricted, already her chest was tight.

The needle stopped, almost touching her left eye. Paradise could smell jasmine. The woman leant in the open window and put her lips close to Paradise's left ear. "Houris are supposed to protect djinni," she snarled. "Not kill them." Pulling at her throat, she banged Paradise's head against the seat headrest. "Next time the needle goes in."

She let go of the throat, drew her hand back and landed a hard punch to Paradise's left temple.

Paradise was gasping for air and falling sideways at the same time, dizzy, hurting.

The next thing she was aware of was the passenger door opening, and she knew she had to fight back. A hand touched her head, and she flailed out hoping to make contact. Then she heard a voice say, "Sister! Sister! What happened? Are you all right?" She could see Love holding the left side of her own head.

Paradise grasped her sister's hand. "It was her," she croaked. "She's here." She felt the hand pull away sharply.

Love ran around to the other side of the Jeep, looking up and down the street. There were cars everywhere, people going about their business. A woman driving a beige Ford Explorer with three children inside suggested that her mother had made love to a camel. But there was no one running, no one hurrying away.

The prey had disappeared.

Coastal Highway, Lebanon 13:00

"You are all right, sister?" asked Love as she drove the Jeep northwards over the Nahr Ibrahim (River Ibrahim), her hand touching her own left temple.

"Just a slight ache, probably nothing you can feel," said Paradise reaching out and turning up the air conditioning. "But it is so hot with the roof on. Sometimes I wish we could sweat."

"We'll soon be home," consoled Love. She pulled out to overtake a slow-moving Mitsubishi van. The coastal road was as busy as always, perhaps even more so on this unexpected public holiday.

Love had shaken her hair back down in Beirut after she had gently pushed her stunned sister across into the passenger seat, belted her in and then climbed into the driver's seat. As she had driven eastward out of the city she had managed to remove one of her contact lenses but then she had hit the highway and needed both hands for driving, so one lens remained in, making a peculiar sight.

In a while, as they were passing the town of Halat, Love said, "I am sorry."

"What for?"

"For what happened. For you getting hurt."

"You got hurt too, sister. You feel what I feel."

"This woman," Love shook her head in frustration. "I should have converted her in New York."

Paradise touched Love's arm. "But how were you to know?"

"I wish I had seen her eyes then."

"Well, you didn't. You thought she was just Convert Arif's girlfriend. And our instructions are not to make any unnecessary conversions, only the selected ones who deserve it. Only those who know The Secret."

"And now we find out she is a Lebanese agent! We know she knows The Secret. Therefore she qualifies. She is being clever, elusive. She will not be converted easily."

"And..." Paradise looked at her sister, wondering how she would take what she was about to say. "She let me live."

Love eased the car to the right, ready to turn off the highway. She sighed. "Yes, she did... She did. Why did she do that?"

"I do not know. There is something about her..."

"I know what you mean. What is it, do you think? Why is it we feel unsure about her? In the past, we have converted many.

But this one...? Do we feel... a kinship?"

Paradise frowned, shrugging. "She is not one of us, we would know. But yet, we do feel, don't we..? She said something about *djinni*."

Love raised a cautionary finger. "Not a word about this to Malek tomorrow."

"Of course not."

They had reached Jbeil, passing the town clock and bearing left onto Boulevard al-Mina.

"But I failed today," admitted Love. "Just as you did yesterday." She pulled into the parking area just beyond the Seven Seas Restaurant, found a space and turned off the engine. "So," she continued, "you must punish me like I punished you." One brown and one white eye turned to her sister. "Only worse."

7 July 2010
25 Rajab 1431

Verdun, Beirut 11:00

Captain Jihad Merhi of the Internal Security Force stood at the edge of the Food Court on the second floor of The Dunes Shopping Mall, his mind awash with memories. It had been over five years since he had last been here. Five years since those dreadful events, when he had almost – almost – prevented the most horrendous Lebanese political assassination of recent times.

He sighed. Not pleasant memories.

Meeting at The Mall was the idea of his counterpart who was in charge of policing at the Beirut Palestinian refugee camps. The Mall was one of the oldest shopping complexes in Beirut, and the Verdun area over near the west coast and on the same block as the Holiday Inn Hotel was an easy drive from the Palestinian's base in the Bourj el-Barajneh refugee camp in the south of the city near the airport.

When Merhi met officially with his counterpart, it was in Merhi's own offices in Jonblat. The Food Court of The Dunes Shopping Mall had been used for unofficial meetings when they did not want to be monitored, overheard or even seen. There was a period when they met here frequently, but such a circumstance had not arisen for those full five years.

But now somebody else wanted to meet him here and it seemed like the last five years had never happened. Over there was *McDonald's*, *DipnCrunch*, and the *Frizzy Center*. The *Haagen Dazs* booth was still in the middle. All as he remembered. Was *Doodle Doo* over in the corner new?

The Food Court was not yet busy. Even if it was, Merhi's uniform white shirt and blue trousers, and all the accoutrements around his waistband including his gun, would have ensured him a quick passage along any queues.

He went over to *Cup Cake* for a double chocolate special and a coffee. There was one person ahead of him, a youth probably going to a bargain early showing at the Cine Empire opposite.

Merhi could tell it was early. The food odours had not yet encroached, he could still smell the cleaner's polish. Jasmine.

"Captain Merhi."

Inwardly he jumped and his right hand just gave the slightest twitch towards his gun. The low voice came from behind but he had not heard anyone approach.

He turned, looked and recognised.

"Well, well. Agent - "

Her soft finger went to his lips. "Please. Do not say it."

Merhi's eyebrows rose, then he nodded in acceptance. The finger was removed. "May I get you something?" He indicated the kiosk.

"An espresso please."

"Anything to eat?"

"*Merci.*" She shook her head.

"Do you mind if I do? It has been a long time since I have been here."

"Please."

As they sat at a table in a far corner of the court, she with her tiny polycup containing an even tinier amount of espresso, he with his black Americano and double chocolate cup cake, she said "My name is Carla Chedid."

Merhi slowly peeled the case from his cake. "Is it?" he said. "Not - "

"If you think I am anyone else, you are mistaken. That person has been exiled from Lebanon. For what happened."

"I see." He broke off a piece of cake and put it in his mouth.

For a moment there was silence between them. Merhi looked at the small, black-haired, black-eyed, olive-skinned, exotic creature opposite in her knee-ripped blue jeans and pink T shirt, and wondered what on earth she wanted with him. Their time was in the past.

She drank her espresso in one and said, "I need your help."

Merhi nodded, in understanding not in agreement. "With what?"

"You are the only person I can trust."

"I say again, with what? Is this an ESU matter? Or a personal matter?"

"Possibly both." Carla looked around the Food Court, satisfying herself that there were no Listeners or Watchers about. Then she asked, "Do you know Sajida?"

Merhi frowned. "Sajida? Didn't she appear at the *Casino du Liban* recently?"

Carla couldn't help but smile. "No, really. Do you know who Sajida is?"

Merhi shrugged and held his palms open.

"In which case," said Carla, "it is perhaps better that I do not tell you what this is about."

"Hold on, hold on," Merhi leant forward, putting down the piece of cake he was about to pop into his mouth. "You want me to help you? You come back to Lebanon after five years, you come back into my life after five years, you ask me to help you and you won't tell me what it is about?"

"Bluntly, yes."

Merhi sat back. "Is this conversation over?"

"I hope not. Let me explain to you. If you knew Sajida, if you knew what I was talking about, then I would explain everything. But as you do not, I am protecting you by not telling you."

Merhi raised an eyebrow. He popped the final piece of cake

into his mouth.

Carla went on. "Have you heard of Captain Maroun Khoury?"

"No. What district is he in?"

"He is – was – my boss at the ESU."

"Was?"

"I went to him with what I know and the next day he was killed."

"As a direct result of what you told him?"

"I am almost certain. That is one of the first things I want to find out. If my suspicions are confirmed then I must take action to avenge him - and protect myself. And to stop what is going to happen."

"What is going to happen?"

"I will tell you when I need to. When I can be sure you will be safe."

Merhi pulled out a packet of Cedars King Size cigarettes from his shirt breast pocket, offering them to Carla with an inquiring look. She shook her head.

He took his time lighting up. Then, looking at the glowing tip of his *seejaere*, he asked "What would you want of me?"

She looked relieved. "Thank you. *Merci ktir.*" She reached across and touched his arm, sending a mild tingle through his bicep. Taking her hand away slowly, she asked "Firstly, do you have access to street CCTV?"

Again Merhi shrugged. "For sure."

"If I gave you a street and a time, could you arrange for me to look at it?"

Another shrug, used as a silent confirmation.

"If it proves what I think it will prove," said Carla. "Then I will need to take action. And I may need the help of your intelligence resources."

"Well, one step at a time, eh?" He took a long drag on the cigarette.

"Yes. Okay. May I buy you a coffee?" She nodded at his

empty cup.

He looked at it, considered, shook his head. "*Merci.* Give me a day, time and street and I will see what I can do about the CCTV. You will need to come to my office to view it."

"No problem. There is, though, just one other thing."

Merhi blew smoke. "What is that?"

Carla pouted. "I need somewhere to stay."

Jbeil District, Lebanon 14:30

Although it is designated a primary road, the route from Jbeil to Annaya is bumpy, especially if you have a sore bottom.

Love fidgeted uncomfortably in the passenger seat of the Jeep. She had asked to be punished for failing in her conversion yesterday, but perhaps Paradise had been just a little too rough last night. A little too keen.

Love was glad her sister was driving, the stinging in her currently mottled-purple cheeks would have distracted her. Full concentration was needed for this drive high up into the mountains, the road meandering, curving, often bending back against itself as it made the ascent.

They passed through the villages of Hboub, Kfar Qouas, Breij, and stopped just the other side of Ras Osta. It was the beginning of high summer, the sun was intense, but it still felt cooler up here; they were glad they had worn long-sleeved tops.

Love smiled as she rummaged in a holdall and brought out the two contact lens cases, offering them to Paradise on the palm of her hand.

Paradise smiled and pulled the Jeep over, stopping close to the edge. Looking at the cases, she put a finger to her lips, thinking. She stretched over towards the case furthest away, then at the last moment pulled her fingers back and touched the one nearest to her. "This one."

Love let her take the case and then slowly opened the one she was left with, raising the lid away from her so that her sister would enjoy the exquisite anticipation until the very last moment. She looked and then let the case flop open in her hand. She had her own lenses, the brown ones.

"Yes!" Paradise gave a little air-punch of triumph. "I picked right. Three wins in a row! Thirty-three thirty-two."

Love nodded. "Congratulations, *habibi*. It is your time. You are on a roll."

Paradise was self-deprecating. "It is nothing. Just our little game." She leant forward, balancing one of the lenses on her index finger and pulling her eyelid open with her other hand.

"Yes, but Allah is favouring you," insisted Love. "That is good for the next conversion."

Paradise came back up, one green eye one white eye. "You think there will be more?"

Love shrugged. "We still have this djinn to deal with. And who knows? Malek might have others. He said the time is close now. The re-birth cannot be disrupted."

"No," said Paradise. "It cannot. The world has waited too long."

They both finished putting in their lenses. Shortly the Jeep was moving off again with the two identical women inside, separated only by the colour of their eyes.

They drove higher, to 1350 metres above sea level.

To the Deir Mar Maron.

The Monastery of Saint Maron.

Annaya, Lebanon 15:45

The orange-roofed monastery of Saint Maron is Lebanon's most visited pilgrimage site. It is where Youssef Antoun Makhlouf, Lebanon's revered Saint Charbel, lived and died. So popular is the saint that the monastery is often incorrectly referred to as the Deir Mar Charbel by the tens of thousands of people who come each year, an error uncorrected by Charbel's followers who give service in the new church housing the saint's tomb, or in the bookshop, the restaurant or the monastery shop.

Although it was midweek, the parking area was busy. The two tall blonde women in camouflage combat trousers, desert boots, white vests under black hooded tops, hairs in simple ponytails, attracted some glances from the devout visitors, but they were looks of the *oh-look-twins-aren't-they-sweet?* variety. They avoided the new church and walked eastwards to the monastery itself.

Love had her mobile phone to her ear. "We are here," she announced. "Yes... *oui, d'accord*." She pressed the End icon and put the phone into a thigh pocket. "He will meet us outside," she said to her sister. "They are not keen on having young women in the monastery – even if we are novitiates, which is what he told them." She smiled. "Sister Paradise."

"Sister Love," Paradise nodded. "It suits you."

"Perhaps we should take the cloth when he comes again."

"I think our rewards will be much greater than that, dear one. Much greater."

"Not long now and we will find out. Ah, there he is."

The tall, hooded figure had come out of the main monastery door and was walking towards them. Sandaled feet poked out from beneath the full-length *burnus*.

"*Salaam, oh Malek*," greeted the twins in unison.

Brother Malek raised his right hand in a gesture of blessing. "*Salaam*."

"The place is to your satisfaction?" asked Paradise.

Malek's face was hardly visible beneath the cowl. His grey-black beard moved up and down as he spoke. "Come, walk with me."

He turned back and the twins caught up and went either side of him. Like bodyguards. They walked casually along the side wall of the monastery, shaded from the midday sun.

"It will suffice," he said in his curious way of talking without acknowledging any pause in the conversation. "I have my own cell well away from others, befitting for a monk with hermit inclinations. And they have asked me if I would like to work, as you said they would." Suddenly he was gruff. "Of course I do not wish to work!"

Paradise and Love exchanged glances.

"But," Malek went on, calmer. "I must fit in. So I have asked for something where I do not have contact with others, just like a hermit would. Tomorrow I start work harvesting vegetables. Physical work. It will be good for... my soul."

"Your soul is mighty," said Love softly.

"Mighty," agreed Paradise.

"The conversions," Malek went on as if they had not spoken. "They were successful?"

"Your collection of spirits has increased," confirmed Love, hoping he had not noticed the very slight pause before she answered.

"Good. That is good. The Secret remains safe. God is pleased. Do you have anything for me?"

They had reached the end of the monastery and Malek paused, looking at the holdall on Love's shoulder.

"Of course," she said, turning her back so that Paradise could get into the bag.

Paradise brought out a paper bag and gave it to Malek. He did not look inside it.

The three of them turned and began to walk back the way they had come. They were silent, walking in the tree-lined shade, respectful of the tranquillity.

When they reached the main door of the monastery, Malek held up his hand. He said "I have been in contact with the disciples. I have some news. It is close now, very close. After all this time."

"*Allahu Akbar*," said Paradise softly.

"The preparations are made. We have a date for The Second Coming. Satan is running with his spiked tail between his legs. In eight weeks. Just eight weeks and The Secret will be revealed. The world will be saved from itself."

"Ma Sha' Allah!" Love was genuine in her surprise. "You must tell us what you want us to do."

"I will, I will," the voice from beneath the cowl was benign. "You will be with me, my sisters. My right and left hands."

"You are too good to us, Malek," said Paradise.

Malek looked into the top of the bag they had given him. "Now it is time for prayer," he said. "Go in peace, sisters, I will call you. Soon the world will be at our feet."

"Insh'allah," agreed Love. Both women knelt down as Malek held out the backs of his hands. They kissed the hairs above his knuckles.

As Paradise looked up she could just see his eyes in the shadow of the hood. They were bright, anticipatory, almost excited.

Without further word, Brother Malek turned and went back into the monastery.

The twins rose and turned to each other. *"Yalla,"* said Love, taking her sister's hand. "Time to go."

Back at the Jeep, Paradise said "We did right not telling him about the djinn. Wouldn't want to spoil his excitement, would we?"

"No," agreed Love. "What *al-Mahdi* does not know - "

"*ad-Dajjal* does not grieve over."

They climbed into the Jeep and soon were heading back down the mountain.

As Brother Malek mounted the stairs to his cell on the third floor of the monastery, faint singing was coming from another part of the building, a joyous Maronite holy song. But he did not hear it. All he could hear was the *azan*, the Islamic call to prayer, recited by the muezzin in his head. It was time for *'Asr salat*, afternoon prayer.

In the bag was strawberry-flavoured *ma'asel*. He would wash, pray, and then enjoy a leisurely *argileh* before his evening meal. He would not join the other pilgrims in the refectory, his meal would be brought to him.

After all, he was a monk with hermit inclinations.

Jounieh, Lebanon 18:00

"How could you do this?" Gisele Merhi spoke lowly, her tone on the cusp between not-at-all-pleased and outright anger. "You know Samer and Sary are due home for the summer soon."

"It will only be for a few days," reasoned her husband. "And what was I supposed to do? Refuse a colleague in distress?"

They were standing in the kitchen of their mountainside apartment, high above the town. The summer evening sun was streaming in across the Mediterranean beyond the coast. Jihad still wore his uniform shirt but he had swapped his trousers for an old pair of jeans.

"And it's not as if you don't know her," he reasoned, cigarette propped in the side of his mouth, glass of whisky in hand. "She was one of your students once."

At one time, Gisele had been a member of the Lebanese security service – that was how she and Jihad had met – and she knew that her husband was right. You do not leave a colleague in the field in harm's way. But now she was a wife and a mother – and a Lebanese wife and mother at that – she knew she had to make a fuss, it was part of the job description.

"So?" she asked. "Are we to accommodate all the students I have ever taught if they come knocking?"

"Actually," Jihad took a long swill of his Johnnie Walker. "Yes. If necessary. You know that, Gigi. It's how we work in our job."

With one downward stroke of her kitchen knife, Gisele cut the head off a sea bass on the chopping board in front of her. Jihad winced and subconsciously moved his groin backwards.

She slit open the fish's belly and began to gut it. "Well, as long as you are sure it will only be for a few days," she was giving in, playing the indignation through. "What if she is here when the boys arrive?"

"Then we will have a full house. It is not like we do not have the space."

"And what will we tell Mama and Baba? And Joe and Jacqui will be arriving soon from Dubai."

"We tell them the truth! Sort of... she is an old friend, not been back home for many years. Last minute decision to come back. You know."

Gisele turned, holding a handful of fish entrails. She nodded. The scene had been played out. She was satisfied. She said, "I've heard of bringing your work home with you, but you, dear husband, take it to extremes!"

She smiled and bipped him on the nose with her index finger, leaving a round fingerprint of fish blood above his right nostril.

Jounieh, Lebanon 19:45

"I'm truly grateful, Gisele, thank you. Thank you both." Carla spooned fish and rice onto her plate. "And this *sayadieh* looks delicious." The three of them were sitting at the table in the dining area.

"It is her special way," said Jihad. "She removes the fish head before cooking."

Gisele nodded thanks to her husband as he poured white wine. *"Beyti beytak,* Carla. You are welcome here. And you won't tell us what it is about? Who this Sajida is?"

"Not until I need to. Not until I have to. You are my gracious hosts. I need to ensure your safety. If I establish that Maroun was not killed because of what I told him, then I will tell you. But I have a strong suspicion that he was." Carla took a mouthful of fish. "I need to see that CCTV, then I will know for sure. This *is* delicious, Gisele."

"I will call for it tomorrow," Jihad also ate as he spoke. "It should be with me pretty quick. Will you be safe coming to my office?"

"Nobody knows me in Internal Security – except you. As long as you can get me through the doors."

"I will meet you and escort you in personally. The team might wonder who you are but no one will ask. And if they did, I would tell them the truth. You are a liaison from the ESU. Keep it as simple and as truthful as possible. In falsehood lies confusion."

"One of Gisele's lessons," smiled Carla.

"Er... yes. *Sahtik*. Cheers." Jihad swilled down some wine

Gisele grinned at her husband's forced acknowledgement.

"There is one thing though," said Carla, touching Gisele on the arm. "I had to check out of the Hotel Albergo by telephone. To preserve my cover I had to ask them to ship my case back home to New York. The only clothes I have are these ones I'm wearing. Gisele, you don't fancy going shopping with me in the morning, do you?"

Gisele's grin became wider and Jihad inwardly groaned as dollar signs rolled before his eyes like the loaded drums on a casino slot machine.

8 July 2010
26 Rajab 1431

Jbeil, Lebanon 11:45

Private investigator Abu Yussuf drove his old, battered, rusting, burnt orange, over thirty years old, apple-of-his-eye, Datsun Bluebird south out of Jbeil down the coastal road. He was following a tivoli blue Citroen C4 Picasso driven by its owner, the sexual animal and octogenarian Monsieur Albert Gourhant.

The sun was over the coastal cliffs to Abu Yussuf's immediate left and was beaming straight into the Bluebird, which meant he had to drive with the car's sunshade down and his *Ray-Ban*s on. He drove one-handed, his left arm hanging out the open window, cigarette between his fingers, warm air blowing into his face.

Yesterday had been a quiet day. Sex God Albert had stayed at home - or he had been confined indoors. Today he had been let out – or he had escaped. It would be interesting to see where he was going. South to Beirut?

Soon the Citroen slowed as a modern five-storey building came into view on the right. The Hotel Victory Byblos, its name emblazoned in large green letters on the roof. Albert kindly indicated he was turning.

Throwing his cigarette away, Abu Yussuf brought his left arm back into the car, turned in after Albert and parked three spaces away from him.

Well now. A just-out-of-town hotel in the middle of the day? It had 'tryst' written all over it.

Was Madame Gourhant, his esteemed and very generous client, right after all?

Picking up his iPhone from the passenger seat, Abu Yussuf got out and followed Albert Gourhant into the hotel.

Annaya, Lebanon 12:30

Brother Malek was not happy.

Because of his publicised hermit inclinations, he had been given work in a secluded corner of ground near the monastery. Pulling up potatoes. He could see others at work further away, but no one was near him. No one was helping him. It was his responsibility to bring in several sacks of *batatis* before vespers, the daily Christian evening prayer.

He would do it, but he was not young any more. All the bending was making his mortal bones ache already. And it was so hot under the hooded cloak. He felt dirty, sweaty, unclean.

He needed to work because he needed to fit in, but he did not like it. He was Malek – the King. The King of Kings. He had come to save the earth – not work on it.

But, like a good hermit, he kept his head down and got on with his task. But he was not happy.

And an unhappy Brother Malek was not good for any one.

Jbeil, Lebanon 12:45

Well it was a tryst of sorts, but not the kind that would interest Madame Gourhant. Monsieur Albert Gourhant was in the Health Center of the hotel having a massage!

As Abu Yussuf sat in a low chair in a corner of the Health Food Bar trying to pretend he was enjoying the carrot juice he had ordered, he wondered how Madame would interpret this. She would probably say he was toning himself for his slut tart, his fast-becoming-imaginary bit on the side. In reality it seemed that Monsieur Albert was simply an old man going about his business, looking after himself. Getting out of the house.

Abu Yussuf smiled. And who could blame poor Albert for wanting to get out of the house!

He was only three days into his investigation and he had given himself a month. Just in case. But already he was reaching a conclusion of innocence regarding the unfortunate Albert. The next twenty-eight days would drag, and although his boredom was assuaged by thoughts of the daily fee he was earning, he would need to find something to fight off the *ennui* of the waiting-and-watching times. He wished he had his playing cards with him.

Or perhaps he should read a book. He had read one once. At least he thought he had, couldn't remember.

He played with his iPhone, many of the apps unavailable because he was not online. He went to reach for his cigarettes in his pocket and then thought better of it, looking guiltily around the Health Center. Instead he took another very small sip of his juice.

Five minutes later, Monsieur Gourhant came out from somewhere in the back, accompanied by a local girl in a white uniform dress with 'Victory Byblos Health Center' in green on her left breast. Gourhant shook her hand, slipping her the expected few notes tip, and went over to the main counter to settle his account.

Abu Yussuf casually stood up, pretended to take a final long swig from his juice, left a low-denomination note on the table, and followed Gourhant out. Now, which way would he go? Back to town, down to Beirut?

Gourhant stopped by the elevator in the lobby, pressing the Call button. Abu Yussuf stopped, surprised, and pretended to read something on a notice board about beach facilities. Well now, he wondered, what was this?

The elevator door pinged open. Gourhant went to get in but

then stepped back with a nod to let three people out.

Abu Yussuf walked over behind Gourhant and followed him into the small elevator, just the two of them. As the doors closed, Gourhant asked over his shoulder "Floor?"

"Top," said Abu Yussuf, watching closely to see what other button Gourhant pressed.

"The same," said Gourhant, pressing just the one button and then staring straight ahead at the doors, as people in elevators do.

The elevator was slow but there were only four floors. As it juddered and then stopped at its destination, Gourhant stepped back to let his fellow traveller out first.

Abu Yussuf was expecting a floor of rooms but instead he stepped out into a bright, spacious area with a magnificent view through a semi-circular glass doorway out onto a terrace and the Mediterranean beyond.

He was in the rooftop restaurant and lunch was being served.

Jonblat, Beirut 13:30

Jihad Merhi sat at his desk, cigarette between his fingers, Johnnie Walker in his mug, looking at the latest pile of *ilishael* that had been dumped upon him by Major Ghanem. Apparently the Israelis had released photographs and maps purporting to show Hizbullah training sites in the south, together with details of arms and rocket locations below the Litani river. The Jews were threatening a pre-emptive strike against the training sites. Problem was these 'training sites' were in fact villages and the alleged weapons depots were in fact schools and hospitals. Although Ghanem had acknowledged that this was a matter for the Lebanese army, Merhi had been asked 'to comment'.

Merhi had one two-word comment, the second word being 'off'. He had enough to do.

His mobile was in his right hand, and as he listened to it

ringing at the other end his eyes travelled over to the closed door of his office with the cracked pane of glass that had not been repaired in five years.

"Hello, light of my life. I hope you've spent all our money for the month on something frivolous which you don't need," he said, still listening to the ring tone. He took a swig of whisky, avoiding burning his forehead with the cigarette in the same hand with the deftness of a hardened smoker.

Eventually Gisele answered and he put the mug and cigarette down as if she could see him. "Hi, Gigi. Had a good time? Great. Tell your cousin everything's okay. Tomorrow at 16:30." Which meant today at 14:30, in one hour's time. "Yes. Okay. I'll see you tonight. Yes, I love you too."

Jbeil, Lebanon 14:15

Sometimes life just gives you an unexpected bonus, reflected Abu Yussuf, stifling a burp. A little reward for being a good boy.

It had been a surprisingly sumptuous Italian meal in the rooftop restaurant of the Victory Byblos Hotel. It was too hot to sit outside on the terrace, but he was given a good table for one just inside the semi-circular glass doorway, facing inwards. And facing Albert Gourhant three tables away.

He had not dined alone, he had been accompanied by a bottle of imported Barolo wine and then by two limoncello liqueurs and two double espressos. And best of all, he wouldn't have to pay for it. The delightful and rather-beautiful-the-more-alcohol-you-drank Madame Gourhant would see it on her bill.

Albert Gourhant had also dined with just liquid company. Now, as Gourhant put down his coffee cup and wiped his mouth, Abu Yussuf counted out a sizeable amount of US dollars and put them on top of the check in the plastic cover.

He watched Gourhant pay by card, and then he rose, deliberately ahead of his subject. The small bar was near the elevator, and he stopped to exchange small-talk with the barmaid until he was sure Gourhant was leaving. He was waiting at the elevator when Gourhant got there.

Abu Yussuf entered the elevator first then nodded in faux mild surprise when he saw Gourhant, acknowledging their previous encounter. He pressed the button for the ground floor. Gourhant did not reach across for an alternative.

When the elevator thumped to a stop at its destination, Abu Yussuf stepped back and Gourhant left first with a nod of *"Merci."*

Feeling a food and alcohol induced pleasantness, he followed Gourhant outside and watched him climb into his Citroen, start the engine and move off.

Up at the main road, Gourhant signalled left.

Starting the Bluebird's engine, Abu Yussuf had the first pangs of guilt about drinking the alcohol. But he was on a case, he reasoned, under cover. Allah would understand.

Jerkily he drove off, also turning left at the main road. Going back to Jbeil. Back home.

Nothing discovered today.

Jonblat, Beirut 14:30 – 18:00

"No shopping bags?" asked Jihad Merhi as he walked Carla Chedid up the stairs to the ISF offices on the second floor of the State Security building.

"Gisele has taken them home," her deep voice echoed up the stairwell. "We could only just get them all into the car." She gave him an impish sideways look.

Merhi raised an eyebrow, knowing she was teasing him. The Merhi's car was a Toyota Land Cruiser, an ex-official issue on which he had got a good deal. To fill that with shopping bags of girlie things was... she *was* kidding, wasn't she?

Carla laughed. "Do not worry, Captain, I am playing with you."

That comment set his mind off on completely different thoughts, and as he stood back holding the door open for her he cast a quick downward glance at her small, fit body. She was dressed in all black, tight T shirt above jeans which she must have been poured into, black Reebok trainers. Across her body she carried a dark grey Barbour wax cotton messenger bag. Her hair was down and held back with a black and gold hairclip.

They walked down the corridor past the General Office.

"I'll be busy for about half an hour, Sergeant," called Merhi through the doorway.

"Okay boss," el-Gharib was busy on a computer, carefully tapping something out on the keyboard, and did not look up.

As he closed his own office door, Merhi offered "Coffee?"

"No, I'm fine, thanks."

"Cigarette?" He indicated the packet on his desk.

"*Merci.*" She shook her head.

"Please, sit down." Merhi indicated a wooden chair in front of the desk, taking a cigarette from the packet and putting it in his mouth. Carla sat.

"So my darling wife has gone back?" He lit up, feeling instantly more relaxed as the nicotine hit.

Carla took off her bag and draped it over the chair back. "She said you would bring me home."

"Did she now?" Merhi looked at his watch. He went behind the desk and sat down. "I thought of asking The Watchers but I didn't want them asking questions, so I went to the Traffic Division first on the off chance. They've sent over two discs." He held up a brown envelope. "I asked for the intersection of Ashrafieh Street facing north and Abdul Wahab Street facing south, between 14:00 and 16:00. I don't know what we've got, I haven't had time to look at them yet."

"I can look at them on my own. If you are busy. Looking through two times two hours of CCTV might take some time."

"Could you? I do have one or two other things that need my attention."

"Just put me somewhere where I won't get in the way."

Merhi nodded back to the General Office. "Most of the team are out, I'll find you a desk out there."

Carla looked quizzically at the cracked glass in the office door as he held it open for her. "History," he mumbled, following her out. "The last time we met actually." In the General Office he called across to the Sergeant. "Deeb, this lady is from the ESU. Which desk is best for her to use?"

"The Lieutenant's," el-Gharib said without looking away from his screen. "He won't be back today."

"D'accord. That's this one," Merhi gestured to a nearby desk, handing over the envelope containing the discs. "Let me know if you need me. The Sergeant will show you where the coffee is. If you can call it that."

"Thank you, Captain," Carla said loudly then, as he turned away, she reached out and touched his arm. She smiled sweetly and said softly, "You won't forget to take me home, will you?"

She dismissed the disc looking north from Ashrafieh Street after five minutes. It was blurred and occluded (it looked like a bird had done its business right on the camera lens), and anyway Maroun's apartment building was too far down the street.

She hoped for better from the second disc, otherwise she was going to be thwarted before she even started.

The computer hummed, thought about it, did what computers do, and then the picture came up on the screen.

The view was in colour, which was encouraging, better than the other disc, clearer but not clear, and she could distinctly see Moro's block a few buildings down on the left. The top of the screen told her that the date was 040710, the time was 14:00:00, and the time interval was 10SEC - so viewed as a movie it would be jumpy.

She did a quick calculation in her head. Two hours with a picture every ten seconds viewed as continuous...

6 frames per minute x 60

= 360 frames per hour

= 720 frames for the 2 hours.

Viewed at 1 frame per second

= 12 minutes to view it all.

Not bad, but she didn't want to miss anything. She would slow it to half speed, one frame every two seconds. It would still take only twenty-four minutes.

As she suspected, because of the long time interval, movement was fuzzy and jerky. She could just make out humans; passing vehicles were just smudges.

At 14:30:11 a pink fuzz came out of the building, turning left and appearing in just three frames. That was her, going to the Hotel Albergo to pick up the taxi to take her to see Hariri's memorial.

She continued watching.

At 15:00:52 a dark smudge in the road slowed and metamorphosed into a car. It found an empty place further along the street and a fuzz got out. The fuzz came back down the street towards the camera. She could see a bald head. It was Moro.

Oh Moro, Moro, Moro...

She watched, wrapped up in her thoughts.

Then a pink fuzz entered the picture again coming from Ashrafieh Street. Carla frowned and looked at the time on the screen. 15:58:26. It was her, returning.

At precisely 16:00:00 on the screen, the disc stopped and the computer politely asked *Play again?*

What? Carla sat back in the chair. Had she missed something? Had something been cut out, edited? She looked at her watch. *Non*, her calculations had been correct. It had been twenty-five minutes since she started watching the disc.

She had seen no one else leave the building except herself, no one else enter except herself and Moro. What did this mean? Had the assassin been there before 14:00, lying in wait? Carla had been there on her own, but she had not been attacked. Moro had been.

If it was the same assassin who attacked her the next day, why hadn't she done her then in Moro's apartment. Why had she been left for a day? It did not make sense.

Unless it was not the same assassin.

Sighing, she stood up. "Excuse me, Sergeant. The Captain said you would show me where the coffee is?"

"Over there, *madame*." Eyes still fixed on his screen, Sergeant el-Gharib waved a hand to a far corner of the room.

"*Ah oui, merci*. Would you like one?"

"*Merci*. You can use the white mug."

Carla went over to a low filing cabinet upon which was a tray with an encrusted spoon, an old kettle and a Nescafé jar containing hardened granules. Not quite the freshly-ground she was used to, but it would have to do. Next to the tray were five mugs. She assumed the dirty one with brown liquid stripes was the 'white' one.

Back at the desk with a thick, hot brew which tasted nothing like coffee, just a beverage, she clicked on the play icon then immediately clicked the pause button. She would go through this frame by frame until she was one hundred per cent satisfied.

She looked back down the glass-walled corridor to the closed office door. Captain Jihad Merhi might be late home tonight.

Now she viewed the disc in real time, one frame every ten seconds, using the pause button when she needed to. She stopped after the first hour of disc for more coffee. Disappointingly, the slower viewing confirmed that in that first hour no one had come out of the building except herself, no one had gone in except Moro.

So either the assassin was invisible or moved at lightning speed or, as she had suspected, had arrived in the building before 14:00. Which meant that Moro had been the sole target that day, not her. The assassin was waiting for him to come home. Again the question: why had she been left until the next day when she had been in the apartment on her own and 'available' for assassination?

She topped up her mug for the third time and then embarked on the second hour.

Forty minutes later she almost missed it. She had the mug with the last mouthful of her fourth coffee tipped to her lips when the frame for 15:33:30 came on. A bit screen-drunk by now, she glanced casually at the monitor, looked away then quickly looked back again, banging down the mug, leaning forward.

There was a shadow coming out of the building. It looked like one of those photographs of ghosts that regularly appear online and sometimes in the newspapers.

She went back to the frame before. Nothing. She advanced to the frame after. Nothing. One shadow on one frame. Whoever it was must have been moving rapidly to have been captured on just one frame, out of the building and away in nineteen seconds.

There was no vehicle smudge so the person must have left on foot. Therefore in order not to be caught on the next frame, they must have come towards the camera and disappeared underneath it. North to Abdul Wahab el-Inglizi Street.

Carla nodded. That was do-able. But did whoever it was know about the CCTV camera or was it just luck? Did they move at that speed anyway? Or could it be that the camera could not pick them up because of some other reason?

Could she zoom in on this frame? she wondered. Did they have picture-enhancing software on the ISF system?

She opened her mouth to call across to Sergeant el-Gharib, who looked like he was packing up for the day, but then she thought better of it. No need to spark any curiosity. She would play with the software herself.

There was a zoom facility, that was easily found, but after a few moments looking she realised that there was nothing that would enhance the picture. So be it. She clicked on the magnifying glass icon and dragged it to the shadow on the screen.

No good, it just seemed like the enlarged shadow that it was, the zoom didn't really help at all. But she had her own natural internal picture-enhancing software! She squinted her eyes real tight and concentrated, staring at the screen...

And there she was. Still fuzzy but the features were distinct enough when you knew what you were looking for. Female. Tall. Long blonde hair. It was the person, the creature, that had attacked her at the hotel the following day. The one she had allowed to live when she had seen her outside the hotel because she was not one hundred per cent sure she was Maroun's killer.

The *houri*.

Beirut, Lebanon 18:45

"I knew it but I had to confirm it," said Carla above the blast of the full-max air conditioning. They were in Merhi's new official-issue decuma grey Toyota Land Cruiser V8, the upgrade to his old LC5 model which Gisele now had. It was top-of-the-range, as befits a Captain of the Internal Security Force, and, just like most cars, had many features which its owner would never use. This one had built-in sat-nav which had never even been turned on.

"So you can now tell me what this is all about?" he asked. They were driving east on General Fouad Chehab Avenue, heading for the coastal highway which would take them north to *chez Merhi* in Jounieh. This was their first chance to speak since leaving the State Security building. Although the likelihood of Merhi's telephone being tapped was great, it was less likely that his office generally was bugged. But Carla had not wanted to take any chances, and she had shaken her head and made eyes when she had returned to his office and he had asked the question.

"*Non.* But I can confirm that the same person killed Maroun

Khoury as tried to kill me. So it is all connected to the reason I came back."

"You have a positive ID?"

"Oh yes."

"Then I can run him through the system, see if we've got anything."

Carla shook her head. "The picture is too blurred, too vague. But I know it is the same person. And it is not a 'he'."

"It's a she?" Merhi drew on his cigarette

Carla gave a deep breath, almost a sigh, as she looked at the ABN Amro Building passing on her right, with the name Tufenkjian Frères announcing the famous jewellers underneath. "Maybe," she said.

"Sorry?" Merhi frowned.

"Nothing, nothing. A 'she', yes. Perhaps if I make up a composite you can run that through the system?"

"*Oui. A demain.*"

"*A demain,*" she agreed. She settled back into the leather seat. "That is enough work for one day. I think Gisele may have a surprise for you when you get in."

"Really?"

"But you're not to say I said anything. Something we bought today."

"Something I can eat?"

She laughed. "Well, not directly! But you might want to eat what it encloses. It is a little gift, from me to her. An outfit."

"An outfit?"

"How long has it been since you enjoyed a *raqs sharqi* belly dance?"

As they crossed the Beirut River, the Toyota Land Cruiser V8 accelerated heavily. Merhi smiled. And it was not even his birthday!

Jbeil, Lebanon 20:00

"For a moment I thought something was wrong," said Paradise as she pressed the End icon on her mobile phone. The twins were walking back to their accommodation in Rue St John, each carrying a *shawarma*, a small carton of *fattoush* salad and a can of Coca-Cola, which they had purchased in one of the fast-food outlets in the souks. Love's *shawarma* was chicken, Paradise's a mix of lamb and goat. Love had already started to nibble hers.

As usual they were attracting glances, which they acknowledged with gentle smiles when eye contact was made. They were wearing their lenses (it was now thirty-four thirty-four).

"Another conversion?" asked Love.

"No, he wants some mint tobacco."

"Mint?" Love took her sister's Coke so that she could tuck the phone back into her cargo pants. "That's unusual. He only asks for that when he is distressed or something big is about to happen. Like when we left the Promised Land."

Paradise took back her drink. "Well, The Second Coming *is* upon us."

"But it is still weeks away. He must be stressed. We must see if there is anything else he needs."

"He just wants the tobacco. If he had wanted anything else he would have asked for it. We'll take it to him tomorrow."

They walked on, past the wax museum on their right, the Church of Saint John the Baptist visible on their left. Paradise took a sliver of goat from her wrap and put it in her mouth.

"I'm glad it was not another conversion," mused Love. "He does not realise how much they take out of us. We put our soul into taking their souls. That's why we can only do one a day."

"It is not his problem," reasoned Paradise. "We have been sent to protect The Secret and convert *kafirs*, until the glorious day - which will soon now be upon us after all these years. He is not interested in our weakness. Only in our strength."

"And talking of conversions," Love took a full bite of her *shawarma* and spoke as she chewed. "We still have this djinn to deal with. Or should we just leave it?"

"No," Paradise sounded stern. "Malek has issued conversion instructions, therefore we must obey them."

"She might be gone by now."

"You think so? *Djinni* do not run away."

Both of them touched the left side of their heads remembering their last encounter.

"You are right," agreed Love. "But how will we find her?"

Paradise stopped, her sister turning to look at her. "Don't forget, we have a disciple who can help us with these things. It may be time to awaken him."

Love smiled. "Yes, I had forgotten."

They walked on, the evening sun shining on their pale faces as they headed west.

After a minute, Love said *"Sabah a Allah."*

"Indeed," agreed Paradise. "God is good."

They turned left into Rue St John.

9 July 2010
27 Rajab 1431

Jounieh, Lebanon 07:00

"*Sabah el-khair mes amis,*" greeted Carla as she entered the kitchen. "Good morning." She suppressed a grin as the Merhis pulled away from each other, Jihad flustered, over-compensating by fiddling with plates and cutlery. They had been in a romantic embrace, so obviously the outfit she had bought Gisele had worked last night!

"*Bonjour* Za – Carla," smiled Gisele (oh yes, she had the look). "Sorry, can't get used to your new name."

Carla was dressed in a just-long-enough loose white T-shirt – and nothing else. "I hope very soon it won't matter." She held up a piece of A4 paper. "I have done this. It is a good likeness."

Jihad took it, trying not to stare at the T shirt and what was beneath it, as Gisele asked, "Coffee?"

"Please."

"And help yourself to whatever we have. There's *labneh* in the fridge, some meats. Cheese. There's lemon cake. Or we have Jihad's good, healthy, traditional Lebanese breakfast – donuts!"

"Just the coffee for now, Gigi, thank you." As Gisele turned away to pour, Carla asked Jihad "What do you think?"

He was nodding positively. "Very good. You are a talented artist. Look, Geeg." He held up the drawing. The lifelike face of a young woman with long light hair stared out into the room. She was pretty but there was something disconcerting about her.

Gisele handed Carla her coffee. "What is wrong with the eyes?" she asked.

"Nothing. That's how they are."

"Sorry?"

"Her eyes are white."

"Well, shouldn't be hard to find her then," Jihad bit into his traditional Lebanese breakfast, jam oozing out over his fingers. "Might not even have to run the picture, just the description. She is blonde?"

"Yes."

"A blonde haired, white-eyed female assassin. Not too many of them in the world." He licked his fingers. "We could have a quick result. You want me to make it official now?"

"*Non.* Let us identify her first, then we will decide what we will do." Both Jihad and Gisele noted the 'we' but they did not say anything. "I will have my shower now, if that is all right? Then, Captain, could you give me a lift into Beirut? There are places I would like to visit."

"If you're quick."

"I will be. Like a djinn!" She smiled as she span away, taking her coffee with her.

Jihad watched her go, the T shirt gripped in the crevice between her gluteals. "Nice..." he was aware that Gisele was looking at him. "Weather today."

The slap around the back of his head nearly knocked his traditional Lebanese breakfast back out of his mouth.

Jbeil, Lebanon 14:00

Was Albert Gourhant addicted to going in different directions? wondered Abu Yussuf, the best private investigator in Jbeil (in fact, the only private investigator in Jbeil). On Tuesday the alleged adulterer had gone north up Rue Cheralam to the barber's shop. Yesterday, Thursday, he had gone south for his massage and meal at the Victory Byblos Hotel. Today he was going east.

Was he a compass-obsessive?

Abu Yussuf drove his Datsun Bluebird in his usual manner, one-handed, left arm hanging out the open window, cigarette between his fingers. He was dressed in a short sleeved, open-necked white shirt, light brown slacks and loafers. A co-ordinating jacket was on the back seat in case he needed it, which he might do. It looked like Albert was heading into the mountains.

Was this to be the big reveal? Was this where his lover lived? Or at least, one of his lovers. Madame Gourhant had alleged that her husband was both prolific and serial.

Frankly, Abu Yussuf was surprised Albert had been allowed out today. With excursions from the house on Tuesday and Thursday, he had thought an every-other-day pattern was emerging. But he had been wrong. Just shows one never knew what to expect in this game.

And talking of game, to make sure he did not get bored if he had to wait outside somewhere while Albert sated his lust with one of his harem, today he had brought along his playing cards. He could play solitaire or maybe challenge himself to a game of poker (although he regarded solo poker akin to solo sex: an end result was achieved but you knew the outcome beforehand. It was better when at least one other person was involved). Or he could practise some card tricks he had been learning recently, to impress his cousin's children. He was becoming quite adept at making a card pop up out of his breast pocket.

And, of course, he had his iPhone.

Through a cloud of cigarette smoke, he looked at the blue Citroen C4 Picasso a little way ahead. So, where were you going, dear Albert? It looked like today might be a longer journey...

The road became bumpy as it climbed up into the mountains, with some sharp curves that made Abu Yussuf drive with both hands on the wheel, cigarette now lodged in the corner of his mouth. He followed the Citroen, up through Hboub, Kfar Qouas, Breij, Ras Osta...

Annaya, Lebanon 15:00 - 17:00

The Deir Mar Maron.

Being a Muslim, Abu Yussuf had never been here before but he was aware of the significance this place had for Lebanon's Christians. Wasn't one of their prophets or saints or something buried here?

He pulled in at the opposite end of the parking area, well away from Gourhant's Citroen which had parked up near the monastery. He watched as Gourhant got out of the car and went through a door to the left of the large statue of a bearded, hooded figure.

Throwing his cigarette onto the ground and discreetly treading on it as he got out, Abu Yussuf put on his jacket. Not only was it cooler up here, but a jacket was a sign of respect.

There were many people about, evidenced by the number of vehicles, parked either facing the mountains or looking out over the stunning view towards the coast. Abu Yussuf hoped he did not stand out, did not have *I am a Muslim* written in large letters on his forehead. He surveyed the other people, who were paying him no attention whatsoever. No, they looked just like him. One woman was even wearing a *hijab*. He would blend in, as a good *muhaqqiq khass* should.

He walked casually, like the other visitors. This was a place of pilgrimage, reflection and prayer – a sort of local Christian *hajj* – it was not a place for rushing. A few children were running around, ignoring their parents admonishments to be careful. He smiled. God bless them, whatever their creed.

The statue was impressive. Modern yet traditional. Its right hand was raised in a blessing, the left hand carried a holy book – the Christian bible. Two people were kneeling in front of it, praying.

Behind the statue was a raised, bricked area topped with grass and flowers. A wooden sign announced in English and Spanish:

The first tomb of Saint Charbel
In which he was buried on Christmas Day 1898
Few months later lights appeared upon it

Abu Yussuf looked at the door to the left. It was busy, people going in and out. A sign said it was the Tomb Church and Museum.

He went in, still wary that alarms might go off, detecting a Muslim in a Christian holy place. But there was nothing except an air of calm. He followed the general flow downstairs to the museum.

Like the statue outside, the museum was modern yet traditional in style. Behind wooden-framed glass enclosures were liturgical vestments, some heavily stained with secretions, utensils used by the saint, cloths which wiped his face, letters from believers worldwide, and even a wax tableau depicting the saint's family.

To the left of the entrance was a small kiosk-style shop. And one of the two people behind the counter, selling small items, accepting donations, and giving out relics, was Monsieur Albert Gourhant.

This could be a long wait, thought Abu Yussuf as he applied the parking brake. He had just moved his car so that it faced outwards and he could enjoy the views.

How long would Albert Gourhant be here? Probably until the museum closed in the evening. That could be four or five hours yet. Should he just give up for the day and return to Jbeil?

It was tempting, but he had resolved to give the distrusting Madame G a timetable of Monsieur's movements, so he would stick it out. It was highly unlikely Albert Gourhant was conducting an affair in the church! But he would be thorough. It was possible the old man could have a little respite stop somewhere back down the mountain on his way home. Possible but unlikely.

Abu Yussuf had placed his playing cards and telephone on the passenger seat next to him in the car. If this wait was as long as he expected it to be, before the evening was through he would be adept at all the games on the phone and well-rehearsed in the card tricks to show his cousin's children.

He picked up the phone, pleasantly surprised that he could get a signal on it up here, and accessed the apps. Casually glancing in his rear-view mirror, he saw a Jeep pull into the parking place he had just vacated facing the mountains. Two identical blonde-haired young women got out and walked off towards the monastery.

Twins, thought Abu Yussuf. How sweet.

Brother Malek stank.

Even if the twins had not had ultra-sensitive noses, they would have whiffed him anyway. The *burnus* seemed limp and clinging. And his mood was black.

Paradise and Love were wary as they walked either side of him along the shaded side of the monastery.

"This was not a good choice," he growled lowly. "I know I need to fit in but this physical work is too much. I have come to save the world. And look at the state of me. You have it?" He scratched his beard.

Love took a brown bag out of her rucksack. Malek took it without thanks.

"Hurt yourself," said Paradise.

Malek stopped walking. Without forward movement, his stench became even stronger. "*Maa?*"

"Hurt yourself. Say you have pulled a muscle, hurt your back or something. You are only working to fit in. It's not like we have not paid the monastery well for your stay. They will not quibble if you just spend your days in prayer and contemplation. You have tried to work but you have hurt yourself."

For quite a while Malek was silent. The women exchanged glances.

Then he said, "The twenty-second day of Ramadan."

The twins waited but he did not elaborate. Paradise gave a gentle nod of encouragement. "Yes, brother?"

For a moment, nothing. Then the hood moved from one to the other of them. "Fitting, don't you think? The Second Coming during the Holy Month. Satan has been vanquished, even now he is retreating. The first of September is the day, my sisters. Prepare yourselves for triumph."

Love breathed in through flared nostrils. "*Allahu Akbar. Sabah a Allah,*" she said softly, euphorically, grasping her sister on the forearm. Paradise patted her hand.

"Yes, it is a good idea. My back aches, so I will not be lying." Seamlessly Malek returned to the previous conversation. "But I must wash now and wash these robes as well. It will soon be time for '*Asr salat.*" He reached out and touched each woman on the shoulder. His mood had changed dramatically. "You have pleased me, my sisters. My right and left hands. My dexter and sinister. I bless you."

The twins went to turn back towards the monastery entrance, but were stopped by Malek's non-movement. "There is one thing I would like you to do for me, right now," he said.

Paradise put her arms by her side, a gesture of readiness. "Anything, oh Malek, you know that."

"I have left a sack of potatoes out in the field. Retrieve it. Fill it until it just closes and then leave it at the end of the monastery wall over there. I will say that is where my back gave up and I could carry it no further. One of the Christians will move it later. The earth will be changed on the twenty-second day of Ramadan. Rejoice."

Brother Malek nodded towards the nearby field, then, reaching into the hood and scratching his beard with both hands, he turned and walked quickly back towards the monastery entrance, head bowed, not wishing to be seen.

Like a hermit.

Abu Yussuf was bored. He had been in the car an hour and a half now. All the games he could access on his iPhone had been played, the card rising out of his top pocket had been rehearsed to perfection, two packets of cigarettes had been smoked as could be witnessed by the pile of butts beneath the car door. And he could be here a few more hours yet.

He climbed out of the Bluebird, stretching his legs and flexing his back. This was the worst part of surveillance, the waiting. In many cases, waiting was rewarded by the culprit eventually revealing himself, getting found out in the sin. But he doubted that Albert Gourhant had ever done anything naughty in his life. He was a volunteer at the monastery, for goodness sake. His wife was just a suspicious, jealous harridan.

But she was paying the piper. He needed to move, but he couldn't go far from the museum. Sod's Law said that the minute he turned his back, Albert would slip out and be away, beyond pursuit.

The idea of puncturing one of the old man's tyres flashed into his mind but was immediately thrown out like the unwelcome thug it was. That was not a nice thing to do – and anyway he could be stuck up here all night if he did that.

He needed a drink and perhaps a bite to eat. This time he had brought his phone and his cards to stave off boredom but he hadn't given a thought to his physical needs. Next time he would bring food and drink as well. Might even treat himself to a little picnic hamper.

There must be a café or some sort of restaurant facility around here somewhere. He would have a little look around, always keeping one eye on the front of the museum...

It took Paradise and Love thirty minutes to find the abandoned sack of potatoes, fill it up to its required level, tie it and haul it back to the rear wall of the monastery. They did not sweat (never had, never would), but their hands and white vests were grubby, and Love had a black smear across her nose as they stood by the dumped sack, trying to brush off the earth from their cargo pants.

They did not voice any complaints, they had been sent to protect The Secret and obeying Malek was part of that protection, but they had worked up an appetite and Love joked that a quick conversion of two of the huge potatoes via a microwave oven would be good for the cause!

Paradise gently wiped her sister's nose with a tissue as she laughed at the conversion suggestion. "Come *habibi*. Let us return to Jbeil. He will not want to see us again today. I will ring him and tell him we have done as he asked."

They moved off towards the front of the monastery.

Brother Malek felt human again – which, as he considered himself divine, was not really as good as it sounded, but at least he felt better than he had before. A full fifteen minute shower had washed away the grime and sweat of his toil, but he did not feel completely clean. His beard still itched. It had been a long time since its last trim and it had grown into the long, straggly Maronite style of old. It was time to take it down to modern levels, maybe even take it off and let it grow back evenly during his final weeks here.

He did not have washing facilities in his cell upstairs, he had to use one of the monks' two communal washrooms on the ground floor, just like the others. He had chosen the smaller of the two and had wedged the door closed with a bible. So he had time. First scissors, then razor.

Wispy grey and black hairs fell into the sink as he began to snip...

That was better.

Abu Yussuf had found a small refreshment kiosk in the park

area and he was now on his second bottle of orangina and third packet of Oreos. In his pocket he had a wedge of cake. He needed the sugar.

He had had to lose sight of the museum while he found the refreshment kiosk but as he came back into the parking area he was relieved to see Gourhant's Citroen was still there.

He walked slowly. Now that the immediate pangs of thirst and hunger had been sated, he could eat and drink his remaining items leisurely.

The late afternoon sun was still warm on his face as he walked down the side of the monastery. He could hear singing from somewhere inside. Must be some Christian song; it sounded melodious.

Way down the other end of the building he saw two figures turn the corner, coming his way. One of them was on the telephone. Idly, without much thought to what he was looking at, he glanced in at an open window in the monastery wall.

And he stopped dead in his tracks.

Brother Malek, wet hair pushed straight back, beard removed, lines of foam still on his face, was speaking on his mobile phone and looking straight out of the window. He stopped talking abruptly when he saw the man outside staring at him, open-mouthed.

Their eyes locked. Malek's were dark and malicious. Abu Yussuf's were wide, incredulous, like an *arnab* caught in the headlights.

Still with his phone to his ear, Malek said "I have been seen." The person on the other end spoke, then Malek said "Yes, him. Deal with it."

Abu Yussuf could not believe what he was seeing. At first he thought his mind was playing tricks, the effects of a malevolent sugar-rush. In a micro-second he blinked, shook his head, then blinked again. *No, it was impossible.*

Then he became aware of people running to his right. Glued to the spot, he turned his head. It was those two young women he had seen parking earlier, the identical twins.

He looked back at the window. The man was still there, staring at him blankly.

The women reached him. One stopped two metres away on his right, the other moved around to his other side. What would they think when they looked in the window? "Look," he said breathlessly, a tremble in his voice. "Look!" His fingers shook as he pointed.

But they ignored him. From the other side of the window an accented voice said, "Convert him."

Abu Yussuf frowned. Convert? He was a good Shi'ite, he did not want to be converted. He would never be Christian.

Then something happened that made him doubt his sanity. The two women brought their hands up to their faces and then leant forward. *In the name of Allah, they were taking out their eyes!*

The two heads snapped back up. Bile rose in Abu Yussuf's throat as he gasped at the white eyeballs and black pupils focused on him, the heads inclined to one side, curious.

The woman on the right moved. But so did Abu Yussuf. Instinctively, without thought, he threw his bottle of orangina at the approaching woman. It cracked onto her brow but weirdly there were two gasps, one from her, one from the woman behind him. Both women leant forward, holding their heads.

What on earth...? Had the bottle bounced off one onto the other?

Abu Yussuf ran. He did not understand but he knew he needed to get out of there. Something mad was happening. Something evil.

Up ahead, people were still going in and out of the museum. He would be safe in a crowd.

Still running, he risked a look back. Both women were on their haunches, still holding their heads. It looked like one of them was bleeding – but he would not stop to find out!

He ran past Albert Gourhant's Citroen but it did not even register with him. Back at his Datsun Bluebird he fumbled with the keys, got them into the lock at the second attempt, got in, slammed the door and quickly locked it.

The engine started on the first turn. Breathlessly, he engaged the gears – and jerked forward. Just in time he slammed his foot on the brake before he took off over the mountainside.

He found reverse and turned in his seat – to see the two women running round the corner up by the museum.

Rubber smoke from the tyres and cinders from the track flew into the air as the Bluebird shot forward and away.

Coastal Highway, Lebanon 17:30

Three times Abu Yussuf nearly drove off the mountainside on his way down. Once one of his back wheels actually went off the edge on a hairpin bend, but the speed of the car kept his momentum forward, saving him. He prayed to almighty Allah that he would see a Jeep Wrangler Ultimate somersaulting down the ridge behind him - but his prayers went unanswered.

They were in pursuit, but he knew if he could reach the highway the Bluebird had enough power to at least match the Jeep, if not outrun it, despite the Bluebird's age.

He still could not believe what he had seen up at the monastery. He needed to tell someone. Someone he could trust. Someone who could help him.

He reached the coastal highway, speeding onto the south-bound carriage to a cacophony of blaring horns from the other drivers. It was busy as always, but at this time of day the north-bound side was busier. Was that a consolation or a hindrance?

Half a kilometre behind, he saw a black Jeep also careen into the traffic flow, immediately pulling out into the far left lane. The chase was on.

He needed to do something, just in case he didn't make it to his destination. He looked at the playing cards and his iPhone on the seat beside him. He had an idea.

Keeping his eyes on the road and keeping his left hand on the wheel, he fumbled in the glove compartment for his pen...

Beirut 18:10 – 19:30

He kept them at bay all the way down the highway, just about matching the pursuers for speed, the Jeep only gaining on him by about three cars on the forty kilometre journey.

The background of irate horns continued all the way down into the capital – once he even took someone's wing-mirror off. Many drivers were on mobile phones, but were any of them reporting him? Unlikely knowing the drivers of Lebanon, they'd be too afraid their own sins would find them out! Where were the police when you needed them? Where?

The sheer volume of traffic made him slow down as he entered Beirut, but what slowed him would also slow his followers. He would stay on the highway for as long as possible and then use the major boulevards through the city. The last thing he wanted to do was to get caught in traffic in the narrow side streets.

The Dora Highway became Charles Helou Avenue. The traffic was maintaining a strong pace. He couldn't see the Jeep in his rear-view mirror but he knew it could not have gotten any nearer to him.

He would be looking to turn south, probably along George Haddad Street.

But he never got that far.

As he approached the entrance to the Port of Beirut on his right, the Bluebird stuttered. It caught its speed back then stuttered again.

What the hell?

He looked at the dashboard.

No, he did not believe it. He had not been aware of any warning lights. Perhaps the car did not have any – he had never run out of fuel before.

Now he needed to get off the avenue quickly. If he stopped here they would get him in no time. He wrenched the wheel to the right taking the road that led down into the port. The Bluebird stuttered, slowed, stuttered, slowed. Soon he would be running on fumes only.

Another right took him onto the narrow road running underneath Charles Helou Avenue. Slowly and more slowly he rolled along it, taking another right into Berberi Street.

At the junction with Pasteur Street, the car stopped. He swore, turning the key, knowing it was futile. Clunk, shudder, clunk. Grabbing his phone, he jumped out of the car, looking back down the road, the busy avenue above him.

There was no Jeep. Had they missed him turning off? If so, they would have gone speeding off into Gemmayzeh and then into the downtown district and they would have lost him. Perhaps running out of fuel had been the best thing that could have happened!

He had lifted the phone in his hand, ready to make a call, when he heard the sound of a vehicle coming down the same way as he had. He shouldn't worry, he told himself, it could be anybody. Casually he looked back.

And saw the Jeep.

He took off at a run, hearing the engine accelerate behind. He crossed Pasteur Street. He couldn't hope to outrun a car, he needed to get somewhere where they couldn't follow... Ah, he knew!

He ran left down a narrow street into the Rmeil District. He heard the Jeep turn after him, but he knew it would have to go slowly to avoid people and parked vehicles.

His breath began to go. What he would do for a cigarette right now!

He turned right into Gouraud Street by the post office. If he remembered correctly, there was a police station a little way down. But he wasn't heading for that.

He crossed over the street and raced up onto the Saint Nicholas Stairs.

Also known as Daraj el-Fen, the Artists' Stairs, it is a street of stairs connecting Gourand Street with Sursock Street. One hundred and twenty-five stairs divided into twenty-three flights and stretching for half a kilometre, it is lined either side by apartment blocks and houses, and twice a year is used for art exhibitions.

After two flights of stairs, Abu Yussuf had to stop, leaning on a waste bin, catching his breath. His legs were beginning to shake. There were people about but no one was paying him any heed. Still with his phone in his hand, he tapped his jacket pocket for his cigarettes then remembered that he had smoked them all up at Annaya.

Warily he looked up and down the stairs. Well, the Jeep certainly couldn't climb up here. Looking back, it seemed quiet down on Gouraud Street this Friday evening.

Except for the tall, blonde young woman coming up towards him.

Adrenaline shot through him as he straightened up, injecting power into his weak legs to keep on climbing but making him drop the phone. It smashed onto the ground, the back flying off and both parts spinning off in different directions.

He made it up one more flight and stopped, looking back. Now he was afraid.

The woman seemed to be in no hurry as she walked up the stairs. Her white eyes were looking at him curiously, dispassionately. But surely she couldn't kill him here, with people about?

He looked upwards to see if there was anyone who could help him. Surely there was somebody...?

But what he saw made the tension leave his body and he knew it was all over.

The other twin was walking down the stairs towards him. He was cut off, one coming down, one coming up.

He began to pray. *"Ash-hadu alla ilaha illaha illa llah. Ash-hadu anna Muhammadan-rasulu llah..."* I testify that there is no deity except God. I testify that Mohammed is the Messenger of God...

The women met on the stairs next to him, embracing each other, laughing. For a moment it seemed like they did not know he was there. Then the four white eyes turned to him, the two faces smiling. One of them patted him on the shoulder and then, linking arms and still laughing, they walked down the stairs, not looking back.

Abu Yussuf shook his head, bewildered. He couldn't believe it. No knives, no guns? Had this just been a warning all along?

He had an urgent desire to pee, but that would have to wait. This was a respite, a let off. Allah was protecting him. *Allahu Akbar.*

He needed to find a taxi and fast.

Back down on Gouraud Street he found a service taxi, identified by its red licence plate. Beirut's service taxis pick up and carry more than one passenger, but a generous *pourboire* for the driver as he got into the decrepit old vehicle ensured that Abu Yussuf would travel alone.

He did not give his exact destination, just told the driver to head south towards the airport area. He would direct him further later.

Five minutes into the journey he began to feel ill.

By the time they reached Annan Street, Abu Yussuf's chest was heavy and a thick red fog was swirling over his eyes. Sweat was beaded on his brow. His mouth felt dry and tasted foul, and he just managed to say *"Hon"* to the taxi driver before his tongue ballooned up.

The driver was mumbling, swearing. He did not like to come down this far south. This was on the edge of the hell-hole that was the Bourj el-Barajneh Palestinian refugee camp, and this was not a place anyone wanted to be unless they had to, even on a light, warm summer's evening.

The taxi pulled over and Abu Yussuf dropped a bundle of notes over the front seat, which shut the driver up for ten seconds. He opened the taxi door, tried to step out but found himself sprawled on the ground. He had alighted at a terrace of shops and service providers, but the place he wanted was... What was it? He couldn't remember... Oh yes, the small two-storey house...

He got up, reeling like a drunk. The buildings were swimming in the thick red fog. He saw the door he wanted. Wondering why it was getting dark so early, he staggered over, raised his hand to knock, and missed the door completely.

He hit it on the third attempt, slapping it pathetically. Summoning up his last gram of strength, he struck the door harder. Harder, harder, harder...

A pain ripped through his stomach and he fell backwards, bent in half.

Then a voice boomed from down the road and a large shadow was running towards him. No, he thought, no. Not the women again. Hadn't they killed him already?

Another pain, making his bowels move violently, and he fell to the ground, rolling in agony, gripping his stomach. His tongue was so swollen he was unable to breathe through his mouth. Snot was shooting in and out of his nose as he tried to inhale.

The shadow reached him. "Chadi?" said a voice. "Chadi? Chadi!"

Abu Yussuf opened his eyes but he couldn't see the figure kneeling next to him. But he knew the voice and his cheeks twitched in a smile. He tried to say something but all he could manage was a grunt. So he moved his left arm.

The kneeling figure gasped in bewilderment as a playing card rose out of the breast pocket of Abu Yussuf's jacket.

The door behind opened to reveal a fat Palestinian woman dressed in a black *jilbaab* with no head covering, a small child of about three looking out from around her legs. "Who is it, husband?" she asked.

The kneeling figure looked up, shaking his head, perplexed, unbelieving. "Nada. This... this is my cousin. Chadi. The one from Jbeil... And he's dead," said Captain Fadi Lattouf of the Civil Police of the Palestinian Security Force.

PART THREE
الجزء الثالث

THE TAKING
أخذ

10 July 2010
28 Rajab 1431

Jonblat, Beirut 09:00

Jihad Merhi did not like attending the office on a Saturday, but he acknowledged that being a Captain of the Lebanese Internal Security Force was a 24-7 job and sometimes needs must. And, he had to admit, there was the advantage that the office was quieter – unlike the street outside which was the lead-in to the Hamra shopping district and was already crowded and noisy. Out there, somewhere, Gisele and Carla were once again preparing to donate inordinately large sums of money to the poor shopkeepers of Beirut.

Yesterday had been one of those frustrating days when he was constantly busy but had seemed not to get anything done. In Parliament, the March 14th coalition of parties was preparing to re-present Walid Jumblatt's bill on Palestinian rights[*] - nothing to particularly worry the ISF except that Prime Minister Saad Hariri had called for national unity on the conferring of civil rights to Palestinian refugees, and a call for national unity often gave ideas to people with ill-intent.

And yesterday had also been the annual Miss Lebanon contest and, as always, certain sections of society objected to such things. If the mood took them, they might have wanted to

---

[*] The bill would allow many of the 425,000 Palestinian refugees living in Lebanon (mostly in the country's 12 refugee camps) to obtain work permits for professions from which they were currently barred under Lebanese law, for example doctors, dentists, lawyers, engineers, and accountants. It had not been passed when first presented the previous month.

express their complaints in a tangible way - but thankfully the event had taken place without incident.

So he had been unable to proceed with Carla's drawing of her assailant and the alleged assassin of the DGS captain. She had been understanding when she came in late last night (she had been out all day, she did not say where, he did not ask) and he had promised to clear the decks this Saturday morning and get down to it.

When he came in he had placed his mug of so-called coffee on top of the notepad on his desk. Picking up the mug while his computer was booting up, he found a note underneath. It was in Sergeant el-Gharib's handwriting.

Lt Himo rang 18:00

Merhi's eyebrows raised. Lieutenant Himo? Selim Himo? Good heavens, he had not spoken to him since he knew not when. Himo was in the Bekaa Inquiry Brigade of the *Gendarmerie* and had helped him out with the serial killings investigation five years ago.

The raised eyebrows reformed into a frown. Five years again...

Well, Himo would have to wait. Carla was his priority today.

Out in the General Office it took him fifteen minutes to scan Carla's drawing into the system (el-Gharib would normally do it but he was off duty). He filed it under 'Unknown female' and forwarded it to himself.

Back at his desk, he opened the national database (it was now much more user-friendly than in the past; it had been updated last year when the government had decreed that religious affiliations need no longer be shown on national identity cards). Then he brought up the scanned drawing, linked it into the database, inserted 'Female' and 'Under 50' filters, and pressed Search.

Faces shot onto and off the screen, and he turned away, reaching for his cigarettes.

He had time to go outside and make another so-called coffee

and then return to enjoy it with a leisurely Cedars King Size while staring down at the traffic on Bank of Lebanon Street before the screen stopped its maniacal face churning.

NO MATCH FOUND

Well, no surprise there. Most of the assassins operating in the country were not Lebanese, and this one was no exception. He would try the national criminal database.

This search was quicker.

NO MATCH FOUND

Now his task became more difficult. He wished he could look at the databases of other countries, especially Lebanon's neighbours. He had heard rumour that the Israelis had a universal hacker that, with the right input, could search any system anywhere in the world, by-passing all firewalls and other security features. The Jews might have shared it with their allies but Lebanon would never get it. Which meant that he might have to make verbal, written or electronic requests of other countries. Which meant his enquiries would have to become official. He would need to run that by Carla first –

His mobile phone rang.

As he stretched out for it, the landline telephone on his desk rang. My, wasn't he popular all of a sudden!

Assuming that the mobile would be Gisele seeking his agreement to spend money, he picked up the landline.

"Merhi, excuse me just one second." He pressed the reject button on his mobile to shut it up. "Yes, hello."

"Jihad, I wondered if you would be in. It's Selim Himo."

"Selim, *kifak*? They left me a message that you rang. How are things in the Bekaa?"

"I'm fine thanks, as I hope you are."

"I'm good, *merci*. Busy, of course, as always, but good."

"Jihad, I'm in town. I wonder if we could meet? There's something I really need your help on."

Shit, thought Merhi. This was not needed, not right now with the work he had on – not to mention the Carla business. But he owed Himo, owed him big for the help he had given him five years ago. "For you, any time. When would you like to meet?"

"Can we make it Monday morning, at your office?"

"If you are happy with that, yes." They both understood Merhi's oblique reference to The Listeners. "Around nine?"

"Perfect. Enjoy the rest of your weekend. *A lundi.*"

As he put the phone down, Merhi wondered whether he should return Gisele's phone call. She hadn't called back, she had probably bought whatever it was she was going to buy, taking his non–answer of the phone as tacit agreement. Deciding to meet the challenge to his bank account head on, he reached for his mobile – just as it rang again.

He answered without looking at the screen. "Hi."

"Morning of light, Jihad my dear friend!"

Merhi nearly dropped the phone in shock. In the name of Jesus Christ, the Almighty in Heaven above! The voice, the shout, was unmistakeable. He felt his strength draining away.

"Fadi Lattouf, how are you?"

"I am well, my friend, well. And you and the charming Gisele?"

"*Shukran*, we are good. And Nada and your family? How's the little one?"

"Everyone is well, thank you. Little Wissam looks more like his father each day!"

Feeling nothing but sympathy for the poor child, Merhi asked "Number seven not on the way yet?"

"Pah! Chance would be a fine thing. Nada thinks that abstinence will bring us nearer to Allah. I told her Allah will be seeing us soon enough and in the meantime we should honour Him by doing what comes naturally, but she was having none of it."

Well she certainly had some of it three years and forty weeks ago, thought Merhi. He said, "I wish you well in your continued quest, my friend."

"Thank you, thank you. Jihad, I need to say something to you that I thought I would never have to say again."

"What is that?"

There was a pause, then Fadi Lattouf said "Jihad, I have a body."

Sodeco, Beirut 14:00

Gisele Merhi smiled at the waiter as she handed back her menu, then she turned to her husband and said, "Fadi Lattouf. I cannot believe it. After all this time."

"As if I do not have enough on." Jihad pointedly did not look at Carla, sitting next to his wife opposite.

They were in *La Piazza* restaurant. It was one of Jihad's favourite eateries and he had surprised the women by offering to take them here when he had met them up at Hamra. He was in need of the familiar – and good food. Carla had never been in the restaurant before, but she had heard of it from a close friend. She was amazed at the setting. They were inside but were sitting in an Italian town square; on the walls around them were murals of houses, some even with laundry hanging out to dry. It was quaint, charming and, unusually for a restaurant with such a strong theme, Jihad had assured her that the food was excellent.

"It is Ramadan soon," continued Gisele.

Jihad dragged on his cigarette and pulled a face. "What of it?"

"What comes at the end of Ramadan?"

The pulled face dropped as he realized. "*Eid*. Oh no, not again." They had gone through a three-year phase of being invited to the Lattouf's to celebrate *Eid* and, in return, having to invite the Lattouf's to Jounieh for the New Year's celebrations. It had started during the events of five years ago but had then dropped away during Madame Lattouf's sixth pregnancy. Jihad did not want to resurrect the tradition.

"Was he that Palestinian you were with?" asked Carla. "The huge one. In Nejmeh Square."

"The same. The giant. He is supposedly in charge of the refugee camps in the Beirut area, but we all know who really runs them. I think even Fadi now accepts that he and his men are nothing more than window dressing. We used to meet officially twice a year, but even that has gone now, when we realized the meetings were pointless."

"What does he want?" wondered Gisele.

"I'll find out tomorrow." He had not mentioned those ominous four words: *I have a body*.

An appetizer of garlic dough balls was delivered to the table, together with other bread and separate olive oil. As they began to eat, Jihad asked Carla, "So do you want me to make official enquiries?"

"She is not local, we could have guessed that." Carla dipped bread into oil and took a small bite. "Which means she has been brought in from abroad. Just to kill Maroun?"

"That would be very extravagant."

"To kill me?"

"Still extravagant. With respect."

"No, no, you are right. And she has failed with me. Perhaps she has gone. Quickly in, quickly out." A small dribble of olive oil ran down her chin. She caught it with her little finger and smoothed it back upwards into her mouth, dabbing the residue with her napkin.

"Or perhaps Maroun and you are just sidelines," suggested Gisele. "Think broadly." Once a trainer always a trainer. "Maybe you are not her main purpose. She was just conveniently here to deal with you while doing something else."

Knowing what she knew, it was a conclusion Carla had also come to. "Yes, I agree. And that means she is still here. So," she rubbed crumbs from her fingers over her plate, looking at Jihad, "can you make enquiries without specifying a reason?"

"There is another route I can take. I can be vague," he nodded.

"Then please do so."

Meantime, she thought, I shall enlist help of my own.

11 July 2010
29 Rajab 1431

Jounieh, Lebanon 02:30

The night was warm, the stars shimmering in the cloudless sky. It was a new moon so natural light was sparse, but the coastal highway way down below was well-lit by traffic despite the hour. Beyond the road, way out to sea, a boat bobbed, small lights fore and aft.

Jihad and Gisele were in bed and asleep, at least one of them snoring for Lebanon as Carla had glided soundlessly past their bedroom door. Now she was outside on the balcony and for a moment she closed her eyes and lifted her face, absorbing the air and warmth, as if she was being recharged by the stillness of the dark. She was completely naked.

Then a light shone from her left hand as her cell phone trembled. Right on time. She lifted the phone to her ear.

"Bon soir," she smiled, speaking low, looking out westwards into the night...

Verdun, Beirut 11:30

Captain Fadi Lattouf of the Civil Police of the Palestinian Security Force was two metres tall and seemed to measure the same around his stomach. How he had not spontaneously combusted - or simply burst - in any one of his fifty years was a mystery to many people.

Jihad Merhi could see the Palestinian in the Food Court of the

Dunes Shopping Mall as he came up the escalator. Lattouf's backside was so big that it consumed the chair beneath him and gave the impression he was squatting on thin air. He still had the severe comb-over of the remaining strands of his hair, which served to emphasise rather than hide his bald dome, but they were greyer than the last time the two men had met. His beard was greyer too, still of the unshaven-look rather than the cultivated variety.

Lattouf was dressed – *oh my goodness*. He had on the same clothes as he did when they used to meet here five years ago! Rough blue denim jeans, for which he was about twenty-five years too old and fifty kilos too heavy, and a loose pink and blue checked shirt. He used to wear them to blend in with the other shoppers. He failed then and he failed now. Giants did not blend, giant Palestinian policemen even less so.

The state of the table in front of him looked like McDonald's would have to send out for some more burger wrappers before the lunch-time rush began.

Merhi decided to go straight up to *Cup Cakes*. When he was a few metres away, a voice from behind boomed out *"Ay, ay!"* making cups rattle on trays, and he looked back to see a beaming Fadi Lattouf with his right hand in the air. Merhi half-raised his hand and gestured with his head towards the counter. Lattouf nodded (was the Pope a Catholic? Was the President of Lebanon a Christian?).

A few minutes later Merhi was placing a tray down onto the now empty table, the floor beneath littered with the McDonald's wrappers.

"Morning of joy, my dear, dear friend!" Lattouf stood up and Merhi knew what was coming. Lattouf grabbed him and planted five kisses on his cheeks. "Mwah, mwah, mwah, mwah, mmmmmmWAH! It has been a long time. It is good to see you."

Merhi thought that three ribs were broken. "And you, Fadi. You're looking well."

"Pah! Nada has me on a diet," Lattouf tapped his gut which

looked bigger than ever. "I am wasting away, look at me!"

"Then you won't want these cakes," Merhi gestured to the tray on which sat ten cup cakes, two supersize coffees and one double espresso.

"It would be rude to reject your hospitality," reasoned Lattouf. "Bless your hands." He sat down, once again making the chair below disappear.

Merhi sat down also. "One of the chocolate ones are mine." He took the espresso off the tray and helped himself to a cake, pushing the tray and its remaining contents towards Lattouf.

"Of course," smiled the Palestinian. "You Lebanese and your sweet teeth!" He picked up one of the coffees, steam rising from the polycup as he took off the lid. Much more quietly he said, "To you, my friend."

Merhi gestured with his espresso cup. He had to admit, it was good to see the fat, stupid, ebullient bastard again. Perhaps another *Eid* celebration with him wouldn't be so bad after all. "And to you, Fadi."

Half the contents of the polycup had vanished when Lattouf put it back on the table. Sweeping two cakes up in his hand and peeling off the cases, he said "Jihad, you find me a sad, sad man."

"Oh? Why?"

"I have had a death in the family."

"I am sorry to hear that."

Lattouf shrugged. "*Shukran.* He was my cousin. I could not say we were close, but a family death is a family death."

"Of course."

The two cakes were placed in his mouth, one on each side. "He lived up in Jbeil. Moved up there in 2006 after his wife and son were killed by the Jews when they bombed Beirut."

Merhi did not say anything. The constant, regular destruction of Lebanon on an any-excuse basis by the Israelis was a source of hatred for all Lebanese.

Lattouf picked up two more cakes and began to peel them.

"His *kunya* was Abu Yussuf, but his name was Chadi."

Merhi quickly rammed the remains of his cup cake into his mouth. How did Lattouf manage to do this, to bring out such a range of emotions in him? The flare-up of anger at the reminder of the Jews had been replaced by the urge to burst out laughing. Chadi? Chadi and Fadi Lattouf? Sounded like a vaudeville comedy act! Quickly he sipped his espresso then reached across and took another cake from the tray.

"My – my condolences," he coughed, stifling the giggles, reaching in his jacket pocket for his cigarettes.

"Thank you, my friend, thank you." Lattouf reached across and touched his arm, mistaking his watering eyes for an expression of sorrow.

Both men ate cake.

"You said you had a body?" Merhi prompted.

Lattouf frowned. "Yes. My cousin."

"Oh, sorry, sorry! I didn't realise he was the... erm..." Merhi looked around, cigarette in his hand. "Do they still allow you to smoke in here?"

"I am sure nobody is going to argue with you." Lattouf nodded at Merhi's uniform.

"No, I suppose not." He slid the packet of Cedars King Size across the table. "I'm sorry, Fadi, perhaps you had better start from the beginning." He lit up.

Lattouf's eyes were full of sadness – as he looked at the cigarettes. "I had better not. She will smell it on me." He pushed the packet back.

"You could say the smoke got on you from me."

The packet was grabbed back and a cigarette removed. Merhi passed over his lighter.

As he inhaled smoke, Lattouf said "There's not much to tell. Two nights ago I was coming home from work. Around seven-thirty. I was walking down the street towards my house and I saw a *service* pulling up. Someone fell out of it, got up and started banging on my door. I realised it was my cousin. As I got to him he fell back onto the floor, clutching his gut. He was trying to say something to me but he couldn't. Then he died. Right there in the street."

"Did you call the emergency services?"

"Why? He was dead."

"The street is under Lebanese jurisdiction. You should have reported it."

"The street might be. My house isn't."

"Ah, I see. A Palestinian problem then. So why have you called me?"

Lattouf sucked a full two centimetres from the cigarette then stubbed it out in one of the cup cake wrappers. "Chadi was in his forties, no illnesses that the family knew of."

"Death happens, my friend. Sometimes very abruptly."

"As I was washing the body prior to burial last night I noticed something on his left shoulder. A distinct puncture mark. Fresh."

Oh heavens, here we go, thought Merhi.

"I think my cousin was murdered," said Fadi Lattouf.

Annaya, Lebanon 11:35

The Monastery Church of Saint Maron was quiet, deserted except for the three people sitting near the first wall alcove on the right, beneath the two pictures of Saint Maron with the vase of flowers underneath. Visitors rarely came to this 1840s church, even on a Sunday, most preferring the new, round Saint Charbel Church on the other side of the monastery.

Brother Malek was dressed in his full black *burnus*, hood up, only his stubbled chin visible. Because of the heat he wore nothing underneath. But no one would know that.

Paradise and Love knelt on the pew in front, facing him, their green and brown eyes (thirty-five thirty-six in Love's favour) looking at the chin moving as he talked.

"If necessary we will convert the world. I have done it in the past, I will do it again." Although his voice was deep and low, every word was distinct. "Soon now we will no longer have to keep the secret, we will reveal it to the world. Those disciples left behind are now preparing for the second coming. The way is being cleared. It feels like they have been waiting millennia, but they will be rewarded for their patience."

"What can we do?" asked Paradise.

"You are already doing plenty," his voice softened as he reached out and patted their arms. "Follow me, my daughters. Keep the faith."

"Should The Secret be moved?" asked Love. "There was a breach."

The hood turned in her direction. "Was The Secret compromised? Did you not deal with it?"

"Of course we did, Brother," said Paradise. "As always it is your decision. But we would be failing if we did not bring it to your attention."

There was silence. The twins could detect the change in mood, the change in aura, coming from the cowled figure. Eventually he said, "You have somewhere in mind?"

Love looked at her sister. "We were thinking somewhere near the triumphal road. To prepare for the journey come the time. Beyond Baabda. Jamhour perhaps, maybe even Bhamdoun."

Again silence, this time for quite a while. Then: "No. The Secret has moved enough. The time is so close now we will not move again until we begin our journey. The breach was an accident. A *kafir* passing, a chance happenstance. He has been converted and I will not be using that washroom again. I am satisfied The Secret has not been compromised."

Paradise nodded. "Your decisions are always infallible. But take this." She nodded to Love who put her hand into a front pocket of the rucksack on the pew next to her and brought out a tiny object, no more than two centimetres long by one centimetre wide. She placed it in Malek's outstretched palm. "We have the number," continued Paradise. "Naturally no one else does."

Malek closed his palm over the new SIM card.

"We did not bring any more *ma'asel* because you did not request any." Love now had her hand in the main part of the rucksack. "But we thought you might like these." She passed over a folded yellow and green *Spinney's* carrier bag.

Malek felt it without looking inside. The hood moved up and down, nodding. He tucked the bag under his arm and stood up.

Before the twins could rise he had placed a hand on each of their heads. "The Secret is safe. All conversions have been achieved. I will let you know further details of The Second Coming once the disciples have prepared the way. Our route will be strewn with palms..." He took his hands off their heads. "And the bodies of the unbelievers."

Silently he walked back down the church. He stopped by the door, the hood turning back towards the women. He spoke no louder but his voice carried. "You have pleased me, my daughters. Soon now I will please you."

The door creaked open and the hooded monk glided out.

Paradise and Love were left looking at the shaft of bright sunlight piercing through the half-open door.

"Did you feel it?" asked Paradise.

"Yes," said Love, touching the top of her head. "He almost burnt our scalps."

Verdun, Beirut 11:45

"And you want me to investigate it?" asked Jihad Merhi disbelievingly. "A man dies in Beirut, you drag him into Palestinian jurisdiction and now you want the Lebanese authorities to investigate it because you think it might be suspicious? You can't have it both ways, my friend. You should have reported it in the first place."

"And have strangers' hands over my cousin's body? Maybe

cutting him up? And anyway, I did not know he had been murdered - "

"You still don't."

"I think I do. But I need you to confirm it." Lattouf finished the second cup of coffee and stifled a burp down to sonic boom proportions.

"You want another?" Merhi could not believe he had just asked that.

"I will get them." Lattouf fumbled for money in his jeans pocket.

"No, no, I will."

"Okay then. *Merci ktir.*"

When Merhi returned with one large and one medium Americano plus a four-pack of chocolate chip cookies, he asked "In what way can I possibly help you? Your cousin is dead, you have buried the body, what can I do?"

"Bless your hands." Lattouf pulled the lid off his coffee like a man in the final stages of dehydration, slurping it, mixing it with air like a fine wine, confirming Merhi's opinion that he had an asbestos oesophagus. Lattouf shook his head. "You are wrong, my friend. I did not say my cousin was buried. I was preparing him for burial when I found the puncture mark. So I didn't bury him, I've kept him somewhere safe. Please Jihad, come take a look. Tell me if I am imagining it." Lattouf's huge fingers adroitly pulled open the wrapping on the cookies. He offered the packet to Merhi who raised a hand in refusal.

"Where is he?"

"In the *mashraha.*"

"You have a mortuary?"

"We have had one for some time now. Hardly ever been used. Usually the groups, you know, take care of their own."

"And the mortuary is in the camp?" The one place where the Lebanese authorities could not go.

"*Taban.* Of course. You know it. You've been there. Used to be the butcher's shop."

Annaya, Lebanon 11:45

Back in his cell, Brother Malek pulled off his *burnus* and stepped out of his sandals. He stood there naked, his body hairy, carrying the weight of age but by no means fat. A sheen of sweat covered him, his body hairs matted where they were thickest. He should wash, it would soon be time for *salat al-Dhuhr*, noon prayer. But first there was something he must do.

Next to his mattress against the wall was the square, dark blue carrying case with his golden *argileh* inside. He knelt on the floor, flicking up the clasp of the case as he pulled it over. Gently, almost lovingly, he took out the separate pieces of the shisha, placing them carefully on the floor beside him.

But he did not assemble the pipe. Instead, when all the parts were out, he put his hand back into the case. And brought out a Sony Vaio netbook.

It was a chore using one-time-only e-mail accounts, but it was effective. And, when he needed them, he had his one-time-only *Skype* accounts too, with *Windows Messenger* as a fall-back.

One of the benefits of being in Lebanon was that the country was technology-obsessed. There were more mobile telephones in the country than there were people, there were more satellite dishes than there were houses, the social networking sites were more popular here than anywhere else in the world, every one under a certain age – and most people above it – had a computer, and, if they could, their own website. And that included the monasteries.

All the monasteries of any note had their own website, often run by one of the younger brothers of the order. And where there was a web domain there was access to the internet. WiFi.

Malek lifted the lid on the netbook and pressed the On button.

Jounieh, Lebanon 14:30

Gisele Merhi had been less than impressed when her husband had appeared at the door half an hour earlier with the huge Palestinian, but being the perfect hostess she had pretended to be pleased to see him – and so suddenly and unannounced too – enquiring after his family, his health, how was the new baby? Three already, good heavens, God's blessings upon him. Yes, she would love to visit and see him sometime.

Now she asked, "Are you sure you cannot stay for dinner, Fadi?"

Fadi looked up from the two-seater leather sofa which, with him in it, looked like it was a scaled-down chair from a kindergarten. In his hand he held his third glass of apple juice. "My dear Gisele, there is nothing I would like more. But alas, your husband and I have business. But soon, perhaps."

"Yes soon." Under her breath she added, "Perhaps."

Jihad appeared. He had changed from his uniform into casual gear: blue 'I ♥ Dubai' T-shirt (a present from his brother-in-law), light beige jeans, socks and trainers (he had wanted to wear sandals but they would not be suitable). When he had told Gisele where he was going (as if she hadn't guessed already), a classic Merhi *sotto voce* discussion had ensued in the kitchen, with Jihad winning but feeling like he'd lost ('twas ever thus). And, by the way, asked Gisele with the last word as always, just how many waifs and strays from the past was he intending to bring back to the apartment this weekend? That was two now and counting.

"Okay Fadi," Jihad said. "Let's go." Pecking Gisele on a reluctantly-offered cheek, he said "I'll text you when I'm on my way back."

Lattouf poured the remainder of his apple juice into his body and stood up, looking for somewhere to put the glass then giving it to Gisele.

As they walked towards the front door, there was the sound

of a key in the lock. The door opened to reveal a small, olive skinned, black haired woman whom Lattouf instantly recognised. He gasped. "The lady! The lady from Nejmeh Square." He grabbed her hand, raising it to his lips. "My dear, how are you?"

Who said chivalry was dead? thought Jihad. "Z – Carla. Captain Fadi Lattouf. You remember him? My Palestinian cohort."

"My goodness, yes." Carla raised her other hand and discreetly stroked Lattouf's palm in the guise of turning the hand-kiss into a hand-shake. Bluff called, Lattouf let go instantly. She said, "It is good to see you again, *monsieur*."

"Carla is staying with us," mumbled Jihad. "Come, let us go."

"And it is an honour to see you again, *madame*," called Lattouf over his shoulder as he was dragged down the stairs.

Bourj el-Barajneh, Beirut 15:45

The Palestinian refugee camps of Lebanon are not 'camps' as such. A local politician had recently gotten into trouble for calling them 'slums', but it was an accurate description.

The Bourj el-Barajneh camp in southern Beirut is one square kilometre of basic brick and block constructions which pass as dwellings, packed so tight together that most paths between the buildings are less than half a metre wide. There are no maps, no street signs. You have to know where you are going to find your way through the tight alleyways, over the broken water pipes, under the sagging cables, past the broken windows which might at any minute open into your face, through the sewage...

Posters or drawings, nowadays mostly of Hamas leaders or martyrs, were everywhere.

The camp, and the others like it, was set up after *al-Naqba* – the catastrophe of 1948 when three hundred thousand Palestinians fled their homes in Palestine. It was built to deal with the 'temporary crisis' of the refugees. It was originally constructed to house ten thousand people, and the camp is forbidden to expand physically. By 2010, it was housing over twenty thousand human beings.

Jihad Merhi had changed out of his uniform because the camps in Lebanon are no-go areas for the Lebanese authorities. Lebanon is forbidden from interfering or intervening in the camps and from sending troops or other officials inside, including police. He was risking his job – not to mention his life - just by being here.

The place had not changed in the five years since his last visit. Still the sagging cables going from building to building, still the cracked, dripping pipes... still the smell.

He walked with Lattouf, unsure which was causing him the most discomfiture: being back in the camp or having accepted Lattouf's suggestion of popping in to visit his wife and children after they had conducted their business, which would also mean the offer of food and drink.

Five minutes in and he knew where he was, but not how they had gotten there through the complex maze of alleys. They passed the old butcher's shop, still boarded up. "We use the back way," explained Lattouf.

They turned left then left again. Lattouf could only just fit down the narrow alley between the buildings which led on to a small courtyard area.

Only one door led out into the yard, obviously the back of the butcher's shop. The other sides of the yard were blank walls with windows above, through which came sounds of habitation: talking, shouting, babies crying, radios, televisions, cooking noises. The wooden door was rotting but there was a huge for-show padlock on it which Lattouf unlocked.

As he pushed the door open, the stench dashed out to meet them like a long-lost relative. Merhi staggered backwards, hand going up to his face. "Satan's bollocks, Fadi! You've not installed climate control then."

"I told you. It is hardly ever used. *Yalla.*"

Still covering his face, Merhi followed him in. The room on the right had not changed. In the dim light Merhi could see the wide, shallow gulley in the floor with a deep hole at one end. A drain for the blood of chopped up carcasses when this used to be a butcher's, and probably the same now for its human clientele. Against the opposite wall was a table on which lay a covered shape.

Lattouf went over and pulled off the *kafan* with a flourish, like a magician's reveal. The corpse was at a slightly odd angle, corner to corner on the rectangular table. "*Allahu Akbar*," said Lattouf softly, pulling the cloth back up to cover the genitals. Noticing Merhi had turned his head to align it with the corpse, he explained "I have tried to face him towards the *qiblah*."

"I see." Merhi knew that Muslims should be placed with their head facing Mecca, at least when they were buried.

Lattouf seemed to read his thoughts. "I did it now because there will not be a burial." Merhi raised his eyebrows and looked a query, but did not say anything. Lattouf shrugged. "He had no family, not since the murders by the Jews. We were his only relatives. Where are we supposed to bury him here?"

Merhi glanced over to the gulley opposite, thought thoughts which he didn't want to think, and then turned back to the body. He put on his reading glasses which had been hooked over the neck of his T-shirt.

Chadi Lattouf had been just an average male in his forties, slight paunch, gentle balding, moustache, nothing out of the ordinary. His fingers showed nicotine stains. There were a few moles and other marks on the torso but nothing to indicate a violent death. The face was calm. Rigor mortis had passed but there were signs of lividity on his underside where he had been laid out.

"Look. There." Lattouf nodded towards the left shoulder.

Merhi had no intention of touching the body but he brought his head closer, squinting through his glasses. From a metre away the mark looked like any of the other moles or blemishes, but as he got nearer he could see it was different. It was about half a centimetre wide and looked like the mark that sometimes appears after a blood test. Death had stopped the spread of the bruise. And in the centre, sure enough, was a distinct puncture mark.

"I see. Hmm..." He sniffed (not the right thing to do, the body had not been perfumed) and straightened up. "You think that killed him?"

"I saw him die. It was not a natural passing. There are no other marks upon him."

"Really there should be an autopsy, you know."

"For what reason? He is dead. Dead because of that. Dead is dead. Nothing will be achieved by knowing *exactly* what killed him, only *how* he was killed. This obsession with cutting open the dead is an affront to Allah."

Merhi was surprised at the strength of his friend's opinion, and to some extent he agreed with him. He turned back for another look at the wound. After a few moments he took hold of the edge of the *kafan* and gently raised it back over the body.

"Thank you," said Lattouf. "Bless you."

"Can we go?" asked Merhi. "I guess you will be..." He made a gesture towards the body.

"Yes, I will. *Yalla*. Come."

Back out in the small yard, Lattouf refixed the padlock on the door.

"So who would murder your cousin?" asked Merhi as they walked away. "Was he involved with the groups?"

They went back down the narrow alleyway. "No, no, he was not political." Lattouf's voice was amplified by the closeness of the walls. "The family has never involved itself in such things. That is why we make good policemen! But after 2006 we came close to joining the groups. Very close. Chadi even went so far as to quit his job."

"What did he do?"

Lattouf sounded surprised. "Did I not say? He was a police-man."

"No, you didn't say."

"Well, he was. Then after his family were murdered he quit and went up to Jbeil."

Merhi trod in something and was momentarily distracted. He did not look down but he was so pleased he had not worn his sandals. There was no rising smell, for which he was grateful.

They reached the edge of the camp and turned right into Annan Street.

"And he did not work now?" asked Merhi.

Lattouf looked affronted. "Of course he worked! He was a *muhaqqiq khass*. A private dick, as they say on TV. And a damn-ed good one."

They reached a doorway which Lattouf opened with a key. "Wife!" he called. "Nada! You will never guess who is here, who has come to see us! Our old friend Jihad! And he has come to dinner!"

Jounieh, Lebanon 23:59

Jihad Merhi sat on the edge of his bed casually stroking his wife's thigh under the cotton sheet. "They mean well, bless them, but oh my God. *Kibbeh nayeh!* The *Fattoush* was fine, but the raw meat!"

"Was it awful?" asked Gisele, leaning against the golden leather headboard.

"Actually, no. It was very nice. But it's just the thought of it. Nada prepared it especially for me, so I felt obliged to eat it. Why do people assume that if you're Lebanese you must like raw meat?"

"Well, apparently you do, you've just said so." She smiled, reaching out for her husband's hand. "How were they?"

"Fine, fine. Really it wasn't bad seeing them again. Little Mini Me is cute. Farts like his father though. The rest of the kids are getting bigger, I hardly saw them."

"So what did he want?"

Jihad looked down at their joined hands. He sighed and said, "He has a body. Again."

"What of it?"

"It's his cousin."

"And it involves you how?"

"A jurisdictional crossover thing again. Looks like murder."

"His cousin was murdered?"

"It seems so."

"That is sad. But we all know the problems in the camps, murders happen all the time."

Jihad rubbed his thumb over the back of Gisele's hand. "Not like this one. He wasn't shot, stabbed or beaten. Not even strangled."

"What then - ?"

Both their heads turned as they heard movement outside. There were footsteps on the tiled floor. A door opened and closed. Gisele said, "She's back. She has been out all evening. Left just after you and Fadi."

"Really?" Jihad stared at the bedroom door. Then turning back to his wife, he said "I don't know what she's involved in, other than this murder of her boss. This thing about – what was the name?"

"Sajida."

"This thing about Sajida I just don't understand."

"So what happened?"

"What?"

"To Fadi's cousin."

He let go of her hand and rubbed his nose. He wished he was allowed to smoke in the bedroom. "You're not going to believe this. The old poison dart."

"Ricin!"

"Maybe."

"On the streets of Beirut?"

"Seems like it, but Fadi won't allow an autopsy, so we can't be certain. Might be this new ricin-abrin compound our neighbours but two have produced. I've seen the mark." He touched his shoulder.

Gisele was shaking her head. "That's not playing fair."

"No. Not like the good old days of shootings and bombings. At least then you knew where you stood – unless your legs were blown off." He did not smile at his own macabre humour. Gisele grimaced and looked heavenward.

"So, as usual," continued Jihad, "I don't know what's going on. It's like the gods of confusion and ignorance are laughing at me again. There I was, coasting along, when suddenly two faces from the past drop back into my world, both bringing death with them. But at least this time, dear wife...." He took her hand, raised it to his lips and sucked the end of her index finger. She did not pull away.

After a moment, she asked "But at least this time, dear husband?"

He took her finger from his mouth. "At least this time they're unconnected."

12 July 2010
30 Rajab 1431

Jonblat, Beirut 09:00

"Jihad! How nice to see you again." Selim Himo was shown into Merhi's office by a young officer from downstairs. Sergeant Deeb el-Gharib, who would normally act as his captain's reception, had already been called out to a bomb scare up at Rmeil along with most of the team.

The first thing Merhi noticed was that the tall, slim man he knew as Lieutenant Himo of the Bekaa Inquiry Brigade was not dressed in the uniform of the *Gendarmerie*. Nor was he wearing the epaulettes of a lieutenant on his uniform shirt. He was dressed exactly the same as Merhi.

They shook hands. "Selim, it's nice to see you too," smiled Merhi. "What's this?" He tapped Himo's left epaulette. "Are congratulations in order?"

"Sort of."

"Coffee?"

"That's very kind, thank you."

"Sit, sit, I won't be a minute."

Out in the General Office, Merhi found the two least dirty mugs and spooned in granules as the kettle boiled. Normally he would have 'real' coffee brought in from outside but because of that damned bomb scare he had no one here to run errands.

He hoped this would not take long. Himo had obviously been promoted. Had he come here just to elicit the obligatory praise and approval? He was about fifteen years younger than

Merhi and, ever since they had first met on a training course many years ago, Merhi had realised Himo was a high-flyer destined for the fast track.

Apart from any professional jealousy (which, of course, he did not have), Merhi wanted to start the wider-field enquiries regarding Carla's attacker. Not only that but today was the fourth anniversary of Operation Sincere Promise[*], and celebrations were expected on the streets. The bomb scare might be the beginning of the festivities.

Back in his office, coffees on his desk, Merhi said "So, you are no longer in the Bekaa?"

"I moved a few months ago."

"Promotion to...?"

"Originally a level transfer, but I've just been made up, acting at the moment."

"Not acting for long. I'm sure it's only a matter of time until it's substantive." Merhi held up his packet of cigarettes in query.

"Thank you. And *merci*." Himo shook his head.

Merhi lit up as Himo continued. "I'm now with the DGS. The guy whose role I've taken has been found dead. Murdered. That's why I'm here." He took a swig of coffee. "There's something you might be able to help me with."

Jounieh, Lebanon 09:15

Carla pressed the End icon on her mobile phone and sighed. She was disappointed but she well-understood. Money did not

---

[*] On 12 July 2006 Hizbullah captured two Israeli soldiers to trade them for Lebanese prisoners in Israeli jails and for the remains of resistance fighters that had been held for decades in Israel's infamous Cemetery of Numbers. In retaliation, Israel waged war on Lebanon, bombing the country for 33 days, destroying much of south Lebanon and south Beirut. At least 1300 people were killed and 1 million Lebanese displaced. The hostilities officially ceased on 12 August 2006 after the adoption of UN Security Council Resolution 1701. Two years later, on 16 July 2008, the bodies of the two captured Israeli soldiers were swapped for four captured Hizbullah fighters, one former Palestine Liberation Front member (Samir Kuntar) and the bodies of 200 Lebanese and Palestinian militants.

grow on trees. Work was work and took priority. Naturally he had not said where he was going but he said it would only take a few days. So she would have to wait for assistance, and waiting was not a strong characteristic of *djinni*. She only hoped that the other string to her bow, Captain Jihad Merhi, brought back some results quickly.

She was out on the balcony of the Merhi's apartment, dressed only in a small red cotton thong. Jihad was at work and Gisele had gone down to Kaslik to do some shopping. The sun was already hot as it crept over the mountain behind her.

Laying down on the towel she had placed on the tiles, she brought her right leg up, crossing it over the left and linking her hands under her thighs in a piriformis stretch. She changed over legs, performed the piriformis again, then lay flat on her back, feet on the floor, knees bent, thighs opening and closing in hip abductor stretches.

This was a routine he had taught her, and, as her legs parted and the sun's rays went into intimate places, she smiled at how often they had not gotten any further than this move!

Twenty minutes later she finished with a standing hamstring stretch, first her right leg up on top of the balustrade, then her left. Sweat glistened on her olive skin. She had worn as little as possible but perhaps she should not even have worn that. The soaking wet thong would need to be peeled down her legs.

As she warmed-down with a few little hip movements, she looked out to sea. It was hazy out over the Mediterranean, but inland it was clear. She could see the traffic down on the coastal highway.

What she could not see, even with the eyes of a djinn, was the topless black Jeep Wrangler Ultimate with two women on board heading down into Beirut...

Jonblat, Beirut 09:15

Shit, thought Merhi. Shit, shit, piss and shit. The gods really were having a laugh, weren't they?

He decided on the naive approach. "Someone has been murdered?"

"My captain, Maroun Khoury." Himo put his mug back down on the desk. "Know him?"

"No. How was he killed?"

"Garrotted."

Merhi grimaced. "Oh dear. My condolences. You have any-one for it?"

Himo shook his head. "Not yet. That's where I hope you can help me."

"If I can help you in any way, I most certainly will. But I don't see - "

"Five days ago you asked the traffic police for CCTV recordings of a street in Ashrafieh. Why?"

Merhi took a long drag on his cigarette, staring across at the younger man. Then he said slowly, "Don't much like the tone, Selim."

Himo held the gaze. "And I don't much like having my captain murdered."

"Even if it means you step into his shoes? You always were ambitious."

"What the fuck are you implying?"

"What the fuck are *you* implying? How dare you come in here demanding that a senior officer explain his actions. I am a captain of the Internal Security Force. I can ask anyone for anything I want, and I don't have to give a reason."

Another drag on the cigarette, another swig of the coffee.

"But," continued Merhi, "if you are asking rather than demanding...?" He waited.

Ten seconds of stand-off, then Himo conceded. "I am asking."

"Then I can tell you that we are in a heightened state of alert at the moment, concerning various things that I am sure you can guess at. Have you looked at the CCTV in question?"

"Yes."

"Then you will have seen the traffic in the street, how crowded it was. We have a tip that a car bomb might be going off in the city sometime soon - our friends in the south. Even now my men are out after an alert this morning. Intelligence at the time suggested that the target was somewhere in Ashrafieh. We were trying to examine parking patterns. Comparing historical from four days previously to immediate eyes we had on the ground. To see if any cars had not been moved for a few days. Maybe there was a dud bomb sitting around."

"And was there?"

Merhi shrugged. "The CCTV was so blurred and unclear we could not undertake any useful comparison. Our eyes on the ground did not find anything."

"And if I question your team they will confirm this?"

"Don't push it, Acting Captain."

The landline telephone on Merhi's desk rang, which was perhaps just as well. He answered it with his name and listened. "*Oui... oui... d'accord... alors, j'arrive.*" He put the phone down.

Stubbing out his cigarette as he stood up, he said "I am wanted up at Rmeil. The car bomb. I take it there was nothing else?"

Himo also stood up. "For now, no. If there is anything else - "

"Send me an e-mail. Now, if you'll excuse me?" Merhi gestured towards the door, not offering a hand shake.

Rmeil, Beirut 10:15

The traffic was heavy but Merhi was surprised that it was moving at all as he drove east down Gouraud Street and took the first left after the post office. Even stopping traffic in a small section of Beirut usually had a disproportionate butterfly effect over the rest of the city.

At the end of the small street, at the junction with Pasteur Street, a police officer was standing next to the tape spread across the road, beyond which Merhi could see members of his team mingling with more of the local force. Things seem to be happening just to the right, out of his view.

He flashed his lights, the officer looked at his uniform and then pulled the tape up high on tiptoe so that the Toyota Land Cruiser V8 could pass underneath. Merhi pulled up at the top of the street, the action – or, more properly, inaction – over on the right now visible.

The local police were milling about, pretending to be important but actually doing very little. A sniffer dog was sitting chewing intently on a treat. Three members of Merhi's own team were standing near an old sports car at the fork with Berberi Street.

Sergeant Deeb el-Gharib raised his hand as he saw Merhi climbing out of the Land Cruiser.

"Standing a bit close, Sergeant?" commented Merhi as he came across.

el-Gharib shook his head. "Nothing to worry about, Captain. It's clean, at least for explosives."

Merhi spoke as he walked around the vehicle. "What is this old rust bucket?"

"A Datsun Bluebird. Not made anymore. Probably worth something, even in that state."

"An orange Bluebird. Must be some irony there somewhere. Situation report?"

"According to locals its been parked here since Friday. Was only reported this morning, by the priest from Saint Antoine's Church down there, who became a bit worried, what with the anniversary and all. The local boys called us as a matter of course."

"Of course. Keys?"

"No. Doors unlocked though. But they'll have to move it by truck, they don't have ignition keys on hand for something like this. It will be a special request. And we don't want to hot wire."

"The dog been over it?"

"Yes."

"Printing?"

"Probably not necessary."

Merhi pulled open the driver's door with his fingertips and leant in. The car smelt like a burnt-down tobacco factory. Or was that him? He sniffed his shirt.

The leather seats were worn and cracked, even split in places, stuffing hanging out like the intestines of a stab victim. The door to the glove compartment came away in his hand. "Meant to tell you about that," said el-Gharib from behind.

"You find anything in here?" asked Merhi over his shoulder as he refitted the door and then backed out.

"The usual stuff in the glove compartment. Empty cigarette packets and sweet wrappers in the driver's door, nothing in the other door. Something interesting on the passenger seat though."

"What?"

el-Gharib moved closer, speaking quieter. "A notepad. I've got it in my car."

"Informative?"

"Not particularly, but I thought you might like to have a look at it."

"Anything else?"

"Just some playing cards, a pen and a pair of sunglasses."

Merhi folded his arms, studying the Bluebird. He nodded. "Much as I appreciate being involved, Deeb, being kept in the loop, why did you call me out on this? You could have handled it, or the Lieutenant."

"We've been together a long time, Jihad," el-Gharib looked around, making sure no one else was in ear-shot. "I thought you might want to see it because there's something you should know. I haven't told the Lieutenant. I ran a registered owner's check." He paused.

"And?"

"It is registered to someone called Chadi Lattouf."

Jonblat, Beirut 11:45

Back in his office, Merhi looked at his watch, unable to believe that it was not yet even the afternoon. This day already contained more shit than the nappies in a nursery hit by an outbreak of infant diarrhoea.

On his drive back he had thought more about the upstart Selim Himo. His immediate anger after he had left for Rmeil earlier had now been moderated by the acceptance that Himo was not only investigating a murder, which he was perfectly entitled to do, but a murder of one of their own kind. Not only that but he, Jihad Merhi, had played the ignorant card – a murder? Really? – and yet truth be told he knew more about it than anybody.

Why hadn't he been open? Why hadn't he told Himo about the returned exile now known as Carla Chedid, and the fact that she had been staying with Khoury at the time of his death? Why hadn't he mentioned the fact that she had been attacked shortly afterwards? Why hadn't he shown Himo the lifelike drawing he had in his drawer of the attacker, the tall blonde woman with the white eyes?

Why? Because he should have reported the whole thing straightaway when Carla had first contacted him. He should not have let himself be beguiled into secrecy and complicity.

But he had. And when you were deep in the shit, and even if you were adding to it yourself, the last thing you wanted to do was to encourage others to dump upon you too.

Carla knew the body would be found and she knew there would be an investigation. He would tell her of Himo's involvement tonight. It would be up to her whether she contacted him or still ploughed her own furrow. Really, he had enough on his plate without this.

Opening the drawer, he brought out Carla's drawing. He would initiate enquiries with Interpol, see if anyone anywhere knew of the woman with the white eyes, and that would be the end of his involvement.

This was actually the easy part. Interpol Beirut was in this building, in a suite upstairs, he had been seconded there once himself. He knew that for a few years now they had used the Global Communications System I-24/7, so his request for 'Anything Known' would be out there in no time and results should come back quickly. Then perhaps he would have Carla out of his hair.

He placed the drawing in an envelope and left his office.

He was back within ten minutes. The great, all-powerful, all-singing, all-dancing Global Communications System I-24/7 was down. It was a problem at Interpol HQ in Lyons, France, he had been told, nothing to do with us. But if he cared to leave a copy of the picture and a note of his request, they would get round to it as soon as they were able to.

He cared to and he did.

Right, one down. How many more to go?

He needed to contact Fadi Lattouf, to tell him his cousin's car had been found. He had taken the notepad off of Sergeant el-Gharib and had told him to tell the local police that the ISF considered it to be just an abandoned vehicle but that the ISF would retain jurisdiction because of certain sensitive matters that had arisen relating to its ownership.

He frowned. Good heavens, that was the truth! At least at this time. But of course there would be more to it. Only he knew that the owner was dead.

He had already examined the notepad. Didn't seem to be any clues in it, but he would discuss it with Lattouf.

He picked up his landline phone and then put it down again. He didn't know Lattouf's number, it was plumbed into his mobile. Actually, that was the better option, what with The Listeners. He would go out, grab a bite to eat, and phone Lattouf from out in the street.

Hamra, Beirut 12:30

Although it was a Monday, Hamra Street was as busy as ever. In times past Hamra was *the* shopping district of Beirut. Many of the famous names had now moved to other locations, such as the malls and back into the rebuilt city centre, but the area still buzzed. The retail shops and the sidewalk stalls were as popular as ever, the shouts from the street-hawkers vying with the noise from the traffic to see who could be the loudest.

Merhi waited until he was in the relative calm of Hamra Square before he pulled out his mobile. It seemed to take ages to connect and then it rang for a long time. He was about to disconnect when a voice answered, "*'eeh?*"

"Fadi?"

"Who is it?" The reception was not good, Lattouf sounded as if he was deep inside a cave.

"Jihad."

There was a pause and Merhi heard the sound of metal clinking. Was Lattouf having his lunch?

"Jihad, you have caught me at a bad time. I am burying my cousin."

Merhi frowned. "But I thought you said you weren't..." His voice trailed off as realisation dawned. He did not want to think what that metallic sound had been. Lattouf was in the butcher's shop morgue, that's why the reception was bad. "Oh I see. I won't keep you."

A resigned sigh came down the phone. "No, it does not matter, my friend. Abu Yussuf is not in a hurry. In fact wherever he was going, he has arrived there already. This is just his shell."

Merhi could feel the Palestinian's sadness. "Actually, he's the reason I'm calling. We've found his car."

"You have? That was quick. Thank you for giving it priority. I always knew I could rely on you, Abu Samer."

Merhi did not have the heart to tell him that it was pure

coincidence, that they had been investigating a potential car bomb and that he had forgotten about his cousin until el-Gharib had discovered the name of the owner of the vehicle. "Fadi, we need to meet. There are things to discuss."

Lattouf said something but he was drowned out by a shrieking sales pitch from a stallholder near Merhi.

Glaring at the man, Merhi said loudly "Sorry I didn't hear a word of that."

Now it was Lattouf's turn to shout. "I said, Wednesday at midday?"

Merhi drew long and hard on his cigarette, swallowing the smoke. Was that really Wednesday midday or was Lattouf using their old twenty-six hours earlier code, which meant tomorrow at ten?

"Fadi, clarify. Do you really mean Wednesday at midday?"

"No."

"Okay. My office, not the other place."

"Really?"

"Yes, this is official." And it will be good for your waistline.

"Okay then. Should I be identified?"

Knowing that the giant would be more noticeable in his ridiculous 'street clothes', Merhi answered "Yes. You can be in uniform."

"Okay. Wednesday at midday at your place. Jihad, what is all that noise? I can hardly hear you."

Without thinking, Merhi replied "I'm outside. In Hamra." As soon as he said it, he regretted it. Oh how easily a man forgets!

"Hamra!" exclaimed Lattouf, all sadness gone. "My friend, you couldn't pick me up some pickles from that stall on the square, could you?"

Ras en Nabaa, Beirut 17:00

As he left the Directorate of General Security offices that evening, Acting Captain Selim Himo was still fuming at the treatment he had received seven hours previously from Jihad Merhi. Fuming and curious. Their paths had crossed infrequently in the past but when they had the two men had seemed to get on well. Hadn't Himo helped him out with those serial killings five years ago? Okay, they might not be friends, they moved in different circles, but until that morning he had thought that they were at least close colleagues.

So why the aggression from Merhi?

Merhi had claimed ignorance of the murder of Maroun Khoury. That may or may not be true, the DGS had kept it quiet while it was being investigated. But was it really feasible that a captain of the Internal Security Force had wanted to see CCTV recordings covering the same street where the victim lived at precisely the time of the murder, the time supposedly chosen by Merhi at random for an historical check for a current sweep for a car bomb?

And had Merhi really expected him to accept it, say "Oh, okay, thanks" and clear off? Himo knew when he was being played.

He reached the parking area at the back of the building, his GMC Yukon Denali bipping as he pressed the key in his pocket. Throwing his case on the back seat, he climbed in.

So what should he do about Merhi? He did not want to go running to Merhi's boss, Major Ghanem, like a tell-tale. That would be childish. But he wasn't satisfied, he needed to look into this further. In his case he had copies of the same CCTV footage Merhi had requisitioned. He had already sped-watched it twice in the office. There was little activity in the street during the two hours in question save for one woman entering the building. She was small and dark, probably a local. Who was that? Was she the killer?

Now he was taking the discs home to watch without the everyday interruptions of a workplace. He would watch them on slow speed, to see if there was anything his initial viewing had missed.

Key in the ignition, he started the car.

He drove off, turning right into Damascus Street, pulling out in front of a Jeep Wrangler Ultimate that had just moved away from outside the French Cultural Centre next door.

Then he turned right again onto Abdallah el Yafi Avenue.

As did the Jeep.

Raousheh, Beirut 18:00

It was a straight journey to Himo's apartment just off Beirut's western corniche. At this hour the traffic was heavy as Abdallah el Yafi Avenue became Saeb Salam Avenue. The traffic moved slowly and then stopped completely when he was in the Verdun underpass. Eventually the GMC crawled out at a snail's pace, passing the three-vehicle smash at the junction with Rafic el Hariri Avenue that was causing the tailback.

Once he was heading north on General de Gaulle Avenue, the shore of the Mediterranean over on his left, he was able to pick up speed. Up the hill, by Pigeon Rocks[*], he turned right then right again just west of Australia Street, pulling into the small underground parking area beneath a 1960's (1380's) apartment block.

Internal stairs led up to the ground floor where he could take the elevator to his apartment on the fifth floor.

So he did not see the Jeep Wrangler Ultimate pull up outside.

Himo's apartment was in need of some small cosmetic refurbishment and minor repairs, as could be expected in a building now fifty years old which had survived the events of 1975 to 1990, but because of its location and views it still commanded a high rent. From his small balcony he could just

---

[*] Beirut's most famous natural landmark, two massive calcareous rocks just off the coast. The larger, southern, rock has an archway at the base made by waves and wind. The sixty metres high rocks are famous not only for their natural beauty but also for diving competitions and suicide attempts.

see the northern Pigeon Rock beyond the sea-front buildings.

Pulling open the glass door to the balcony to let in some air, he took his gun from the holster on his waistband and locked it in a drawer of his modern desk. He pressed the On button of his Hewlett Packard computer and then went into his kitchen for food.

His freezer yielded a carton of *yakhnit el samak* (fish stew), which he preferred to eat hot rather than the usual cold. He turned on his oven and then took a bottle of local lemonade from the fridge, pouring himself a large glass. Kicking off his shoes, he went out onto the balcony with his drink. The waning sun was still hot and blazed directly at him from the west, making him shield his eyes.

As he thought about Merhi and what to do, his eyes wandered down to the street below. Cars were parked on either side and he was grateful he had paid the extra for a private parking space under the building.

Deciding to shower, he walked back inside. The oven had nearly reached its temperature so he put his carton on a small baking tray and put it inside, turning the timer for twenty minutes.

He stripped, throwing his sweat-soaked shirt straight into the washing machine, together with his underwear and socks. He carried his trousers over his arm into the bedroom and hung them up.

As the spray of the shower hit him, first too cold then very hot, he closed his eyes, soaking his hair, feeling the water run down his body, dripping off his nose, his chin, his genitals, washing away the grime of the day.

He was not aware of the bathroom door opening, then closing again.

Jounieh, Lebanon 18:30

"Well of course it was only a matter of time until Maroun was discovered." Carla was sitting on the leather couch, bare feet curled up under her, holding a glass of orange juice. She was dressed in blue back-in-fashion leggings and a long black linen top open one button more than was necessary.

Jihad Merhi stood in front of the balcony doors with his back to her, smoking, looking out over the view down the mountain to the coast, glass of red *Massaya* wine in the same hand as his cigarette.

"What is this Lieutenant Himo like?" asked Carla.

"Acting Captain," said Merhi. "He would be the first to correct you. And that sums him up really." He turned, blowing out smoke. "Sure of himself. Knows where he's going. He probably has a - " he made bunny ears in the air, awkward because of the glass and Cedars King Size, " – Life Plan. He's as decent as a high-flyer can be, but Selim Himo is his number one priority."

Carla nodded. "I see. So you don't think he would be interested in a partnership with me?"

"Not the sort you mean."

A smile spread across Carla's face as she uncurled her legs and stood up. "What sort do I mean, Jihad?" she asked softly as she walked across and stood next to him, facing the balcony.

"The professional sort." He glanced down at the too far unbuttoned top and then quickly looked away, noticing mischief in her eyes.

"That would still need clarification." She looked out over the view.

Merhi coughed and drank wine, swiftly followed by a drag on the cigarette.

"Could you introduce me to him?" she asked.

"Are you sure that's wise?"

"I did not kill Maroun, I have nothing to hide."

"You haven't? What about this Sajida business that you won't tell me about?"

She put her hand on his shoulder. "It is not that I won't tell you, as I have explained. I am protecting you. Regard it as need to know. Perhaps Acting Captain Himo already knows about Sajida. If not, perhaps he is one who does need to know. Can you arrange a meeting, just between him and me?" In the reflection in the glass she noticed Gisele standing in the doorway of the room, a large chopping knife in her hand. Carla turned, letting the natural movement take her hand from Jihad's shoulder.

"The *shish tawook* is on," announced Gisele stonily. "There is *tabouleh* and *falafel* and things on the table. Whenever you two are ready." She swung round and went back into the kitchen.

Jihad sighed. "I have a feeling my own *falafel* might be on the table very soon," he said wearily. "I'll give Himo a ring later. *Yalla*, let's eat."

Raousheh, Beirut 18:30

Selim Himo wiped the water from his eyes as he stepped out of the shower cubicle, reaching for his towel.

He dried himself vigorously, leaving his head until last, his short hair sticking up in spiky style. When he was not on duty he liked his hair like this, made him feel younger, more attractive, especially in his favourite club over in Sin el Fil. He would flatten it down when he shaved in the morning.

He opened the bathroom window wide. Although the shower had washed away the grime of the day, it had done nothing to reduce his temperature. Beirut in the summer was hot, and the air conditioning in the apartment was so old that it was always destined to be fighting a losing battle. He was glad he had left the balcony door open.

Naked, he walked out into the bedroom. He could smell his stew cooking nicely out in the oven. Any moment now the timer bell would be going off.

Deciding against getting dressed, he went out into the living room.

And stopped dead.

His small table for two over against the wall had been set, cutlery, condiments, his refilled glass of lemonade, flat bread, some hummus from the fridge - and his fish stew steaming in a bowl.

He tensed, feeling totally vulnerable. He was literally completely exposed. With two leaps he was over at his desk, pulling open the drawer – to find it empty, his gun gone.

"Looking for this?"

He straightened up slowly, facing the wall. Carefully, to show he was not making any sudden moves, he turned around.

A woman was leaning against the open kitchen doorway, his gun swinging from her left index finger. She was tall, long frizzy blonde hair falling down over her shoulders, eyes a deep brown. She was wearing a white vest, combat pants and desert boots.

Himo said nothing, weighing up the situation. Was this a hit? The second External Security Unit captain within days?

As if she was reading his mind, the woman span the gun on her finger with the precision of an expert, catching it so that it pointed towards him.

"Who are you?" he asked. Although she was pointing the gun at him she had made no move to pull the trigger. "What do you want?"

The woman looked pointedly at his hairy groin, smiled, then looked back up into his face. "You."

His eyebrows raised. Who was this, the local recruiter for the Raousheh swingers society? Well, she was barking up the wrong tree with him. At the very least she would have to turn round.

Again she seemed to read his mind. "Don't be silly. I know you are not interested in the likes of us."

"Us?"

"Us," said a voice from his bedroom.

Himo jumped, looked then looked again. An identical

woman was standing in his bedroom doorway. Identical except that she had green eyes. Where had she appeared from?

He looked from one woman to the other. This was spooky. And professional. He was in a total checkmate position. All his exits were covered – literally and figuratively.

Then he jumped again as the cooker timer went off.

As the woman from the bedroom walked over into the kitchen, the one with the gun said, "You should only do *yakhnit el samak* for fifteen minutes, not twenty."

The other one had turned off the timer and now stood next to the one with the gun. Obviously twins. Or clones.

"What do you want?" asked Himo. "Apart from dispensing unwanted culinary advice?"

The women bent their heads to the side, one one way one the other, looking at him. Suddenly he was not hot any more. In fact he felt cold.

Then the one with the gun straightened up, lowering the weapon. "Brother Malek sends his blessings," said Love.

"And you will show us respect, Disciple Selim," said Paradise. "Our advice was good. Come, eat your food before it gets cold."

"And don't bother to get dressed," advised Love. "We like you just the way you are."

Jounieh, Lebanon 20:30

Jihad Merhi took his mobile phone away from his ear, looked at the screen then put it back to his ear again. "No answer," he said.

The three of them were sitting out on the Merhis' wide balcony, facing the setting sun far out at sea. Humours had mellowed with the intake of wine over dinner, Jihad now augmenting his with a post-prandial *arak*. Background music was playing from inside.

"It might not be the right number," he continued. "This was

the one he gave me five years ago."

"You don't have his office number?" asked Gisele.

"I have it at work." He ended the call and put his phone down on the glass coffee table in front of them. "I'll call him in the morning." He looked at Carla, sitting on the other side of his wife. "Are you sure you want to do this? Maybe his non-answer was a sign."

Carla shook her head. "I don't believe in signs. I was directly responsible for Maroun's death and I am going to find the person who did it, this woman with the white eyes. Acting Captain Himo is the only option I've got at the moment."

Jihad noted the 'at the moment' but he let it pass. Next to him, Gisele was running her fingers gently over the scar on her neck. She said, "And what about the wider picture? This Sajida?"

"Himo needs to know, I've decided."

"Won't you be putting him in danger?"

Carla shrugged. "Maybe. But at least he will be prepared. Maroun was not. We did not know that people with the knowledge were being eliminated."

"How about elimination by association?" Gisele leant forward, stubbing out her cigarette in the ashtray (only one, to be sociable, as a treat) and picking up her glass. "Something I used to instil into my students. Leave no loose ends."

"You mean...?" Jihad let the question hang.

"Us. If this assassin finds out Carla is staying here, surely we are loose ends. Even if we don't know what is going on."

Jihad looked over at Carla with raised eyebrows.

"She seems to be very meticulous," reasoned Carla. "And personal. No bombs to cause collateral damage, not even shooting. She's a hands-on killer." She smiled at her literal metaphor. "I do not think you are in danger. But be careful, of course."

Gisele gave an ironic little laugh. "Being married to a captain of the ISF, I am always careful. Comes with the job."

Jihad feigned protest. "It is a job being married to me?"

"Sometimes more than you know, *habibi*." Gisele smiled sweetly. "But I took you for better or worse."

"Till death..." Jihad knocked back the remains of his *arak*.

"But not yet," reassured Carla. "It is me she's after. She has tried twice, I am sure she will come again." She reached forward, picked up the bottle on the table and poured herself some more wine. "But she's got to find me first. And before I find her."

13 July 2010
1 Sha'ban 1431

Jonblat, Beirut 09:00

"*Bonjour* Selim. Jihad Merhi." A pause, the silence conveying an apology for yesterday which would never be spoken. "Selim, I have some information for you. We need to meet. Can I suggest this afternoon, fourteen hundred in my office...? I look forward to seeing you then. *Salaam.*"

"Hi Carla. Jihad. Still no response from Himo so I've left a message on his office phone. I've suggested we meet this afternoon at fourteen hundred here in my office, as we agreed. I'll let downstairs know you're coming and I'll come down to collect you when you arrive. Enjoy your morning."

What would the world do without voicemail? wondered Merhi. Telephones might be the invention of the devil but voicemail was a gift from God. Think of all the time saved leaving messages rather than having to keep calling back.

He was still not certain introducing Carla to Himo was the right thing to do, but she had insisted that was the way she wanted to progress. So be it. He was a mere male, he knew better than to argue.

But fourteen hundred was five hours away. Before then he had other matters to attend to. The world went on and so did his other cases.

He reached for his cigarettes which were sitting on his desk next to the three jars of pickles...

Jonblat, Beirut 10:15

Merhi knew Fadi Lattouf had arrived even before he had entered the building. The sudden cacophony of car horns outside did not disturb him at first, he was too engrossed in an intelligence report that suggested Hizbullah had invited Iranian President Ahmedinejad to visit Lebanon in three months time (surely no coincidence that right now was the anniversary of the Israeli war?), but the constant background blaring suddenly registered and he got up to look out the window.

Sure enough, down on Bank of Lebanon Street was the dented, rusting light blue police Ford Transit van with the distinctive red number plate of the Palestinian military. It was badly parked and was causing chaos as drivers tried to get round it.

It was two minutes before he heard the sound of feet in the corridor, one set thudding louder than the other. Then Sergeant el-Gharib knocked on his door, opened it and – with an Allah-help-us look – stood back to let the giant Lattouf enter.

"Morning of light, my dear Captain!" boomed Lattouf, casting an eye backwards to watch el-Gharib closing the door then doing a double-take when he saw the cracked glass. It had been like that the last time he had been in this office five years previously! He said more quietly, "How are you, my dear friend?"

"I am well, Fadi." They shook hands. "Peace be upon you."

"And upon you."

"Come, sit."

Lattouf carried his uniform jacket over his arm. His blue shirt had damp patches of sweat underneath the arms, down the centre of the back and underneath his breasts. Lebanon in the summer was not a place for man-made fibres.

"Would you like some water?" Merhi handed over a two litre bottle of *Sohat* mineral water, the outside damp with condensation, as Lattouf hung his jacket over the back of the chair. "They'll bring coffee in in a moment."

"Bless your hands." Lattouf cracked open the bottle and drank it. All of it. In one go.

Emitting a satisfied burp, he sat down, the wooden chair cracking with the strain. "Ah ha!" he exclaimed, noticing the jars of pickles. "The finest *mekhallel* this side of Gaza. Thank you. How much do I owe you?"

"We'll settle up later."

"Okay. It is good of you to give this case priority, Jihad. I thank you."

Merhi sat down behind his desk, pulling open a drawer and bringing out a large manila envelope. "We found the car up at Rmeil. Abandoned."

"What sort was it?"

"You don't know?"

"My memory."

"It is a Datsun Bluebird. Probably worth quite a bit even in its poor condition."

Lattouf was nodding. "Oh yes, I remember vaguely. Chadi liked his modern things. High-powered cars, technology. He was useless with them but he liked them."

There was a knock on the door and Sergeant el-Gharib entered carrying two steaming mugs.

"Thank you, Deeb." Merhi watched as the mugs added to the ring stains on his desk. "And the other?"

"The boy has just returned with them."

On cue there was another knock on the door and 'the boy' (a junior officer) came in and placed a bulging bag on his captain's desk. The colourful writing on the side of the bag said *Dunkin' Donuts*.

Lattouf's eyes lit up like Satan welcoming a new batch of virgins to Hades. But there was also a sadness in them.

Once the door was closed again, Merhi opened the bag. "Dive in, Fadi," he encouraged, then he frowned at the look on his friend's face.

"Alas, I wish I could Jihad. But my weight." Lattouf patted the vast, protruding expanse of his stomach. "Nada has me on a diet. I am doing well, no?"

"Positively svelte. So you will insult me by refusing my hospitality?"

"No! That I would never do." Grinning, Lattouf's hand went into the bag like a grab-a-teddybear crane at an amusement arcade and came out with three donuts. "Thank you."

"Okay." Merhi picked up the envelope from his desk and tipped out its contents, corralling the playing cards as they attempted to flee all over the place. "We found these in the car. Some cards – "

"He always liked his cards. He would do tricks for the children when he came to visit." Lattouf's beard was already sprinkled with sugar and streaked with jam.

"A pen." Merhi held it up. It had a picture of a girl in a swimsuit on the shaft.

Lattouf turned his head. "Does it...?"

Obligingly, Merhi inverted the pen, Lattouf smiling as the swimsuit came off. Merhi pushed the pen and cards across the desk. "And a notepad. Have a look." He threw the pad on top of the pen and cards.

Lattouf brushed sugar from his hands and then wiped his fingers on his trousers for good measure. He reached out and picked up the pad, flicking over the pages.

There wasn't much, but what there was was written in Arabic and French. The first sheet was headed *6/7*. Underneath that on separate lines were *0930 Départ, 0950 Hallaq, 1130 Retour*. The second sheet was headed *7/7* and had a line straight across the page. The third sheet started *8/7* then *1130 Départ, 1145 Tadlik, 1415 Retour*.

The fourth sheet was headed *9/7* then *1400 Départ*. And that was it, nothing else.

Lattouf flicked through the remaining pages of the pad. Blank. He sniffed. "He was following someone."

Merhi reached out and took a donut from the bag. "But who, why, where?"

Lattouf poured the entire contents of his mug down his throat, giving a satisfied lip-smack as he put the mug back on the desk. His hand went into the bag and commandeered the last two donuts. "He specialised in marital problems and workplace pilfering."

"Specialised?"

"It was all he could get."

Merhi took a bite out of the sole survivor of the Lattouf rampage. "So it looks like he was following someone."

"Someone who didn't want to be followed?"

Both men ate, giving themselves time to think. Finishing, Merhi rubbed the sugar from his hands and said, "So tell me again how you found him."

Lattouf licked jam from the corners of his mouth. "I was coming home from work. I saw a taxi pull up near my house. Chadi staggered out. Knocked at my door. The taxi drove off. Chadi fell backwards. I reached him. He was dead. Murdered, as we now know."

"What about the taxi? Was there anyone in it?"

"Of course! The driver."

"Fadi!"

"I did not see anyone else, but I was not looking." Lattouf picked up the *Dunkin' Donuts* bag and looked inside to make sure it was empty.

"You didn't get its number?"

"Please." He screwed up the bag and launched it towards Merhi's waste bin, missing it by about two metres.

"Okay. So, as good investigators we have to ask all the questions, even those we know the answers to." Merhi reached out for his cigarettes. "Firstly, what was Chadi doing in Beirut?"

Lattouf shrugged. "He had come to see me?"

"Why? Was he in the habit of making unannounced visits?"

Lattouf shrugged again, reaching out and helping himself to

a cigarette, quickly raising his other hand. "No, no, don't light it. I just want the feel of it." He rolled it about between his fingers. "No, we didn't see him that often. Two or three times a year and never unexpectedly. *Eid* would have been the next time. Talking of which, what are you and Gisele doing?"

"Secondly, why leave his car in northern Beirut and come all the way south in a taxi?"

Lattouf put the unlit cigarette in his mouth, ignoring the ignoring of his question. "Perhaps he did not want to bring his car into that area. Maybe he did not trust the locals."

"A possibility – if he had left his car in a car park. But it was abandoned at a road junction. Look." Merhi stood up and went over to a map of Beirut on the wall. With a grunt, Lattouf rose and came over. Merhi could smell his sweat as he stood next to him.

Merhi pointed at the top of the map. "It was left here at the junction of Berberi Street and Pasteur Street."

Lattouf squinted. "I haven't got my glasses..." He could smell the stale cigarette odour from Merhi. "Okay, so let's invert the question. What was he doing *there*?"

"Yes. Good one. There is something we only found out after we'd carried the car to the pound and obtained keys. It was out of fuel."

Suddenly Lattouf leant sideways, his hand going into his trouser pocket. It came out with some car keys. "These will probably fit. I found them in his jacket."

He went to hand them over but Merhi said "You keep them. The car's yours now."

"Mine?"

"You are his only surviving relative. We can release it to you."

Lattouf nodded pensively. "Yes, I suppose I am... Okay, he runs out of fuel. Gets in a taxi to continue his journey to see me. Logical."

"And, for all intents and purposes, falls dead from the taxi on arrival. So who killed him? The taxi driver?"

"Unlikely. A murderer waiting in a taxi just in case he ran out of fuel?"

"Exactly. So he must have been mortally wounded before he got into the taxi."

Lattouf tapped the map, talking with the unlit cigarette in the side of his mouth. "Where does that road go to?"

"Which one?"

"That big one there, coming in from the right." Lattouf squinted at the writing. "The Dora Highway." He laughed. "The road for explorers! My children watch her on the television."

"Who?"

"Dora The Explorer. No? No, your boys are too old." He patted Merhi on the back.

"It goes north. Becomes the Coastal Highway. We were on it the other day, when you came to my place."

"So it heads north."

"All the way up the coast to Tripoli."

"Passing through Jbeil. Where he lived. And worked."

"Was he done there or in Beirut? If it was Beirut, his killer would have to have been waiting for him. But how would he know Chadi would be running out of fuel at that particular spot?"

"Unless he was following him," said Lattouf.

Merhi was still, looking at the map. Then he tensed. Without looking sideways, he asked "Fadi, have you farted?"

"Donuts on an empty stomach," reasoned the Palestinian. "That will do it every time."

"Unlike you to be silent. Deadly, yes. Silent, no."

"To break wind is a gift from Allah."

"If you say so." He took a longer than usual drag on his cigarette. "Okay, your cousin was being followed. All the way from Jbeil?"

"That would sound more like a chase than a follow."

"And there is one other thing we have to address. Why you?

What was so important? What had he discovered to make him run down from Jbeil, with someone chasing him, to see you?"

"Did he know he was dying? Did he want to say goodbye?"

"To a cousin he only saw two or three times a year? What are you, Fadi?"

"I'm sorry?"

"What are you?"

"I... I... am a Palestinian... a husband... a father... his cousin... hungry..."

Merhi put his hands on his hips. "You are a policeman. Just like Chadi used to be. You are the one person he knew he could trust. He may have been assaulted in Jbeil or it may have been in Beirut. Doesn't really matter. What you have to find out is what had he discovered that made him dash all the way down from Jbeil, with someone chasing him, to come to tell you?"

"Something that someone was willing to kill for. He tried to say something to me when he was lying on the ground, but he couldn't speak. If only."

Merhi went back to his desk. After a further moment in front of the map, Lattouf came back over, the chair cracking again as he sat down."So what do we do now?"

"We?" asked Merhi. "It is not my case. You took the body, remember. You should have reported it. My only interest was a questionable abandoned vehicle. We have since discovered it was abandoned because it ran out of fuel. We know who the owner is, unfortunately deceased. But we can release it to his next of kin, as I said."

"But I need your help."

"Fadi, I am busy. You just don't know the amount of work I've got on."

"I understand. And what is one Palestinian life, eh? What is it worth? Nothing."

"Oh no, don't you dare. Don't you dare play the Palestinian life is worthless card." Even if it was true.

"How can I investigate it on my own?" reasoned the big man.

"Will you give me jurisdiction? Write me out a *laissez passer* to operate outside the camps?"

"I cannot."

"Of course you cannot." Sad eyes looked at Merhi. "My cousin has been murdered and there is nothing I can do." His bottom lip trembled. Grains of sugar fell onto his lap from his beard.

Because your friend has refused to help you, thought Merhi. Shit. Shit, shit, shit.

He sat back in his chair, wiping his hands down his face. With resignation, he asked "What do you want to do?"

Lattouf looked up, tears around his puppy-dog eyes. He sniffed and brushed a strand of comb-over back over his head. "You are truly a friend. A good friend. I thank you. Chadi thanks you. Allah thanks you." He reached out and took one of the jars of pickles off the desk. "You and me as a team, eh? Me and the best Lebanese investigator I know." He looked like a small child who had just been told that he can, after all, have that expensive toy he wanted for *Eid* (after Daddy had paid his *fitra*, of course). He popped the lid on the jar of pickles. "I think we should go to Jbeil," he said. "See what we can discover."

His hand plunged into the jar, emerging dripping with oil and holding a pepper which promptly slithered into his mouth. He held the jar out to Merhi. "Have some," he said. "The finest *mekhallel* this side of Gaza."

Jonblat, Beirut 13:45

The traffic outside cleared instantly just before midday when a light blue Ford Transit van was driven away by its keeper, back to the southern suburbs. Merhi spent an hour in a forlorn attempt to reduce the mountain of paperwork on his desk then popped down to Hamra Street for a walk, a drink, several cigarettes, and two slices of *mana'eesh* from his favourite eatery.

As he was walking back, mind elsewhere, a soft voice said

from his side, "*Massah el-khair*, Captain."

His head snapped to his right to see a smiling Carla Chedid. He had not been aware of her approach. "Carla! Where did you spring from?"

"I was just looking in the shops. Then I saw you come out of the café. You did not feel me behind you?"

"No."

"Good."

Not good, thought Merhi. He was getting rusty. Or was he just getting old? He said, "*Yalla*. Himo is due at two."

Carla was dressed in a short, elegantly-patterned beige dress and co-ordinating slave sandals. The dress was button-through, her usual open one-button-more-than-necessary style at the top augmented by the same at the hem, revealing her olive inner thighs as she walked. Her dark grey Barbour messenger bag was over one shoulder. When they entered the State Security building, more than one head turned as Merhi walked her up to his office.

"Please sit down," he said once they were in his inner sanctum. "But be careful, that chair has started to creak. Coffee? Or rather, sludge?"

"Sludge would be fine, thank you. Perhaps, as a way of thanks for your help, I should donate a coffee machine to your office?"

"It would be too good for those Neanderthals. They wouldn't know the difference."

When he returned five minutes later with two mugfuls of brown liquid, she was over by the window looking out. She looked over her shoulder. "I had forgotten how busy Beirut is. Reminds me of New York."

"You like being over there?"

She shrugged. "No one likes being in exile. But better that than dead. And there are compensations." She did not elaborate but she was thinking of her man and how he was when she had left him, unconscious on the bed after twelve hours of love-making. She was missing him.

She came back over and sat down, the dress slithering off her thighs like a snake, revealing a glimpse of her white pants beneath.

He coughed. "So how do you want to play this?"

"Leave it to me. I need to find the woman that killed Maroun. But I must also remember why I came back. I have important information and, as he is now my boss, Capain Himo must be told. Whether we then involve you and the ISF will be up to him."

"If you wish to speak privately, I can make myself scarce."

"*Merci bien.*" She sipped from the mug, then said "Goodness, you are right. Sludge."

"I should have made one for him at the same time." Merhi looked at his watch. "Where is he? He's late. I hope he got my message."

Jonblat, Beirut 14:20

Now Merhi was standing by the window, smoking, impatient, irritated. He looked at his watch again. "He's not coming, is he?" Was the bastard getting his own back for yesterday? "This is a waste of time, Carla, I'm sorry."

She came over and stood next to him. "Is he usually this late?" Reaching up, she took the cigarette from Merhi's lips, took a drag, then replaced the cigarette where she had found it.

He was glad he did not have to turn round right at that moment, he was doing an impression of a drawing pin on its side. "Actually, I don't know him that well," he said to the window. "Our paths have just happened to cross once or twice. But he's a high-flyer, they're usually prompt and by the book."

There was a knock on the door.

"*Tfaddal,*" called Merhi. "Come in."

The door was opened by Sergeant el-Gharib who then stood back to let Acting Captain Himo enter.

"Sorry I'm late," said Himo smiling, charming. "There was a hold-up caused by some Palestinian police van parked down by Hamra Square. Near the food stalls." He was dressed in an open-necked white shirt with captain's epaulettes, and the usual blue uniform trousers.

Merhi went over, glad his reaction to Carla was subsiding (Himo would probably think it was his mobile phone in his pocket), hand outstretched. As they shook, Himo looked at Carla.

"Selim, may I introduce you to... Carla - "

"Carla Chedid." She held out her hand. "*Charafna*. Delighted to meet you."

"*Heureux de vous rencontrer, mademoiselle.*" He squeezed her hand as she smiled. "Have we met before?"

"No."

"You look... familiar."

"I often have that effect." She held onto his hand longer than was necessary as he laughed.

"Well it is a pleasure anyway."

"Thank you. And for me."

Merhi had pulled up another wooden chair and held it out for Carla to sit down. He nodded at the one in front of Himo. "Be careful of that one, it's beginning to creak." Merhi sat down. "Coffee, Selim?"

"Thank you, no."

"Okay." Merhi steepled his fingers in front of him. "Selim, I was not particularly forthcoming yesterday, for which I had my reasons. I do know more about the death of Captain Khoury. In fact, it might be best if I let Carla tell you. Carla?"

"*Merci*, Jihad."

She explained at length about how she was actually a member of Himo's team, the External Security Unit, albeit she had been on permanent assignment at the United Nations in New York for five years. She had found out information that had led to her returning to Lebanon to report it personally to

Maroun Khoury. She was convinced this had led directly to his murder, by a tall blonde woman with white eyes.

"A tall blonde woman with white eyes?" queried Himo.

"Yes, she tried to eliminate me the next day."

"White eyes?"

"Yes."

Himo frowned. "Okay, perhaps you'd best fill me in on all of it. What was the information that made you come back?"

"Do you know who Sajida is?"

Himo tensed, controlling the sudden rush of adrenaline, hoping they did not notice his reaction. He frowned, "Sajida?"

"Sajida."

"Why don't you tell me."

Carla looked across at Merhi.

"I'll leave you two alone." He stood up. "Call me when you're done. I'll be outside. Making sludge."

Jonblat, Beirut 15:30

Merhi was sitting on Sergeant el-Gharib's desk, talking football (they were both hoping Racing Beirut would improve on their eighth place in the Premier League last season) when Himo and Carla appeared in the doorway.

"We're finished, thanks Captain," nodded Himo.

Merhi pushed himself off the desk. "All done? Good." He went out into the corridor with them. "Nothing else you need me to do?"

"No, that's fine. Carla will be helping me directly now." Himo looked at Carla. "I'll be in touch. Jihad, thank you. I appreciate your help." The men shook hands. "I know my way out."

They watched him go. As they walked back to the office, Merhi asked "Everything okay?"

She nodded. "Yes. He knew about Sajida."

Well, he would, wouldn't he? thought Merhi. High-flying

twat.

"Makes it easier," said Carla. "And that gets you out of it now."

"That's good news. And you?"

"He's going to let me know what, if anything, he wants me to do. I had a feeling he would like me to go back to New York and as quickly as possible. Wants all the glory for himself."

"Why am I not surprised? And will you? Go back?"

"Not until I've ripped that bitch's head from her shoulders."

"That's my girl." He tried to catch himself before he said it, but he didn't.

She grinned. "Thank you... my boy. But I'll be out of your hair soon, I can't implicate you any further. If he orders me back to New York, I'll find some other place to hole up. You can tell him I've gone if he asks."

"You're welcome to stay, you know."

"Thank you, but you and Gisele have your own lives to lead."

"My brother-in-law has an apartment up near Jamhour. He's hardly ever there. Lives in Dubai for most of the year. You could have that."

Carla did not tell him that she knew the block, that she had had an apartment there herself for a while five years ago. "Let's see what happens over the next couple of days and we'll take it from there." She picked up her bag. "Right, I've still got some shopping to do. Gisele asked me to pick her up a little something."

"She did?" He thought she was talking about food.

"Mm. You like red lace?"

Merhi sat down quickly before his mobile phone appeared in his pocket again. For God's sake, he was fifty-one years old. His wife and his lodger were going to kill him at this rate!

"What time you shooting off tonight?" she asked innocently.

He squeezed his legs together. How about right now? "F-five. Maybe six."

"Can I cadge a lift back?"

"*B- bien sûr.*"

"*Merci.* I'll see you shortly." With a swirl of the undone dress, she left the office.

Merhi sat back in his chair, thinking thoughts for which in some parts of the world he could be stoned to death. Then he reached out and opened the bottom drawer on the right side of his desk. The small digital recording machine, connected wirelessly to the pin-prick microphone disguised as a knot in the wood on the front of his desk, was still recording. He turned it off.

In the corridors of politics, power and security in Lebanon, everyone spied on everyone else, or at least tried to. Why should he be any different?

The only question was, should he now listen to what was on here? Would he be protecting himself by doing so?

Or would he be signing his own death warrant?

Bourj el-Barajneh, Beirut 20:00

"I am going to Jbeil," announced the patriarch of *La Famille Lattouf* as he sat down at the old wooden dining table. "Me and Jihad. We are joining forces to investigate Chadi's murder."

The six children seated shoulder to shoulder, three on one side of the table, three on the other, couldn't really have cared less but they knew to be quiet when Baba was seated and pontificating. The older ones even tried to look interested.

"Are you really? You are officially working with the Lebanese police?" asked Nada Lattouf as she brought in a large, steaming bowl of *lubya* (bean stew). She was nearly half a metre smaller than her husband in height but proportionately she was the same volume, a big Palestinian Mama. On the very rare occasions when she and her husband mated, the earth had no choice but literally to move for both of them. She was dressed in her usual black *jilbaab*, head uncovered as she was at home, greying hair pinned up.

"Not the police," explained her proud husband. "Better. Jihad is the Internal Security Force. When the ISF says jump, the police ask 'How high?'."

"So they are recognising you at last?"

"I knew it would be only a matter of time after I helped them solve the Hariri murder."

Five years was a long matter of time, thought Nada as she went back and retrieved the bowl of rice from the kitchen. As she came back in, she said "That is good. Your genius deserves recognition, husband." She sat down at the other end of the table, making the older children giggle as she looked heavenward. The children began passing their plates towards her.

"Who knows where this might lead?" pondered Fadi as he spooned a mountain of rice onto his plate then picked up the bowl of stew. "Maybe a merging of forces. Or perhaps they might want me as a consultant." He stared dreamily into the future. "Paid by the hour. When all else fails, call in Lattouf! I will be known throughout The Levant. Maybe it will get us out of here."

Nada knew better than to dampen her husband's spirits with a reality check. He would be brought down to earth soon enough, as he always was. She said, "Insh'allah" and nudged the nearest child, nodding at the bowl of stew. The nudge went down the line and Lana, the eleven year old at the end, lifted the bowl from in front of her father and passed it back down to her mother.

"Apparently we are Chadi's only known relatives." Fadi looked back down, looked at his plate of rice and then wondered where the stew had gone. "We inherit his stuff."

"Really?" Now Nada was interested. "Here, children, pass this down to your father." Back came the bowl of stew.

"Not that there will be much. The Israelis destroyed everything when they bombed his place in Bir Hassan." He slathered the stew on top of the rice, then passed the bowl back up the table on the opposite side to which it had come. "In fact, I have something already. Lana, pass me my jacket."

Lana smiled, grown up before her time. "You are leaning on it, father."

"I am? Oh yes!" Fadi turned around, rummaging in the pockets of his uniform jacket draped over the back of his chair. He brought out a pen which he quickly put back into a pocket with a sheepish look towards Nada. Then he brought out some loose playing cards, handing them over to Lana as if he was giving her the keys to the *Kaaba* itself.

She was less than overwhelmed, but dutifully she said "Thank you, father."

"Now you can practise those tricks Uncle Chadi used to show you," Fadi ruffled the top of her head. Then he said more quietly, "In his memory." He looked up at his wife, sadness on his face. He nodded. "We will find out who did this, Nada. And why. Me and my friend Jihad."

Jounieh, Lebanon 20:00

"I am going to Jbeil," said Jihad Merhi as he sat down at the modern glass dining table. "With the idiot Lattouf. He wants me to investigate his cousin's murder."

"Really? And you have time for this?" asked Gisele as she brought in a platter of *samak mishwi* (kebabs of monkfish, lemon and pepper).

"Well, now that Carla will be working back with her own team, that relieves me of that duty. With all respect." He looked across the table at their guest as he opened a packet of flat bread. "But do I have time? No."

Carla smiled, taking bread from the offered wrapper. "It is good that I am out of your hair. Perhaps Captain Himo can progress matters more quickly than I have been able to."

Gisele put a bowl of rice on the table and sat down. "Then why do it if you don't have time?" she asked her husband.

Jihad poured wine, a Chateau Ksara chardonnay. He shrugged. "What can I do? Refuse him?"

"Yes."

"It won't take long, we won't find anybody, I'll just be going through the motions." A picture of the butcher's shop morgue in the refugee camp flashed suddenly into his mind. "At least I can show him that the death of a Palestinian matters to at least one person in the lower echelons of authority here." He helped himself to one of the kebabs. "We'll just nip up there tomorrow, won't take long. Deeb el-Gharib is covering the office. Just one thing, though." He looked over at Gisele. "As he's up this way, I thought we could invite Fadi for dinner."

Gisele sighed, but it was not the negative reaction he was expecting. "Of course. It is only right." She sipped her wine. "You know, you are too good, my husband."

"I am?"

"Oh yes. Am I not right, Carla?"

Carla nodded as she chewed on a piece of fish. "Too good."

"One day," said Gisele, "it will be the death of you."

14 July 2010
2 Sha'ban 1431

Annaya, Lebanon 03:50

"*Subhana Rabbiyal A'ala*. Glory be to my Lord, the most high."

Brother Malek was kneeling in his cell, forehead and nose on the floor, elbows raised in the *raka'ah* posture of submission to God. The cell was in darkness save for a small tea-light candle in one corner. Malek wore nothing except a cloth around his waist.

He rose into a sitting position, saying the first of the three *takbir* that would end his *Fajr* prayer. Prostrate for the second *takbir*, back up again for the third, he then sat back on his haunches for a moment's reflection.

Reaching out, he unwound the hose of his golden *argileh* and sucked on the end. The charcoal was still alight, the water in the bowl bubbling. Two-apples flavour. He was calm.

But even at this early hour, he was warm. He ran a hand over his five-day growth of beard. He would not shave it off again, that had been a mistake and his *houri* had had to deal with the consequences. He would be bearded for his return to the Holy Land, but his followers would know him, they would know *Yawm al-Qiyamah* had come and they would rejoice.

He smoked for half an hour, in reflection and personal prayer. At 04:30 he removed the Netbook from the *argileh* case and turned it on.

He knew by heart the user name and password for the single-use e-mail and *Skype* account for today's date (it included the numbers 281431). He signed in, making friends with the similar single-use account at the other end.

It took a few moments to connect, and then he smiled as the face of his favourite disciple appeared on the screen. Malek was pleased. He never knew which of his twelve followers would be at the other end, they varied it for security and locational purposes, but this one he had the most affection for.

As the sun rose in the east they began to talk.

Bourj el-Barajneh, Beirut 07:30

As a captain of the Internal Security Force of Lebanon, it took a lot to shock Jihad Merhi. But at that moment he sat in his grey Toyota Land Cruiser V8 and stared open-mouthed as Fadi Lattouf came out of the front door of his house,

Lattouf was dressed in a suit! Dark grey, probably polyester, off the shelf from somewhere in Bourj Hammoud as could be witnessed by the slightly too short trousers. Underneath was an open-necked white shirt. His sparse hair was plastered over his head and his beard had been trimmed to an unshaven, rather than unkempt, look. Wraparound counterfeit *Ray-Ban* sunglasses completed the ensemble. On anybody else, the outfit might look smart; on Lattouf it just looked... weird.

As the sun's early rays hit him, Lattouf immediately removed the jacket and undid another two buttons on the short sleeve shirt, his grey and black chest hairs falling out like commuters from a Tokyo subway train in the rush hour.

"Morning of light, my dear friend!" The Land Cruiser dipped to the side as Lattouf got in. "A joyous day to start our fruitful collaboration."

Merhi, who perhaps had had one too many *arak* the evening before, wondered what the hell he was doing here. Why didn't he just throw the Palestinian out and go have a normal day's work protecting the unprotectable? "Morning Fadi."

Merhi sniffed. Lattouf was wearing cologne! "You look - "

"Thank you. It is good to be out of uniform for once. To be myself."

Merhi slipped his own sunglasses on, coincidentally also *Ray-Ban* wraparounds but genuine. He hoped the two of them didn't look like The Blues Brothers. Or Laurel and Hardy.

Suddenly Lattouf leaned to the left, coming closer to Merhi, almost as if he was going to kiss him. A stentorian roar emitted from his backside.

"Left over *lubya*. That will do it every time." Lattouf was pressing buttons on the armrest, trying to open the window. Merhi was only too pleased to oblige from his side.

"The fresh air will do us good," said Lattouf as they pulled away. "How long till we get to Jbeil?"

Annaya, Lebanon 09:00

Brother Malek stood on the step in front of the altar of the Monastery Church of Saint Maron, hood up, arms outstretched, holding the hands of Paradise and Love who were kneeling in front of him. "Rise, my daughters, rise," he said deeply, gently.

Touching their lips to his hands, the women stood.

Malek locked his fingers in front of his waist and pushed his elbows out as he stepped down. The twins linked him, one either side. Slowly the three of them began to walk around the church.

"Seven weeks," said Malek. "There will be no reversion. It is as if the dates have been set by Allah himself. Satan has been defeated. The Messiah will return to the Holy Land on *Laylat al-Qadr*. The holiest night of the holiest month. The Night of Power, the Night of Destiny."

"*Sabah a Allah*." Love squeezed his arm.

"Indeed God is good, my daughter," the hood nodded. "But so am I. Soon now we must move The Secret. We will be travelling overland, across The Levant. The journey will be as important as the arrival, it will be talked about forever. The journey that saved mankind, the true resurrection, the true renaissance. It must take forty days and forty nights to cross the desert – which means the journey must start in ten days time. The Secret will cross the desert on camel."

"On *jamal*?" queried Paradise.

Malek stopped, pulling them up sharply. "Did I not make myself clear?"

"Yes, brother," Paradise cast her eyes downward. "I am sorry. Please forgive me."

For a full thirty seconds Malek did not move. No sound came from under the hood, not even breathing. He was perfectly still. The silence of the church enwrapped them.

Then he resumed walking as if nothing had happened, their arms still linked. "The Secret will cross the desert on camel. There will be some waiting on the other side of the mountains. We must be there at the desert on twelve Sha'ban. You may chose camel also or you may travel by car. But when we reach the Holy City, The Secret will not enter it on a camel, not even on a donkey. This time it will be on a white stallion. And The Messiah will have a sword in his hand. This time there will be no turning the other cheek." Now they could hear his breathing and it was becoming heavier.

"*Yaatik al-aafieh!*" whispered Love.

"God *is* my strength, daughter." Malek's chest was rising and falling. "After all these years, the time is here. Soon the world will know that the prophesies have been fulfilled. Soon the world will know *al-Mahdi* has come to save them. Soon the world will know that The Secret..." He disengaged their arms and leant forward, his hands coming up to grasp the rim of the hood. Straightening up, he threw the hood backwards off his head, revealing the ageing mortal face and the black immortal eyes. He looked from one woman to the other. "... is me."

Mount Lebanon 09:30

"What do you think will happen?" asked Love, the wind blowing her hair as Paradise drove the open-topped Jeep Wrangler Ultimate back down the mountain. "When he returns. Will the world recognise him as *al-Mahdi*?"

"It must. Everything is as prophesied."

"And there will be peace?"

"Eventually. It is written that when he comes again it will be Armageddon, but after that there will be peace for thousands of years."

Love was quiet, contemplative, as her sister negotiated a particularly sharp hairpin bend. Then she asked, "And what about us? Do you think we will be with him as he promised? His right and left hands?"

Paradise shrugged. "Why not? He would not deceive us. Our commander has said that we are permanently assigned to him until we are instructed otherwise."

"We will truly be his companions, his *houri*."

"And his protection."

Another hairpin bend then they were on the straight run west of Hboub, heading down into Jbeil.

"Should we ride with him on the camels, sister?" asked Paradise.

"No," Love shook her head. "That must be his glory. We will follow in a car. This one. Open-topped. So we are ready to confront any non-believers."

Love stretched forward for her mobile phone as it began to ring. "I bet this is him. I knew we should have brought him more tobacco – Oh, it's not." She brought the phone to her ear. *"Bonjour mon frère... Oui?... Vraiment? Alors, c'est merveilleux... Tu es un vrai croyant... Oui... Oui...D'accord. Nous arrivons. Merci."*

She ended the call, relaxing her head on the headrest, eyes closed. "God truly is good, sister."

"Who was that?"

A wide grin spread across Paradise's face as Love gave her details of the call. "No way! Is God on our side or what? Time to take out the lenses?"

"Maybe," said Love. "We cannot convert with them in. But there is another thought..."

By the time Love had told her sister of her idea, they had reached Jbeil. They entered on Rue Jbeil, slowing to a crawl behind a grey Toyota Land Cruiser V8 that looked like it was lost (tourists!), then overtaking it and heading down Boulevard al-Mina towards the parking area.

Their day had started early but it was far from over yet.

Jbeil, Lebanon 09:45

"See that?" Fadi Lattouf swivelled in his seat as Jihad Merhi turned in to the car park just beyond the Seven Seas Restaurant.

"What?"

"Twins! Two women. They look identical! A rare sight. I must tell Nada later. Did I ever tell you that they thought Wissam was going to be twins - ? "

"Where is your cousin's office?" Merhi applied the parking brake and turned off the engine.

Grunting, Lattouf slid out of the car, the vehicle noticeably rising on the passenger side. "Down in the souks, near the cemetery. I've only been there once, I think I can remember the way." He pulled his underwear from out of his crevice and shook his leg.

The Toyota's lights flashed as Merhi pressed the lock button on his key fob. "*Yalla* then. And we've got his house to examine after that."

"He had no house," Lattouf shook his head sadly as they began walking. "Not after his family was murdered. Had no need. He lived in a couple of rooms above his office."

"Well, that makes it easier."

They turned left onto Boulevard al-Mina.

"My friend, look!" Lattouf nodded.

A little way ahead, the twins were walking side by side. One of them carried a rucksack on her shoulder.

"Same height, same hair, same bodies, same way of walking. Even the same clothes. Amazing. Having a child is a gift from Allah, but having twins is a double-blessing."

"If you say so." Merhi lit up a cigarette and offered the packet to Lattouf, who shook his head and patted his waistline incongruously.

Beyond the Seven Seas Restaurant, the women crossed over the road, walking parallel with the medieval town wall. Lattouf eased Merhi across the road with his body.

The women turned right through the ramparts into Rue St John.

When Lattouf turned right also, Merhi exclaimed "Fadi! What the hell are you doing?"

Lattouf looked puzzled. "This is our way. The souks are down here."

"If they turn round they'll think we are two dirty old men on the pull."

Lattouf sniffed under his own arm. "Not dirty. And I am happily married, my friend. And so are you. Cannot a man simply admire one of nature's splendours?" The women turned into an alleyway by an old bookshop. "There, you see, they have gone."

They walked on and turned left at the end of the road. Tourists were already milling around outside the wax museum on their left. Lattouf pointed down the road where there was another gap in the ramparts. "The cemetery, see? I knew we were heading the right way."

"We're all heading to the cemetery, Fadi. It's only our journeys that are timed differently." Merhi drew on his cigarette without appreciating the full irony of the action.

"Yes. Very good." Lattouf suddenly seemed distracted. "Abu Samer, may I ask you something?"

"Of course."

"Before we begin our search of Chadi's place, can we get something to eat? I'm starving."

Jounieh, Lebanon 09:45

Carla was sitting on the Merhis' balcony drinking her third coffee of the day, enjoying the sun's rays as they slid over the mountain behind her. She was dressed only in a thin white cotton T-shirt and matching pants, her bare legs stretched out in front of her, tanned and firm. Once again she was on her own, Gisele having gone out to meet some friends for a coffee morning down in Kaslik.

Her telephone rang, the opening bars of *Hey Soul Sister*, and she knew it wasn't him. It wasn't his ring tone.

"*'ehh?*"

"*Bonjour*, Carla. It's Selim Himo."

"Good morning, Captain. *Kifak?*"

"*Bien, merci.* As I hope you are."

"Sure."

"I've been thinking about things. Can you come in to discuss?"

She had been expecting it. He was going to order her back to New York. "Sure. I'll get a taxi. Give me two hours just in case, you know what the traffic's like."

"Okay, but don't come to Ras en Nabaa. I've discovered something but I don't want to put it on the Department's system, eyes and ears and all that. Can you come to my apartment in Raousheh? It's clean and uncompromised."

"*Bien sûr.*"

He gave her the address.

"Okay Captain, give me two hours. Say *muntasif an-nahar?*"

"Midday will be fine. You might be surprised at what I've discovered."

I don't think so, thought Carla. The biggest surprise was that

Sajida was right. Anything else after that was insignificant. She said, "Sure."

Jbeil, Lebanon 10:15 – 11:15

"This is it," said Fadi Lattouf over a mouthful of goat *shawarma*. They were standing outside an old wooden door in the furthest part of the furthest souk in the old town. The area was quiet, not many tourists would venture down this far.

Jihad Merhi was holding Lattouf's other two *shawarmas* and his two remaining cans of Coca-Cola. He stepped back, nodding at the door.

"What?" A piece of goat bobbed on Lattouf's lower lip.

"You kick it in, you're bigger than me."

"Why should I do that?" Lattouf crammed the remaining half of the *shawarma* into his mouth and put his hand into his trouser pocket, bringing out a set of three keys on a ring with a small silver thirty-three ring *tasbih*.

Merhi raised his eyebrows at the prayer beads. "He was a religious man?"

"He was a worried man. Like we all are. These were in his jacket along with his car keys." Lattouf handed the keys to Merhi in exchange for his second *shawarma* and a can of drink.

The second key fit. The door creaked opened onto a small office. A musty smell came to embrace them.

The office contained an old desk, two chairs, a four-drawer filing cabinet and a fan in a corner. A closed door lead to another room, probably a kitchen or a lavatory, they would find out. To their immediate left a set of stairs led upwards.

A fly flew around the bare bulb hanging from the ceiling, oblivious to its several dead compatriots on the small sill below the window looking out over the cemetery.

"Well, well, look at that," Merhi nodded, impressed. On the desk sat a state-of-the-art iMac computer complete with a 27-inch monitor. "I think this is going to be easier than we expected."

But, of course, it wasn't. Lattouf was assigned the physical search while Merhi sat down at the desk.

The filing cabinet was unlocked but it was empty except for an old box of hardened baklava in the second drawer which looked like it had been there since before the French mandate. The closed door indeed revealed both a kitchen and a lavatory – in the same room. The lavatory was a hole in the floor in one corner with a shower hose coming out of the wall at waist level, the kitchen was nothing more than a water tap, a sink and a cabinet supporting a plug-in two-ring electric hob. But the room was spotlessly clean.

While Lattouf went upstairs, Merhi cracked his knuckles like a concert pianist and started on the computer. Nothing happened when he tried to turn it on, until he discovered that it was not plugged in. Situation rectified, he started again.

Lights twinkled, the monitor flickered, there was an almost-inaudible hum from the processor – and Merhi stared at the screen in disbelief. "No," he said loudly. "Shit."

Grey polyester-covered legs came halfway back down the stairs and Lattouf's voice asked, "You have found something, Abu Samer?"

"It's bloody asking me to register! This is the first time this machine has been turned on, Fadi. It's brand new! I don't believe it."

"I told you he liked his modern things. He was useless with them but he liked them."

"Shit." Merhi sat back in the chair as the legs turned around and went back up the stairs.

The floorboards above began to groan in agony as Lattouf moved about upstairs. Merhi heard drawers being opened and closed, then a door was opened, there was grunting, and the door was closed again. The legs came back down the stairs.

"Nothing." Lattouf popped the ring on the last can of Coke.

The disappearance of the final *shawarma* had not been witnessed and would remain a mystery for all time. "Just one room. A bed, unmade, a small chest of drawers, only clothes, and a wardrobe, one suit and one shirt. Nothing else."

Merhi lit up a cigarette, sighing and breathing out smoke at the same time. "So that's all we have? Nothing? No papers, no records, not even any bank statements?"

Lattouf shrugged as he sat down in front of the desk. "He was Palestinian. Even now it is not easy for us to get bank accounts here. And what good would papers be to a man who does not exist? Papers can be more trouble than they are worth. Possibly the last papers he had were the death certificates of his wife and children – if they had been issued, which they probably weren't."

"So we've come all this way for nothing?"

Another shrug. "We had to check, to see for ourselves."

"He had nothing else on him when you found him, just the two sets of keys?"

"Some money, not much. Nothing else. So, where do we go from here?"

Merhi wanted to say "Straight back to Beirut to get on with our lives", but he bit his tongue. He pulled a folded sheet of paper from his back pocket. "So all we have are these notepad entries." He unfolded the paper, spreading it flat on the desk. "On 6 July someone was at the barber's at 09:50. On 8 July someone had a massage at 11:45. On 9 July someone went out at 14:00." He looked up at Lattouf. "And that's it. He has no case records, nothing. Who is this someone?"

"Can we make enquiries of barbers and health spas?"

"Where? In this street? In Jbeil? In the district? In Beirut? In the whole of the f... in the whole of Lebanon?"

Shrug number three.

"And even if we did progress this logically," continued Merhi, "say by starting with the barbers and health clubs of Jbeil, we would need resources. We couldn't do it ourselves. I don't have time and you don't have jurisdiction. Do you really want to get the local police involved? Because that would be the only way."

Lattouf was shaking his head. "No. They wouldn't want to know, anyway."

"The death of a Palestinian private investigator would not be top of their list of priorities, no."

Lattouf looked sad but resigned. "I'll have one of your cigarettes if I may, Abu Samer." Merhi took one from his packet and threw it across.

Lattouf caught it, waited, and then said "And I'll have a light this time, please."

He leant forward over Merhi's proffered lighter and then sat back. After his second lungful of smoke he said, "We've given it our best shot, haven't we? There's no place else to go."

"Yes we have and no there isn't."

"Well at least I have a new car, and the clothes upstairs might fit my thirteen year old," Lattouf laughed humourlessly. He looked about. "I guess I will have to see about the rent on this place. A refund might be due. Or could he have owned it?"

"Unlikely and certainly not officially. But I'll look into it for you. The enquiries will be better coming from me."

"Thank you, my friend, thank you." Lattouf looked at his wrist even though there was no watch on it. "We might as well go. It must be lunchtime by now."

Raousheh, Beirut 12:15

Rather than try to negotiate its way through the centre of Beirut, the taxi had taken the coastal route over the top of the city, approaching Raousheh from the north down General de Gaulle Avenue. It had driven directly over the spot where Rafic Hariri had been assassinated five years ago and where Carla had paid homage ten days previously.

Again she had looked at the statue as they had passed by,

and she had become sad. Sad and angry. She could have stopped it, she told herself, she could have. But the assassin had been so, so clever. He still was.

She smiled. And who would have thought things would turn out the way they did? With life, one never knew. Never.

Now she paid the driver and climbed out of the cab, looking up at the 1960s apartment building. She was wearing her button-through patterned beige dress, but today she had left the top and bottom one-button-too-manys done up – at least for the start of this meeting. If things did not go her way or she thought that some persuasion was needed, they would discreetly become open again. The slave sandals might be a bit exotic for a meeting with her new boss, but she had nothing else to co-ordinate with the dress. Her Barbour messenger bag added a touch of *gravitas*.

Captain Himo's apartment was on the fifth floor, one from the top. As she walked into the building, Carla wondered what awaited her. Would she be sent back into exile? Would she be reinstated, with or without honours? Would she be fired...?

The ageing elevator stopped eight centimetres above the level of the fifth floor, and she stepped out. There were four doors in the expansive foyer. Himo's was number 20, over on her left.

She pressed the front door bell, standing back so that he would be able to see it was her when he looked through the spy hole. She straightened herself, flicked her long hair over her shoulders, made sure her hair clip was in place, and put on a smile.

The door did not open.

Okay, maybe the bell was not working, she had not heard any ring or buzz when she had pressed the button. She knocked on the door – and it moved ever so slightly as she hit it.

Immediately she was alert. What was this?

Her hand went into her bag, bringing out the solid wooden Holding Cross. The down beam of the cross poked out between her first and middle finger, the cross beam held within her fist. She put the end of the down beam against the door and pushed. The door eased open silently.

She stood in the doorway, not moving. One part of her – the sane, rational part - was screaming at her to go, to leave this place, to get away. But what would that achieve? And this might be a test, who knew?

All senses alert, she entered the apartment.

The small hallway led into the living room through a doorway with no door. Tentatively, slowly, carefully, back to the wall, she stepped through the doorway, eyes scanning.

Then she smiled and relaxed.

Captain Himo was out on the balcony, sitting in the sun. No wonder he hadn't heard her knocking! And maybe this was a test, that's why he had left the door open. To see how close she could get before he knew she was there. Okay, she would show him how good she was.

Soundlessly she walked across the floor, now pleased that she had worn the slave sandals – no heels to click on the tiles.

She reached out to open the glass door. This might be tricky, this would show how good she was. He hadn't given any indication that he knew she was there, but the door might give her away.

Slipping the Holding Cross back in to her bag, she curled her fingers around the door handle. Careful now, careful... careful...

Her mobile phone rang.

Hey Soul Sister.

Dammit!

She grinned, resigned. Okay, she had gotten this far. Nine out of ten. You win this one, Captain.

Pulling the phone from its dedicated pocket on her bag, she looked at the screen. It was Gisele. *Not now, habibi.* She pressed the reject button –

And then frowned, staring out at the balcony.

Himo had not moved. In fact he was still. Far too still.

Throwing the phone back into the bag, she grabbed the door handle. Then a voice from behind her said, "Hey, Soul Sister."

Carla froze, eyes searching for a reflection in the glass.

"I wouldn't bother going out there," continued the voice. "He's been converted. He is with Allah."

Carla could see the inanimate objects of the room in the glass but there were no reflections of living objects. If the object was living.

She turned. "You."

"Me," smiled Love.

The two women were silent, sizing each other up. The woman – the killer – with the long blonde hair and crazy white eyes had her head cocked to one side. She was by far the bigger, but Carla had bested her before. This time she would need to finish it.

"Why?" asked Carla.

"Why what?" Love straightened her head.

"Why kill him? I did not tell him the secret."

"He had served his purpose. al-Mahdi ordered that he be rewarded with full conversion. He is with Allah in *firdaus*."

"*al-Mahdi*? You call him *al-Mahdi*?" Carla laughed, shaking her head. "He is *ad-Dajjal*, he is Satan."

"You will believe. You will be converted."

Carla nodded backwards. "And what purpose had Captain Himo served for his 'full conversion' if he did not know the secret?"

"He knew the secret," Love was speaking calmly, having a reasoned conversation. "Just because you didn't tell him doesn't mean he didn't know. All the disciples do. He was not a *kafir*. His purpose? Was to bring us you."

Carla had slipped the bag off of her shoulder, letting it drop to the floor. She so wished she had done her nails before coming out, but this bitch wouldn't know they were empty. She moved her fingers, easing the micro-needles down. "So how do you want to play this?"

Love raised her hands level with her shoulders, her fingers forming claws, her needles also showing. She smiled and turned her head a little to the side, the white eyes staring.

"Okay, a cat fight." Carla also raised her claws. "Are you sure you want to do this?" She took a step forwards. "I chased you off last time."

"But you didn't chase me off," said a voice from the kitchen doorway.

Carla looked to her left, mouth dropping with shock. There were two of them! Her eyes jumped from one woman to the other. They were the same. Absolutely and positively identical in every way. What were they, some sort of genetic mutation? Look at the eyes!

Carla's face hardened. God, if you exist, protect me now. She flicked her fingers threateningly, one hand towards one mutant, one towards the other. As she took another step forward, she reached up to her hair.

"The hairclip!" shouted Love. "Stop her!"

Then they were on her. Like a real catfight, it happened in silence, only the thumping of feet, the slapping of flesh, quick gasps as injuries happened.

A clump of Carla's hair was ripped out as the hairclip was yanked from her head. Arms moved, fingers poked, scratches were made, blood was drawn, teeth were bared.

A twin whimpered as Carla viciously striated needled fingers down her face.

Buttons flew into the air as Carla's dress was ripped open. She spat blood as she was punched in the mouth. They were all over her. Hands, knees, heads, legs everywhere. She felt flesh against her throbbing mouth and bit, hard. She heard a high-pitched yelp as the flesh came away between her teeth.

Then she was falling backwards, something was around her throat and it was getting tighter. She crashed down, grasping at her neck, scratching under her chin with her own needles. It was her bag! They were strangling her with the strap of her own bag!

She kicked out, hit someone, but she knew she was getting weaker. The pressure on her neck became heavier, tighter.

Paradise was sitting on the floor behind Carla's head, pulling and pulling on the bag. A breathless Love was now on top, moving from side to side, kicking back at the flailing feet.

Carla felt her kicks weakening, her strength failing, her life ebbing away.

Love was now astride her. Paradise had managed to grab Carla's hands above her head. Love plunged her needled fingers into Carla's exposed stomach.

As the strap bit into Carla's neck and pain flooded her gut, her sight began to blur, Love leant forward, body to body, her face next to Carla's. She stared curiously at the dying woman. Her tongue came out and she lapped at the blood running from Carla's cut mouth. Then she kissed her full on the lips.

Love pulled her head away, not knowing if the glazed eyes below her could still see. There was blood on her face from the kiss. She put her mouth to Carla's ear, panting. "*Houri* will always triumph over *djinni*. It is written. That is the way of things. Now we want your soul, sister..."

PART FOUR
الجزء الرابع

THE SECOND COMING
المجيء الثاني

Coastal Highway, Lebanon 14:45

The black open-topped Jeep Wrangler Ultimate sped northwards, weaving in and out of the traffic. In the driver's seat, Paradise was grim-faced but satisfied. The intercession had gone as planned. The *houri* were invincible. But she was in pain, her right forearm hurt like hell. She stole a look across at her sister.

Love had her eyes closed, letting the sun's rays caress and calm her. Her right arm was held across her body, a towel from the disciple's apartment wrapped tightly over the forearm covering the bite wound. Thankfully no blood was seeping through, which was a good sign.

They had a Field Medical Kit back in Jbeil. They were both fully trained field paramedics, but neither of them had had to use their skills for a long time (not since the incident at Jebel Uweinat on the Libyan, Egyptian, Sudanese border six years before which had led directly to them being ordered to guard the body of *al-Mahdi*). Well, today Paradise would tend to her sister. The pain in her own arm might be empathetic but the pain in her sister's arm was real.

And they would both need antibiotics. Only Shaitan knew what infections the unclean djinn had been carrying...

The speed of the vehicle, the noise of the traffic, the roar of the wind over the open top, and each sister's preoccupation with their pain meant that neither of them heard the music that suddenly came from the floor in the back of the Jeep.

It was coming from the dark grey Barbour wax cotton messenger bag that they had flung there when they had left the apartment in Raousheh.

It was not *Hey Soul Sister*, it was Shakira's *Hips Don't Lie*.

A caller ID ringtone, specific to one person.

Murray Hill, New York City, USA 07:45 (local time)

The man with the long black hair falling either side of his face stood naked at the window of the 30th floor apartment on East 39th Street, looking north over Midtown. His hairless swarthy body was hard, fit, but flawed by the various scars, gouges and burns on his torso and down his legs. These marks were years old now but they would not fade, and neither would his memories of how he had received them. On the orders of a man who was once dubbed The King of Lebanon. A man who had blasted off his left ear when trying to shoot him in the head. A man now long dead.

The Damascene looked at the Nokia cell phone in his hand. He and the woman who now called herself Carla both understood that sometimes a call could not be answered. Their fail-safe procedures were that one call could be ignored, it was just a *Hi, how are you?* A second call within ten minutes meant *I want/need to talk* and should be responded to at least by text giving a time when they could speak. A non-response to the second call would mean a third call within half an hour of the first, which must be answered. If it was not, something was wrong.

He had made three calls in the last half hour and she had not responded. Something was wrong.

She had asked for his help two days ago but she had understood when he explained that he could not leave instantly, he had a job to do in Washington (as a result of which there was now a vacant seat in the Senate). Now he was back.

But where was she?

Bourj el-Barajneh, Beirut 21:00

"Well, we tried, my friend, we tried." Fadi Lattouf and Jihad Merhi were sitting in Merhi's Land Cruiser outside *chez Lattouf.*

Merhi nodded. "We did."

"Bless you for that. And thanks once again to Gisele for the *jawani*, the meal was delicious."

The chicken wings in a lemon, garlic and coriander sauce were one of the many specialities of *la cuisine de Madame Merhi* but neither she nor her husband had ever seen anyone eat the bones before.

"So, we will see you at *Eid*?" confirmed Lattouf. "We used to have such a good time, didn't we? This year it will be better than ever."

"We look forward to it," lied Merhi.

"I will make arrangements to pick up the Bluebird. Will there be any charge?"

Merhi shook his head. "I'll make sure there isn't."

"Thank you." He nodded at the back seat. "Will you give me a hand? Just to the front door."

Merhi carried the monitor, Lattouf carried the iMac processor. They put both components of the computer on the ground by the front door.

Merhi offered his hand. Lattouf took it and then yanked the Lebanese forward in a crushing bear hug. The smell of garlic encased Merhi's head like a bubble. "It was good to work with you again, my friend," said the Palestinian. The hug was maintained (unilaterally) longer than was necessary. It was as if Lattouf didn't want to let go. Then he pulled back and said, "See you in a few weeks."

Lattouf watched the Land Cruiser drive off, giving it a final wave as it disappeared north. Then he opened his front door, bent down, balance the monitor on top of the processor and picked them both up in his huge arms.

"Children!" he called as he went through the door, kicking it closed behind him. "Come see what your Baba has bought for you!"

16 July 2010
4 Sha'ban 1431

Jounieh, Lebanon 07:00

"That's two nights now and she has not returned." Gisele was leaning against a kitchen unit in her dressing gown, eating a yoghurt. Jihad was at right angles to her, leaning against the sink, dressed in his uniform, eating his typical Lebanese breakfast (a sugared ring donut, no jam today). On the work surface next to him was a double espresso.

He shrugged with his shoulders, mouth and hands. "She is not our problem anymore. She is with Himo now, working with her own people. Perhaps she is staying with him."

"You would have thought she would have let us know. Some of her clothes are still in her room."

"Maybe she left them for you." Jihad brushed the sugar off his fingers into the sink.

Gisele raised an eyebrow. "You would like me to dress like her?"

Oh-oh. Seven a.m on a Friday morning and he could be seeing his weekend disappear before his very eyes. "I love the way you dress." Did he hesitate too long?

"Do you even notice the way I dress?"

"Of course. I am in a constant state of arousal whenever I'm with you."

"What is your favourite outfit?"

"Sorry?"

"If you know them so well, which of my clothes do you like

the best?"

Well, he hadn't made any plans for Saturday or Sunday anyway. Might as well spend them in the dog house. And he had a backlog of work. "That is easy," he knocked back his coffee. "If I tell you, will you put it on for me? Right now?"

"What?"

"Will you put it on for me right now?"

She sniffed. "What is it? Which outfit do you like best?"

He put his cup down on the side. "Isn't it obvious, my little siren from Jamhour? I like your birthday suit the best!" He grabbed hold of her, his hand slipping inside the dressing gown, over her small left breast.

She squealed pushing him away. "You filthy bastard!" But her hand was around the back of his neck, and her dressing gown had opened up, and somehow they were falling onto the floor.

They fought, they kissed, they made love. Right there in the kitchen.

An untypical Lebanese breakfast.

17 July 2010
5 Sha'ban 1431

Jonblat, Lebanon 09:30

Still no word from Carla – but no word from Himo either. No doubt they were far too busy to grant Jihad Merhi even the courtesy of telling him what was going on. The External Security Unit always thought it was a cut above its colleagues in the Internal Security Force.

Well it worked both ways. He, Merhi, was also too busy. If they came knocking at his door today, he would have no time for them. Today was the tenth anniversary of Bashar al-Assad becoming President of Syria and celebrations were expected by certain factions in certain parts of the city. As usual, Merhi had been put in charge of security.

Yesterday, after a relaxed and benign Merhi had arrived at the office, his boss, Major Ghanem, had called him in to brief him on the expected celebrations and to issue orders that all his team had to be on duty that weekend. The order did not apply to Ghanem himself, of course, who only worked weekends in the direst of emergencies.

Which was why it was another two days before Jihad Merhi found out the news.

18 July 2010
6 Sha'ban 1431

Bourj el-Barajneh, Beirut 19:30

Captain Fadi Lattouf was the last to leave the conjoined cabins that acted as the camp's police station that evening. It was a regular occurrence nowadays since his team had been reduced by fifty percent over the previous two years. Recession was even having an effect in the Palestinian refugee camps!

It was 19:30 when he padlocked the door of the police station from the outside and began the ten minute walk back to *chez Lattouf*. The streets were quiet as they often were on a Sunday evening, and in these hard times fewer and fewer people were populating the nearby café.

As usual he waved at the café proprietor, shook his head at the come-inside hand signal, and helped himself to the newspaper that always seemed to be left on the table outside just as he was passing. That day's *Al-Mustaqbal*.

As soon as he opened his front door, he could hear the noise, shouting, encouragement, moaning. Time was his children would be in bed by the time he got home, but the combination of closing the police station an hour earlier because of lack of staff and the children's increasing age, meant that they were always up when he arrived home. Which, as every hard working father worldwide knew, was a mixed blessing.

Nada popped her head out of the kitchen to greet him and then went back to her – what was it? Lattouf sniffed the air. Mmm, smelt like chicken livers.

Picking up the wandering three year old Wissam in one hand, he went into the living room. Most of the noise was coming from the other three boys playing a game on the new computer. Lana, at eleven the elder of his two daughters and the image of her mother, was seated on the floor with the playing cards spread out in front of her. She leapt up when she saw her father.

"Baba, Baba! Look, I can do it!"

"Do what?" smiled Lattouf, gently placing little Wissam on the floor and wondering when his dinner would be ready.

"Uncle Chadi's trick!"

"His trick?"

"You know, the one he was always trying to do. Making the card come out of his pocket."

Lattouf nodded sadly, remembering that was the last thing his cousin had done when he lay on the pavement outside. What a man, what an uncle. Dying and his last thoughts were for the children. God bless you, Abu Yussuf.

"It's all to do with the card," enthused Lana. "You can't do it with just any one. Watch! I'll show you?"

Lattouf was tired and his lower back was aching where he was bending forward. His gut rumbled. My God, he would die of starvation in a minute!

"Come down, Baba." Lana was pulling on his arm.

"What?"

"I haven't got a jacket. It is best if you have a jacket."

There were two sonic booms as Lattouf's knees hit the floorboards, then Lana was tucking a card into the top pocket of his jacket. "This is the first card you gave me," she explained. "Before you gave me the others. It is different. Watch." She fiddled in his pocket, manoeuvring the card, getting it just so. Then she lifted her father's left arm.

Lattouf felt like an idiot, kneeling on the floor, arm out raised, on the point of wasting away through hunger.

Lana tugged his arm down. "Now as your arm comes down,

squeeze it close to your body. Go on Baba!"

Hoping he was giving an avuncular smile and not looking bored, Lattouf squeezed...

And the card popped up halfway out of his pocket.

He raised his eyebrows in genuine amazement. "My darling, that is clever. So, so clever. Uncle Chadi would be proud of you." He pulled the card out of his pocket to hand it back to her. "You must learn some more - "

He frowned, looking at the card in his hand. He turned it over, looking at both sides. "This was the first card I gave you?"

"Yes, you gave me the others a few days later. They all look the same but that one is different, isn't it?"

Fadi was nodding, thinking.

Then he said, "Yes, it certainly is my darling."

19 July 2010
7 Sha'ban 1431

Jonblat, Beirut 09:30

There are days when the fan of events moves slowly and you take things leisurely. There are days when the fan of events moves quickly and you have to be on your toes. And there are days when the fan of events is moving so fucking fast that if it coincides with the biggest pile of shit mankind has ever known heading for it at the speed of light then no one, no one, escapes an ordure mud bath.

This was destined to be just such a day for Jihad Merhi.

He liked to be in by 08:00 but heavy Monday traffic on the Coastal Highway had delayed him, so he was already grumpy when he arrived at work. As he walked down the corridor past the General Office, Sergeant el-Gharib called out *"Sabah el-khair, rais.* The Major has been calling you since eight."

"The Major knows what he can do," mumbled Merhi as he walked into his office. First he needed a cup of sludge, the more awful the better. Did everyone really have to come south into Beirut at the very same time as he did? His knees were already aching from the slow drive, and the week had hardly started.

Or, he wondered as he turned on his computer, were his aching knees nothing to do with the drive? Was it just down to that one horrible, nasty, inevitable three-letter word: age?

Empty mug in hand, he was walking back towards the door when his desk telephone rang. It was the ring of an external call, so it was not the Major. Telling himself he should leave it and go get his sludge, he picked up the handset. "Merhi."

"Morning of light, Jihad my dear friend!"

No, really, this he did not need, not at 09:35 on a Monday morning. Hadn't they said their farewells five days ago until *Eid*?

"*Bonjour*, Fadi," he said flatly. "Morning of peace." Oh if only it were.

The Palestinian sounded excited. "I have found something. To do with my cousin. Maybe all is not lost after all."

Merhi sighed. "Really?"

"I think he may have left us a clue."

"A clue?"

"A clue. I had better not say too much over the phone."

"No."

"We should meet."

Now how did he know Lattouf was going to say that? Well if you start your week with the worst thing that could happen it could only get better from there. "When?"

"Tomorrow at fourteen hundred?"

"What? Can't you make it later?" Today at midday was pushing it, and he didn't yet know what new shit the Major had for him.

"No, this is important."

Merhi sighed. "My office."

"Can't we meet at the other place?"

"Just think of it as me helping your diet."

"Diet! I am wasting away. It is not good for a man to be size zero."

"That's a clothing size, Fadi, not the shape of your stomach. My office. I might be busy so you may have to wait."

"If I do I will enjoy one of your splendid coffees."

Merhi wondered whether he was being sarcastic but, knowing Lattouf, he probably wasn't. "Can you tell me what this clue is?"

"No. Later."

*

Merhi enjoyed two cups of sludge while carrying out a verbal autopsy on the weekend's soccer results with Deeb el-Gharib. Then, buoyed by the caffeine, he went upstairs to the office of Major Ghanem.

Ghanem was seated behind his desk, neatly trimmed greying head buried in a file in front of him. He looked up as Merhi entered, flapped a hand at a chair and returned to the file, stroking his equally neatly-trimmed moustache in concentration. Five minutes later he looked back up.

"Everything go all right with the weekend's celebrations?"

Merhi shrugged with his mouth. "As we know, there are those that support Syria's influence in Lebanon, there are those that do not. Not everyone wanted to wish Bashar al-Assad a happy anniversary. But there was nothing to worry you with."

"Good. You probably know that the Prime Minister is in Damascus meeting with President Assad today. He's expected back tonight and he might give a press conference. Keep an eye out on the streets, just in case."

In case of what? wondered Merhi. In case someone had an objection to the improving of Lebanese-Syrian relations? Ghanem was obsessed with 'trouble on the streets'. What harm was there in a little protest? Or was that a thought that had also crossed minds on the morning of 13 April 1975?*

"Sure." Merhi went to stand up.

"Just one other thing," Ghanem motioned him back down. "You had that External Security Unit Captain visit you recently."

"Selim Himo. Lieutenant. Acting captain."

"Anything I should know about?"

"He'd seen I'd requested CCTV footage of some streets in

---

* On 13 April 1975, Palestinian guerrillas fired on a church in the Christian East Beirut suburb of Ain el Rommaneh, killing four people. Later that day a bus carrying armed Palestinians was ambushed by gunmen belonging to the Christian Maronite Phalange party; about twenty-six people were killed. The attack against the bus is regarded as the official beginning of the Lebanese Civil War.

Ashrafieh, for a random parked vehicle security check. He was interested in the same streets at the same time. Just wanted to liaise."

Ghanem nodded and picked up a piece of paper from his desk. Almost as an aside he said, "He was found dead on Friday evening."

Merhi's anal sphincter tightened like the rectum of a virgin with constipation. *"What?"*

"Suicide apparently. Hung himself on his balcony." Ghanem frowned. "You all right? You look grey."

"That's... that's... It's just a shock, that's all."

"You weren't close."

"No, no. It's just the usual, you know, you're talking to the man one minute, the next he's dead. And suicide? Are they sure?"

"Why shouldn't they be? He probably couldn't hack the increased responsibilities that come with promotion, not everyone can."

"It was just him, nobody else?"

"What do you mean?"

"Well, er, his predecessor was murdered a couple of weeks ago. That's what he was investigating."

"Strange, I'll grant you. But I only know what's on this memo. Suicide."

"So they'll be looking for another new captain, three in the same month."

"I hope you're not thinking of applying?"

Merhi gave what he hoped was an ironic laugh, disguising the turmoil and confusion he was feeling inside. "Three times a charm? I don't think so."

"Good. Let the ESU sort their own house out. We have enough problems of our own."

Hamra, Beirut 11:00

Shit, thought Merhi. Shit, shit, shit. He was walking west, looking at the shops and stalls but not seeing. After Ghanem's casually-imparted news he had had to get out of the office. To think, to clear his head, to smoke at least two packets of Cedars King Size. The noise, bustle and madness of Hamra Street was the ideal place to lose himself.

Think, Jihad, think. Progress it logically.

Himo had been found dead. A death disguised as a suicide. He knew enough of the man and his high-flying confidence and arrogance to know that he was not the sort to do away with himself. So there was only one obvious answer: a death made to look like a suicide equalled murder.

By whom? Was it obvious?

His anal sphincter twitched just a little to expel a whistle of air. Nobody would notice it out here in the street.

Carla. Carla, Carla, Carla. What have you done? You come back to Liban with a cryptic message that Sajida was right, but you won't expand on it to anyone who doesn't know what it means. Your boss is murdered. You vow to track down the killer. You confide all to your new boss. You go off with him...

Your new boss is found dead.

In anyone's book you are the Prime Suspect.

But why? Why would you kill him? He didn't kill his predecessor, surely...?

Merhi drew on his cigarette and swallowed the smoke.

No, no, no. This was wrong, all wrong. The white-eyed assassin, that's who we were looking for here. The one who attacked you at the Hotel Albergo. Yes, that was logical. She had killed Himo because you had told him the secret, just as she had killed the previous guy.

But only one body had been found in Himo's apartment. Which begged the question: where was Carla now?

Or rather, where was her body?

*

He reached Hamra Square and, turning back the way he had come, crossed the road by the Eldorado Shopping Centre.

So what should he do? Should he go to Ghanem and tell him what he knew? Or maybe even go to the Major in charge of the External Security Unit? But that would put him right up to his neck in the shit. Two captains murdered, an exiled agent clandestinely returned and herself either a murderer or a victim. He would have to confess that he had been helping her, not to mention giving her somewhere to stay. Goodbye bollocks if not his career.

No, no. Right now he was in the clear, and he must stay that way. His reason for Himo coming to see him was neat and simple. He would repeat it to anyone who came asking. Not that they would, he realised with relief: the death was a suicide, no investigation needed.

A thought suddenly struck him, right in the middle of his forehead like a bolt shot by William Tell on an off-day. He slapped his palm on his brow as he walked along the street.

The memory card! The recording he had made of Carla and Himo in his office. It was in his drawer. Should he listen to it? Did he *want* to listen to it? Would he be signing his own death warrant? Should he just throw it away...?

Above the human and vehicle noises, he became aware of a loud beeping. There was probably a road rage fight brewing somewhere behind him. He picked up his pace. Being in uniform, he did not want to be dragged into any fray.

The beeping became louder and closer, coming from a van crawling along, now level with him. He looked to his left. It was a light blue van of the Palestinian Civil Police.

And waving across from the driver's window, two jars of pickles in his massive right hand, was a beaming Fadi Lattouf.

Jonblat, Beirut 12:00

The lid on the pickle jar opened with a satisfying pop. Contrary to expectation, Fadi Lattouf did not plunge his hand into the jar to pull out his first vegetable victim. Instead, Jihad Merhi watched from behind his desk in horror as Lattouf lifted the jar to his mouth and drank the vinegar and brine solution like a man who had just been rescued after a month in the desert.

He brought the jar back down from his mouth with a contented sigh, moustache and beard glistening. Noticing Merhi's stare, he said "This Beirut traffic is hell. Makes a man thirsty." Then his fingers went into the jar and pulled out some pepper and cauliflower. "And hungry as well."

Merhi shook his head."I don't suppose you'll be wanting any coffee then."

"Yes, please."

Five minutes later, with two cups of sludge on the desk and two empty pickle jars in the waste bin, Merhi said "So, you've found something?"

"Yes, yes!" Lattouf wiped his hands on his trousers and patted his jacket breast pocket.

"Take it off if you like," said Merhi. "The AC's not very good in here."

"No, no. I have it on for a reason," smiled the Palestinian. "Watch!"

Merhi's eyebrows disappeared into his hairline in disbelief as he watched Lattouf raise his left arm with a flourish, wave his hand in the air like a magician and then slowly bring his arm down.

"How about that?" asked Lattouf, his eyes wide, expecting praise. "Impressive, no?"

Merhi shook his head, puzzled. "Congratulations, you can raise your arm into the air. What the hell are you doing, Fadi?"

With a frown, Lattouf looked down at his pocket. Nothing had happened. "No, no, wait!" He tried it again, flapping his arm up and down, again and again, with increasing frenzy, looking like a chicken trying to take flight. "I did it at home, Lana taught me."

"Fadi!"

Lattouf stopped, looking abashed. "I am sorry. I wanted to show you. It raises up out of my pocket." He put his fingers into the pocket and pulled out a playing card.

"You came here to show me a magic trick?"

"Not just any magic trick, my cousin's magic trick."

Merhi sat back in his chair, at a loss at what to say. "Fadi... I'm sorry about your cousin's death... but... you know, I have things to do..."

"No, you don't understand. At first I thought it was just a trick too. It was the last thing Chadi did."

"Sorry?"

"As he lay dying. He couldn't speak, but he did this trick. You move your arm and the card raises from your pocket. I thought it was his farewell to the children."

Merhi was shaking his head, in sympathy, sorrow and bewilderment. For the moment, words really had failed him.

"But he was doing it for me," continued Lattouf as if it was obvious. "It was a clue. Look." He leant forward and flicked the card onto the desk.

At first Merhi did not pick it up, in case he might be affected by the madness that accompanied it. But then he saw writing on the patterned side of the card. He frowned.

"Numbers," said Lattouf.

Merhi slid the card nearer with his finger. Written across the card from corner to corner were the numbers 340715354514. He looked up.

"It matches the pack of cards you gave me from his car," Lattouf's eyes were ablaze with excitement. "But this one was in his pocket. As he died he made sure I got it." The eyes turned sad. "But I missed his intention, may Allah forgive me."

Merhi shrugged, one shoulder and mouth. "They mean

something to you, these numbers?"

"No, I thought you would know what they mean."

"How the f – how should I know what they mean?"

It was Lattouf's turn to shrug. Seizing his mug, he swilled down the remains of the lukewarm sludge. "A code or something?" He wiped his mouth with his hand.

"A code? The man is dying and he gives you a code?"

"Maybe he wasn't dying when he wrote it on there."

Merhi nodded. "Point. Did you have codes between you when you were young? Boys often do."

"No, we were too busy throwing stones at the occupiers."

"Coded messages on walls, anything like that?"

Again Lattouf shook his head. "They would have shot us."

"Okay, let's have a look." Merhi opened a drawer and pulled out a notepad. He took a pencil from the caddy on his desktop. "Let's just see, try the basic." Down the paper he wrote the first seven letters of the Arabic alphabet and put numbers against them:

ا	1
ب	2
ت	3
ث	4
ج	5
ح	6
خ	7

"So, disregarding the zero, 34715354514 gives us..." He held the pad up. " ت أ ج ث ج ت ج أ خ ث ت. Can we make anything of it...?"

The Arabic alphabet is consonants only. Vowels are not letters, they are symbols placed on top or below consonants to create words and sounds. For ten minutes and two cigarettes, Merhi tried the code consonants with three main Arabic vowels and some vowel derivatives and combinations. Then he sat back, shaking his head. "Meaningless. Let's try Western."

a	1
b	2
c	3
d	4
e	5
f	6
g	7

"Cdgaecedead. Hm! Well, look, we have the English 'dead' at the end. Did he speak English?"

"Arabic and French. Very little English."

"So, whether he knew he was about to die or not, he wouldn't have sent you a code in English?"

"No."

Both men were quiet, reflecting on the numbers. Merhi finished his sludge and Lattouf looked into his mug and wished there was more in it.

After a while Merhi said, "Of course, there are other combinations. One and five could be fifteen, o in Western. One and four could be fourteen, n in Western. That gives us..." He scribbled again. "Cdgoceden. Great." He reached for his cigarettes, throwing one to Lattouf. The Palestinian caught it and leant forward for a light. They both sat back, drawing in the smoke.

"It's the zero that bothers me," said Merhi. "Seems to indicate the numbers are, well, numbers, not coded letters."

Out of the blue Lattouf suggested, "It's a bank account! In all good mysteries there is a secret bank account! Perhaps he has left me a fortune somewhere!" He looked at Merhi's 'Yeh, right' eyes.

"Careful of those flying pigs, Fadi," advised the Lebanese. "And anyway, there's too many numbers for a bank account, too few numbers for a bank account with sort code."

Lattouf took three centimetres off his cigarette in one suck. On the exhale, he said "Telephone number?"

Merhi looked down at the pad. "Again too long... Or is it? Hold on. Let's work backwards." He wrote right to left across the paper. "Hm. Well, we have 34 071 535 4514. Or 3407 1535 4514." He showed the pad to Lattouf. "I like the first one. Could be an international number."

"Shall we try it?"

"Who has international dialling code 34?"

"Oh, um..." Lattouf put on a pensive face, giving the impression he was trying to recall something which he patently did not know.

Merhi picked up his phone and dialled four figures. "Deeb? Have you got the telephone books out there? Can you look up to see what country has dialling code 34? Thanks." He looked across the desk. "Don't worry, Fadi. He'll have it in a minute."

"Oh, okay."

Sergeant el-Gharib was back within thirty seconds. Merhi listened and nodded, said "Okay, thanks" and put the phone down. "Did your cousin know anybody in Spain?"

"Spain?" Lattouf shook his head. "Not that I know of. The family has never travelled far."

"Shall we try it? I have to leave out the zero, apparently."

Lattouf shuffled to the edge of his chair, intent and keen, as Merhi dialled.

Merhi hadn't finished dialling the full number before he put his fingers across the phone cradle, instantly lifting them off again and redialling. He did this twice more, then said "Shit. I'm getting the no-such-number tone. It won't even let me finish dialling."

Lattouf flopped back, deflated. "As you say, my friend. Shit. What can it be? What do the numbers mean?"

Merhi stole a quick look at his watch. They had been at this for an hour, a lot of time wasted in a busy day. And he still had a decision to make about a certain memory card. "Maybe it's nothing," he said. "You have jumped to the conclusion it is a clue. What if it isn't? What if it is scribble? Or random numbers that might have meant something in the past, written on the card to mark it out as the one that would come out of his pocket. Perhaps it was just a trick for the children after all."

Lattouf was grim-faced but he was nodding in reluctant acceptance. "Another lead, another dead end."

"If it was a lead in the first place. I don't see where we can go from here."

Lattouf stared into Merhi's face, his usual ebullience now flat, a look almost of anger in his eyes. Then he said, "Oh, I know where we can go from here, my friend. And you are going to go there with me. Whether you like it or not." He stood up and for a split second Merhi thought he was in danger. He had never seen this side of the Palestinian. Quickly he stood up too, his chair rolling back against the wall with a thump.

"We will go where there are no secrets," growled Lattouf. "Where all the world's problems can be discussed and solved." He stopped, stared – and then his face broke into a big grin. "Where is the nearest McDonald's?"

For a beat Merhi was shocked, then a laugh burst from his lips as he looked at the huge, grinning, stupid face. "I'd better call them and warn them," he said as he came around the desk, clapping his friend on the back. "They may have to send out for additional stock."

Jonblat, Beirut 15:00

Thank God he was gone. As much as Merhi had to admit to a reluctant, renewed and growing affection for the idiotic Palestinian giant, he had too much work on his plate right now to continue a dead-end investigation into his cousin's death.

They had gone to the McDonald's on Bliss Street in the Hamra district, and Merhi was glad they had decided to walk, otherwise he would have had to increase the tyre pressure on his Toyota on the way back such was the volume of burgers, desserts, drinks and one salad consumed by Lattouf.

They had parted downstairs, and once again Lattouf had seemed reluctant to go. They would meet again in seven weeks to celebrate *Eid* at the end of Ramadan. Yes, Merhi had confirmed, he and Gisele were really, really looking forward to once more coming down to Bourj el-Barajneh to celebrate with the Lattoufs and their six children. What could be better?

Now he was back in his office with the door closed. On the desk in front of him was the memory card from the digital recording machine in his drawer. He stared at it. Was this memory card his friend or his foe? What was on here would explain everything. It would reveal the secret knowledge that had killed who knew how many people, Himo and Carla included. But it could kill him too. Others with the knowledge had died, why should he be different?

But hold on, it was not like the knowledge was cursed, the victims had not suddenly been struck down with mortal diseases – they had been murdered. And murder meant somebody knew they knew.

Well, this time it was different: nobody knew he had this recording.

He picked up his telephone, keyed the General Office and told Sergeant Deeb el-Gharib that he was transferring his calls to him. If anybody asked, he was out of the office. He was not to be disturbed under any circumstances until further notice.

Opening his drawer, he removed the current memory card from the EM voice recorder and replaced it with the one that had been on his desk. He plugged earphones into the machine and then popped them into his ears.

Still not certain that he should be doing this, he pressed the Play key and sat back in his chair.

"Call me when you're done. I'll be outside. Making sludge." It was his own voice, picked up at the start of the recording when he pressed the button under his desk as he stood up. Six days ago. Seemed like a lifetime.

He heard the door close.

"Sajida - " began Carla.

"I know," interrupted Himo. "I was just stalling you to get him out of the way."

"You know?"

"About Sajida, yes. There's is rumoured to be an Eyes Only file at the very highest level with all the details. It is said it never goes below ministerial level. To many of us it is a myth, but you are confirming it is true?"

"I can only confirm what I learnt from my source. Sajida was right and The Second Coming is now imminent. Maroun's murder and the attempt on me seem to be confirmation of that."

"And *al-Mahdi* chose Lebanon."

"*al-Mahdi*?" queried Carla. "I hardly think so."

There was moving about. Then Himo said, "It all depends what you believe. The Saviour against Satan? There are those that have always seen it that way."

"Try telling that to the ones who died."

The voices had become muffled, as if the microphone in the desk had been covered. Merhi wondered if Carla had sat herself on his desktop and he was now listening through her bottom.

"Some will always die for the greater good," said Himo. "To spread the true word. So they say. He has many followers."

"Sounds like that includes you."

"No, no. I'm just putting the case. I am a good Muslim, that is the one true religion."

"If you say so. So if his existence is known and his presence is condoned by our leaders," there was a rustle of movement and the sound became clear again, "why kill Maroun?"

"That I don't know. We'll find out. Will you come back in? Or do you think it would be better if you went back to New York?"

"What do you want me to do?"

There was a pause. Then, "I'll let you know. Bear in mind I'm new, I don't know you. Tell me, why exactly is a member of the External Security Unit permanently based in New York?"

Carla proceeded to tell him, the story that Jihad Merhi already knew and had been a part of.

And that was it. Himo made no direct comment on the story she had to tell. They spoke more about her possible return to the ESU, about the woman with the white eyes and about where they might go from here, and then they left the room.

Merhi turned off the machine and pulled the headphones from his ears. After all that worry and consternation, that was it? He shook his head, baffled. He still didn't know who Sajida was. And what was that they were saying? *al-Mahdi*, the prophesied redeemer of Islam, had returned and was living in Lebanon? And his second coming was imminent? What was that all about?

Carla had been right – he really did not want to know about this. Religious mythology had no connection with law enforcement. He had better things to do than to indulge in legends. He should wash his hands of all of it.

Except, of course, that Himo and Carla were now dead.

But was that his problem? It might sound callous but no, it wasn't.

And, contrary to expectations and although he was disappointed, he had heard nothing on the recording to put his own life in danger.

Thank God.

al-Mahdi indeed. Whatever next?

Jonblat, Beirut 19:00

Jihad Merhi sat back in his chair, exhausted. What a day! Lots of shit had hit that fan but he was pleased that he had managed to avoid all but a peripheral splattering of the brown stuff.

First there had been his report to Ghanem on the weekend's activities followed by the casual announcement of the death of Selim Himo. And, by logical reasoning and known only by himself, the death of Carla too. Then Lattouf and his ridiculous failed card trick and the ludicrous numeric clue which was probably nothing of the sort. Then the anxiety of whether or not to listen to the recorded conversation, his fear of discovering what was on it and the disappointment that it revealed nothing other than the risible idea that in 2010 The Saviour had returned to earth. And in Lebanon!

For the last three hours he had put all the stupidity behind him and had concentrated on his real work. He had delegated Prime Minister Saad Hariri's press conference to one of the Lieutenants, and he had concentrated on finalising the security arrangements for the joint visit of Saudi King Abdullah and Syrian President Bashar al-Assad at the end of the month.

Now it was time to go home. Computer shut down, desk cleared, drawers locked, keys locked in wall safe with combination dial, he had stepped out into the corridor when he heard his desk telephone ringing. He did not even break his stride. The day was over, he was knackered, and it was probably Gisele wondering where he was.

He pulled out his mobile phone and his cigarettes. He would call her from the car, that way he could truthfully say he was en route.

He reached the stairwell and lit up a Cedars King Size as he walked down, leaving the cares and stresses of the day behind him...

Rafic el-Hariri International Airport, Beirut 19:10

The tall, hard man with the long black hair falling down the side of his face to cover his missing left ear, put down the pay phone in the airport arrivals area. No answer. Not unexpected.

He stepped away from the booth, placing his small bag between his feet and pulling a rubber band from his pocket. With two swift movements he tied his hair back in a ponytail, pulling at the sides to make sure the hole was still covered.

He was tired. For security reasons he had not taken a direct flight, instead he had gone New York – Cairo – Amman – Damascus – Beirut. That way he was a Syrian national entering Lebanon on his Syrian passport and he would not be looked at too closely at Immigration and Customs, if at all.

In fact he was not Syrian, he was originally Lebanese, although nowadays he regarded himself as nothing, not since he had been killed ten years before, right here in Lebanon at Aanjar. He had been Captain Marwan Mebarak of the Lebanese army, and records showed that he had died a hero.

Now he had no name. Dead men don't. His existence was known only to a few. But to those people who employed him as a 'problem solver', either locally or on an international level, he was known as The Damascene.

He had returned to Lebanon for the first time in five years, and this time it was personal.

He was looking for the woman he loved.

20 July 2010
8 Sha'ban 1431

Jbeil, Lebanon (time unknown)

Death was supposed to be the end of it. The merciful release, the eternal blackness, the grateful dead. Thank you and goodbye. *Finito.* Once the curtain came down there was nothing.

Or was this God-thing for real? Had all the teachings down the ages been true and not just humankind trying to make sense of a senseless moment of existence? Was there life beyond death? Was there a heaven? There must be – because she was in hell.

The pricks in her arms and legs annoyed her, the ones between the toes even more so, like the thorns of the *zaqqum* tree being pressed into her. They were an irritation, disturbing the darkness of her oblivion. But it was when her fingernails were prised out, slowly, one by one, rip rip rip, that she knew she had been sent down below. It felt like the demons of *Jahannam* were burning the tips of her fingers on the orders of Maalik, the guardian angel of the gates of Hell. Hadn't she heard his name mentioned?

Soon they would be making her eat the thorned and bitter fruit of the *zaqqum* and drink boiling water.

If you believed in such things.

Which she didn't. She was dead. Why couldn't they just leave her alone?

Hazmieh, Beirut 06:30

The Damascene woke early in his room at the Hazmieh Rotana Hotel on Boulevard Chiyah. The hotel suited his purposes for three reasons: it was just four miles from the airport; with one hundred and fifty one rooms it was big enough for him to remain anonymous; and it was on the way to Jamhour in the eastern suburbs.

As he showered, the hot water onto maximum scalding, he wondered if the old motorbike repair shop still existed near the Bejco dealership up in Jamhour.

He had need of their services again.

Annaya, Lebanon 10:00

The cowled figure sat motionless in the front pew of the small Monastery Church. He did not move when the door creaked open and the two women entered, and he gave no indication that he knew they were there as they walked silently down the central aisle and stopped in front of him.

"*Salaam*, Brother," greeted Love.

The hood rose but they could not see the face underneath.

"You are well?" asked Paradise.

The hood turned towards her. "This mortal body aches with age," said the deep voice from within. "But I am ready. Allah will give me strength for what is to come. I will not be forsaken."

"Everything is arranged?" asked Love.

The hood nodded. "I have had my final contact with the disciples in the Promised Land. The Circle of Haouch Moussa have arranged for the camels to be waiting on the other side of the mountains together with supplies for our journey. There are three members of the Circle and you will honour them with full conversions after delivery."

The twins smiled.

"I will give you further details when we are on our way. When do we leave?"

"To get you to the desert by Saturday, we will need to leave on Friday," explained Paradise. "Today is Tuesday, so we thought we would come to collect you Thursday and you can stay the night in Jbeil with us. We will look after you."

"That is acceptable."

"And we have a little surprise for you. Something you might enjoy," said Love.

Malek tensed. "I do not like surprises."

Love reached out to touch him and then thought better of it. "This one you will, Brother. I promise. You will be pleased with us."

He ignored the comment. "There are two things I want you to do. Take this." He bent forward and pulled the small blue case out from under the pew. "My *argileh*. Guard it with your lives. I will enjoy it Thursday night. Underneath it you will find the Netbook. I have deleted as much as I can. Do not turn it on. Destroy it by breaking and burning."

"Yes, Brother."

Malek stood up. He did not quite reach the height of the twins. "And buy a camcorder. A good one with plenty of memory. Hard disk with memory card option. High definition. Our journey must be recorded for history."

Jamhour, Lebanon 11:00

The old motorbike repair shop was still there and, judging by the amount of second-hand (or more) bikes outside for sale, it was still doing good business in these times of recession – at least on the buying side if not the selling. The bikes would have been bought for a fraction of their second-hand value and would be sold for full used list price.

The Damascene produced one of his Lebanese ID cards, gave a false address, handed over a huge wad of US dollars, extracted a promise that they would buy back the bike if he was not satisfied with it after a week, and drove away on a one year old 1340 cc black Suzuki Hayabusa.

Jonblat, Beirut 11:50

Jihad Merhi had just countersigned a report on street-level reaction to last week's parliamentary discussions on *tawteen*[*] when the phone on his desk rang. An outside call.

"Merhi."

"Captain Merhi, al-salaam 'aalaykum.'"

Merhi frowned. The voice was deep, the accent local. Slowly he said, "'aalaykum al-salaam?"

"Captain, I am a friend of your niece."

"My niece?"

"Carla."

Merhi said nothing.

"I am looking for her."

Another moment of silence, then Merhi said "Do you have a name?"

"No, I do not."

"I see. You work for General Security?"

"Currently I work for nobody."

"Why are you phoning me?"

"You know why."

More silence. Then Merhi said, "Call me on my mobile." He gave his number. "Do you need to write it down?"

"No."

"Give me ten minutes."

---

[*] The naturalisation and resettlement of Palestinians from Lebanon's refugee camps. Parliament was debating whether to accord Palestinians three rights - unrestricted employment, social security and medical care, and ownership of property. The issue had divided opinion and had even caused a split between the previously politically-inseparable allies of Michel Aoun's Christian Free Patriotic Movement and the Shi'ite Hizbullah.

Hamra, Beirut 12:05

"What makes you think I have a niece called Carla?" Merhi was sitting at a table in busy Hamra Square, triple espresso in front of him, third consecutive Cedars King Size between his fingers, phone to his ear.

"You do not. But do you really want her to be fully identified for The Listeners?"

Merhi sucked on his cigarette. "Who are you?"

"I am no one. Just a friend looking for a friend."

"I cannot help you."

"I would like to talk with you anyway."

"No."

"Yes."

Merhi swallowed smoke, stifling a cough.

"Let me take you to dinner," said the voice. "You and your charming wife Gisele."

"What has my wife got to do with this?"

"Gisele Merhi, *née* Ibrahim but known in the business as Gisele Joudeh. One time senior field operative of the Department of General Security, latterly a trainer before she resigned. Still, I am told, a very formidable ally. I would like to meet her."

"No."

"Yes. Both of you. Tonight. The Burj al-Hamam restaurant in Antelias. You know it?"

"If I wanted to I could find it."

"We have a reservation for 20:30. Please be there."

"Or...?"

"Or you don't want to know. But let me give you some advice, Captain. Enjoy your espresso, it has already been paid for. But cut down on the cigarettes, they're not good for you."

The chair clattered backwards as Merhi stood up, looking from side to side at the shoppers, phone still held to his ear. People were looking in windows, buying from the stalls, some were on their mobiles, one or two were texting, nobody was paying him any heed. He did not notice the black Suzuki Hayabusa motorbike pull away into the traffic of Hamra Street.

After two more visual sweeps of the area, he picked up the chair and sat back down, unhappy, looking at the screen of his phone to see that the call had ended. He went to put his cigarette back into his mouth and then stopped, looking at it and thinking of the advice he'd just been given.

With a curse he stubbed it out in the ashtray on the table, stood up and walked away.

Coastal Highway, Lebanon 15:00

"Are you mad?" Gisele's voice echoed around the Toyota as Jihad drove north, his mobile phone bluetoothed into the car's audio system. "Do you know who he is?"

"Someone who knows Carla. And he knows us too. Knew all about you." He dragged on the cigarette between his fingers then put his hand back on the wheel.

"I don't like it."

"What can he possibly do, in public, in a restaurant? Perhaps it's his way of reassuring us."

"Well I am not reassured."

"And there are two of us." He reached forward and turned up the fan on the air conditioning. Was it becoming hotter in the car or what it just him? "*Habibi*, he's looking for Carla. Says he's a friend. Whether he is or he isn't, he can't do her any harm now. And I know, even from the few words I've had with him, that he won't leave us alone unless we meet him as asked."

"I don't like it," she said again.

"But you'll come?"

"Of course!" she said it as if it had never been in doubt.

"I've heard it is a good restaurant."

"Even better when you are not paying, eh my husband?"

"It always makes the food taste that much nicer! We'll leave at seven-thirty. Could you get my suit out of the cupboard to air, the light one? And perhaps iron a white shirt for me?"

"*Tayyib.*"

"And just one other thing, darling."

"What?"

He pulled out, overtook a lorry and pulled back in again.

"Make sure you choose a handbag big enough to put a gun in."

Antelias, north of Beirut 20:25

They were a respectful five minutes early, more by the grace of the god of traffic than any accurate timing. Jihad was wearing a fawn suit with an open-necked white shirt, Gisele wore a short-enough-to-be-noticed-but-not-too-short-to-be-indecent red dress with gold lamé vertical pattern and co-ordinating six centimetre heels. She carried a red shoulder bag which, to a practised eye, looked slightly on the heavy side.

The place was big with probably room for a hundred covers or more, décor of wood and cream-beige. It was busy but not full, and they had to wait in line to be greeted.

Their turn came, a black-suited *maître* greeting them as if he had known them for a long time. "*Bonsoir, m'sieur-dame.* Thank you for coming to the Burj al-Hamam. Your name please?"

"We don't have a reservation," said Jihad, "we are - "

"Ah, Captain and Madame Merhi. We have been expecting you. Please, come this way."

They were guided across the large main dining area towards the wall on the right with the impressive back-lit faux-stained-glass windows with drawn scenes of old Lebanon. Underneath a scene of the ruins at Baalbeck with Mount Lebanon in the background, a tall man stood up from a round table set for three. He wore black slacks and a loose white collarless shirt, long black hair draping the sides of his hard, tanned face, untied, no ponytail.

"Your guests, sir," the *maître* announced and then discreetly disappeared.

The man gave a half smile and held out his hand. "Captain Merhi."

Jihad paused and then, with hesitation, shook his hand, extending his left palm towards Gisele. "My wife, Gisele."

"Of course. Madame Merhi. I am pleased to meet you." He raised Gisele's hand to his lips."Please. Won't you sit down?"

There was a scraping of chairs. "And your name?" asked Jihad, sitting down, placing his cigarette packet on the table.

"I don't have one."

"Everyone has a name."

"I don't. Let us order," his hand went into the air. "Then we can talk." A waiter appeared, handing out menus. "The last time I was here the *farouj meshwi* was particularly good. I shall try it again. But please, have what you want."

Jihad was really in no mood for studying a menu, so he plumped for the first thing that sounded interesting: *kastaleta*, lamb chops with fries. Gisele took a bit more time, eventually ordering *mallifa*, a barracuda steak.

When the waiter was gone, Jihad lit up a cigarette, not offering the packet to his host. *"Alors, Monsieur No-Name.* You are Lebanese, from your accent I would say you are from the north. Tripoli?"

"If you say so."

Jihad blew smoke. "You are obviously fit. Strong. Ex-army?"

"You make a good detective."

"But what are you now?"

Water was delivered to the table and poured, sparkling for the lady, still for the men.

The Damascene sat back, arms behind his chair, smiling. "Now? I am nothing."

"That I do not for one moment believe."

"As you wish."

Pickles, raw vegetables, dips and bread were placed onto the table. Gisele handed out the bread, being Mum, letting the boys play out their pissing contest. Jihad's stream might be stronger but he was doing it into the wind and it was blowing back all over him.

"Why don't I just arrest you right now?" suggested Jihad.

"On what grounds?"

"I'll think of something."

"Very Lebanese. At least enjoy your food first." The Damascene took a lettuce leaf from underneath the pile of vegetables, dipped it in *mutabal*, aubergine dip, and took a bite. "And while you are doing so, I could reach across this table and have your head off your shoulders long before your wife even has time to get her gun from her purse." He smiled and looked at Gisele. "So, which of us has the biggest dick?"

She couldn't help but laugh as she reddened, quickly taking a sip of water. Then she said, "Okay, okay. You are both Lebanese. You know you have the biggest dicks in the world, that's why we girls love you so."

The Damascene laughed out loud, tapping his hand on the table in mirth. Jihad looked aggrieved.

"As always, the lady wins," The Damascene raised his glass. "*Touché*. Captain, I mean you no harm. I am trying to find Carla, that is all."

Jihad dipped bread into hummus. "What do you know?"

"I was with her in New York. She found out reliable information. That Sajida was right - "

"In the name of Christ!" chewed bread fell out of Jihad's mouth onto the table. "That is all I keep hearing. Who the fuck is Sajida?"

"Language, husband," scolded Gisele, still smiling about their dicks.

"You don't know?" frowned The Damascene. "Carla did not tell you?"

"Only that it was knowledge that was dangerous. She said she was protecting us."

"And so she was. If you don't know then it is best if you don't."

"Oh for God's sake! Tell me."

"No. Carla came back here to Lebanon. Looked you up. You were both kind enough to offer her somewhere to stay, for which I thank you. She said her boss had been killed after she had told him the information, and that she had been attacked."

"How do you know all this?"

"She has been in regular contact with me."

"In New York?"

"Wherever I have been. Modern technology, eh? She said she was going for the person who killed her boss. She asked me for my help, but I couldn't come right away. She told me she had met her new boss and she was hoping to work the case with him. Then – nothing. That was a week ago and I've not heard from her since. "

Jihad swallowed a piece of pepper and wiped his mouth. "You know just about everything we know. More if you count this Sajida thing..." He paused just in case an explanation was forthcoming. When it was not, he went on "There's just one bit to add. A week ago she indeed went off to work with her new boss – he was found dead two days later, hanging in his apartment."

The Damascene was still. Very still. He stared into the glass of water in front of him as Jihad and Gisele glanced at each other. It was a full minute before he looked up and said, "And?"

Jihad sighed, reluctant, knowing he was the bearer of bad news. "And Carla has not been found. No trace of another person in the apartment. It has been put down as suicide. Nobody except me - "

"And me." Gisele.

" – seems to know she was with him that day, or even that she exists."

"No notes, no record of the investigation?"

"Seems not," said Jihad. "So her disappearance means one of

two things. Either she killed him and has fled..."

The Damascene shook his head.

"...or she herself is dead and her body disposed of."

Staff descended to clear away the plates in preparation for the main course. The Damascene was quiet, intent, thoughtful. Jihad did not know what to say, what else he could say.

"What are you going to do?" asked Gisele, touching The Damascene lightly on his arm. The muscles were rock solid.

"I don't know. Do you think she is dead? Either of you?"

Jihad shrugged. Gisele said, "Either that or, as Jihad said, she killed her boss and has fled."

"But no contact? With you, I can understand. All along she has not wanted to incriminate you, that is why she has not explained about Sajida. She wanted to protect you. But no contact with me? No phone call? Doesn't make sense." The Damascene turned to Jihad. "Can you get me copies of the suicide report?"

"I'm sure I could, for what good it would do."

"I cannot believe, I must not believe, that she is dead."

"If she is not," said Jihad, "that begs the question: where is she?"

"That," said The Damascene, "I do not know."

"What is she to you anyway?" asked Gisele, pulling backwards as her *mallifa* was placed in front of her.

The Damascene also pulled back to let his *farouj meshwi* be delivered. "What is she to me?" He looked from one to the other of them. "Carla is my wife."

Bourj el-Barajneh, Beirut 20:45

It had been a long, hot day, and the temperature showed no sign of dropping, even at that hour. As he locked up the police post for the evening, Captain Fadi Lattouf sniffed under the right arm of his sweat-soaked blue shirt. He was as ripe as a two-days-past-its-use-by-date gorgonzola. Thankfully *chez Lat-*

touf had a shower, of sorts (cold water only and the flow rate slower than a tortoise on diazepam), and he would wash immediately after dinner. It would be good to get the blood off his hands too.

He looked down at his now brown-stained fingers, dried blood encrusted down his nails. It had been hard extracting the confession from the eighteen year old, but it had been necessary. You do not, ever, steal from another person's home in the camp. Never. If you wanted to steal you went out into Beirut. The youth had admitted it eventually (they always did) and if he ever woke up from his coma he would be charged and passed on to the camp authorities for punishment.

Lattouf helped himself to the paper on the table outside the café and gave his usual wave to the proprietor, tapping his wrist to indicate his reason for not coming inside for his free coffee and shisha.

As he entered his house, a naked-from-the-waist-down Little Wissam toddled out to meet him. "Hello, young man!" Lattouf bent forward and picked up his youngest son with a blood-encrusted hand. "Why aren't you in bed yet, eh? I hope you have been a good boy for your Mama."

He carried the boy in the crook of his arm into the main living area. The two oldest boys were watching *Deal Or No Deal* on the old television (Lattouf paused as host Michel Sanan asked model Nadine to open Case 21. It was the fifty million Lebanese pounds, the last remaining high number. Tough luck). Lana was on the computer over by the kitchen and Lattouf ruffled her hair with his free hand as he went past, leaving a little flake of dried blood on her scalp which neither of them noticed.

"Evening of peace, dear wife. It is good to be home."

"*Salaam*, dear husband," greeted Nada. "Dinner is only just ready. The power."

"Thank goodness it is ready, otherwise I would have had to eat this young specimen I found in the hallway." He bounced the boy in his arm. "I need to shower but I won't have the strength until I get some food inside me..." His voice trailed off as he felt a sudden warmth against his stomach and hip. He pulled Wissam away from his body, the boy's tiny penis erect and pissing horizontally. Nada just had time to take the saucepan of rice out of the sink as Lattouf held the boy over the plug hole to finish. "Then again," he said, "perhaps I do just have enough strength left to shower first."

He passed the giggling boy to his mother and went back out of the kitchen, past Lana and into the bathroom across the hallway.

Even though the water was cold and flowed as if the house plumbing had an enlarged prostate, he turned it on to run while he stripped off his clothes, throwing his shirt into a corner but treating his trousers with a little more respect, hoping they would dry out and give him a good three months' wear yet before they needed to be cleaned. The shirt almost cringed in fear as massive Y-fronts were thrown on top of it (he'd had a good two weeks' wear out of them, time for fresh ones) and his socks walked into the corner of their own accord.

A stark naked Fadi Lattouf, the stuff of every woman's dreams (in his dreams), stepped under the shower, squealed as the water touched his skin and then let it trickle over his hairy, sweaty, blood and piss-stained body.

Five minutes later he was lathering up his groin and thinking thoughts of Nadine and Case 21, when he stopped suddenly, frowning, soap held somewhere in the crevices of his lower stomach, snugly out of sight. His face contorted in concentration, as it always did when he was thinking... What was it that he had seen...? What had occurred to him...? Something was nagging –

In the name of Allah! Could it be?

He grabbed the shower off its holder in the wall, rinsing off the soap as quickly as the water flow would allow.

Snatching his towel from the pile (Nada always insisted he

use the black towels, for some reason), he quickly rubbed off the excess water and suds. Mankind had not invented a towel big enough to fit round the waist of Fadi Lattouf, but he threw it around his gut anyway, holding the ends with his hand, his right hip exposed, one of only two areas of his body that was not covered with hair (the other being his head).

Nada was just bringing the chicken and rice to the table in the living area when the damp, hairy monster, comb-over flapping away from his head, barged through the door. She shrieked, just managing to hold on to the food.

"Lana!" cried Lattouf, his eyes just a little wild. "Lana!"

The eleven year old on the computer turned around in her chair, fear in her eyes. What had she done, what had she done?

Her father dashed over to her and she flinched away. He bent forward, staring at the computer screen. "What is this?"

She could smell the warmth off him as his flesh wobbled close to her. "U – uncle's computer," she said hesitantly, warily. "You brought it home, Baba."

"No, no. No, no. I mean what is this, this on the screen?" He poked the monitor, making the image bend inwards in the shape of his finger.

"It's... it's a geography thing. I was just looking at it."

Lattouf was staring intently at the bottom of the screen. In a calmer tone, he asked "What is it? This thing?"

"It – it's called Google Earth."

"Incredible," he was shaking his head. "Incredible. And what? It maps the earth, this thing?"

"Yes, Baba. You can see pictures of anywhere. I was just looking at New York..."

To Lana's great relief, her father ruffled her hair again as he straightened up and turned around. Nada was looking at him with raised eyebrows. "Wife," said Lattouf. "My cousin was a genius. I am a genius! God is good." He raised his arms in an expansive, theatrical gesture – and the towel fell to the floor.

The screams of his wife and children could be heard as far

away as the north Beka'a.

Antelias, north of Beirut 21:10

Jihad Merhi pulled back as his *kastelata* was placed in front of him. "Carla didn't tell us she was married."

"On the other hand," smiled Gisele, looking at their dining companion, "she didn't tell us she wasn't."

"True, true." Jihad looked across the table at The Damascene. "People in her kind of work – in your kind of work – normally aren't."

"How long?" asked Gisele.

Through a mouthful of chicken, The Damascene said "We have been together five years. We married on Valentine's Day this year. It is a date that means a lot to us."

"That's nice, congratulations."

"Thank you."

Jihad busied himself cutting his chops. Valentine's Day? Five years? 14 February 2005? The day Rafic Hariri was assassinated...? He didn't want to go there. He stuffed a forkful of fries into his mouth and mumbled, "So where do we go from here?"

"You will get me a copy of the report?"

"Yes, but after that?"

The Damascene shrugged with his mouth. "You will understand that I simply cannot accept that she is dead, not without investigation."

A thought had occurred to Jihad. "There is one thing," he said, waving his fork for emphasis. "She - "

There was a sudden burst of music. Jihad frowned as the other two looked at him, wondering why he was their focus. Then he realised and said apologetically, "Excuse me." As he fumbled in his jacket for his phone, he mumbled "Never off duty." He brought it out and put it to his ear. "Merhi."

"Evening of joy, my dear friend!"

Oh Christ. Jihad turned in his seat as if the action would

make him invisible to the other two. "I can't talk now. I am busy."

"But I have solved it! I know what the clue is!"

"Not now. My office. In the morning."

"Can I just tell you - "

"My office." Merhi ended the call. Turning back round he said, "Sorry about that." He picked up his fork, thinking how he would like to poke it in Lattouf's oversize gut right at that minute. "Another case."

"You were saying?" prompted The Damascene.

"I was?"

"You said there was just one thing."

"I did...?" His thoughts had been knocked sideways by Lattouf's interruption. "Oh, yes! Carla did a drawing of her assailant, the person who attacked her and who she thinks murdered her boss. It was a woman."

"A woman?" The Damascene looked at Gisele then back to Jihad. "You have the picture?"

"I have a copy of it in my office. I'll get it for you tomorrow."

Gisele had gone to the ladies' room.

"So what are you really going to do?" asked Jihad through a mouthful of mango.

The Damascene sipped his water. "You are going to get a copy of the report for me and let me see the drawing. Then I'm going to find this woman."

"Just like that?"

"I have resources."

"Who?"

"You."

"Me?"

"You. You will help me find this woman and you will help me find my wife."

"How?"

"I don't know yet. I will decide on a course of action once I've seen the report and the picture."

"I'll get them for you, but after that you'll be on your own."

"Really?"

"Really."

"No. You will help me in whatever way I want you to. Here." The Damascene held out his clenched fist, palm downwards and dropped five bullets onto the table. All five rounds of Gisele's Smith and Wesson 642 that was still in her handbag.

Jihad opened his mouth. "How the fuck did you do that?"

"It is not the first time I have had to disarm someone in this restaurant."

Jihad didn't know what he was talking about and he didn't want to know. "Bravo. A clever party trick."

The Damascene saw Gisele walking back towards them and scooped the bullets back into his hand. "Have you ever wondered what it would be like if your wife was not there?"

"No."

"Then pray you never find out."

The Damascene stood up, courteously pulling out Gisele's chair for her, and Jihad saw a whole new meaning behind his smile.

Coastal Highway, Lebanon 22:00

"That is one dangerous bastard," said Jihad as they turned right onto the coastal highway, heading north. In his rear-view mirror he saw the Suzuki Hayabusa with its unhelmeted rider disappearing into the night towards Beirut.

"I thought he was charming, in a dangerous sort of way." Gisele settled into the leather seat, resting her head, mellow. "Carla is a lucky girl."

"Really? I don't consider being dead as lucky."

"He thinks she's still alive."

"Well he would, wouldn't he?"

"Are you going to help him?"

Jihad flashed his lights at an innocuous Ford Focus before pulling out to overtake it. "I'll get him the report and the picture."

"And if he asks for anything else?"

For a moment Jihad did not respond. He was thinking of what he had heard in the conversation between Carla and Himo. He cast at glance at Gisele's bare legs stretched out next to him. Had the man threatened her or was it just his imagination, reading things into things? He said, "We'll see."

Gisele lit up a cigarette, sucked on it then leant over and put it between Jihad's lips. There was lipstick on the filter but he wouldn't mind. "I thought of asking if he wanted to stay with us."

"No!" The cigarette bounced up and down, stuck on his bottom lip. Gisele was shocked at his vehemence. "No way. You give him a wide berth, do you understand me? You must have no contact with him if I am not there."

"Oh, so it's all right for you to bring home waifs and strays, but if I make just one offer - "

"That was different."

"In what way? It would be nice for me to have two handsome men in the house for a change." Giving a provocative smile, she let her left hand finger-walk over his thigh. "It's nice for a girl to feel protected..." She poked his bulge with her index finger. "Goodness, who's an excited boy then?"

"Two things," said Jihad. "One, that is my mobile. And two, I mean it. That man is dangerous. You will leave him well alone."

She took her hand back. "He's only trying to find his wife."

"Nevertheless," said Jihad, nodding without elaborating. "Nevertheless... You will do as I say."

"Of course, dear husband. Don't I always? And who was that on the phone, one of your fancy women?"

"It was the idiot Lattouf. Thinks he's going to solve his cousin's murder. Won't leave it alone. *L'imbécile.*"

21 July 2010
9 Sha'ban 1431

Jbeil, Lebanon 07:00

With a loud gasp her body shot upright into a sitting position as the blast of adrenaline hit her system. The needle was still in her chest, pulling the skin outwards, the syringe flopping between her naked breasts like a plastic phallus.

"Lie down, lie down," said a soft female voice. There was pressure on her forehead, someone pushing her back down, and she had no strength, no will other than to obey.

She was confused. Where was she? Who was she? She couldn't remember. Wasn't she dead?

Someone was stroking her hair. Who was it? Had someone come to see her in her coffin before her final journey?

But if she was dead, she would not be having these thoughts. Or was that what death was? A cessation of the body but the continuance of the mind, the spirit?

The person stroking her hair was speaking to her softly but she couldn't understand what was being said, it was just a faraway gabble. Did the dead have their own language?

Where was the long tunnel with the light at the end? Why wasn't she floating on the ceiling, looking down at her own body? Had it all been a lie? Was life just a giant con?

There was a gentle tapping on her face, first one cheek then the other. She frowned.

Then there was a really sharp scratch in her chest and she moaned.

"There now," said a voice, and she could understand it. Something soft and damp was rubbed between her breasts. She tried to pull her arms up but they would only move a few centimetres. There was a metal on metal sound.

Slowly, warily, she opened her eyes. She expected to see nothing except the blackness of eternity, but there was a soft, very subtle, ambient light. Was this Heaven's waiting room? There were two angels with her, but they were blurred, out of focus.

Then she felt herself peeing and there was nothing she could do about it. How embarrassing, they would never let her into Heaven now. Then she defecated.

"Don't worry, don't worry," said the angel who had been stroking her head. "It happens when you come back. It's a good sign."

"We'll clean you up," said the other angel from the end of her – what was it? A bed? A cot? A mortuary slab? She tried to move her feet but again there was the metal on metal sound.

"Here, drink." Her head was lifted. "But only a little, and sip slowly."

She did as she was told, tasting the most delicious liquid she had ever experienced. Pure water. "Thank you. Thank you." She didn't know whether she had said the words or just thought them. She was put back down.

And then her system jolted again, the secondary rush of the adrenaline. Her eyes focussed, her mind cleared, and she remembered everything.

She was lying completely naked on an old bunk bed, her wrists and ankles handcuffed to the metal frame.

And this wasn't Heaven's waiting room and they weren't angels. It was more like the ante-room of hell. These were the identical murdering bitches, the *houri*.

And she was The Djinn.

And she was very much alive.

Jounieh, Lebanon 07:10

"I'm off, *habibi!*" Standing in the bathroom doorway, Jihad had to shout to be heard above the shower. Behind the glass screen he could see tantalising glimpses of Gisele as she soaped her body. The room was heavily-scented, warm and steamy, and he wished he could stay and get under the water with her.

"Okay. See you tonight."

"Remember what I said," he cautioned. "Be circumspect."

"Husband, I wrote the book on it." She had. Literally.

As he left the apartment and walked down the stairs, he wondered what the day held for him. More shit from Major Ghanem, no doubt, to add to the piles of shit sitting neatly and metaphorically on his desk already. Then Lattouf would be making an appearance at some stage with his latest crackpot theory. And, of course, there was the man without a name, who for now he would call Mr Carla.

Why, oh why, had he ever got mixed up in this? *al-Mahdi* and The Second Coming indeed. Fantasy. Madness. Murder. Why hadn't he just said no when Carla had first contacted him?

He would get the copies of Carla's picture of the assassin and the report on Himo's death, and maybe try to tap Mr Carla to reveal this Sajida business, whatever that was. No doubt he would be in touch today. But it would be nice to know exactly who he was dealing with...

With a small smile, he tapped his pocket. Maybe he would find out.

He climbed into the Land Cruiser, started up and switched on the radio underneath the unused GPS screen on the dash. He would let the music of *Voix du Liban* accompany him in to Beirut today.

During the near hour-long journey, he never once noticed that, several vehicles back, he was also accompanied by a black Suzuki Hayabusa motorbike.

Jbeil, Lebanon 07:20

"There, that's better." Love spoke sweetly, almost lovingly, caressing Carla's face gently with her right hand while her left hand held a vicious-looking stiletto to the captive's throat.

Paradise had finished cleaning her bottom, holding Carla's legs in the air like a baby while she wiped and dried. They had already removed the thin waste-covered mattress and cleaned and disinfected the floor.

"Sorry we only had one mattress," said Paradise as she reconnected the ankle cuffs to the bed frame. "Hope the springs aren't too painful."

They were more irritating than painful, little pokes, little scratches all down her back and legs. Like lying on a bed of nails. She had clenched her buttocks a couple of times but had then decided the best course was to keep still.

She moved her head, looking around. She was in a small room, musty, bare of furnishings except for the bed. Light was coming in through a small window high in one wall giving the white eyes of her captors an eerie glow.

"We'll let you up if you promise to behave," said Love. "I'll get you some food, you must be starving. We have tomatoes, *labneh, mana'eesh* and some *kunafi* if you're up to it, and coffee when you're ready. But be careful, your stomach will probably process it quickly." To emphasise the point she moved her hand from Carla's face and slowly ran her fingers down her naked body, stopping at her stomach and making soft, gentle circles around the belly-button with her fingertips. It felt like the gossamer caress of an angel – or the deception of a she-devil.

"I am hungry," understated Carla. She was ravenous.

"Well, here's the deal." Paradise leant over next to her sister, touching Carla's thigh. Carla looked up. The *houri* were spookily identical, it was like she was seeing double, hallucinating, the drugs not yet out of her system. "You promise to be a good girl and we'll let you up. You will remain restrained because we do not trust you, but believe us when we say we mean you no harm."

"We could have killed you," reasoned Love. "You could be dead by now."

"Why aren't I?"

Paradise ignored the question. "Will you be good?"

"Yes. Yes, I will."

The twins looked at each other, exchanging thoughts. Love nodded. She held up the stiletto in her left hand. "Remember, I have this – and these." She held up her right hand and made a small flicking movement with her thumb against the top of her index finger. The tiniest needle poked up from beneath the false nail. "You, of course, have been disarmed."

Carla tried to move her wrists, raising her head to look down at her hands. Yes, she remembered her nails being prised off. The ends of her fingers were raw and bloodied.

Paradise took keys from her cargo pants pocket and unlocked first one leg then the other, rubbing Carla's ankles as she did so. Then she stood back, as if trying to decide which wrist to unlock. "I presume, like us, you are ambidextrous, with a favour towards your left?" She stretched over and undid the right wrist.

"Now move slowly." Love was kneeling on the floor, holding Carla's legs in case of kicking and moving them around and down so that she was in a sitting position. Then she rubbed her thighs, massaging life back into them.

"May I put some clothes on?"

"No. Not yet," said Love.

"We like you like that," said Paradise. "Are you naturally smooth or do you shave? And anyway we have nothing in your size. Your clothes had blood on them, we had to throw them away."

Carla watched as Love continued massaging her legs. She asked, "Why am I alive?"

"Because we didn't want to waste you," Paradise replied,

Carla raising her head upwards to look at her. "We should really have freed your spirit but we though for once that we should try a proper conversion."

"Who are you?"

"We're just soldiers of The Saviour. His trusted disciples."

"You really think he is The Saviour?"

"We know he is. He has saved his believers before and he has come to do it again. This time those who believe in him will not perish."

"And we want you to join us," said Love, stopping her hands at the top of Carla's thighs at the crease with her groin. "You are beautiful, you are talented. Become one of the chosen ones, like us. This is the time of *al-Mahdi*. Many will be called."

"But only a few will be chosen." Paradise unlocked the final handcuff as Love grabbed Carla's face, her needled nails against the skin.

"Okay," said Love, her face just centimetres away. Carla could feel her warm, sweet breath. "Now stand slowly as I raise you, as if you were newborn. Your legs will be weak, we will hold you." Hands still on her head, she pulled Carla forward and up, Paradise quickly grabbing both her wrists and pinning them behind her. Supporting her but restraining her also. "Good girl," said Love. "Good girl. Now slowly slowly let your legs take your weight. Carefully... that's good. Put one foot in front of the other... Good." She took her hands down, looking to see that Paradise maintained her grip behind. "Okay. *Yalla.* Let's get some food inside you. Then afterwards we will give you a complete pamper. You look like you've been through the wars."

Or have come back from the dead, thought The Djinn.

Jonblat, Beirut 08:15

And there indeed was today's pile of shit, awaiting him on his desk. A file and a note from Major Ghanem about the pending

Gaza boats crisis*, asking for his comments on the intelligence reports that Israel was preparing to attack Lebanon once again and seeking his proposals for street-level safety.

This time it was easy. Israel had attacked Lebanon so often in the past – either by threat or actual deed – that all he needed to do was dust off some of his old situation assessments and tweak them for the current risk.

Which was good because he had other things to do.

After pouring himself a cup of sludge and exchanging banter with Deeb el-Gharib, he returned to his office, closing the door behind him. Back at his desk he retrieved his mobile phone from his jacket pocket, pressed five buttons (three of them erroneously, which meant he had to come out and go back in again) and managed to activate the phone's Bluetooth.

The Bluetooth on his desk computer was easier to turn on. His mobile and his PC sought each other out, requested permission to connect, raised a four-figure code which he typed into the PC, and then joined like old friends.

He smoked and drank his sludge as he found the images file on his phone. He chose the two pictures he wanted and sent them to his computer one by one.

The man, Mr Carla, might be clever with his party trick of removing the bullets from Gisele's gun, but he hadn't spotted the two quick snaps Merhi had taken of him as he had put his phone away after the call from Lattouf last night.

I have your face, Mister. Let see if the entire security system of Lebanon has anything on record about you...

He had just pressed the Enter button on the third of the three programs he was using when the telephone on his desk rang. An internal call.

He looked at his watch as he picked up the receiver. 09:00.

---

* Certain factions were intending to send two ships, the Junia and the Julia, from Lebanon to the Gaza Strip in defiance of the Israeli naval blockade of Gaza. Through the United Nations, Israel was 'requesting' that Lebanon prevent the boats from departing.

It was the front desk downstairs. "Captain Lattouf is on his way up to you, sir."

"Thank you," said Merhi. "Great."

Really great.

Jbeil, Lebanon 09:00

The *houri* had been right. Eating was difficult and she had wretched several times when she first tried to swallow, her stomach wondering why someone dead would need to eat and trying to reject the attempt. Thankfully she had not actually brought anything back up. She had already embarrassed herself enough in front of these two.

Over breakfast she had noticed that one of the women had a chunk missing from her right forearm. A ragged, dried but bloodied hole, a bite mark. Around the wound was a thin line of black adhesive residue, which meant it had been covered with a dressing until recently. It took Carla only seconds to remember that she had bitten the bitch's arm in the fight. What had happened to the piece of flesh...? She couldn't remember... Oh yes she could, she had swallowed it.

But at least now she had a way of telling them apart. *Houri 1* was the one with the injured arm, the one who had seemed to take great pleasure in massaging her. *Houri 2* was the one who had restrained her, the one interested in whether she shaved her body.

Now she was standing in an old, metre-wide metal bath filled with scented soapy water, her left arm raised and chained to a pipe against the wall. She looked like a perverse Venus de Milo. *Houri 1* was washing her with a sponge, every nook, every cranny, every crack. *Houri 2* was standing back, watching but also guarding.

After the final rinsing, *Houri 1* placed a pink bath towel over her glistening shoulders while *Houri 2* took her right arm, ordering "Step out of the bath." There was a small mat on the floor.

Carla stepped out, having to stretch slightly because her left arm was still cuffed to the pipe. *Houri 1* slid the bath away to the far side of the room and then came back and took hold of two corners of the towel, saying "Come, I will dry you." *Houri 2* kept hold of her right wrist.

Houri 1 was very close, her arms around Carla from the front, rubbing the towel across her back. "After this we have some scented oils which you may like, even some make-up – but you are so beautiful you don't really need any. Make-up is for mortals."

"Why are you doing this?" asked Carla.

"We told you," smiled *Houri 1*, surprised at the question. "We want you to join us."

"And what if I don't want to?"

"We have never failed in a conversion," said *Houri 2*. "It will simply mean yours takes another form."

"The other form being?"

"The freeing of your spirit."

Houri 1 rubbed the towel gently but thoroughly between Carla's legs, staring into her eyes as she did so, smiling.

"Why didn't you just kill me?" asked Carla softly.

The *houri* frowned. "We never kill anyone. We just convert them."

"Okay, why didn't you convert me then?"

Houri 1 knelt, rubbing the towel down her legs. *Houri 2* said, "Self-conversion is always more pure. We respect you as one of us. We wanted to give you a chance for redemption."

Houri 1 left the towel on the floor and stood back up, her hands running up the outside of Carla's legs, stopping on her hips. "And we are going to grant you the greatest honour anyone could ever have."

"You are?"

"Yes. Tomorrow *al-Mahdi's* journey will begin. The liberation of the believers will commence. The world will never be the same again. Tomorrow you will meet The Saviour in person. You will bow down and kiss his robes, his hands, his feet. Not because you are made to but because you will want to."

"And," said *Houri 2*, "you will do whatever he asks of you."

Jonblat, Beirut 09:05

Merhi stood in the doorway of his office and watched Fadi Lattouf rumble down the corridor like a boulder dislodged from a mountainside. He was coming closer and closer and there was nothing Merhi could do to get out of the way.

"Morning of light, my dear friend!" Lattouf was dressed in his blue police uniform, this time without a jacket to conceal the sweat-soaked shirt. He stopped abruptly at the doorway to the General Office. Looking in, he said to somebody inside "I think your Captain will need coffee, please. I'll have one too while you're about it." Then he continued on.

"Morning, Fadi." They shook hands.

As Merhi closed the door, Lattouf said proudly "I have solved it. Did I not say that you could rely on Lattouf?"

"No, you didn't."

"My cousin was a genius.."

"Sit down, Fadi, sit down."

The wooden chair disappeared under the folds of Lattouf's arse.

Merhi took his notepad out of his drawer. The numbers were still on there from two days ago together with his attempts to solve the alphabetical code. 340715354514. He wondered what hare-brained idea Lattouf had come up with now.

"We were going down completely the wrong track," enthused the Palestinian. "It wasn't a code. My cousin was a genius but he wasn't that clever. It isn't a bank account. The phone number was nearer."

"But we dialled it, there was no such number."

"Of course not. Who would my cousin know in Spain?"

Lattouf spoke as if he had ridiculed the theory all along. "But it is a number!"

Merhi was bewildered. "Yes, it is a number."

There was a knock on the door and Sergeant Deeb el-Gharib entered carrying two mugs with a small cardboard carton balanced on top of them. "Your coffee, gentlemen."

"Thank you, Deeb."

"Bless your hands... Deeb," said Lattouf.

el-Gharib placed the coffee on the desk and removed the carton, placing it next to them. "Thought you might like a few baklava. Don't know how fresh they are, left over from the birthday do the other day."

"Thanks," said Merhi, knowing that the birthday do was at least two weeks ago. el-Gharib went back out, closing the door. "You have them, Fadi. I am not hungry."

"Are you sure? Look there are four. Will you not have one?"

"Thank you." Merhi shook his head. "Careful, they might be a bit stale."

All four disappeared into Lattouf's mouth in one go. "No," he mumbled, crumbs in his beard. "They taste fresh enough to me. Could have been made this morning." Swallowing, he licked his fingers one by one then wiped his hands on his trousers.

"Okay," Merhi waved his hand at his notepad. "It's not a code, it's not a bank account, it's not a Spanish telephone number. What is it?"

"What do you have on your computer?" Lattouf nodded at the PC on the desk.

"What? What do you mean?"

"What programs do you have on there?"

"What's that to do with you?"

"Do you have Google Earth?"

"Do I have...? In the name of Christ and your prophet, what are you talking about?"

"You know my cousin's computer? You helped me take it

home."

"*Bien sûr.*"

"My eldest girl, Lana, was on it last night."

"Good, I'm glad it works."

"She was on Google Earth."

"I'm glad she's getting use out of it..." Merhi's voice trailed off as he looked down at the numbers on his pad.

340715354514.

He looked back up. Lattouf was beaming, nodding, his eyes glassy with imminent triumph. "Ah ha, there it is, yes? You can see it? Now you understand?"

Merhi looked down again. "Holy fuck." He grabbed a pencil from the caddy and wrote the numbers on the pad once again, this time in two lines of six, one above the other.

340715

354514

Then he changed it to

+ 34.07 15

- 35.45 14

He sat back in his chair. "They're bloody map co-ordinates. Thirty-four degrees, seven minutes, fifteen seconds north, thirty-five degrees, forty-five minutes, fourteen seconds east. My God."

"And mine too," nodded Lattouf. "He is good."

"Have you looked them up?"

"Ah no," Lattouf looked slightly abashed. "I don't... You know. Can we do it now? Do you have Google Earth on there?"

"Fadi, we don't need Google Earth. We have more sophisticated GPS programs. Wait."

Lattouf drank his coffee (good stuff this, just as he liked it: thick, strong... gritty) while Merhi's fingers played across the keyboard. The fingers paused, played again, paused. Then they were drumming on the desk. Then Merhi said, "Shit, not working. Okay Fadi, Google Earth it is!" More finger movement, more waiting. Then, "Okay, come round."

Lattouf came around, bringing his chair with him. He sat close, leaning forward, staring at the screen. Slightly ripe but not overpowering. He said, "I don't have my glasses."

"Okay," Merhi had the sidebar open, cursor in the *Fly to* box. "How do I do this?"

The first attempt put him in the middle of the Atlantic Ocean, the next somewhere in South America. He humphed. "On the assumption that your cousin wasn't in either of these places, I must be putting it in wrong. Let's see how they do it..." He scrolled around the screen, watching the co-ordinates changing at the bottom. "Okay, let's try this."

He typed in 34 07' 15.0"N, 35 45'14.0"E and pressed enter.

The picture on the screen raised up from South America, heading east at speed. Then it was falling. Falling, falling. Over north Africa. Over the Mediterranean. Over Lebanon.

It stopped.

"Where is it? Where is it?" Lattouf craned forward.

Merhi sat back to let him see. Then he said, "It is Annaya. Saint Charbel."

"Who? What?"

"It is a Christian monastery, Fadi. The Saint Maron Monastery, the tomb of Saint Charbel. At Annaya. Inland from Jbeil."

"Jbeil!"

"Indeed. I think this is the answer, my friend." He nodded in thought. Then he said, "But it raises more questions."

"What was my cousin doing at a Christian monastery?"

"Yes. Working, presumably? I assume he didn't restrict his clients to one religious persuasion?"

Lattouf shook his head. "Not as far as I know."

"So what we have to ask is: what was it he found at this monastery that made him dash down to see you, leaving you this clue on a playing card?" Merhi put a cigarette in his mouth and pushed the packet to Lattouf. The big man took one, bending over the flame from Merhi's lighter.

After each of them had taken a drag, Lattouf said "What had

he found, what had he seen, to get himself killed?"

Jonblat, Beirut 11:00

That was a turn up for the books, thought Merhi, and an unwelcome turn up at that. He could do without this, he had too much on. The murder of Chadi Lattouf was unrecorded, a local death, the body had been disposed of, no longer any proof of foul play – why couldn't it have been left at that, what was one more dead Palestinian?

But no, it couldn't be left at that. The victim was the cousin of the local Palestinian police chief, who also happened to be a friend of his. A friend who, despite his idiotic bumbling, gluttony and unfortunate personal habits, had solved a major clue the victim had left for him.

Shit.

Merhi watched from his office window as the light blue Ford Transit van with the red number plate pulled out into the traffic with much honking of horns and flashing of lights. Lattouf had wished he could stay for lunch (Merhi hadn't offered) but he had to get back. He said something about an eighteen year old who had died in police custody. Had to take the body to the morgue. But he would see him tomorrow, around 08:30. They were going to Annaya to have a look around.

Merhi watched the van go west and then disappear south (two pedestrians crossing the road narrowly escaping with their lives), then he went back to his desk.

Right, what next? He would cut and paste his situation assessment on the Gaza boats crisis and print it out for Major Ghanem (the boss preferred not to have classified documents sent via e-mail) – but first there was something else requiring his attention.

One of the facial recognition programs he was using was flashing orange on the Taskbar on the screen. Two of the programs were still feverishly working away. The program that had reported back was the new system, the custody suite Digital Image Register with the Colossus facial image search engine inside. With anticipation, Merhi clicked on the Taskbar. Okay, Mr Carla, let's see who you really are...

Merhi's face dropped.

He was nobody.

The new system was by far quicker than the other two, but that only meant that it brought him the bad news sooner.

NO MATCH FOUND.

Shit.

That meant that Mr Carla was not in the criminal database of Lebanon, so he had never been naughty here, or at least had never been caught being naughty here.

Merhi drummed his fingers on the desk. If he was Carla's husband, it was logical that he had been living with her in New York (or was he being old-fashioned?). Should he instigate another Interpol check? No, that would be declaring his interest too publically. This one he needed to keep tightly under wraps.

Clicking that he did not want to start a new search, he came out of the program and opened *Word*, clicking on his *Security Assessments* folder.

He saved a new blank document under the title *July 2010*, opened up three old assessments and began to cut and paste.

At 11:50 his mobile phone rang as he was checking a printed copy of his Gaza boats assessment. It was a number he did not recognise.

"Merhi."

"Do you have them?"

For a nano-second he was confused, his attention being on the boats assessment. Was this Major Ghanem? Then he realised it wasn't. "Yes, I have them."

"Good. Hamra Square in half an hour. Have a coffee."

Silence. Merhi looked at the screen. The caller had gone.

Squinting at his phone, he pressed the Menu button and then

the Call Logs. The app opened and he smiled. Well, well, Mr Carla, not so clever after all, are we? You've left your number. It began with code +961 which meant he was using a Lebanese SIM card.

He pressed the Call icon.

And almost immediately an automated voice told him that his call could not be connected.

He tried again. Same result.

Shit. Okay Mr Carla, you were clever, his apologies. You were using the SIM once only, it was probably destroyed by now. No call back and, importantly, no triangulation detection. He shouldn't have expected anything less.

Hamra Square in half an hour it was. He could do with a coffee anyway. It would make a change from sludge.

Merhi left his office at 12:05. Like everyone in the building, he was supposed to shut down his computer when he was going out. Like everyone in the building, he never did except at night. He simply turned the monitor off. To anyone glancing casually, it looked like the computer was turned off.

So he didn't know that, as he began to walk along the corridor, the first facial recognition program on the old facial search engine, the one used by Human Resources, reported back, followed shortly by the second program, Lebanon's national ID card base.

Hamra, Beirut 12:25

Merhi sat at the same table as he had yesterday, triple espresso, a packet of Cedars King Size and a brown A5 envelope in front of him. At midday there was no place in Hamra Square that was not caressed by the sun, so he tilted his head upwards, eyes closed, enjoying the rays.

"*Massah el-khair*, Captain," said a deep voice above his head.

Merhi jumped. Had he nodded off? There had been no one

near when he closed his eyes. He straightened himself up as the man pulled out a chair and sat down.

The man was dressed in jeans and sandals and the same loose collarless white shirt as he had on the previous evening, but it looked like it had been freshly laundered overnight. His long hair was down the sides of his face then tied back in a loose pony-tail.

"This is for me?" The Damascene laid his hand on the A5 envelope.

"The report and the drawing as requested."

"Thank you. I will return them as soon as I can." The Damascene looked up as a woman from the café hovered next to him. He smiled. "A triple espresso please and a mineral water. In the bottle." The woman nodded and went back inside.

"I've got some more information for you," said Merhi.

"You have?"

"But I thought we could make a little trade."

"A trade?"

"I tell you my information, you tell me who or what Sajida is."

The Damascene sighed. "My wife did not tell you about Sajida for a reason. She was protecting you. The knowledge is dangerous."

"Shouldn't I be the judge of that?"

"In this case, no. I think we should both respect my wife's wishes."

"Okay," said Merhi.

There was silence. Merhi took a cigarette from the packet and lit up.

"Well?" nudged The Damascene.

"Well, what?"

"What information do you have to tell me?"

"Sorry, the knowledge is dangerous. I'm protecting you."

The Damascene sat back, staring hard at Merhi's face. Then he smiled again as he saw the woman coming back with his order. *"Shukran."* She placed the cup and bottle of *Sohat* water on the table and left.

"Let me make a little trade with you, Captain." He pushed the coffee towards Merhi. "For you."

"What do you have to trade?"

The Damascene twisted open the cap and swilled water from the bottle. "The information you have for your wife's life."

"You fucking bastard."

"Thank you." He screwed the cap neatly back on. "Well?"

Merhi sighed, beaten. "Your wife first met Captain Himo, the one who supposedly killed himself," he nodded at the envelope, "in my office. I have a recording of their conversation."

The Damascene raised his eyebrows, nodding. "You have a transcript?"

"No. But I can tell you what was said, if you can believe it. Carla told Himo that Sajida was right and The Second Coming was now imminent. The Second Coming! Of The Saviour! Or *al-Mahdi* to you."

"To me? That's very presumptuous of you. Did she say it was The Saviour? Did she use those actual words?"

Merhi paused, thinking. Then he said, "No, actually, she didn't. That was Himo. Carla seemed to think otherwise."

"Himo said it was The Saviour?"

"He said *al-Mahdi* had chosen Lebanon."

A humourless laugh burst from The Damascene's mouth. "Of course he had. Had to be Lebanon, didn't it? It figures."

"It does?"

"Our country is one long mountain with a valley on one side and a coast on the other. Plenty of places to hide, in the mountains."

Merhi really didn't know what he was talking about. He stubbed out his cigarette in an ashtray and pulled over the second cup of coffee.

"I want a copy of the recording," said The Damascene.

"Why? I've told you what's on it."

"You say my wife is dead. I do not believe that." The Damascene stood up, his hand going into his pocket. Merhi tensed. "But if you are right, that is the last recording of her voice. And I want it." He pulled a fold of US dollars from his pocket, peeled off a generous quantity and threw them on the table. "I will be in touch." He picked up the envelope and his bottle of water and walked away, north towards Makdissi Street.

Jonblat, Beirut 13:30

Merhi was back in the office, staring at the voice recorder that he had pulled from his drawer. The memory card with the Carla-Himo conversation was still in the machine from the other day. He considered what he should do. It would serve that bastard right if he wiped the card, that would teach him to threaten Gisele. But what would that achieve, other than to give Merhi a spiteful triumph and perhaps to put Gisele under more threat?

There was no operational need for Mr Carla to have it, but he understood the personal need. His wife was dead. This was a recording of one of her last conversations. It might be the only record ever, anywhere, of her voice.

Telling himself not to be such a shite, Merhi fumbled in the drawer and brought out the voice recorder's USB connection lead. He plugged the smaller end into the machine and the USB into the computer. He switched on the monitor as he unwrapped, with great difficulty, the new memory stick he had bought on his way back from lunch.

The monitor opened on the ISF's official screensaver as he pushed the memory stick into a free USB port.

He then spent several minutes trying to copy the conversation from the voice recorder to the computer. He made a mental note to delete the file from the computer as soon as it had been copied to the stick. He didn't know what he was dealing with but whatever it was it was dangerous and he didn't want this incriminating evidence sitting there, implicating him.

While he was waiting for the import to complete, he noticed the other tabs on the Taskbar, the other two facial recognition programs. Well, he could take a guess at what these were going to say. Nothing. He clicked on the first tab, the national ID card base.

NO MATCH FOUND.

Well now, there was a surprise. Not. So despite Mr Carla 'not denying' that he was Lebanese from Tripoli, he had no national ID card. So he wasn't a Lebanese national at all. Just who the hell was he?

Merhi checked on the download, one minute to go, and clicked on the second tab, the Human Resources database.

And his jaw dropped.

Oh my God!

MATCH FOUND.

There, sitting side by side, was the photo he had put into the program and another black and white picture, obviously some years old. At first there seemed no similarity. The old picture was the sort of one that you would get on an identification or building entry card. Slightly blurred showing that little care had been taken, just another photo in a long line of photos. It was of a man in his thirties, hair cropped short, strong face, staring at the camera.

Merhi's picture was in colour, had necessarily been rushed, and showed a not-quite-full-on picture of Mr Carla, long black hair down either side of his face, looking – disconcertingly – at an out-of-picture Gisele. His face was leaner, stronger, older than the face in the other picture. Was it the same?

The computer said that there was a fifty-five per cent chance of a match, and there were various graphs and charts at the side referencing point-marks on each of the faces.

Fifty-five per cent! What good was that? There was a fifty-five per cent chance Jihad Merhi looked like President Bashar Assad of Syria, less thirty centimetres in height, plus ten years in age, less the moustache, plus a few centimetres around the waist...

Fifty-five per cent was not good enough. Such a percentage would never be accepted as proof of anything in a court of law. Nevertheless, he looked at the biographical information.

```
NAME:      MARWAN MEBARAK
DOB:       01 JUNE 1967/22 SAFAR 1387
RANK:      CAPTAIN
UNIT:      COMMANDO
LOCATION:  BAHJAT GHANEM NORTH
DOD:       10 JANUARY 2000/3 SHAWWAL 1420
```

And there it was. In that last line. Proof that fifty-five per cent was no good. DOD. Date of Death. This poor bastard had been a serving soldier, killed in the line of duty probably. It was just possible, Merhi supposed, that Captain Marwan Mebarak had been some sort of distant relative to Mr Carla, a cousin or something. Maybe he would drop the name in conversation, see what reaction he got.

But Mr Carla was not a Lebanese national, the databases proved it. Which begged the question: what was he? Who was he?

Realising he would probably never know, Merhi went back to the Voice screen, confirmed the import was complete, and clicked on the *Copy To F: Drive* icon.

Jbeil, Lebanon 23:59

Carla had slept well. Not the nightmare oblivion of her previous *faux* death, but real, proper sleep. But she only ever slept in three hour bursts, always had, so now she was awake.

She was on the bunk bed in her small, cell-like room, staring through the supports of the upper bunk into the blackness of the ceiling. She was no longer handcuffed to the bed frame, and a new thin mattress had appeared during the day, so she was in relative comfort for her situation. But she was still naked.

As the *houri* had promised, she had been pampered. A full, lingering body massage (the hands of *Houri 2* lingering just a little too long in certain parts, trying to ascertain whether she shaved or was naturally without body hair), a scalp massage, a hair wash and condition and blow dry. It was almost as if she was the twins' pet, a plaything. A living doll.

They had fed and watered her, gradually and carefully, throughout the day. All three of them had been pleased that there was no more bodily rejection of its intake.

But the one thing they had not touched were her hands. She couldn't have a manicure, she had no nails, just flaking scabs. When she got back to New York her nail technician, Emma at Middleton's on Madison Avenue, was going to have a fit.

Carla smiled at the subconscious positivity. *When* she got back to New York, not *if*. That was good. But how she was going to do it she did not know. She was captive, stark naked, without fingernails or her hairclip against two extremely proficient – what were they? Soldiers, like they said? Killers? Disciples?

The thought of disciples brought Selim Himo into her mind. They had admitted he was one of them, so all the stuff he had told her about there being an Eyes Only file at the highest level, about people knowing that the so-called *al-Mahdi* was in Lebanon, was a crock of shit. No one knew. She should have realised that, alarms bells should have rung when Himo said about the file, but she had no reason to distrust the guy who was her new boss. Of course there would not be a file, the secret was too dangerous. Only the chosen few would know it until the time was right. And Lebanon was incidental, chosen because of its terrain and its convenience and for no other reason. Soon it would be just a backdrop in the story. This time the Wise Men need not come from the east, their Saviour was going to them.

Their Saviour! She laughed ruefully. Well, there were many who would think he was. One man's *al-Mahdi* was another man's *ad-Dajjal*.

And tomorrow she would be meeting him...

She got up off the bed and went over and peed in the small commode in the corner.

As she lay back down, she thought of Marwan. How many days had she now been out of contact? He would have instigated their contingency procedures the third time she had failed to answer his calls. He would be looking for her. Without doubt he would be in Lebanon by now. He might even be close by.

Please find me, my husband.

Gently, she drifted off back to sleep.

22 July 2010
10 Sha'ban 1431

Jbeil, Lebanon 07:30

For breakfast, *Houri 1* prepared *baiid baladi,* fresh country eggs, fried in *awarma,* preserved meat fat, saying that they had a busy day ahead and they needed their strength. There was also yesterdays' leftover *mana'eesh* and *kunafi.*

Carla ate well, sitting naked at the table with the two fully-dressed women. She understood the reason for her continued nakedness and she had not queried it. It was standard procedure with prisoners considered dangerous. Keeping them naked was not only intended to humble and psychologically weaken them in front of others, it also ensured they had no concealed weapons (or easily-accessible weapons if they were considering internal concealment). It did not worry Carla one bit.

"Have you considered our offer?" asked *Houri 1* at the end of the meal, wiping her mouth on a tissue.

"What offer?" asked Carla, knowing only too well.

"Will you convert?"

"Or," said *Houri 2,* "will you be converted?"

Carla rubbed crumbs off her fingers onto the paper plate in front of her. "I am flattered that you consider me like you."

"You are a trained soldier, no?" *Houri 2.*

"In a manner of speaking. I am also loyal."

"As we are."

"You've killed people."

"We've converted people."

"Okay. Whatever."

"We are sure you have killed people," said *Houri 1*. "We have experienced your skill."

Carla said nothing.

Houri 2 stood up. "We have to go out today. The great journey is beginning." With a swift, unexpected movement she grabbed Carla's arms, pinning them behind her.

"And as you are not yet one of us," said *Houri 1*, also rising. "We must take precautions."

Houri 2 lifted Carla off of the chair and, before she could kick out, *Houri 1* had grabbed her feet.

"Don't worry," said *Houri 1*, "we're not going to hurt you."

"We just need you restrained till we get back."

Carla tried a token buck but she knew it would be useless. Please, she thought, no more drugs.

Houri 1 seemed to read her mind. "We want you fully alert," she said as they carried her back to her room. "But we can't have you making a noise or causing a fuss while we're not here." She dropped Carla's legs next to the bunk as *Houri 2* increased her grip, pulling her closer.

Houri 1 went over to a box in the opposite corner of the room to the commode. Carla stared, frowning. That had not been there before. The *houri* pulled out a fold of heavy textile with rope on the top. Turning back, she said "We'll be gone a few hours, no more."

"And he will be with us when we return," said *Houri 2* close to her ear. "*al-Mahdi*, Brother Malek, will wish to convert you personally."

Bourj el-Barajneh, Beirut 08:30

Jihad Merhi bipped the horn as he pulled up in his Land Cruiser outside *chez Lattouf*. Already the day was hot and the car's air conditioning was roaring dutifully in the background. No matter that he was a native, the high summers of Lebanon still roasted him alive, and at this time of year it would be only marginally cooler up in the mountains. He had dressed in a blue cotton *Lacoste* polo shirt and fawn linen trousers.

A few minutes later the Lattoufs' front door opened and, to much shouting of goodbyes and Allah's blessings, Fadi came out.

Merhi's eyes shot heavenwards. He was dressed in his grey polyester suit again! Full jacket, the works – this time including a garish tie, which might have been in fashion forty years ago – and of course the counterfeit *Ray-Ban* sunglasses. In his hand he carried a bulky package.

"A little over-dressed, aren't we?" commented Merhi as the big man slid his award-winning arse onto the passenger seat.

Lattouf stopped, his right cheek still half out of the car. Pushing his sunglasses up onto his dome, he looked Merhi up and down then looked at himself. "I thought I would dress respectfully. We are visiting one of your major religious shrines."

"Fadi, it is more of a tourist destination. Yes, it is a shrine, yes it is a monastery, but dressed like that you will stand out like... like a Muslim trying not to stand out."

"Shall I go change?"

"No, no. Damage limitation. Take off the jacket."

Lattouf stepped out, took off his jacket and threw it onto the back seat on top of a folded road map.

"Now lose the cat's vomit."

"The what?"

"That thing around your neck. It cannot be called a tie."

Lattouf yanked it off but Merhi stopped him throwing it onto the jacket. "No, no. I said lose it. You should never be seen in that, have some self-respect."

Lattouf looked around, confused. Then he simply dropped the tie in the gutter.

"Good," nodded Merhi. "Now undo a few buttons on your

shirt – not too many, we don't want to scare the mountain wildlife... There, that's better. You'll feel cooler too."

Lattouf climbed back in, car dipping to the right, door slamming.

"What's in there?" Merhi nodded at the package on Lattouf's lap as he released the parking brake and checked his mirrors.

Lattouf smiled. "Our lunch. Nada made it for us – she sends Allah's blessings, by the way. Do you like goat and rice?"

"I can never think of anything else." Merhi pulled away into the traffic, the slight jerk as the car moved making Lattouf's sunglasses roll back down his sweat-soaked head and plop back onto the bridge of his nose.

Annaya, Lebanon 10:00

Paradise and Love sat in the Jeep Wrangler Ultimate, hard top on, windows open, staring at the main monastery door, one set of brown eyes, one set of green eyes (Love was now in the lead thirty-nine to thirty-seven). As soon as they saw Brother Malek emerge, they got out, bowing reverentially.

"*Salaam, oh Malek,*" they greeted in unison.

Malek was in his full-length *burnus*, hood up, feet sandaled, and he was in a no-nonsense mood as he hurried over to them. "*Salaam.* Let us go." He climbed into the back of the Jeep as Paradise held the door open. "I do not like dealing with these people," he said, referring to the fact that he had had to give the Father Superior the final farewell donation himself. "That should be your task. Why they will not let you in there I do not know. They are *kafirs,* I wish I could convert them all."

The twins exchanged looks as Paradise went round to the driver's side and Love climbed into the passenger seat. Once they were settled inside, Love said "It is over now, Brother. After all these years, your final journey has begun."

The Jeep moved off, Paradise driving slowly out of the complex, avoiding other visitors and their vehicles. Malek kept his head still in the back seat, not looking out of the window, hood up and falling forward over his face.

"You have disposed of the Netbook?" he asked.

"As you instructed," said Love. "It has been broken like the bread of the eucharist and scattered to the winds."

"And my *argileh*?"

"It is safe and waiting for you"

They reached the exit and Paradise picked up speed, braking firmly again as a car came round the first hairpin too far into the middle of the road. She negotiated the bend herself and then accelerated again.

"Do you have anything for me now?" asked Malek.

Love opened the compartment on the dashboard and held up two items of equal length: the silver tube containing a cigar and a blue and white wrapped candy bar. "Which would you like?"

Malek's hand reached forward. "I'll take both."

"And we have something else for you at base," said Paradise over her shoulder. "As promised. We think you will like it."

Without commenting, Malek unpeeled the top half of the candy bar and it disappeared up into his hood.

At the next hairpin Paradise slowed to avoid a motorbike heading up the mountain, then the three of them settled in silence for the journey down into Jbeil.

"Hell's teeth," mumbled Merhi as he swerved right to avoid the Jeep then over-compensated back again. "Bloody tourists."

Lattouf had dropped the opened, and nearly finished, packet of goat and rice onto the floor as he rolled first one way then the other, also popping out a small fart. He turned in the seat, looking back down the mountainside. "Did you see who it was?" he asked.

Merhi sniffed. "Is that you or the food?"

Lattouf turned back. "Probably both. Sorry. Are you sure you won't have some?"

Not if it smells like rotten eggs with a sulphur sauce, thought

Merhi. He shook his head, "Thank you."

With great effort Lattouf strained forward between his own legs, gathered together the food that had spilled onto the car mat and rolled it back into the package. He straightened up, package in hand and once more began to eat, using his fingers.

"Who was it?" asked Merhi.

"What?"

"You asked me if I saw who it was, in the Jeep."

"Oh. It was the twins."

"What twins?"

"Do you remember? When we were in Jbeil. The two women we saw, we walked behind them along the street."

"I wouldn't know, I only saw the back of them."

"It was them. Small world, eh?"

"Indeed."

Lattouf finished the rice and screwed up the paper, looking around for somewhere to put it. They pulled in to the parking area.

"Leave it in the door," instructed Merhi as he applied the parking brake. "I'll see to it later. But - " he fiddled on his arm rest and the back window behind Lattouf popped open just a centimetre. "I think we need to let some air into the car." *I'll have a full valet and fumigation done later.*

They both got out, the car's lights flashing twice as Merhi pressed the remote locking button on his key fob. "Right," he said, admiring the view out over the mountainside and then looking to his right to Saint Charbel's church. "So, what did your cousin see here that was so shocking?"

"What did he see here that got him chased down into Beirut?" pondered Lattouf as he hitched up his too-short trousers then pulled them back out of his anal crevice.

"What did he see here that got him killed?"

"And who was it that chased him? Let us find out."

Merhi and Lattouf set off up the slope towards the church.

Jbeil, Lebanon 11:00

Paradise stopped the Jeep on Boulevard al-Mina opposite the top of Rue St John. Love got out, holding the back door open for Brother Malek. Although robed monks were not an uncommon sight in Jbeil (many were pilgrims visiting the Church of St John the Baptist and the Greek Orthodox Church, or just visitors from the mountain monasteries), one with his hood up on such a hot day might attract attention, especially if he was accompanied by two tall, blonde, young female twins. So they had decided to pull up as close to base as possible and to have only one twin accompany him. From here it was just a short walk down Rue St John to the old boarded up shop behind the Mayadoun Bookshop.

They waited for traffic to pass then Love and Brother Malek walked across the boulevard and passed through the entrance in the rampart walls.

Paradise drove off to the car park up by the Seven Seas Restaurant.

"Welcome, Malek," said Love as she unlocked the padlock and pushed open the front door.

"May Allah's blessings be upon this abode." Brother Malek entered into a large, dim room, which used to be the public area of the shop.

"We have electricity," said Love. "They never turned it off, you know what the Lebanese are like. Although it does go off when they have their daily power cuts. Mind your eyes." She flicked a switch on the wall and a bare bulb hanging from a threadbare wire in the ceiling radiated forty watts illuminating a small table containing breakfast remnants.

"You are hungry?" asked Love. "I will be preparing dinner later, but I can ask my sister to bring in *shawarma* and pastries." She took her mobile phone from her belt.

"I have eaten." The hood turned towards Love. "But thank

you." He seemed calmer now he was here. Now the final journey had begun.

Love put her phone back on her belt. "You would like something to drink?"

"Water."

From a small coolbag below the table she produced a small bottle of *Sohat*, handing it over to the monk. He cracked it open and drank.

"We have a room especially for you for tonight," said Love as he put the bottle down. "*Yalla*, come please." She led the way down a narrow corridor to the very back of the premises, stopping by a door padlocked on the outside, key still in the lock. "Naturally we no longer need this," she said as she turned the key and removed the padlock. At that moment they heard the front door opening. Love smiled. "Perfect timing." She raised her voice. "We are back here, sister!"

Paradise appeared at the other end of the corridor, a paper carrier bag in her right hand. As she walked towards them, she said "I bought some *shawarma* and *baklava* anyway. We must all retain our strength for the journey to come."

From underneath the hood, Malek said "But she did not phone you."

"She didn't need to," said Paradise.

"Saves a fortune on phone bills," said Love. "Sister, I was just about to show Malek his present."

Paradise nodded and Love pushed open the door. The light from the corridor cast an oblong into the room. Malek gestured for Love to enter ahead of him.

"There is no light in here," explained Love. "Just a small window. But we have lanterns if you require them later."

The light from the corridor and the light from the small window cast as much light as the forty watt bulb outside. Malek stepped into the room. In front of him a small figure was standing, tied with rope by both wrists to either end of the frame of a bunk bed. The figure wore a white, hooded towelling robe, the hood up covering the face. It moved as they entered, raising its head, trying to see. The feet below were bare and obviously female.

"Our latest disciple," said Love. "She wishes to convert. We think she is worthy."

"But of course she needs your vetting," said Paradise.

Love stepped forward and put both her hands on either side of the hood. Gently, almost tenderly, she pushed it back off the head, caressing and tidying the long black hair as she lifted it out.

The captive's mouth was gagged with a tight swatch of silk, thick red lips not quite able to join together over it. Heavy mascara and dark eyeshadow enhanced the blackness of her actual eyes.

Love undid the belt, allowing the gown to fall open, revealing the naked body underneath. Her face close, she reached behind the captive's head and undid the gag. She removed a lipstick smudge from the captive's chin with her thumb and then stood back, as if she was showing off a prize pet. She said, "Let me introduce you to The Djinn. She is one of us. She is skilled. Djinn, meet Malek, your king. Our Saviour."

"Leave us," said Malek after a few moments.

"Do you wish us to untie her?" asked Love.

"No, I will do that when I am ready. Go."

Obediently the twins left the room, closing the door behind them.

Carla looked at the robed figure as she moved her jaw, loosening it after the restriction of the gag. She noticed the hood go slightly up and down as he looked at her body. Apart from that he did not move at all. After a few moments he asked, "You are like them?" He had an accent but she understood him perfectly.

"They say I am."

The hood nodded. "Good answer. Do you belong to the

Colonel?"

"No."

"But my *houri* rate you."

"Apparently."

A pause, then he asked "You will join us?"

"Do I have a choice?"

"I think the choice would have been explained to you. You will join us of your own free will or an alternative conversion will take place. It really doesn't matter which. Soon the whole world will be converted."

She looked at the hood and asked softly, penitentially, "May I join you?"

Malek raised his hands, palms outstretched. "I will test your worthiness. If you pass, who knows? You may be my favourite disciple of all." He raised his hands further, grasped the edge of his hood and casually pushed it back and off.

Carla stared at his face, at the proof. All along.

That Sajida was right.

Annaya, Lebanon 12:00

"Can't you ask them?" suggested Fadi Lattouf.

"No I bloody well can't," said Jihad Merhi grumpily. Another two hours of his life wasted. They were walking back down the side of the monastery, having walked up as far as a field and then deciding to turn back. It was quiet here, visitors didn't come up this far. "What am I supposed to do? Go and knock on the head guy's door and say 'Excuse me, but do you have anything up here that will scare a man so much that he will be chased down the mountainside into Beirut and murdered?' I feel as frustrated as you do, Fadi, but short of staking out the place I don't see what further I can do. We have looked everywhere, seen nothing."

They passed the open window of a monastery washroom but neither of them thought anything of it.

"Will you do it then?" asked Lattouf.

"Do what?"

"Stake the place out."

"On what grounds? I'd need a good reason, which I don't have."

"My cousin."

"Not good enough. So he writes these map co-ordinates on a card. Might not be anything to do with his death. We might be barking up the wrong mountainside."

"I don't think so. Lattouf feels it in his gut. Something happened up here."

"Like what?"

"Who knows? A ghost? You liked that little church but I found it scary."

"That's because you're used to a mosque. Our 'idol images' as you call them frightened you."

"That museum was scary too. The saint's robes with his body secretions and stains on it, I didn't like that at all."

"No, there I know what you mean. You think Chadi was frightened by the ghost of Saint Charbel? Or, being a Muslim, just by this whole place?"

Lattouf shrugged. "I don't know, I am not Christian."

"Well, Christian saints are not normally in the habit of appearing to people and scaring the shit out of them." Actually, on reflection, maybe they were, but he wasn't going to go there.

"But isn't it one of your major concepts that the dead shall rise again?"

Merhi shook his head. "Oh God, Fadi, you are walking proof that a little knowledge is a dangerous thing. It doesn't mean that at all."

"Oh."

To avoid further theological discussion, Merhi asked "Hungry?"

"Of course."

"There's a refreshment place down here. *Yalla*. Or are you too full from the rice?"

"What rice?"

Within ten minutes the staff of the refreshment kiosk were telling customers that they had run out of food, only drinks would be served for the rest of the day.

After thirty minutes sitting near the refreshment kiosk they walked back down the slope towards the car, Lattouf finishing off the last of the kiosk's potato chips. Merhi smoked.

"So, that is it?" Chip slivers bounced around on Lattouf's beard. "We are giving up again? Another dead end... just another dead Palestinian."

"Unless you can give me any form of probable cause, any new evidence, there is nothing more I can do. This is an unreported death, remember, and you were quick to dispose of the body."

"In accordance with our teachings."

"Well, sometimes teachings and criminal investigations don't go well together. I have no body, no tangible evidence of murder - "

"You saw the wound on the body yourself!"

"My examination of a body which no longer exists is not tangible evidence. We do not even have photographs."

"But you know he was murdered."

"Me knowing is not good enough. Is there nothing else, Fadi?" *Please let there not be.* "He didn't do any other little trick? Nothing popped out of anywhere else?"

Lattouf gave him a sideways look.

They reached the Land Cruiser, the vehicle's lights flashing as Merhi pressed the key fob. Lattouf screwed up the empty chip packet and threw it over the mountainside.

"Not very respectful," scolded Merhi.

Lattouf looked chasten. "I am sorry. I just feel frustrated. Please excuse me, Abu Samer." He shook his head. "My cousin must have left that clue for some reason. Have we missed something?"

Merhi took one last drag on his cigarette, pinched the end and launched the butt over the mountainside to follow the chip packet. "Come on, Fadi. Let's go home."

They climbed in and were soon negotiating the hairpins on the downward run.

Neither of them noticed the envelope on the floor in the back behind Lattouf. The one that had been slipped through the open back window of the car.

Bourj el-Barajneh, Beirut 15:00

Much to Merhi's relief, Lattouf had not moped or kept on about his cousin on the drive back. He was more interested in why Merhi did not use the inbuilt satnav on his dashboard. "It is marvellous what these things can do," said the expert. "You witnessed Google Earth yourself. It unravelled my cousin's clue for us."

"Satnav is pointless, Fadi," argued Merhi. "Just something else that everyone's been conned into thinking they cannot live without. What's wrong with a good old map? And they always have women's voices. There is only room for one woman's voice in this car."

"Please tell Gisele I wish her Allah's blessings."

"I will. Thank you. She'll be seeing you at *Eid*." Merhi could sense that Lattouf wanted to be invited back for dinner today but that was not going to happen, he had far too much work on and he was expecting a call at any time from Mr Carla asking for the voice recording.

Merhi slowed as they cruised down Annan Street, stopping just short of Lattouf's front door. They clasped hands. "Thank you, my friend, thank you," said Lattouf, sorrow but appreciation in his voice. "Believe me, I truly know that I ask a lot of our friendship. You are very gracious."

"Fadi..."

"If I think of anything else I'll give you a call." He stepped out of the car.

"Fadi..."

"Yes?"

"Allah's blessings upon you, my friend."

Lattouf nodded. "Thank you." He opened the back door, picked up his jacket which had fallen onto the floor, then slammed the door closed.

He stood on the sidewalk, smiling, raising a hand as Merhi pulled back out into the traffic and drove away. As the Land Cruiser disappeared, the smile turned into a grin. A big, naughty grin. He draped the jacket over his arm.

As he opened his front door he let go a stentorian breaking of wind. "Surprise, my family!" he called out. "Baba's home early. Isn't that nice?"

After embracing his wife, throwing Little Wissam into the air three times and (thankfully) catching him, and being ignored by the rest of the children who were jostling around the new computer, Lattouf went into his bedroom.

He had been naughty and he knew it. But he told himself he had done it as a favour to his friend Jihad, to force him to use new technology like the Lattoufs did. Once Jihad had tried the satnav in the car he would use it forever. And now he would have to – because Fadi had swiped the map he had seen on the back seat of the car!

Cousin Chadi had not been the only member of the family that was adroit with his hands. Fadi had seen the map on the back seat earlier. It had fallen on the floor along with his jacket when they were negotiating the curves on the mountainside. When he had retrieved his jacket he had purloined the map also, draping the jacket over it so it could not be seen. A master prestidigitator!

He threw the jacket onto the bed and looked at the map in his hand.

The map and the envelope.

His eyebrows rose and his mouth opened. He had not seen an envelope in the car! How had that happened? He must have picked it up when he picked up the map. Hiding it under his jacket had concealed it not only from Jihad but from himself also!

Shaitan's scrotum!

He would have to give his friend a ring, apologise, say it was accidentally picked up with his jacket (which was true), arrange to return it. Maybe Jihad would ask him to drive up to Jounieh with it tonight. Around eight o'clock, the time when the Merhi's had their dinner...

The thought made him realise he was on the point of expiring through starvation. Nada would not have started their evening meal yet, but he wondered if he could persuade her to bring it forward. He might have wasted away by tonight. He would eat first then phone Jihad afterwards.

Leaving the jacket, map and envelope on the bed, he went back to the family room, thoughts of Little Wissam on toast with a mustard relish popping into his mind. Not seriously, of course. Well, only in extreme circumstances...

Jonblat, Beirut 15:50

Merhi had pulled into the parking area behind the State Security offices. Now he sat in his car, engine running, looking up at the building, then looking at his watch, thinking. It was nearly four o'clock. Really, after his day with Lattouf up at Annaya, he didn't feel like going in to the office. The reports on visiting heads of state, street security, parliamentary discussions, press conferences, threatened attacks by the Jews, you name it, could wait until tomorrow. And no doubt there was today's shite waiting for him on his desk upstairs.

He looked at his phone, in the well next to him behind the transmission stick, his mind going off on a different tack. Why hadn't Mr Carla phoned? The memory stick with the copied Carla and Himo conversation was burning a hole in his pocket.

He lit up a cigarette, the nicotine helping him to make the decision.

Putting the transmission into Drive, he manoeuvred back out into Bank of Lebanon Street. Soon he was heading east. Going home.

As he had not gone up to the office, Merhi did not know that on his desk, along with today's shite, was the response from Interpol relating to the facial composite drawing he had submitted. A positive identification had been made.

Jounieh, Lebanon 17:45

He was looking forward to a shower and then maybe an hour on the balcony with Johnnie Walker, watching the sun reluctantly setting over the Mediterranean. Then he would enjoy a good bottle of wine and whatever delicious concoction Gisele was preparing for dinner. She was already in the kitchen. As he came through the front door, he could hear the voices on the radio, she liked to listen to *VDL* while she cooked.

Smiling, he crossed the hallway and went into the kitchen – but she was not there, and the radio was not on. She must be in the living room with the TV.

He walked further down the hall, opened the living room door, and stopped dead.

"Husband," Gisele looked up smiling from one of the couches, large glass of red wine in her hand. "You're home early. We have a visitor."

Sitting on the couch opposite, tumbler of mineral water in his hand, was the man Merhi called Mr Carla.

"An unexpected pleasure," said Jihad insincerely, picking up a glass from the cabinet against the wall and sitting down on the couch next to his wife. On the table between the two couches was a bottle of *Massaya* red wine, olives, nuts and savoury biscuits.

"Yes, isn't it?" said Gisele.

Jihad picked up the bottle of wine and filled his glass to the brim.

"I was passing. Thought I'd pop in," explained The Damascene. His long black hair was down, hanging loosely either side of his face. He was wearing a black T shirt, usual jeans and sandals. "Kill two birds with one stone... as it were. I spent the day up at Annaya." His eyes held Jihad's.

Jihad took a mouthful of wine. "You been following me?"

"In a manner, yes. I wanted to talk to you, to give you back the report and the picture. But you had that large gentleman with you. A friend of yours?"

"Another case. Nothing to do with you."

Gisele leant back into the corner of the couch, pulling her legs up under her. The day was hot, she was wearing denim shorts and a yellow cotton vest. "You boys getting your dicks out again?" she asked, amused.

The Damascene smiled. Jihad said, "My dick stays right here. Where it belongs." He glanced at his wife's bare thighs.

The Damascene let the moment hang while he drank some water, then he asked "Did you get the envelope? I slipped it through your car window."

"What envelope?"

"I was returning the report and picture."

"Didn't see it. Must be on the floor, maybe under one of the seats."

"The report tells me nothing. An interesting picture, though."

"You know who it is?"

"I've heard of them. Thought it was a myth. Didn't think they would operate outside of their own territory. He must be sub-contracting."

"Them? There is more than one?"

"Oh yes."

Jihad waited, expectant, feeling more enamoured with the visitor. At last he would be told something. He drank more wine. When Mr Carla remained silent, he said "Well?"

"Well?"

"Aren't you going to tell me who it is? I can find her and arrest her. Put out an ATL*, make it official."

The Damascene gave a small laugh. "You think it is that easy? You will not locate this one unless she wishes to be located."

"Who is she?"

"I have no name."

"What is she?"

"That, my friend, is a good question. A bodyguard. An assassin... A *houri*?"

"A *what*?"

"Never mind."

"Jesus Christ, this is getting too mystical for me. *al-Mahdi, ad-Dajjal, houri*. What the hell is going on?"

The Damascene frowned. "How do you know these things?"

"Here," Merhi pulled out the memory stick from his trouser pocket and threw it onto the table. "The conversation between Carla and Himo."

The Damascene leant forward and picked it up.

Unfolding her tanned legs, Gisele stood up. "I'm going to make dinner. Will you stay? I'm making *samkeh harra*. You like spiced fish?"

"Yes, I do. And I would be honoured to stay, thank you."

Gisele turned to her husband. "Jihad, why don't you let our guest listen to that on the computer?"

"I - "

"It's no good to him otherwise, is it?"

Jihad stared at her legs and bottom as they left the room.

---

* Attempt To Locate

Then he looked back at Mr Carla and asked, "Who is Sajida?"

"It is best - "

"If I don't know. Yes, yes, yes. You're protecting me, blah, blah. Jesus!" He was shaking his head as he stood up. "Come. The computer is in my study. I'll leave you to listen to that. I have an appointment out on the balcony."

Bourj el-Barajneh, Beirut 20:30

Despite his pleading, demanding, cajoling, shouting, and whimpering, Nada Lattouf was not going to prepare the evening meal any earlier than usual. Had her husband forgotten he was on a diet? Nevertheless, the puppy dog eyes made her take pity on him and she had given him some nuts and the very last remnants of yesterday's goat and rice, which had tided him over until dinner (she never knew that by those actions she had saved Little Wissam Lattouf from a fate worse than could possibly be imagined).

After a dinner of giblets, bread and rice, Fadi announced that he was going to the bedroom as he had work to do. Nada knew that this was a euphemism for having a nap, getting some peace and quiet from the children. The day her husband brought work home was the day she would know it was time for him to quit his job.

Closing the door, Fadi sat down on the bed, the mattress collapsing its usual twenty-five centimetres as The Arse descended upon it. He lifted his jacket and threw it to one side, flicking away the map and picking up the envelope. He turned it over in his hands. It had no address or any other writing on it. The flap was unsealed.

He must phone Jihad, tell him he had it safe; he might be missing it. The Merhis would have eaten by now so it could wait until the morning.

Wonder what was in it? The open flap called to him like a siren enticing sailors onto the rocks. No, he mustn't look at another person's mail, it was private.

He put his hand inside and brought out a stapled A4 document and a loose sheet. The document looked like an official report of some kind, an investigation into a death. Well it wasn't Chadi so he didn't care.

The loose sheet was blank on the side he was looking at. He turned it over. It was a drawing of a head –

He frowned, squinting, bringing the sheet closer to his face and then holding it at arm's length.

He went over to a drawer and fumbled inside for a pair of Nada's eyeglasses. He put them on, pink horn-rims, and stared at the drawing once more.

Well, Allah be praised, what was Jihad doing with a picture of her...?

Jounieh, Lebanon 21:00

Gisele was bringing fruit to the table when they heard Jihad's mobile ringing out in the hall. Normally he would have left it, checking on the Missed Call later and ringing back if necessary. But it was a good excuse for him to leave the table. He was getting mightily pissed off with the attention Mr Carla was receiving. Sympathy only went so far. Carla might be missing, or even dead, but that did not mean that Gisele had to step into the breach.

"Excuse me," he left the room as Gisele was unpeeling a banana, laughing at something Mr Carla had said.

He lifted his phone from the hall table, looking at the screen. Oh good heavens, it was Lattouf. He looked back at the dining room, looked at the phone, and decided to answer it.

"Merhi."

"Evening of joyous discovery, my friend!"

"Merhaba, Fadi." *Not another meaningless clue, please.*

"I am sorry to call you at this hour, you must be having your dinner, no?"

"Just finished."

"Oh." He sounded curiously disappointed. "Good. I was going to call you in the morning, but I thought you might be wondering where it was."

"Sorry? Wondering where what was?"

"The envelope."

"What envelope?"

"I accidentally picked it up from your car when I picked up my jacket."

"Envelope...?" He remembered what Mr Carla had said. "Ah yes, never mind. You can give it to me when we meet."

"It is not urgent?"

"Just some reports that... I left there. I have copies. But thanks for ringing."

"The papers slid out of the envelope... I, er, dropped it."

"Never mind, there's no state secrets there."

"Are you sure there are no secrets, my friend?"

"What do you mean?"

"You are a sly one, you know. I think you have been kidding Lattouf."

Merhi heard laughter from the dining room. "Fadi, I have a guest for dinner. I need to get back. What are you talking about?"

"Those twins, the ones from Jbeil, who we saw in the Jeep today."

"What about them?"

"You said you have only seen them from the back."

"Yes?"

"You crafty dog, you have a drawing of their face!"

Merhi literally staggered backwards.

"I have what?"

"This is a drawing of the twins' face. I have it here in my hand right now. The eyes are a bit funny, but it's them all right. Have you been doing doodles and having naughty thoughts?"

"Have I been...?" Merhi was aware that his mouth had dropped open but there was nothing he could do about it. His muscles had frozen. *What?* "I..." He was classically confused. Reason, thought and speech were fighting a raging battle in his head with nobody winning.

"Hello? Are you there, my friend?" There was a thumping as the phone was bashed up and down at the other end.

"Y-yes... Yes, I'm here," said Merhi. He couldn't believe it. *What?* "Fadi, I'm... I'm... What are you saying? Are you sure? That is the twins from Jbeil?"

"As if you did not know, you bull. Naturally your secret is safe with me, fellow men and all that."

"My secret...?" Merhi was standing in the middle of the hallway, phone held to his right ear, his left hand held to his head. "I don't... Well, fuck me."

"You should be saying that to the picture!" raucous all-boys-together laughter boomed out of the phone.

Merhi was breathing heavily, his heart pounding. Not again, surely? Surely The Idiot Lattouf had not bungled his way into solving another case? "Fadi, listen to me. My office, nine o'clock in the morning. Bring the drawing with you."

"And the report."

"I don't care about the report. And tell no one. Don't mention it to Nada, or any one of your team. Keep it to yourself."

"Mother is the word. But there are two of them, these twins. One isn't spare, is she? Sticky seconds? Or leftovers of any kind?"

"What? Don't... don't be such a filthy bastard. I don't know how you do it but I think you've just cracked another case."

"I have?"

Merhi was shaking his head. "Nothing short of amazing."

"I am, thank you. I keep telling Nada that."

Merhi gave an ironic, sarcastic laugh. "You're a crazy man. Don't happen to know who Sajida is as well, do you?"

Lattouf gave a loud laugh, joining in the fun, co-conspirators, a crack team, him and his mate Jihad. He said, "Sajida? Of course I know who she is, doesn't everybody?"

Five minutes later an ashen-faced Jihad Merhi returned to the dining room. Gisele had the stones of two plums on the plate in front of her, and she and Mr Carla were enjoying a little humour (something about Syria and the King of Lebanon). She looked up, smiling. "Who was it?"

"Lattouf." He stared at Mr Carla, his face hard. Then he went over to the sideboard and took two bottles of Johnnie Walker whisky from underneath. Reaching further in, he brought out a packet of two hundred Cedars King Size cigarettes. He tucked the cigarettes under his arm and carried a whisky bottle in each hand.

"I'm going outside," he said. "I need some air."

Jbeil, Lebanon 23:00

Brother Malek sat cross legged on a mat in the centre of the small room he had been allocated. He still wore his *burnus*, but the hood was off of his head. Next to him his golden *argileh* bubbled as he sucked long and slow on the pipe. The room was dim, lit only by a small candle in a saucer on the windowsill.

He held the smoke, letting it trickle down his nose naturally. His eyes were closed as he rocked back and forth in contemplation.

There was a gentle tap on the door and he stopped rocking. The smoke was still trickling out of his nose. Only when it stopped did he open his eyes and say, "Come."

Love opened the door, entering and stepping to one side. Behind her Paradise guided Carla into the room by the forearm. Carla's face was heavily made-up, eyes dark, lips red and full. Her black hair was down, falling over her chest and covering her naked breasts. Below she wore red diaphanous harem pants. Her feet were bare.

"Your djinn for conversion," announced Love.

Malek took another pull on the pipe, making the women wait. Then he said, "Leave us."

The twins gave a small bow and left the room, closing the door.

Carla stayed still, feeling his eyes travelling over her, inspecting. She in turn was studying the *argileh*. Was that solid gold? The apple and mint smell of the tobacco fought with her own heavy jasmine perfume.

After two more languorous inhalations, Malek draped the hose over the plate of the *argileh* and put his hands on his knees. He asked, "Do you still wish to be converted?"

"Yes, I do."

"This is your free choice?"

"It is."

He looked at her some more. Then slowly he stood up. "You know who I am?"

"Yes."

"And you wish to be part of The Second Coming?"

"I do."

Malek undid his belt, the *burnus* falling open. "We must all appear before the seat of judgment, so that each one may receive what is due for what he has done in the body, whether good or evil. Whosoever shall deny me before men, I will also deny. Do you deny me?"

"I do not deny you."

Malek put out his hands. "True conversion starts from within. I believe you are worthy. Come to me, my child. You are welcome."

23 July 2010
11 Sha'ban 1431

Jounieh, Lebanon 02:30

Normally two large glasses of red wine and half a bottle of whisky would have him pissed out of his mind, unaware even of his very existence. But not tonight. When he craved for oblivion it would not happen. For hours he had lain on the sun lounger in the dark, slapping off the mosquitoes, willing himself into unconsciousness. But no.

Flat on his back, Merhi stared up at the diamante night sky. A few minutes ago he had watched the waxing gibbous moon setting out over the Mediterranean. In two hours the sun would be rising behind him.

His mind was a raging cascade, thoughts, ideas and memories bouncing off each other in a maelstrom of confusion. Oh Lattouf, why had you ever entered his life? One phone call and Lattouf had given him the double tap whammy, as efficient as any executioner, killing his sense of reason. Killing his sanity.

Disembodied phrases swam in his head, over and over. "Had to be Lebanon, didn't it?" – Mr Carla. "The dead shall rise again" – Lattouf. "Plenty of places to hide, in the mountains" – Mr Carla. And always the one word, the name: Sajida.

Sajida, Sajida, Sajida.

Well, he just did not believe it. He would not believe it. It was ridiculous. Preposterous. The Second Coming was a myth, a religious lie to give the gullible a reason for living, to help them make sense of the nonsense that is life.

A thought struck him and he raised himself up onto his elbows, frowning. He looked around for his phone before realising he had left it on the hall table. What time was it anyway?

Slowly he moved into a sitting position. His hips ached after the hours on the lounger. On the floor tiles next to him was a pile of cigarette butts, too numerous to count. Knees creaking, he stood up, avoiding the butts, expecting the world to spin. But it remained steady. He took a tentative step... no loss of balance.

He was pleasantly surprised. No feeling of drunkenness, no hangover symptoms – except for his mouth, which tasted like a mountain lion had crept over his balcony while he was asleep, shat down his throat and then run off. He tried to wet his lips, but his tongue felt like a desert cactus. Only one solution. He bent down, picked up the open bottle of whisky, filled his mouth and swilled the nectar around before swallowing it.

He walked over to the sliding glass door, opening it carefully, trying not to disturb the man asleep on the couch inside. He had been unable to disguise his displeasure when Gisele had suggested Mr Carla stay for the night but he had won the subsequent clenched-teeth low-growl argument in the kitchen: they would not make up a bed for him, he would sleep on the couch.

Soundlessly he opened and closed the door leading to the hall. It was dark but he did not want to risk putting on the light. His hands flap-fumbled across the top of the table until they landed on his phone. He pressed a random key and the phone lit up, sending a powerful beam straight up into his eyes.

Squinting, he found the Phonebook, scrolled halfway through the alphabet and pressed the Call key.

Bourj el-Barajneh, Beirut 02:45
Jounieh, Lebanon 02:45

Fadi Lattouf was flat on his back, mouth wide open, snoring like a Harley-Davidson doing top speed with a broken silencer. Occasionally his mouth moved and his cheeks twitched. Next to him Nada knew that this would be yet another night in her very long marriage when she slept only intermittently.

Lattouf was dreaming he was being interrogated by a set of naked blonde female triplets; he was tied down, also naked, and at their mercy. One girl was tickling his feet, one was squeezing his pineapples and the other one was tweaking his nipples. They kept asking over and over *Who killed Chadi? Who killed Chadi?* He tried to tell them he did not know but they ignored him. *Who killed Chadi? Who killed Chadi?* The one at his feet stopped tickling and opened a bag of potato chips. She placed a chip between each of his toes and then leant forward and began eating them. *Who killed Chadi? Who killed Chadi?* The one squeezing his pineapples got to work unpeeling his banana. *Who killed Chadi? Who killed Chadi?* The third one stopped tweaking his nipples and turned, backing up towards him. *Who killed Chadi? Who killed Chadi?* Her bottom was just ten centimetres away from his face, and he was sticking out his tongue trying to reach it, when music started playing. That was nice, how thoughtful - what the...?

Lattouf's eyes shot open, confused. His tongue was still poking out of his lips, prodding the air. His throat was sore. The triplets had gone but the music was still playing. Something was covering his left eye, he couldn't see out of it. Was this his punishment for impure dreams? Panic slapped him awake and he sat up in bed, his hand coming up to move his fallen comb-over away from his eye and back over his head. The music was still playing. If that was one of the children at this hour he would beat their hides raw.

Then he realised it was his mobile. In the name of Allah, who was calling him at this time of night?

He got up off the bed, causing Nada to bounce like flotsam on a stormy ocean. Retrieving his phone from next to his glass of water, he sat back down, Nada bouncing some more.

In this light and without Nada's glasses, the screen on the phone was a blur. "Yes?" he barked, thinking he was talking quietly, waking all light sleepers within a ten block radius. "Who is this?"

"Fadi, it's Jihad."

"Jihad? My friend, are you okay? Do you know what time it is?"

"Were you asleep?"

"Asleep? Me? No, no, I... I was just preparing for *Fajr* prayer." With three naked blonde triplets.

"I need to ask you something. To do with Chadi."

"You have found something? You have another clue?"

"No, but you might."

"Me?"

"The card that popped out of his pocket. The one he wrote the co-ordinates on. What was it?"

There was a puzzled pause. "It was a card. I'm sorry, I don't know what you mean."

"Yes but what card was it? You know, two of diamonds, three of clubs?"

"Oh. I don't know. Hold on, it is still in my jacket."

Lattouf got back up off the bed and went over to his old wardrobe. The door opened to much creaking and clunking. "Where the hell is it?" he mumbled to himself. "Where did she hang it...?"

He reached out and turned on the light. On the bed, Nada moaned and rolled onto her side, her hand coming up to shield her eyes.

"Ah, here it is." He pushed other clothes aside, some falling off their hangers, and stuck his fingers into the top pocket of his jacket, pulling out the card. After a moment he said, "Jihad, it is the ace of spades."

There was silence on the other end of the phone.

"Jihad, are you there? Hello?"

"Fadi, I want you to bring that card and the drawing of the

twin to me right now. I'm at home."

"Now? But we are meeting in the morning."

"Not any more we're not. We have things to do. I need you to bring them to me right now."

"But I cannot."

"You can. You know where I live, you know how to get here."

"I can't."

"Don't worry about your prayer, Allah will understand. Say it on the way."

"I really can't."

"Fadi, have I ever asked you for anything? Think of all the stuff I've done for you. Really, I need you to bring the card and drawing to me now. You and I have things to do. The roads will be emptier at this hour, it will be good driving."

"I... I can't."

Merhi was angry. "Why?"

"I... I have no lights on the van. They don't work."

There was a stunned silence. Then, with a sigh that could be heard as far south as Sidon, Merhi said "It will be light in two hours. Come then. Don't let that card out of your sight. And tell no one."

"Are we going to find Chadi's murderer?"

"My friend, I think we are."

Tears welled in Lattouf's eyes. Emotionally, he said "May Allah bless you, my friend."

But Merhi had already clicked off.

Nada turned in the bed, raising her head, her eyes still screwed up against the light. "Who was that?"

Fadi was standing by the wardrobe, fallen clothes at his feet, holding the playing card in his hand, wearing just his outsize boxer shorts. Wet eyes looked across at his wife. "That... that was Jihad." He tapped the card. "He thinks he has found Chadi's killer. I am to go to him at daybreak."

She laid her head back down on the thin pillow. As she turned away from him, she said "Husband, I think it is time you quit your job. Find something better to do. Something more suited to your incredible brain power..."

She fell asleep.

Without turning around, Merhi asked "Like listening in on other people's conversations?"

"I assume the drawing you were talking about is the one done by my wife?" said the voice behind him.

The light from Merhi's phone had dimmed by fifty per cent but, as he turned round, it gave him enough light to see the shadow leaning against the living room door jamb.

"And what is this about a card?" continued The Damascene.

"Just something I've discovered."

"Who were you talking to?"

Merhi smiled, enjoying having the upper hand. "My fat friend. He is a Palestinian police chief."

The light on the phone went out completely.

"He is coming here?" said the voice from the darkness.

Merhi waited for his eyes to adjust. "Yes."

"Why?"

"To find the person who killed his cousin."

The Damascene paused, reflecting. "And what is that to do with my wife's drawing?"

Merhi did not answer, instead he said "I know who Sajida is."

Another pause. "Really? Well good for you. What has a Palestinian police chief to do with my wife's drawing?"

"He knows who the woman in the drawing is."

"So do I."

"But do you know where she is?"

The atmosphere changed palpably. Dangerously. The Damascene pushed himself up off the door jamb. "Do we need to talk?"

"Yes, we do," Merhi stood his ground. "My friend will be here in three hours. We'll talk then."

"In the meantime," said Gisele's voice from the doorway of the master bedroom, "do you boys want some coffee? Or is it dicks at dawn?"

Jounieh, Lebanon 06:00 – 07:15

Lattouf was dressed in his old jeans and pink and blue checked shirt. "Morning of joy, my friend!" he pumped Jihad's hand furiously, patting him on the back with the hand that carried the envelope. "Morning of peace, Gisele."

As Gisele reciprocated the Morning of Peace, Jihad said "Come in, Fadi. Your van worked all right?"

"Fine, fine. It's just the lights, no big deal."

"Come through, we're having breakfast." Jihad took the offered envelope and led the way into the living room.

The first thing Lattouf noticed was the table spread with meats, cheeses, *labneh*, tomatoes, cucumber, dates, pastries and donuts. The second thing he noticed was the man standing next to the table, plate in his hand.

"Fadi, this is..."

"An old friend of Jihad and his charming wife." The Damascene shook the fat man's hand.

"Allah's blessings upon you," said Lattouf to the man with the long hair tied back in a ponytail, noticing the scarring on the left side of his face under the hair.

"Thank you. And upon you."

"Please help yourself to food," encouraged Jihad. "We have some talking to do."

Gisele appeared with two pots, one a *rakwe* with Turkish coffee, the other a *dallah* with cardamom flavoured Arabic coffee. Putting them on the table next to the small, handleless cups, she said "Sit down all of you. Be comfortable."

Five minutes later they were seated with their plates,

Lattouf's piled perilously high, coffees on small side tables. Gisele and The Damascene sat on one couch, Lattouf and Jihad on the other.

"Right, where do I begin?" Jihad ate bread and *labneh*.

"Maybe at the beginning?" suggested The Damascene.

Gisele smiled. Lattouf ate.

Jihad spoke. "There are two separate cases here. Completely different, apparently no connection between them. But then as they go on, as they are investigated, slowly slowly they join." He pinched grease-covered fingers together. "First, yours." He nodded at The Damascene. "Case Number One. Just over two weeks ago I am contacted by your wife, Carla."

"Your wife?" said Lattouf, not yet understanding what was going on but enjoying the food enormously. "Congratulations."

The Damascene looked at him but said nothing.

Jihad went on. "I knew her in the past. Five years ago. The Hariri assassination. She was not called Carla then. But she was a member of the ESU, as she is now. That's the External Security Unit, Fadi."

"Oh."

"She asks me to help her. Her boss has been murdered and she thinks she is in danger. She has been attacked. She won't tell me why because I don't know who Sajida is. Saj–bloody–ida. She asks me to get some CCTV footage for her. And she asks if she can stay with me – us." He looked over at Gisele. "Naturally we agreed, colleague in distress and all that. I get the CCTV, she examines it, confirms the same person killed her boss as attacked her. It's a woman. A woman with white eyes. She sketches a composite," he nodded at the envelope on the floor beside him, "I run it through the system. Nothing. I refer it to Interpol. They've yet to report back, systems have been down." He paused to drink coffee. "Then I'm contacted by Carla's new boss, wanting to know why I've requested the CCTV footage. Long story short, I have to tell him about Carla, Carla asks to meet him. They meet – you've heard the conversation. She tells us she is going to work the case with her new boss. Then, while Gisele and I are both out, she disappears. Leaves. Some of her stuff is still in the wardrobe in the bedroom – you'd best take it. That was a week ago." He paused as Lattouf got up and poured himself more coffee from the *dallah*. The Palestinian looked around, holding the pot in the air. The Damascene and Gisele shook their heads, Jihad held his cup up for refilling.

"Okay," continued Jihad, watching Lattouf pile more food onto his plate. "Case Number Two. My friend Fadi here, Captain Lattouf of the Palestinian civil police." Lattouf turned and bowed. "This one I will cut very short. Fadi contacts me to tell me that his cousin has been found dead on his doorstep. We examine the body and confirm he has been murdered, something injected into him. Fadi's cousin was a private investigator operating out of Jbeil. By various methods we establish that he was up at the Annaya monastery the afternoon of his death. We deduce that he saw something up there that made him dash down to his cousin, his only relative, in Beirut. He was murdered before he had the chance to talk."

The Damascene put his empty plate down on top of Gisele's on the side table. "And what is the connection?"

"Ah, this is where Fadi comes in," Jihad looked at Lattouf who smiled, donut protruding between his teeth. "He has solved it. He doesn't even realised it but he has solved it."

Lattouf bowed again. "Thank you. You are too kind."

"When we went to Jbeil to examine his late cousin's premises, Fadi noticed two women in the street. I hardly saw them, we were walking behind them." He noticed Gisele's eyebrows raise. "But Fadi had seen them from the front. They were twins. Identical twins. We commented on how nature was wonderful, didn't we Fadi? Fadi!"

"Yes. Yes." Lattouf had dropped half a pastry on the floor. He bent down, picked it up and put it into his mouth.

"They went one way, we went the other. Thought no more about it. Now this is where it gets interesting, and a little complicated. I'll try to keep it simple. As his cousin lay dying, a card popped out from his jacket pocket."

"Popped out?" The Damascene shook his head, not understanding.

"A trick. Don't worry about it. On this card were some numbers. Twelve of them, written straight across the card, corner to corner. It took us a while to find out but we finally realised they were geographical co-ordinates. And they were pointing us to Annaya in the mountains, the Saint Charbel place. As you know, we went there yesterday. And didn't Fadi see the twins again up there, they were driving away as we got there."

"And they had somebody in the back of their car," said Lattouf.

Merhi frowned. "Did they?"

"Yes."

"You never told me that."

"Sorry. Couldn't see who it was. Didn't think it was important."

For a minute Jihad stared at the Palestinian, then he turned back and continued. "Still one might say so what?"

"I think I see where this is going," said The Damascene.

"Then last night I had that call at dinnertime, remember? It was Fadi. He had accidentally picked up that envelope you had so cleverly sneaked into the car." He leant forward and picked the envelope up off the floor. "The contents fell out and he saw this." He pulled out the drawing and held it up. "Carla's composite. Fadi recognised it. This is the face of the twins. And this..." he put his hand back into the envelope and pulled out the playing card, "is the card his cousin wrote on with the Annaya co-ordinates." He threw it across into The Damascene's lap. "Look at the suit. The ace of spades, the death card. Still I made no connections. Then Fadi told me about Sajida. And it all fell into place."

The room was silent. Jihad looked triumphantly across at The

Damascene. The Damascene was looking at the card, turning it over. Gisele was looking at The Damascene's lap. Lattouf was looking at the final pastry before he put it into his mouth.

"The Second Coming and then some," said Merhi. "It wasn't some thing Fadi's cousin saw, it was some one. And it got him killed. And the twins, who you are looking for, are in Jbeil."

"And we think we know where," said Lattouf, cottoning on, the whole mystery falling into place in his head with the sudden rapidity of a building being imploded.

"If your wife is still alive, she is probably there with them," said Jihad.

The Damascene was breathing through flared nostrils. "She is still alive. I feel it. Do you have weapons?"

"Two guns."

"That will do. Come, we must go." The Damascene stood up.

"Just one thing," said Gisele, unfolding her legs and moving to the edge of the couch. She looked up at all three men now standing. "Who is Sajida?"

The full sun was already up over the mountains behind them as the three men left the apartment block. "Take my van?" suggested Lattouf.

"Yes of course we will, Fadi," said Merhi. "Not. Can you just imagine a Palestinian police van roaming the streets of Jbeil? We'll take my car, get in." He looked at the other man who was heading towards the side of the building. "Come with us," he called.

"No. I have a bike," said The Damascene over his shoulder. "I will follow you."

Merhi climbed into his Land Cruiser, Lattouf already ensconced. "He has a bike?" scoffed Lattouf. "It will need to be something to keep up with us - "

They heard a roar and then the black Suzuki Hayabusa rolled up beside them.

"Maybe not," said Lattouf.

Merhi smiled and made a mental note to get someone to ticket Mr Carla for not wearing a crash helmet. "*Yalla.*"

Gisele watched from the balcony above. She was grumpy because they had refused to tell her who Sajida was, three boys with the knowledge leaving the woman in ignorance 'for your own protection'. Ridiculous. She had more experience in covert activity than the three of them put together. Probably. Jihad and Fadi she knew, but she was unsure of Carla's husband. What was his provenance? He was tall, dark, mysterious – and he emitted an aura of danger. Not someone you would like to come across on a dark night. She grinned. Then again...

She watched Jihad's Toyota head down the mountainside, the monster of a motorbike following close behind. Touching two fingers of her right hand to her lips and then to her heart, she said softly "God speed, my heroes. I hope you know what you are doing."

Jbeil, Lebanon 07:30

Love tapped on the door.

It was a full minute before the voice from within said, "Come."

Brother Malek was sitting cross-legged on the mat, puffing on his *argileh*. His *burnus* was loosely around his body. Love glanced at the floor in front of the mat where a pair of diaphanous red harem pants were crumpled in a ball. "I expected her to be here."

Malek took the pipe from his mouth. "She was a worthy and adept convert. The process was completed quickly. You are now three."

Love nodded without comment.

Malek went on, "She has returned to her room, to pray, give thanks and to rest. I have told her of our plans and of the great journey that begins today."

Love picked up the harem pants. "My sister has prepared

breakfast. It awaits you. We will leave in an hour. With the grace of Allah, we will be at Haouch Moussa by midday, where The Circle awaits us."

Malek nodded, putting the pipe back into his mouth.

Love turned, raising the pants to her nose. She went out and closed the door. Paradise was standing in the corridor."You heard?" asked Love.

"We are three. Your decision to keep her was right, sister. He is pleased with us." Paradise stroked Love's face. "But she will be on probation until we reach the Holy City."

"Forty days and forty nights. Fitting."

"Let's see how she is, he can sometimes be over zealous with his conversions as we know."

They walked down the corridor, knocked on a door at the end and entered. Inside it was dim, just a square beam of light coming in through the high-up window. The room was heavy with the scent of jasmine.

Carla was sitting on the bed and she looked up as they came in.

"Salaam, oh djinn," said Paradise.

Carla stood up, stark naked, her long black hair framing her make-up smudged face. *"Salaam,"* she replied quietly.

Love took her by the arm and guided her into the beam of light. "There is blood on your mouth. Was he brutal?"

"No, it just happened."

Gently, Love raised her hands and wiped the tears from Carla's cheeks with her thumbs.

"Do you hurt anywhere else?" asked Paradise.

Carla shook her head. "He was proper. He was divine. I am just happy. Thank you both for saving me."

Love leant forward and softly kissed her lips, tasting the blood. "He has told you of the great journey?"

"Yes."

"We leave in an hour. Clean yourself. The bathroom is free. We will bring you clothes."

"We think we've got the right size," Paradise was staring at Carla's hairless body.

"Then there is food outside," continued Love. "It will be the last time we eat until Haouch Moussa."

Carla nodded. "Thank you, sisters. You are very kind. I am not worthy of you." She knelt down on the floor, aware of four surprised white eyes looking at her. "But before I do anything, I need to pray." She held out her hands in supplication.

Love stepped back. "Of course. We will leave you."

"I'll be back with the clothes shortly," said Paradise as they went out.

As soon as the door had closed, Carla stood up. She wiped her bloodied lips with the back of her hand, grateful that the one they called *al-Mahdi* had not come in with them. He would have been astonished, because the cuts were nothing to do with him. She had done them herself, couldn't be helped, needs must.

But she was praying. Praying with all her spirit. Praying that her husband was here, that he would come to rescue her.

Otherwise she would have to kill these fucking bitches all on her own.

Jbeil, Lebanon 08:30

Merhi turned into the parking area just beyond the Seven Seas Restaurant on Boulevard al-Mina, pulling up facing the old harbour. As he turned off the engine he watched the fishing boats bobbing on the water. It had been an uneventful drive up to Jbeil. Uneventful but not quiet, because next to him Fadi Lattouf had snored like a rutting boar for most of the journey.

The Suzuki Hayabusa drove in next to the Land Cruiser.

"Fadi," Merhi shook the Palestinian's hairy arm. "Fadi!"

"Mm? What? Oh, we here? That was quick."

"You've been asleep for the last hour."

He rubbed his hands down his face. "Lattouf never sleeps. I

was just resting my eyes."

"*Yalla*, we have work to do."

Lattouf got out, nodding at The Damascene and then jumping as the Land Cruiser's lights flashed as Merhi pressed the lock key. Merhi came round, a bulky rolled up yellow and green *Spinneys* carrier bag in his hand. They wore no jackets and wearing holsters would have been too conspicuous, so the guns were simply in a carrier.

"Are you sure you can remember where the women went?" asked The Damascene.

"I have a photographic memory," said Lattouf, not mentioning that the photograph in his head was one of the twins' backsides as he followed them down the road. "Come."

They could smell the sea air as they walked out of the parking area and turned left onto Boulevard al-Mina. Merhi and Lattouf smoked.

Beyond the Seven Seas Restaurant, Lattouf led the way across the road, like a tour guide. They walked parallel with the medieval town wall then turned right through the ramparts into Rue St John.

"It was just down here, past the bookshop," explained Lattouf.

When they reached the bookshop, Lattouf nodded to the right."They went down this alley."

Merhi threw away his cigarette and began to unroll the carrier bag.

"Not yet," The Damascene raised a hand. "Wait. Let us see what is down here." He led the way, followed by Merhi. Lattouf brought up the rear, feeling at home in the confines of the narrow alley. Its width reminded him of the 'streets' in the camp – but without the broken pipes, sagging cables and crumbling buildings.

The alley was short and widened into a sunny patio area in front of a half-boarded up shop. Merhi guessed that it probably used to be a baker's, with tables outside for customers to relax in the sun. There was nothing else down here, just a dead end.

"It must be here," said Lattouf authoritatively. The Damascene put a finger to his own lips, the corners of Lattouf's mouth dropping like a scolded schoolboy. The Damascene nodded at the bag in Merhi's hand.

Spinneys carrier bags are thick and it seemed to make an unnecessary noise in the alley as Merhi unrolled it. He dipped inside and brought out Gisele's Smith and Wesson 642. The Damascene made silent gestures that Merhi and Lattouf should have the guns. Merhi passed the Smith and Wesson to the Palestinian, the small gun instantly disappearing in the folds of the large hand. Merhi brought out his own official-issue Herstal 9mm. He thought of screwing up the carrier bag and putting it in his pocket but then decided that the better and quieter option was simply to let it drift to the ground.

The front window of the shop was boarded up but the door wasn't. Standing to the side, The Damascene stretched out a hand, carefully, tentatively trying the small round doorknob. It turned...

The door creaked open twenty centimetres, and the three men flattened themselves against the wall in case of gunfire from within. There was nothing. The Damascene stretched out and shoved the door some more. More creaking. No reaction from inside.

Crouching, The Damascene pushed the door wide open, waited, then cautiously leaned inside. Slowly he straightened up. "Seems empty." He stepped inside. "But people have been here, I can smell them. The place is warm." He sniffed the air and was still and quiet. He sniffed again. Jasmine. "She was here." He could not hide the relief in his voice. "She was here and she's alive."

Merhi and Lattouf entered. Merhi screwed up his eyes, straining to see round the large, empty room. "We should have brought torches."

"Wait." Lattouf disappeared back outside. Suddenly there

was a loud ripping sound as he pulled the board off the front window with his bare hands. Light flooded in. The board was discarded to much banging and clattering.

"There," beamed Lattouf, coming back in. "Light!"

There was a small table in the shop area with food detritus on it. Lattouf scooped something out of a foil container with his finger, sniffed it and put it into his mouth. He announced, "*Tahini*."

As well as the front shop area there were three rooms and a small, basic bathroom in the back. One room smelt distinctly of tobacco. The bathroom was damp, warm and heavy, recently used. Another room was empty. The final room, at the back, had an old metal-framed bunk bed against the wall.

The three men stood in the final room, Lattouf leaning against the bed, Merhi standing in the doorway, The Damascene in the centre of the room, tense, senses alert, breathing heavily. He said, "This is where they kept her. I can smell her."

Lattouf sniffed and shook his head at Merhi with a facial shrug.

"So what now?" asked Merhi. "She is alive and that's good. But where have they gone? Where have they taken her?"

The Damascene was quiet. Lost in thought, he scooped his hair up either side of his head, tightening his ponytail. For the first time Merhi and Lattouf saw the hole in the left side of his head where his ear had once been. Lattouf stepped back in shock, grabbing hold of the upright of the bed, looking at Merhi then back at The Damascene. Merhi too was gawking, but neither man said anything.

Ponytail tightened, The Damascene asked "Did your cousin leave any other clues? Anything whatsoever?"

Lattouf shook his head, still grimacing at the now covered hole. Merhi said, "Nothing. That was all. He led us to Annaya."

"And you led us here," The Damascene was nodding in contemplation. "They're on the move, aren't they? But where? To another hide out? Or is this The Second Coming? Has it begun?"

They were quiet, two men in thought, Lattouf staring at The Damascene's head.

After a minute Merhi said, "I have been an idiot." The other two looked at him. "A complete and utter fucking idiot. The Second Coming will be when Satan is cast out. I was asked to prepare a report on this recently, to see if it would have any affect on Lebanon internally. Haven't you been keeping up with the news? The Great Satan is leaving even now, with a deadline of this coming August thirty-first."

Lattouf simply looked bemused. The Damascene said, "My God, yes. It fits. Then it *is* The Second Coming. He is returning, as he said he would. His journey has started."

"But the question is, which way will he go?" pondered Merhi.

"And why does he have my wife?"

Lattouf could not understand a word they were saying, they might have just as well been speaking Slavic rather than Levantine Arabic. He could *hear* what they were saying but none of it made sense. He straightened up, his hand still gripping the bed frame – and he stopped, frowning.

His fingers moved up and down the metal frame, touching, feeling, stroking. He said, "Jihad, can I borrow your lighter?"

Merhi scowled. "Not now. Wait till we're outside."

"No, I don't want a smoke. I want your lighter."

Sighing, Merhi took his disposable *Bic* from his pocket and threw it over. It landed in the bouncy castle of Lattouf's left hand, his right hand still on the bed frame.

Lattouf flicked the lighter once, twice, three times before the flame caught. Then he brought it towards his right hand, at the same time leaning under the top bunk, screwing up his eyes as he looked at where his fingers had been. "There is something here," he said, "but I don't have my glasses. Can either of you see it?"

"What the hell are you talking about?" asked Merhi.

The Damascene stepped across, rubbing his hand on the bed frame where Lattouf indicated. Saying nothing, he took the lighter and bent under the top bunk as Lattouf had done. Then he straightened back up, a small smile on his face. A smile of triumph. A smile of love. "I knew she wouldn't let me down." He nodded at Merhi, nodded at the bed frame and held out the lighter.

Merhi came over, performing the same contortion as the other two had done. The flame flickered as he moved it back and forth, up and down. A word had been scratched into the gray bed frame, probably using a fingernail or something. The letters were shaky and bitty, as if the person who wrote them could not see what they were doing. But it was a word, definitely.

Aanjar

Coastal Highway, Lebanon 09:15

The constantly heavy traffic on the coastal highway is always more intense on Fridays and Mondays. They had been on the road for fifty minutes, sometimes moving fast, sometimes slowing to a standstill, and had just past over the Nahr el Kalb (Dog River) to the north of Beirut. But they did not need to rush, they were in no hurry. They had forty days and forty nights.

The Jeep had its hard top on. Paradise drove, Love sitting next to her. In the back, Carla sat next to the hooded Brother Malek. Carla was dressed in identical clothes to the twins: white vest top, combat cargo pants and boots, but her lustrous black hair and black eyes were in contrast to the blonde haired, white-eyed sisters.

She sat with her arms folded, scabby nail-less fingers screwed into fists and tucked under her arms. Her mouth still hurt where she had carved the word *Aanjar* on the bedpost with her teeth. One of her upper central incisors was chipped but it was too small to be noticed. And The Bitches had thought the blood on her mouth was caused by Malek!

Malek had in fact hardly touched her during the 'conversion', and she had certainly not been violated or abused. They had joined hands, he had mumbled prayers and had then breathed into her nose for five minutes, a warm and curiously sensual experience, his tobacco tainted breath strangely calming. Then he had made her kneel down and lick his feet, the posture making her more aware of her nudity.

After five minutes he had lain on the floor next to her. He was naked under the *burnus* and he pressed himself against her from behind, in the spoon position, his flesh hairy and hot. He had draped the open *burnus* over them and they had stayed that way for probably two hours. She might even have slept.

In the middle of the night he had told her to leave. As she opened the door, he said "Welcome, my disciple. You have chosen the true way."

She had not turned round but she had been aware of his eyes on her. She said, "Thank you," and went out, closing the door, suppressing a giggle and thanking the true God that he had not said she would be sitting on his right hand in Paradise. She might not have been able to contain herself.

Now she gave an inward ironical laugh. They called him Malek, which meant The King. The King of Kings? In his mind he was, and there were people who thought so too. Others thought he was *ad-Dajjal*, the devil who had been responsible for the death of millions in his own name.

She looked out of the window at the Mediterranean on her right and thought of her husband. Was he here? Most definitely, she knew, she could sense his presence in the country. Would he discover the disused shop in Jbeil? Would he find her etched clue? Yes, he would. But how long would it take him?

She watched the gentle lapping of the sun-dappled sea against the coastline as she sipped water from a bottle.

Tomorrow they would start the journey across the desert in another country, which would hold no fear for the man known as The Damascene. But forty days after that, when they reached the Promised Land, it would be a whole different ball game.

Come quickly, my love.

For both our sakes.

Jbeil, Lebanon 09:15

"How long ago did they leave?" wondered Merhi as the three men left the disused bakery and headed back down the alley. He could sense an air of urgency around Mr Carla.

"Not long," said The Damascene. "The bathroom was still warm. There was a residual human aura in the rooms. I'd say an hour."

They turned left into Rue St John.

"Then we can catch them," said Lattouf, slightly out of breath, trying to keep up (both physically and mentally).

"Possibly. We know they are going to Aanjar, but their route after that could be one of many. I wonder if they have changed vehicles?"

"Not here," said Merhi, "but they might be changing on route. Perhaps..."

"When they get to Aanjar," nodded The Damascene.

They walked out through the ramparts and turned left, crossing Boulevard al-Mina.

"So we must stop them." To Lattouf the answer was simple.

"Indeed, my friend," agreed The Damascene. "Obviously they are going across the desert, heading east, which figures. But there are many ways and many means. If we pick the wrong route there will be no way we can stop them."

"You really want to stop him, to change history?" Merhi lit up a cigarette, tossing one to Lattouf. The Palestinian caught it in his mighty hand, the cigarette bending in half on impact. Nevertheless he put it in his mouth, leaning forward for a light, skipping so as not to break stride.

"Or stop him changing history, perhaps," mused The Damascene. "But no. Him I don't care about. What will be, will be. That is for the authorities. For you and your kind. All I care about is my wife. We must take her back."

They entered the car park.

"So Aanjar it is then," said Merhi. "There or before. Before they leave Lebanon."

"Can't you put out an ATL?" suggested Lattouf, smoke rising upwards from the dangling half of his cigarette.

Merhi turned as they reached the Land Cruiser. "Saying what? Think about it, who would believe us?"

"Tell them Sajida was right."

"And who would believe that? And anyway, there are those that want their so-called *al-Mahdi* to return, we could be putting ourselves in danger. No, we're in this on our own. We will find Carla and the women who killed your cousin. The rest we will leave to fate."

The car's lights flashed as Merhi unlocked it. "Get in."

The Damascene climbed onto the Suzuki and once again tightened his ponytail. "I will be able to move quicker than you through the traffic." The bike started with a purring growl. "They will be taking the main Damascus road. If anything should happen, I will wait for you on route. Otherwise I will contact you from Aanjar." With an accelerating roar, the Suzuki drove off.

Merhi and Lattouf stood by the side of the Land Cruiser, cigarettes in mouths, trying not to look impressed.

After a few more quick silent sucks, both men stubbed their butts out under foot. As they climbed into the car, Lattouf patted his gut and asked "Can we stop off for some food on the way? I'm famished."

Mount Lebanon 11:30

Carla began to feel queasy as they drove by Bhamdoun, high up in the mountains. By the time they were passing above Qabb Elias, with the stunning eastwards view over the Bekaa Valley, she felt decidedly strange. At first she thought it could be altitude or motion sickness, but they were not things she suffered from. And she did not feel sick, just... odd.

Now as they descended to Chtaura, her head lolled and involuntarily she leant slowly, gently onto the shoulder of Brother Malek.

Paradise saw it in the rear-view mirror and smiled, nudging her sister.

Love looked round. "Just a little something we put in her water," she explained to the cowled figure. "To keep her docile until we start our journey. We always have to be careful with new converts in case they regress. Once we are out of Lebanon she will have less reason to change her mind."

For a moment Malek said nothing, the hood turned towards the woman leaning on his shoulder. Then he nodded, "As you wish. How many will be waiting for us?"

"All three of The Circle of Haouch Moussa."

"Armenians?"

"No."

"Then that is clever to hide amongst them." Malek shoved Carla back upright. Her head was forward, chin resting on her chest. She stayed up for a moment and then slowly fell the other way, her head coming to rest on the window.

"We will be meeting them at The Factory," explained Love. "Where we will be staying overnight. Then before dawn we travel to the old city and then we will set off into the hills and then the desert. We avoid Dimashq as you requested and pick up the camels at Duma."

"The old city?" asked Malek.

"For the camera," Love held up the Sony Camcorder. "For history. Your journey will start from a ruined city and end in the Holy City which you have come to save and rebuild. Good TV."

The hood turned, looking out of the window. He said no more.

Paradise increased speed as they began the straight twelve kilometre run across the valley. Love turned on the camera and began to film the lush green landscape.

Next to Malek in the back seat, Carla's head vibrated against the window...

Mount Lebanon 12:45

"Haven't we been this way before?" asked Lattouf as they passed through el-Mraijat and began the downward run to Chtaura. "Looks familiar."

Merhi spoke with a cigarette between his lips. "Five years ago. When we went to the wetlands."

"I knew it! Once Lattouf has been somewhere, he never forgets it."

"Which way did we go?"

"What?"

"Which we did we go? We made a turn here."

"Er... that way?" Lattouf pointed to the left, north-east towards Zahlé.

"No, it was that way." Merhi pointed across Lattouf to the right, south towards Qabb Elias. "But today we keep on going straight."

Lattouf finished off the last of several bars of chocolate and opened his window a few centimetres, throwing the wrapper out. He tried to close the window back up but instead it went all the way down, air blasting in noisily.

"For God's sake, Fadi." Merhi stabbed at the controls in his door and the window rose.

Lattouf looked at him. "You seem tense, my friend. I would have thought a mission such as this would be bread and butter to a Captain of the ISF."

"On a level playing field, yes. But the further south-east we go the further we get into Syrian territory. And that could add complications."

"But we are not crossing the border."

"No. But this area was the base of the Syrian *mukhabarat* in Lebanon. Aanjar, right where we're going."

"But they are no longer here. They withdrew from Lebanon after the Hariri killing."

"Maybe."

Lattouf frowned. He opened his mouth to discuss but then closed it again without saying another word. He could see his friend was not in the mood.

Five minutes later, staring ahead down the straight road, he said "Can't see the Jeep."

"No, they will be there by now. We will have to look around the town."

"Is it big?"

"No, but big enough to hide a car if they wanted to. But I don't think they will. They have no idea we're on to them. We'll just have to look around."

"Haven't seen the motorbike either."

"He's probably there now too."

Lattouf nodded. He asked, "Who is he anyway?"

"Carla's husband."

"His name?"

"He never says. He seems Lebanese but I've run him through records and nothing's come up."

Except, he thought, a dead man.

Aanjar, Lebanon 12:45

Haouch Moussa was built in the eighth century by Caliph al-Walid Ibn Abdel Malik of the Omayyads, the first great dynasty of the Arab Muslim empire. The ruins of the old walled city were discovered in the mid twentieth century and are today one of Lebanon's many tourist and academic attractions.

In 1939, France began to build the town of Aanjar on malarial marshland immediately to the south of the ruins. It was built to house Armenian refugees from Alexandretta, a Syrian province which France had ceded to Turkey that same year. The houses were built in an unaesthetic eastern European style, small and squat - but in compensation the French included wide, tree-lined avenues.

One and a half kilometres to the south of Aanjar, on an area of flat arable land, are several single-storey buildings, looking like a farm. The place was known as The Onion Factory, and, for nearly thirty years, it was Syria's main detention and interrogation centre in Lebanon.

The man who crouched on the ground in the sun, back against the wall of one of the buildings, knew that only too well. It was here that he had been killed, shot in the head by Brigadier General Ghazi Kanaan, the man who had been head of Syrian intelligence in Lebanon for twenty years until 2002, the effective ruler of the country.

Captain Marwan Mebarak of the Lebanese Commando Unit had been killed. The Damascene had taken over his body and soul, his missing left ear being the souvenir of Kanaan's bad aim. For five years he had worked for Kanaan, being his personal enforcer, persuader and, when necessary, killer. Then in 2005, at the same time as he had decided to leave Kanaan and work for himself, The Damascene had done something he had thought he would never ever do. Something that he thought he would never feel. Something that was alien to him. He had fallen in love.

And it was that love that now had him crouching on the ground in a place he thought he would never visit again. The place of blood, the place of death. The Onion Factory.

It was quiet. The sun was hot, the ground dusty.

There was farmland all around, but none of the locals would ever venture near these buildings even though Syria had ended its military presence in Lebanon over five years ago. They were too afraid of the ghosts.

He had caught up with the Jeep as they had crossed the Bekaa and had followed it at a safe distance. When he had realised where they were heading, his mood had darkened with his memories.

He had left the Suzuki behind some bushes on the main road half a kilometre back and had crouch-walked across the field parallel to the gravel track leading to the buildings.

Three cars were parked outside the next building along. One of them was the black Jeep Wrangler Ultimate.

Maintaining his crouch, The Damascene moved silently across to the back of the building, hugging the wall next to an open window. The walls were thick but he could hear voices. Carefully he looked inside.

The first thing he noticed was how different the interior was to the other building. The other one was simply an open space with stained, smelly, rotting straw on the floor and a single wooden chair in the centre of it. This one looked like it was the *mukhabarat* living quarters. It was a large room with doors leading off at the far end, probably to catering and bathroom areas. There were five beds down either wall.

In the centre of the room was a long wooden table on which sat fruit, nuts, juice and water. Around the table stood five people. The man in the hooded *burnus*, the identical female twin protectors, and two other men. They were talking, eating and drinking. One of the men was saying, "The contact will come tonight to confirm the final details..."

The Damascene leant back against the wall.

And smiled.

He had caught the faintest whiff of jasmine first and then he had strained to see in. He could just make out a figure on the bed nearest the window opening.

It was Carla, his wife.

The Damascene crouch-ran back to the other building. He sat on the ground on the farthest side, against the wall.

If the contact was coming tonight that meant that this was a Supporter Cell and not a Member Cell. Small fry. But he would take them out anyway. There was no way he could rescue his wife without killing, so they would all go. And, he acknowledged, there was no way he could rescue his wife on his own.

He pulled his mobile phone from his jeans pocket, checked there was a signal, and entered his Contacts list. He found the number he wanted and began to tap out a text message.

Bekaa Valley, Lebanon 13:00

They had just passed the turning for Barr Elias and were nearing the junction with the Rayak road when Merhi's mobile tinkled its message tune.

"Shall I get it?" Lattouf reached towards the phone in the well behind the transmission stick.

"It's probably Gisele." Merhi pulled out to overtake a fruit van.

Lattouf picked up the phone. He held it up to his face, thick fingers poking the screen. "How do you do this?" Poke.

"Just press Read."

Lattouf squinted. "I haven't got my glasses. This one? Ah, no, you don't want to go online. Hold on..." More pressing, then "Ah. There it is."

"What does she say?"

Lattouf moved the phone backwards and forwards in front of his eyes like he was playing an ocular trombone. He frowned, pouted and said, "I think she wants to meet you."

"What? Give it here." Merhi took the phone in his right hand, steering with his left. He brought hand and phone up to rest on the steering wheel.

Located. Meet at Aanjar ruins

Merhi closed the message. "It isn't Gisele, it's our friend. He's found them. Saves us a job. How's your archaeology, Fadi?"

Aanjar ruins, Lebanon 13:45

Even though it was signposted, they went sailing past the turn off for Aanjar. When they began to climb back up into the mountains again towards the Syrian border, they realised their mistake and turned back.

This time they did not miss it. On the far northern side of the town the slender columns and fragile arches of the quadrilateral Omayyad ruins contrasted proudly to the backdrop of Anti-Lebanon mountains. It was summer and there were tourists about but not as many as there would be at Lebanon's other attractions because of the easterly location.

"Keep an eye out for him." Merhi drove slowly along the northern perimeter, the entrance to the site on their right.

"I am," said Lattouf sleepily.

Beyond the entrance they turned right and cruised down the entire eastern side of the old city. At the bottom they turned west. Down here there were far fewer people. They could see the ruins of the Great Palace behind the walls on their right. Over on their left were bunkers and mess huts, not ruins but places abandoned by the Syrian army when it had left five years before.

Suddenly Lattouf nodded. "There. There he is."

The man with the scarred face and ponytail was sitting astride his motorbike outside some shops a little way along. He watched the Land Cruiser as it approached but he did not respond to Lattouf's wave out of the window.

The car pulled to a stop. Merhi leant over, talking across Lattouf. "Located?"

The Damascene nodded.

"What do you want to do?" asked Merhi.

Lattouf looked surprised. "We go get her, of course!" he beamed keenly, rubbing his hands. "And get the bastards who murdered Chadi."

Merhi ignored him, waiting for the other man's response.

"Tonight," said The Damascene. "Until then, we wait. Right now what I want to do is eat. I know a restaurant. *Yalla.* Follow me." Revving the bike, he moved back onto the road and drove off towards town.

Merhi followed.

"My sort of guy," said Lattouf. "I'm liking him more and more. Reminds me of a younger me."

Aanjar, Lebanon 17:00

They ate at the Shams (Sun) Restaurant on the main road into town, enjoying superb local trout, hammour and a selection of grilled meats. The on-site bakery provided a challenge which Lattouf was happy to rise to.

The place was busy and they realised as soon as they arrived that it was no place to talk. They enjoyed their food, drank only water and juice, then nearly three hours later went back out to the Land Cruiser.

Merhi climbed in behind the wheel and The Damascene got into the back. After pausing outside for a breaking of wind that probably shook the fruit from the trees in the Bekaa Valley, Lattouf rolled into the passenger seat, giving a "What?" look to his colleagues.

As soon as the door was closed, The Damascene spoke. "There are five of them. Him and the twins and two locals. A third local is arriving tonight. It is a Supporter Cell, the lowest level of the party organisation. It is unlikely any of the cells above know what's going on and certainly not the Party Divisions or Sections."

"What party?" asked Lattouf. His question was ignored, so he tried "And your wife?"

"She is there. They seem to have her subdued, maybe drugged."

"How many in a cell?" asked Merhi.

"Three to seven. The one arriving tonight is a contact, a full member, therefore I expect there are only the three of them in this cell. You will take them out."

Merhi nodded. "And him?"

"He is mine."

Merhi opened the compartment in the dashboard and brought out both the guns. He held them up one in each hand. "Which do you want?"

The Damascene shook his head. "I do not need a gun. You two have them."

Merhi passed the Smith and Wesson to Lattouf.

The Palestinian weighed the gun in his hand. "My cousin's spirit demands revenge," he said. "I assume we do not take prisoners?

"No. But under no circumstances endanger my wife. Act only on my signal. This is what we will do..."

The discussion went on for some time. At the end, The Damascene reached back and slipped the rubber band off his ponytail. His hair fell down either side of his face like closing curtains. He asked, "Do these seats fold flat?"

"Yes."

"Then I suggest we get some sleep. We will leave here at nineteen hundred. I want you refreshed and alert for tonight. Nothing must go wrong. My wife's life is at stake."

The men in the front nodded.

And it goes without saying, thought The Damascene, that if Carla's life is lost yours will be too.

The Onion Factory, Aanjar, Lebanon 19:15

Lattouf could not keep up with the other two men as they crouch-ran across the field parallel to the gravel track. His gut wobbled on his knees and his arse seemed like it was in the thrall of gravity. He could not see his lower legs or feet and he felt like he was performing an out of breath Russian floating dance.

The sun was beginning its slow setting to the west, making his body cast a distorted oval shadow in front of him. It would be dark by twenty hundred.

He looked up to see how far he had to go. There were three single-storey buildings spread out in the middle of the field. Ahead, Jihad and the other man were heading towards the one on the right, a good way away from the middle building with the cars outside.

Merhi and The Damascene were already sitting on the ground, backs against the wall, when Lattouf finally arrived, sweating and panting. Here they could not be seen from the other building. With a grimace of pain, mouth open in silent agony, Lattouf slowly straightened up, shaking his legs, first one then the other, looking down at his limbs like long lost buddies.

He shook his head. "This is a young man's game. We're too old for this, Jihad my friend."

Merhi looked up at him. "Talk softly. You want to get Chadi's killers, don't you?"

"Of course."

"Then stop moaning." He did, however, totally agree with Lattouf. He was too old for all this. "And take the gun out of your waistband before you shoot your nuts off."

Lattouf accepted the sound advice, holding the gun pointing upwards. "Do we go now?"

"The other one hasn't arrived yet," said The Damascene. "We will wait. Take them all out."

"Will it be long?" asked Lattouf. "Only Nada will be wondering where I am."

"It will take as long as it takes. But I think he will arrive soon."

"Talking of wondering where we are, I'd best call Gisele," Merhi fumbled in his pocket for his phone. "Is it all right? I'll talk softly."

"Yes. They cannot hear us from there." The irony was not lost on The Damascene. All three men were worried about their wives; his was closest, just a hundred metres away, but in terms of contact she could be on the other side of the moon. For now.

The screen of Merhi's phone shone brightly in the fading light so he shielded it with his hand as he pressed keys, then he put it to his ear. He wondered what sort of mood Gisele would be in.

Jounieh, Lebanon 19:30

Gisele pressed the Answer key. "Where are you?"

"Hello Angel. We followed them to Aanjar."

"Aanjar! Why have they gone there? Who are they? I hope to God you know what you are doing, Jihad. I thought you were just going to Jbeil." She was concerned, not scolding.

"Needs must. But it ends tonight."

"Is Carla safe?"

"Apparently, yes."

"Will you be making arrests?"

"No."

She knew what he meant. Softly she said, "Be careful. Please."

"I will. We all will."

"The three of you are there?"

"Yes."

"That is good." Her husband was in hands she trusted, and she did not mean Fadi Lattouf. "How long will you be?"

"I don't know. But don't wait up."

"As if I am going to do anything else! For God's sake be careful," she said again. "Whatever it is you are doing."

"I will. I'll ring you when we're on our way back."

"You make sure you do. Or I will flay you alive. With my tongue."

"Promise?"

"Promise."

There was a pause, then Jihad said "See you later."

"See you then," she pressed the End key. "I love you, husband."

Gisele was sitting on the balcony, staring unseeing out over the Mediterranean, her phone grasped tightly in her hand. She was worried. Jihad was in his fifties now and physically probably not as sharp as he used to be. He was a commander or, if you wanted to be unkind, an administrator. What was he doing running halfway across the country to rescue a colleague? Field work should be left to younger men.

But there was something more behind this, she knew. He had spoken about the murder of Fadi's cousin and how it was linked to the disappearance of Carla. And then there were these twins, The Second Coming, and the mysterious Sajida who, it seemed, had been right!

And they wouldn't tell her who Sajida was, to protect her because the knowledge was dangerous. Yet Sajida seemed to be the link, the explanation as to what was going on. The clarifier.

If, heaven forbid, anything happened to Jihad tonight she might never know the answer. Imagine having to live for whatever remaining years the Good Lord had set aside for her not knowing the full reasons why her husband was never coming home again.

She frowned and turned around in the chair, staring back through the glass doors into her living room. Unless...

Could it be that easy? Was this something she should have done when all this started?

She stood up and went back inside, passing through the living room and going into what had been one of the boys' bedrooms when they had been at home. It was now their office area.

She turned on the computer, waiting a full five minutes for it to do what computers do.

Then she clicked on the Internet icon.

The Onion Factory, Aanjar, Lebanon 19:35

"Right, the sun has gone," said The Damascene. "You understand what you have to do?"

"Yes," confirmed Merhi.

"And you are happy with it?"

"Yes."

"Both of you?"

"Of course," Lattouf was solemn. "If anyone transgresses, transgress likewise. They murdered my cousin."

"We'll move over, then I'll leave you. When the final one arrives you follow my lead as we discussed." Two heads nodded. "No talking, no sound, when we are over there. *Yalla.*"

The three shadowy figures crouch-walked in ant formation away from the building. The bouncing movement made gas move in Lattouf's gut, but he knew this was neither the time nor the place even for a little pop.

They reached the next building and flattened themselves against the wall, Merhi and Lattouf one side of the open window, The Damascene the other. Light came through the window and they could hear low chatter from inside. The Damascene held up his palm indicating that they should not move. Turning his body slowly, he looked inside.

The food and drink on the table was depleted and, as always when humans had been pecking, now looked untidy. The two locals from the Supporter Cell were each resting on a bed, the twins were seated together on another bed and *al-Mahdi* was seated on the floor, his hood off, smoking from a golden *argileh*.

And Carla was sitting next to him.

The Damascene stared.

His wife and *al-Mahdi* did not have body contact but they were sitting very close, in each others' space. She was looking at one of the twins who was talking. She was smiling, attentive, her face fresh, innocent, but her eyes so, so black. It was an expression he knew well. It meant somebody was going to die tonight.

They were opposite the window but at an angle, so they would not see him looking in. Was there any way he could get Carla's attention, let her know he was here? Tell her not to do anything, to leave it to him?

He concentrated hard.

Thirty seconds later Carla stood up and went over to the table and picked up a polystyrene cup, filling it with water. When she went back to *al-Mahdi* she sat noticeably less close to him. Good girl.

The Damascene turned back away from the window. He crooked his finger at Merhi then pointed to his eyes and to the window.

Carefully Merhi turned so that he was facing the wall. Then with silent, shuffling steps he moved sideways until one eye was looking into the room.

And there he saw the proof, as if proof was needed, that Sajida was right.

In the middle of the room, sitting next to Carla, smoking on an *argileh*, dressed in a *burnus* but with the hood down, his head exposed, was Saddam Hussein.

Jounieh, Lebanon 19:35

There were 155,000 results on Google for 'Sajida'. The first and most popular one was a Wikipedia link to Sajida Talfah, the widow and cousin of former Iraqi President Saddam Hussein and mother of his two now-dead sons Uday and Qusay and his three daughters.

Where was this going? she wondered. *Sajida was right.*

Gisele read the article. Interesting, but there was no clue or indication as to what Sajida had been right about! Sajida blamed Saddam for the 1989 death of her brother Adnan, claiming the helicopter crash which killed him had not been an accident but had been a bombing ordered by Saddam because of Adnan's growing popularity – but what had that to do with anything now?

No, was this the right Sajida even? Gisele clicked through page after page of the search results. There were links to people's Facebook pages, many references to Sajidas on the Indian sub-continent, she even found out that Sajida was the 9910th most popular name in the USA! But there was nothing of relevance other than Sajida Talfah so she went back and filtered the search to just her.

Sajida was right.

Gisele clicked on many of the articles. In March 2003 just before the bombing of Baghdad began, Sajida had fled from Iraq, probably to Qatar. In July 2006 she was put sixteenth on the Iraqi government's Most Wanted list for financing Sunni insurgents under her husband's reign – but her mansion in Qatar was empty, she had disappeared.

Gisele smiled to herself. Had Sajida been Most Wanted when the invasion of Iraq had started she would have been on one of those famous playing cards with pictures of the fugitives on them –

She stopped, her finger poised on the mouse, her stomach tightening. *Oh my good God.*

What had happened in this very apartment just last night? The card on which Fadi's cousin had written the Annaya co-ordinates. Jihad had taken it from the envelope and had thrown it across to Carla's husband. The death card, the ace of spades.

On the Iraq personality identification playing cards Saddam Hussein was the ace of spades.

No, this was crazy. Crazy.

al-Mahdi? The Second Coming?

Sajida was right.

Gisele clicked again, article after article, skim-reading when she thought it was necessary. It was another five minutes before she clicked on the link to *Pravda*, the Russian newspaper.

It was an article dated 13 April 2004, two years before Sajida had been put on the Most Wanted list. It was headlined 'Saddam's wife could not recognise her husband'. It reported that the previous week Sajida Tulfah had been granted permission to visit her husband at the American military base in Qatar, his place of detention. Sajida had stormed out of the visit claiming that the person detained was not her husband but a double.

Hand shaking, Gisele now Googled 'Saddam Hussein alive' – and came up with 1,430,000 results.

1,430,000 reasons for believing Sajida was right.

The Onion Factory, Aanjar, Lebanon 20:30

Forty-five minutes after The Damascene had left them, Merhi saw a diffused glow of lights in the distance coming from the direction of the town. The glow became clearer and stronger as it got closer, morphing into headlight beams. He kicked Lattouf who was sitting on the ground sleeping peacefully – and thankfully silently – next to him.

Lattouf awoke frowning with raised eyebrows, looking up, disorientated. Merhi pointed at the lights. Lattouf looked, focussed, realised where he was and nodded his head, stiffly getting to his feet.

A car turned off the road onto the gravel track, the full beams bouncing, illuminating the central building. Merhi and Lattouf flattened themselves against the wall at the side, out of range of the light.

The car pulled to a stop. As the lights were turned off, the large wooden entrance door to the building slid open and the two other locals came out. They shook hands and kissed cheeks deferentially with the man who got out of the car.

Merhi was peeping round the corner. The Ba'ath political party had been deliberately created as a cell-based organisation with contact between cells forbidden unless it was authorised through a higher command level. This cordoned off members from each other but prevented penetrative infiltration by non-Ba'athists. A cell could be compromised but the infiltrator would be able to get no further without exposure. Carla's husband had said this was a Supporter Cell, so the two who had come out of the building would be candidate members, subservient and obedient to the full member who had now arrived. So here was one complete cell, or circle as it was also known. The local circle. The Circle of Haouch Moussa.

The men went inside and Merhi turned back. His gun was in his right hand. Lattouf was standing on the far side of the window, the Smith and Wesson just visible in his large fist. They did not speak but communicated with facial gestures.

Merhi eyebrowed *Ready?*

Lattouf nodded *Now?*

Merhi shook his head, waving the fingers holding his gun. *Wait.*

A few moments later they became aware of a very low, almost inaudible rumble. There was the subtlest of tremors in the ground, as if there had been an earthquake hundreds of miles away in Jordan or Turkey.

The rumbling got louder, the tremors increased. Merhi took a deep breath and nodded to Lattouf.

Now.

They both turned, standing in front of the open window, guns raised out in front of them.

The roar of the Suzuki Hayabusa increased as it came closer at speed. Then light pierced through the open door of the building as the bike's full beam was turned on.

Inside the three locals turned towards the light, bewildered. They began to shout and gesticulate. Then the neck of one of them exploded as shots came in through the window. Carla threw herself down, rolling sideways. Saddam Hussein looked towards the door, confused. The twins leapt across the room, pushing him to the floor.

The hip of another local burst blood and bone as a bullet struck. The Suzuki flew through the doorway, its raised front wheel acting like a circular saw severing the head of the third local, the member who had just arrived.

The Damascene leapt off the bike while it was still in motion, shouting "Carla!" as a bullet zipped past his head. He lost his footing as he landed, bouncing onto one of the beds.

Outside Merhi raised his hand across Lattouf to stop him firing as inside Carla came up in a crouch. "Get the bitches!" she screamed at the men in the window, pointing.

Paradise and Love were covering Saddam, heads raised, white eyes glaring, almost feral. Carla flung herself on top of Love but was met by a raised forearm which knocked her sideways. The twins began to drag Saddam towards the door.

The Damascene rolled off the bed, looking at his wife who was getting back up, rubbing her chest.

Merhi watched, gun raised, aiming through the window.

Carla snarled, ran forward and kicked Love in the side of the head.

Now Merhi and Lattouf witnessed the strangest sight. The woman Carla had kicked flung her head into the air as the foot made impact, unwillingly rolling away from Saddam. But so did the other woman! Identical movements as if she had been kicked too.

The Damascene threw himself on top of Saddam as Carla grabbed Love round the neck from behind.

Merhi moved his gun back and forth sideways, trying to get a clear shot.

Paradise grabbed The Damascene by the hair, lifting it upwards. She saw the exposed mess that had once been his left ear and grinned, plunging two fingers into the hole. Lashing out with his left arm, The Damascene rolled away, blood oozing out of his wound.

Love managed to stand up with Carla clinging to her back with her arm around her throat, her other hand trying to get purchase against the twin's head to snap the neck. Love swung sideways, back and forth, trying to shake off The Djinn on her back.

"It's no good," said Merhi. "I can't risk it. We'll have to go inside."

Saddam was sitting on the floor, bemused, disbelieving. What was happening? He could not fail now after all these years. America, The Great Satan, was leaving his country in forty days. He needed to be there, to reclaim the Promised Land for his people, to save them. To save the world.

Paradise grabbed hold of Carla's hair with her left hand and plunged her right hand between her legs from behind. She squeezed, feeling the cloth of The Djinn's trousers press upwards into the soft folds of her sex. Then she pinched with all her might. Carla gasped and released her hold. Snarling, Paradise raised her in the air and threw her towards the wall.

The Damascene shook his head, seeing his own blood dripping outwards. He spotted the *argileh* knocked over on the floor and he picked it up by the golden body. The heavy half-filled water bowl stayed on the end as he raised it in the air...

"Sister, come!" croaked Paradise, holding her throat in a mirror image of Love. She put her arm around her twin, guiding her towards the door.

The Damascene swung down the *argileh* with all his might. It shattered against the back of Saddam's head, the glass bowl exploding, water, glass, blood and bone bursting in a spraying halo. Hands instinctively reaching upwards, Saddam fell sideways. The follow-through blow with the pipe body smacked into the side of his head, knocking him back the other way.

Merhi and Lattouf ran together round the side of the building – just in time to see the twins stagger out. "Stop!" Merhi raised his gun, still running.

"Police!" shouted Lattouf. "You are under - "

Then he fell over.

As he fell his gun fired and there was a double scream from in front of him. He bounced onto the ground and rolled sideways – taking Merhi's legs out from under him like a tenpin. Merhi went down straight and flat, his face breaking his fall on the sharp gravel.

The Damascene stood above Saddam's body, raining blows down onto his head, into his face, again and again and again, the skull breaking, the face disintegrating, blood, bone and brain matter splashing up into his own face.

Lattouf was on his back like a beached whale, trying unsuccessfully to get up. Merhi was flat out and moaning. His forehead, nose and chin felt like they had been attacked by a sander on full speed.

They heard an engine start up.

"Stop!" said Lattouf weakly. "Police..." He looked to the side to see the tail lights of the Jeep disappearing down the gravel track. He flapped his gun against the ground, trying to get an aim.

Giving up, he turned the other way towards his friend. "Jihad? Jihad!" He moved his arm out to poke his prostrate colleague. "Are you all right? I couldn't stop them, they have gotten away." There was no reply. "Jihad?" said Lattouf helplessly, rolling like an upturned turtle. "I... I can't get up. Will you help me please?"

Merhi moved, very slowly, very carefully, very painfully. Then, face still on the ground, he said, "Fuck off, Fadi."

The Damascene knelt on his haunches on the floor next to the mess that had once been the head of Saddam Hussein. It was now just a shell, a bowl for the soup of blood, brain and bone and now-floating facial hairs within. He had last seen his wife being thrown through the air into the wall. He really didn't want to look round to find what he might find.

Across the room were the three members of The Circle of Haouch Moussa. One was headless, one was dead with his neck blown away, the other was moaning and writhing, his pelvic area a sticky mess of gore and protruding bone. It would take him a while to die. So be it.

The Damascene felt a touch on his shoulder and he looked up.

"I landed on a bed," smiled Carla. Her hair was a mess, there were bruises and scratches on her arms and shoulders, grazes on her face and a distinct cut on her lower lip. Her right collarbone looked more prominent than usual.

She caressed his bloodied face with her hands, not caring about her own pain. "You came for me," she pushed his blood-matted hair back over his head, her thumbs rubbing an ear on one side, a hole on the other.

"Did you think I would not?" He wiped his hand across his mouth, smearing his chin with blood.

"I knew you would." She bent forward and kissed him long and hard on the lips. It was a full minute before she pulled away. There was blood on her face.

"And I always will." He smiled and put out his hand for her to help him up. "You know what I fancy right now?"

Her black eyes widened. "Husband, you are insatiable! Not

here, surely?"

"I fancy a coffee. And the further away from here, the better." He looked down at the body at his feet. "I would have left him, you know, had he not taken you. He was hated by many but there were an equal number who supported him. Look what Iraq was. Look what it is now. I had no feelings about him one way or the other."

"But you have feelings for me?"

"Oh yes. And that's why he had to die. Killed for love." He put his arm around her.

Stepping past the man dying in agony, The Damascene and The Djinn walked out of The Onion Factory.

The place of death.

26 July 2010
14 Sha'ban 1431

Jounieh, Lebanon 08:15

Captain Jihad Merhi had called in sick that morning, giving an upset stomach as an excuse (the Beirut Belly, the Tripoli Trots, the Sidon Shits). Something must have disagreed with him over the weekend.

Now he sat on his balcony watching the blue of the Mediterranean take on the azure of the cloudless sky in a beauty contest.

On the small table beside him were his cigarettes, lighter, a Saint Charbel souvenir ashtray, a covered *rakwe* of Turkish coffee and a small cup. On the floor underneath the table were an empty whisky bottle, a half full whisky bottle, a glass and an empty cigarette packet.

His face looked like it had been pulled through a hedge of brambles. It was slathered with emollients at Gisele's insistence but the cuts, scratches and grazes were uncovered to let the air get to them.

Out at sea he saw a plane with a distinct cedar tree on its tail climbing into the sky having just taken off from Beirut. It would be that morning's 07:55 Middle East Airlines flight to Paris with a connection to New York. He nodded to it, wishing it well.

His mobile phone rang. Ten minutes ago he had phoned Sergeant Deeb el-Gharib and asked him to have a look at his In Tray on his desk to see if anything urgent was awaiting him. This was him ringing back.

"Hi Deeb."

"Hi boss. Couple of bits from the Major. A nine year old boy was badly injured by an Israeli cluster bomb at Shaqra yesterday. Wants your comments. Also he's asked for your opinion on Blackberry phones. The Telecoms Regulatory Authority has identified security issues. Apparently Saudi and the UAE are already threatening to ban Blackberry messenger functions because of difficulties in accessing the data by law enforcement agencies."

Merhi sighed. "Oh, for Christ's sake."

"There's just one other item, in an internal envelope. From Interpol upstairs."

Merhi leant forward. "What does it say?"

There was a rustling of paper, then el-Gharib said "In response to your enquiry... Positive identification made. Two results. Paradise Grace Abu Joade and Love Maria Abu Joade. Age 34. Lebanese Army. Latterly in the *Moukafaha*, the Special Forces Counter-Sabotage Regiment, prior to that in the Republican Guard. Went to Libya on a training course in 2000, never returned. At first thought kidnapped or killed, then known to have deserted. Next heard of in 2002 as two members of Colonel Gaddafi's elite all-female protection unit. Known for their efficiency and ruthlessness. Last recorded sighting as members of Gaddafi's unit in 2004. Suspects in the elimination of various people in Iraq, Syria, Jordan and Turkey over the last five years. There's more detail, of course. Shall I fax it to you?"

"No, no, Deeb. I'm tired. I need a rest."

"Takes it out of you, doesn't it boss?"

"What does?"

"The shits."

"Yeah. Literally. Thanks Deeb, I'll probably be in later in the week."

Merhi ended the call and placed his phone on the table. He leant back and closed his eyes. Feeling the sun on the top of his head, he stood up and turned his chair around to face the mountain behind. Before he could sit back down, he heard the sound of an engine, the pop of a backfire and the complaining of brakes from down below, outside the apartment block.

He went to the side edge of the balcony and looked over. For a moment he stared, face expressionless. Then he shook his head in disbelief and resigned acceptance. Down below was an old, battered, rusting, burnt-orange Datsun Bluebird.

And next to it, looking up and waving, was Fadi Lattouf.

Gisele let the Palestinian giant into the apartment, reluctantly kissing him three times on his proffered cheeks, and then she went back to doing what she was doing in the kitchen.

"Morning of joy, my dear friend!" effused Lattouf as he squeezed through the open balcony door.

"*Salaam*, Fadi," Merhi hoped he projected more enthusiasm than he felt. "Some juice?"

"That would be kind, thank you."

From the kitchen, Gisele called "I'm getting it!"

"And perhaps a morsel to eat?" Lattouf spoke into the empty living room. "It is a long ride from Beirut."

"Of course," called Gisele again.

Lattouf waddled out onto the balcony.

"I didn't expect to see you today," said Merhi. "Here, sit." He pulled over a chair.

"Thank you, I will stand for a while. The long ride makes my bot-bot go numb." He rubbed his massive gluteals. "How are you, my friend?"

"Looks worse than it is," Merhi came and stood next to Lattouf, leaning against the rail, looking out to sea. "How's your ankle?"

"Oh fine, fine. It takes more than that to keep a Lattouf down."

Merhi went back to the table and took two cigarettes from the packet, passing one over. Lattouf took it and accepted the light. Taking a draw, he looked at the glowing end of the cigarette.

"Nada would kill me if she knew I was smoking again."

"She's a good woman, she cares about you."

"She does indeed." He looked round as Gisele appeared in the doorway carrying a tray. "As does Gisele for you. What would we do without our wives, eh?"

"I've been asking him that for years," said Gisele.

Merhi smiled. "We would not be complete," he said sincerely.

Gisele gave him a small, private look.

"Nada says I am getting old," Lattouf went over and took the tray from Gisele, helping himself to some nuts from a bowl in the process. He waited while Gisele cleared Jihad's stuff from the small table then he put the tray down. As he straightened back up he said, "She says I should retire. Nada."

"Can you do that? Are you able?" asked Jihad.

"I can quit," shrugged Lattouf. "They probably won't even know I'm gone."

Jihad laughed. "I doubt that, my friend," he said affectionately. "What would you do? If you quit? What about money?"

Gisele passed glasses of mango juice to the two men.

Lattouf was quiet for a moment, savouring the full glass of juice that he had poured into his mouth. Then he said, "A business maybe?" He held his glass out for a refill as Gisele approached with a jug.

Merhi pulled a face. "It is not that easy for a Palestinian to set up a business in Lebanon. The red tape would be unbelievable."

"Who said anything about *setting up* a business?" said Lattouf. "I already have one. I am Chadi's sole heir. I have inherited his business. In Jbeil." He drank some of his replenished juice and gave a modest belch. "The thing is, it would be a very big leap for me. I don't know Lebanon that well, its nuances, its niceties. I have been too long a policeman in my own little world. Palestine it isn't. Gaza it isn't. I don't think I could handle it on my own. I would need a local partner." He smiled across at Gisele and then looked Jihad in the eyes. "How about it? Lattouf and Merhi, Private Investigators. You could be the brains and I could be the brawn. Or the other way round. Jihad Merhi, investigator first class. In partnership with Fadi Lattouf..." His face beamed and his deep voice boomed down across the mountainside as he raised his glass in a toast. *"Muhaqqiq khass extraordinaire!"*

POSTSCRIPT
حاشية

Spoiler alert! Plot machinations are discussed below.
Please do not read before reading the book.

The use of political decoys is acknowledged practice. History shows that they have been used extensively, usually to draw attention away from the real person or to take risks on their behalf. Literally to put themselves in the firing line. They are people who naturally look like the person they are impersonating or have had surgical assistance. Not all of them have undertaken their duties willingly.

In the twentieth century, the following are known to have used doubles: Joseph Stalin, Adolph Hitler, Heinrich Himmler, Winston Churchill, Field Marshal Bernard Montgomery, Harry S Truman, Indira Ghandi, Henry Kissinger, Boris Yeltsin, Michael Mouskos (Archbishop Makarios III of Cyprus), Uday Hussein, and Saddam Hussein.

Saddam Hussein was probably the most notable of them all, employing many doubles for public appearances, TV appearances and even for meetings with foreign politicians! The most obvious example of this was in the days after the invasion of Iraq in 2003 when 'Saddam' was shown on worldwide television out in the streets of Baghdad in full military uniform being mobbed by his adoring subjects. He was beaming, avuncular, benign – and never said one word.

Is Saddam alive? Did he cheat the gallows? There is a strong theory that he did. But how could that be? Unless they were in on it, surely the Iraqi authorities, if not the Americans, would have thoroughly tested the body both pre- and post-mortem to establish that it was him and to confirm his DNA? Indeed. But with so many Saddam Husseins about (there were believed to be at least eight) how could they ever be sure that they had the right DNA in the first place?

Was Brother Malek ('The King') really Saddam Hussein? Or was he just another decoy?

Perhaps Akhenaten has the answer...

Ma'ak,

David Cullen
ديفيد كولين

To Zalaya, the Man of Damascus.
Know that the king is in good health
as the sun in the heavens. His troops and
chariots are numerous... from the
Upper country until the Lower country,
from the Levant till the sunset,
all is for the best.

- from a letter written by Akhenaten (Pharaoh of Egypt 1353 – 1336 BC) to the ruler of Damascus, on a cuneiform tablet now in the National Museum of Lebanon in Beirut, originally thought to have been discovered at Byblos.

الله هو جيد

GLOSSARY OF ARABIC WORDS AND PHRASES
معجم اللغة العربية الكلمات والعبارات

'aalaykum al-salaam	[And] Upon you peace
Aasif	Sorry
Ahlan	Hello
Allahu Akbar	God is great
Al-salaam 'aalaykum	Peace upon you
Arak	Aniseed-based drink, a relative of absinthe, ouzo and similar
Argileh	Lebanese word for shisha pipe or *nargileh*
Arnab	Rabbit
Asr salat (salat al-Asr)	Afternoon prayer
Awarma	Preserved meat fat
Azan	Islamic call to prayer
Baiid baladi	Fresh country eggs
Batatis	Potatoes
Beyti beytak	'My house is your house'
Burnus	A long, hooded cloak, usually of coarse fabric
Charafna	Delighted to meet you
Dallah	Traditional Arabic coffee pot, curved shape with spout, lid and handle, often ornate
'eeh	Yes
Fajr salat (salat al-Fajr)	Dawn prayer
Farouj meshwi	Grilled chiken
Fattoush	Bread salad
Firdaus	The highest level of Paradise
Fitra	Alms given at the end of Ramadan
Habibi	Darling
Hajj	The annual pilgrimage to Mecca
Hijab	Traditional Muslim head covering for women
Hon	Here
Ilishael	Shit
Insh'allah	God willing
Jahannam	Hell
Jamal	Camel
Jawani	Chicken wings in a lemon, garlic and coriander sauce
Jilbaab	Traditional long, loose-fitting garment worn by some Muslim women
Kaaba	The most sacred site in Islam, the cube-shaped building surrounded by the *Masjid al-Haram* mosque in Mecca, Saudi Arabia
Kafan	Cloth to cover a corpse
Kafirs	Non-believers (in Islam)
Kakhbah	Swear word: equivalent to 'son of a bitch'
Khiyar	Cucumber
Khobz	Arabic flat bread
Kibbeh nayeh	Minced lamb or beef, served raw
Kifak?	How are you? (To a man)
Kunafi	Pastry stuffed with sweet white cheese, nuts and syrup
Kunya	A name honourably given to the mother or father of an Arabic child. Abu (father) or Umm (mother) plus the name of their first

	son, as in Abu Yussuf or Umm Samer
Labneh	Strained yoghurt, very soft cheese made from strained yoghurt
Lubya	Bean stew
Maa?	What?
Ma'asel	Tobacco for *argileh* or shisha
Madrassa	Place of learning
Maghrib salat (salat al-Maghrib)	Sunset prayer
Mana'eesh	Lebanese pizza, a circle of cooked dough topped with a mixture of thyme and sesame seeds
Ma sha'allah	God has willed it (literal)
Mashraha	Mortuary
Massah el-khair	Good afternoon/good evening
Mekhallel	Pickles
Merci ktir	Thank you very much (mixture of French and Arabic)
Merhaba	Hello
Moukafaha	Lebanese Special Forces Counter-Sabotage (Terrorism) regiment
Muhaqqiq khass	Private investigator
Mukhabarat	Intelligence service
Muntasif an-nahar	Midday
Mutabal	Aubergine dip
Qiblah	The direction that should be faced when a Muslim prays, towards the *Kaaba* in Mecca
Rais	Leader, chief, boss
Raka'ah	Cycle or unit of prayer
Rakwe	Long-handled coffee pot usually used for serving Turkish coffee
Raqs sharqi	Belly-dance (literally: 'Oriental dance')
Sabah a Allah	God is good
Sabah el-khair	Good morning
Salaam	Peace (greeting)
Sahira	Witch
Sahtik!	Cheers!
Samak mishwa	Kebabs of monkfish, lemon and pepper
Samkeh harra	spiced fish
Sayadieh	Fish with rice
Seejaere	Cigarette
Shahada	The Islamic creed
Shaitan	Satan
Shawarma	Food: an Arabic wrap
Shou	What?
Shukran	Thank you
Subhana rabbiyal a'ala	Glory be to my Lord, the most high
Taban	Of course!
Takbir	The Arabic name for the phrase *Allahu Akbar*
Tasbih	Prayer beads
Tayyib	Okay
Tfaddal	Come in (To a man)
Uhktee	Sister
Yaatik al-aafieh	May God give you strength
Yalla	Let's go (or 'come' in the same context)
Yawm al-Qiyamah	Judgment Day
Zaqqum tree	A thorned tree that Muslims believe grows in hell. Its fruit is spiked and bitter; those in hell are forced to eat it to add to their discomfort.

The first adventure of Jihad Merhi and Fadi Lattouf

THE BAALBECK DECISION

David Cullen

2004. A dangerous time in Lebanese politics

Prime Minister Rafic Hariri is forced to resign
– but it looks like he will sweep back into power in 2005
bringing in a wave of change for Lebanon.
There are those that want that
and there are those that do not.

The Damascene comes to Beirut to protect Hariri.
Al-Rajul comes to Beirut to kill Hariri.
But who sent them? And why?

And what links a serial killer in the Palestinian
refugee camp of *Bourj el-Barajneh* with the tumultuous
events which are about to engulf the region?

Lebanon will be changed forever by

THE BAALBECK DECISION

ISBN: 978-0-9559911-4-1

All David Cullen books are available from *amazon, Lulu,*
barnesandnoble and other online booksellers and thru all good
bookshops.

DAVID CULLEN

1974. A world in turmoil. Terrorism is rife.
In the Middle East, *El Fateh* plan their first nuclear strike. The Irishman, their hardware supplier, wants a very special item in payment.
In the Mediterranean, Cyprus is an island about to be divided. Resistance leader Grivas is dying. He wants to hit his enemy from beyond the grave.
In Israel, the security services want to finish off their enemies once and for all.
In Europe, Sally wants to find her missing lover.
In a world about to implode, they all have one common link:

THE EYE OF MAKARIOS

ISBN: 978-0-9559911-0-3

1978. Only two people still alive know the explosive dark secret of the British Royal House of Windsor.
One lies in her dotage in France, the other continues to rule the royal household in Britain as she has done for 40 years.
A robbery in Paris. The secret is stolen.
It must be found at all costs. Police enquiries draw a blank. They need help. There is only one man with the skills to locate the secret – Jacques Mesrine, France's Public Enemy Number One.
But there are those that want the secret for themselves and others who will stop at nothing to ensure the secret remains hidden.
Can Mesrine find the secret before the hunters find him?
Death, treachery and double-cross all lead to

THE MESRINE CONCLUSION

ISBN: 978-0-9559911-1-0